The Grown Up To-Do List

Jennifer Joyce lives in Manchester with her daughters. She's been scribbling down stories for as long as she can remember, graduating from a pen to a typewriter and then an electronic typewriter. And she felt like the bee's knees typing on THAT. She now writes her books on a laptop (which has a proper delete button and everything).

JENNIFER JOYCE

the GROWN UP to-do list

hera

First published in the United Kingdom in 2024 by

Hera Books
Unit 9 (Canelo), 5th Floor
Cargo Works, 1–2 Hatfields
London SE1 9PG
United Kingdom

A CIP catalogue record for this book is available from the British Library.

Print ISBN 978 1 80436 856 5
Ebook ISBN 978 1 80436 859 6

This book is a work of fiction. Names, characters, businesses, organizations, places and events are either the product of the author's imagination or are used fictitiously. Any resemblance to actual persons, living or dead, events or locales is entirely coincidental.

Look for more great books at www.herabooks.com

Printed and bound in Great Britain by Clays Ltd, Elcograf S.p.A.

1

To Rianne and Isobel

Today's <u>must do</u> to-do list:

- *Buy Gran's birthday present (Slippers? Perfume? Gin? Ask Mum!)*

- *Find 'something suitable' to wear tonight (Mum insists ripped jeans and a flannel shirt aren't 'appropriate' for a small family gathering)*

- *Help Mum with party prep*

- *Don't be late for work (again)*

Chapter One

I'm late for work again, which is why I burst out through the front door like a reverse bailiff, only one shoe tied and the laces dangling from the other as I hoof it across the lawn towards the gate, Mum squawking about coming straight home after my shift so I can help set up for Gran's surprise birthday party tonight. I wave my hand above my head to acknowledge the request before grabbing the gate and yanking it open. I'm so unfit, my chest is already on fire after the short dash, but I push through it and propel myself out onto the pavement.

'*Oof!*'

I collide with what feels like a massive boulder but is, in fact, a person. I stumble backwards while they stagger to the side from the impact, righting themselves much better than I do as I end up veering into next door's bush, which is the only thing that keeps me upright.

'I am so sorry.' The boulder-like person reaches out to help me straighten up. 'Oh my God. Cleo? Cleo Parker?'

I look from the hand grasping mine to its owner's face. It's thinner than I remember, more contoured, and there's stubble on his chin that wasn't there the last time we saw each other, but it's definitely him. 'Franko?'

My chest aches, but in a good way this time, not in an I'm-about-to-keel-over-from-some-light-exercise kind of way. The way it used to ache when I spotted

3

my crush in the school corridor or loitering around the playground. The way it used to ache when I spotted Paul 'Franko' Franks.

'It's Paul now.' He shakes his head. 'How long has it been? A decade?'

'Seven years.' The last time I saw Franko was the night before I left our little seaside town to travel across the world. I wasn't the only one leaving – Sienna had the seat booked next to mine on the flight, and Peter and Courtney were leaving for university in a couple of days, so we'd organised a final boozy get-together in the Red Lion. It had been an amazing night, where we spilled out onto the beach at kicking-out time and splashed in the shallows without taking our shoes and socks off. Franko walked me home afterwards, our soggy shoes slapping the pavement, and he kissed me on the doorstep, finally, after my three-year crush. I left the next day and I haven't seen him since. Until now.

'Wow, seven years. Only feels like yesterday that we were mucking about in that chippy you used to work in at the weekends, when you used to sneak us free chips so we wouldn't take the mick out of your hairnet.' Franko shakes his head and laughs wistfully. 'Have you kept in touch with the others? I think I'm friends with most of us on Instagram. I haven't seen you on there, though.'

'I'm not on Instagram.'

Franko laughs. '*Everyone's* on Instagram. Even my mum.'

'Not me.' Not since my ex announced his engagement to the girl he cheated on me with and all our mutuals fawned over the couple with their congratulations, as though their relationship was anything other than skanky. I couldn't bear to see their smug faces or the massive ring so I deleted all my social media accounts and have refused to set foot in the Red Lion, where The Skank is a barmaid, or socialise with any of my former friends ever since. I'm not saying they should have taken my side, but they definitely shouldn't have taken Dane's so publicly. Not that I'm still bitter…

'You always were different. Do you remember when you had those multi-coloured dreads? They were pretty cool.'

Cool or cringey? Almost a decade later, I don't think I had any place having dreads, multi-coloured or otherwise, as a white woman, but I was young and stupid and I'd had the rainbow dreads when we kissed on my doorstep. He'd played with an orange dreadlock, twisting it between his finger and thumb while he told me how unique I was, his face moving closer to mine until we were kissing. I wonder if he remembers that?

'I didn't know you were back up north.' I crouch down and tie the loose lace of my Converse. 'Didn't you move down south somewhere?'

'Ashford. In Kent. Moved in with my dad for a bit until I got my own place. I own three gyms down there now.'

'Three *gyms*?' I try not to gape at Franko, but it's quite difficult to remain straight-faced. The Franko I knew wasn't into fitness. The Franko I knew chain-smoked his way through his mid-teens, sat his maths GCSE while hung-over after Shelby's sixteenth birthday party, and spent his pocket money on weed. I think he even sniffed glue for a bit when we were fourteen.

'I know, right? But I cleaned myself up when I moved in with Dad, got into personal training and caught a passion for it. I'm hoping to move the chain on from Kent soon. I want at least ten gyms by the time I'm forty.'

I realise now that Franko wasn't merely passing; he's decked out in shorts over shiny leggings with a skin-tight long-sleeve T-shirt. He's out running, properly, not because a shopkeeper's caught him nicking stuff and he's making a quick getaway like he used to when we were kids.

'Is that why you're here? Looking for new opportunities?'

'Nah. My mum and sister are still in Clifton. Mum's still on Woodland Road, actually. It was my niece's christening so I had to come back for that.' He shakes his head. 'I don't know how people can stay in this crappy little town their whole lives. Not like us, eh? Got out of this shithole as soon as we could.'

'Yeah.' I concentrate on straightening my hair, checking for bits of twigs and leaves after my fall into the bush, so I don't have to look at Franko.

'Did you make it around the world like you always said you would?'

'Sienna did. She met a guy and stayed in New Zealand and married him. They've got kids and everything.' Two of them, the last I heard, but that was a couple of years ago, before the social media cull. How did my best friend become nothing but an Instagram acquaintance?

'It's weird thinking of Sienna as a mum. She was always such a free spirit. Like you.'

'Yeah.' I smile weakly. I'm such a free spirit, I boomeranged back to our sedate home town after a matter of weeks in Europe and failed to escape again. Didn't even try to.

'Shelby had a baby a few months ago. Peter's the godfather. Can you believe it? Peter, who used to get shit-faced every night and drew cock and balls on every surface he came across is a *godfather*. Mind you, he's respectable now. He's a *doctor.*' Franko snorts. 'Peter, a doctor. Mad.' He shakes his head. 'His wife's a doctor as well. Nancy. They're having a baby in a few months. They're down in Buckinghamshire, not far from Spencer in Milton Keynes. Everyone seems to have migrated south, apart from Demi. She's in Edinburgh. She has her own interior design company and she was on telly last year, on that home makeover show on the BBC.' Franko tilts his head to one side. 'How come you didn't stay in New Zealand with Sienna?'

'I didn't make it that far. I had to move back home. My grandad had a stroke.'

'I'm sorry.' Franko places a hand on my shoulder and my stomach flips, just as it would have done when we were teenagers. 'Is he okay?'

'He made a pretty good recovery, but he had another stroke a couple of years ago. A big one and… well, you know.'

'That sucks. I'm sorry, Cleo.' He squeezes my shoulder and my stomach performs a cartwheel. Who knew that my crush on Franko was still there, hidden away all this time? 'Where did you end up?'

'End up?'

Franko's hand starts to slide away from my shoulder. 'You're not still… You don't still live…' His face crinkles up in what looks very much like pity.

'In Clifton-on-Sea?' I snort, really loudly, and regret it immediately. 'Of course not. I'm just visiting Mum and Dad.' I nod back towards the house. My house. Where I live with Mum and Dad, in Clifton-on-Sea.

Franko's face smooths out again and he huffs out a laugh. 'I didn't think you'd still be here. You're the last

7

person I'd expect to stick around in this dump. What was it you wanted to be?' He taps his stubbly chin with his finger. 'A journalist! How did that go?'

'Perfectly. That's what I am now. A journalist. An editor, in fact.'

What am I talking about? I still work in the fish and chip shop in Clifton-on-Sea where I used to sneak free chips to my mates when the bosses weren't looking. I did not add 'lie through your teeth' on today's to-do list, but it looks as though I'm doing it anyway.

'Where are you based?'

I swallow hard as my brain works on another lie. 'Liverpool.'

'Liverpool?' Franko's eyebrows shoot up his forehead. 'That's where I wanted to go to uni. Didn't get in though. Didn't get the grades.' I'm guessing being shit-faced for our entire final year of school had a lot to do with that. 'I bet you have a swanky office.'

'So swanky. It's massive, with big squishy sofas and a top-of-the-range coffee machine and stunning views across the river.'

My nose should be growing because there's no office where I work, unless you count the tiny back room where Jed does the accounts and the only view is of the yard at the back of the chippy.

'What kind of editor are you?'

'I work on a women's magazine.' I scratch the back of my calf with the toe of my shoe. 'A glossy one, not one of the salacious weekly ones with "I Had Sex With My Butcher – And His Sausage Was Massive" type stories.' One of our customers left a magazine behind the other day and it had that exact headline on the cover. 'I won an award last month for North-West Editor of the Year. I'm a proper girl boss, like Meryl Streep in *The Devil Wears Prada*, but nice. But I'm not a pushover. I'm assertive but approachable. Fair but firm. Everyone says so – and not just because I tell them to.' I step forward so I can nudge Franko in jest. I don't know where I'm getting all this from because it's utter bollocks, but I can't seem to stop it spilling from my mouth. My face starts to crumple in dismay, because I don't usually go around spouting lies (making up excuses for being late for work doesn't count) and I press my lips together, really tightly, to smother any more lies.

'Right. That's great.' Franko reaches into his pocket and pulls out his AirPods. 'I should get going. Need to keep the heart rate up.' He pats his chest before slotting his Pods into place. 'But we should get together for a proper catch-up. Are you free tonight?'

My heart is Riverdancing and my feet are itching to join in the joyous jig. It takes great effort to stop them from flickering up and down on the pavement because Paul 'Franko' Franks has just asked me out on a date. *At last.* I have been waiting for this moment since I was fifteen and I can't quite believe it's happening.

Except.

Oh no.

I'm not free.

'I can't tonight.' I pull a face that doesn't even come close to displaying the utter annoyance I feel right now. 'It's my gran's birthday. We're having a party. Just a teeny one – close family and friends – otherwise I'd invite you. Sorry.' I pull another face, but figure it probably doesn't look very attractive and stop. 'How about tomorrow night?'

'I can't. Sorry.' This time it's Franko pulling a face. It doesn't look unattractive. I'm not sure he *could* appear unattractive, with his shaggy blond hair and blue eyes. He still looks like a surfer from a teen magazine poster, even with the light stubble, and I approve. 'I won't be here tomorrow night. I'm heading back home first thing.'

'Oh.' I somehow manage to push a smile through the devastation. 'That sucks.'

Understatement! This could have been *it*. The start of our new life together. First date, second date, fast-forward a bit to proposal, marriage, babies. Maybe babies. Probably not. I wonder how Franko feels about kids?

'I'll be back for Mum's fiftieth though. Couldn't miss that. She'd kill me. I'll be back for the whole weekend so we can meet up then. Go for a drink.' He backs away, already jogging, before raising his hand in farewell. 'Get on Instagram and add me. Or TikTok. I'm mostly on there at the moment. Add the others. I'll message about us getting together.'

'When's your mum's birthday?'

But Franko's already turned and sprinted away in the opposite direction and I'm already severely late for work.

The most embarrassing moments of my life so far:

- *The time the door jammed in the school's loo, and instead of helping me to get out, Sienna gathered all our mates so they could piss themselves laughing at me*

- *My first kiss: there were braces, too much slobber, and all our mates jeering from the sidelines*

- *On the Ferris wheel on a particularly windy day. One of my dreads ended up tangled around the pole. Instead of helping me, Sienna laughed so hard she almost threw up. The ticket guy thought I was messing around and wouldn't stop the ride. I went round three times before I managed to untangle myself – and the ticket guy made me pay for the extra rides*

Chapter Two

Russell and Jed opened The Fish & Chip Shop Around The Corner fifteen years ago, and although we don't have a prime, seafront location, they've built up a set of loyal customers (both local and returning visitors) with friendly service and the best fish and chips in town. I had a weekend job there while studying towards my A levels, and Russell and Jed were more than happy to welcome me back with open arms when I dashed back to Clifton-on-Sea when Grandad was ill. As Grandad grew stronger, I took on more shifts and somehow ended up as assistant manager.

'Sorry, sorry, sorry. I'm late, I know. Russell and Jed aren't about, are they?' I look up at the window of the flat above the shop as I rummage in my hoodie pocket for my keys.

'You're all right.' Claire pushes herself away from the shuttered window where she's been leaning while awaiting my arrival. 'Jed's at curling and Russell's in Manchester.'

'Good.' I heave a sigh of relief as I push the key into the shutter. The shop is due to open in twenty minutes and although I know Jed will have prepped the fish for the lunchtime rush, I'll need to sort the potatoes and get the fryers on the go. There's no time for chit-chat, even though I'm bursting to tell Claire all about Franko, and we set about our respective tasks. I set to work on the spuds, sending them into the 'rumbling' machine to remove the peel before rinsing them. Russell and Jed insist on having hand-cut chips, so once Claire has finished setting out the menus and condiments on the tables, she helps me to slice the potatoes into thick chips ready for blanching. Somehow, we're ready in time for opening, and we even manage to throw a couple of tables out onto the pavement for customers to enjoy their lunch in the unusually warm late winter sunshine. It isn't yet high season so the tourists won't descend for a few more weeks, but there's still a steady stream of customers that doesn't die down until after two. Among our regulars is Fleetwood Jack, who chews the ear off the poor bloke behind him as he waits to be served, relentless in his fury at the way he's supposedly been treated by 'the industry' and 'the justice system'. Jack claims he was a member of Fleetwood Mac back in the day, writing three of their hits (though he won't specify which three) before leaving for unspecified 'creative differences' just before the band went on to become famous. Everyone knows it's bullshit, not least because Jack was only thirteen when their first song was released, and it can be pretty hard going listening to his rants if you don't know how to handle him. I step in to relieve the poor bloke who only came in for a bag of chips, and distract Jack by asking him about his upcoming court case (the source of his 'justice system' rage). It's a relief when he stomps out of the door, belting about going his own way, especially as I spot Babs, smiling away as always. Babs is another regular, though she doesn't usually pop in on a Saturday.

'Don't tell the others.' She presses her hands together as she leans on the counter when it's her turn, and I mime zipping my lips, which makes her beam more than usual. Babs' smile could light up the darkest room and she always manages to lift my mood simply by being there. It's like a superpower and her presence is an antidote to Fleetwood Jack's rage. I'm still feeling cheery when local gossip Gwen arrives with a torrent of stories from the charity shop where she volunteers with Gran. The charity shop is a hotbed of scandal and Gwen has no qualms about whispering about the titbits she picks up. Luckily Bridget isn't on shift with me today as she's fervently against 'muckraking' and won't allow any hint of rumour to be passed on so I'm free to listen to every juicy detail and Claire leans in to hear the latest dirt too. I'm a hot, sticky mess by the time I collapse onto one of the blue plastic chairs by the window, when it's finally my break, a plate of chips drowned in salt and vinegar on the table between me and Claire. You'd think I'd be fed up of chips, but you'd be wrong. Even after all these years of being surrounded by them, I can't get enough of the delicious little beasts, and Russell and Jed's chips really are the best – fluffy on the inside, crispy on the outside, and door-wedge thick. No puny French fries for us, thank you very much.

'Don't let me eat too many of these. It's Gran's party tonight and Mum's made enough food to feed an army.' I reach for a handful of the chips, shoving two in my mouth at once.

'As if I could stop you.' Claire plucks a chunky chip from the plate and dips it into the little dish of ketchup.

'That's true.' I wedge two more chips into my mouth and grab another handful.

'Hey, is this really you?' Claire is nibbling at her chip while scrolling through her phone with her other hand.

She turns the phone around so I can see the screen. It's my new Instagram profile, with the few hastily added photos I shoved on there while I popped to the loo earlier. Although I only created the account to communicate with Franko, I need more friends on there so I don't look like a loser and having only a paltry amount of people to add made me realise quite how small my world has become over the past few years after Dane cheated on me and I cut out our mutual friends.

'Yep, that's really me.' The photo I've chosen for my profile was taken a couple of summers ago, down on the beach on a particularly breezy day. I'm holding an ice cream in front of my face, so all you can see is my mini topknot above the blob of ice cream and swirl of raspberry sauce, while the rest of my hair blows around in all directions. You can't see it, but I was laughing behind that cone, even though I was nearly choking on my own hair, blissfully happy because I didn't know that the person taking the photo was a nasty little cheat who would end up breaking my heart.

'Didn't you say you were never going back on social media again?' Claire dabs her chip into the ketchup again (I can't stand the stuff, so double-dipping is allowed). 'What made you change your mind?'

'It's a boy.' My feet jiggle under the table and I'd clap my hands like a seal if I didn't have a fistful of chips. 'Well, he's a man now, but we went to school together and I had a massive crush on him for years.'

'And it's only just occurred to you that you can get in contact with him?' Claire's pretty face is marred by deep crevices on her forehead. 'And I thought I was the ditzy one.'

'You're not ditzy.' I nudge Claire gently with my foot. 'And neither am I. It didn't just occur to me – I bumped into him this morning – literally. And he's still *so fit*. He told me to add him on Instagram, so I did.'

'No, it can't be.' Claire's brown eyes widen and her mouth droops open. 'Cleo Parker, Miss I'm-never-dating-again, is interested *in a man*?'

'Not just any man.' I lean across the table towards Claire. 'He. Is. A. God.'

'I need to see this god.' Claire wrestles a paper napkin out of the dispenser and wipes the grease from her fingers before wiggling them at me. 'Lemme see his profile.'

My feet are jiggling in excitement again as I load up Franko's profile before handing it to my friend.

'He's pretty cute.' Claire nods before she hands the phone back over.

'Pretty cute?' I'm outraged. 'He's *gorgeous*.' He's grinning at the camera, all toothy and cheeky-chappie, a dimple in his right cheek and his eyes gleaming. 'And he's super-fit. He was a personal trainer and now he owns three gyms. *Three* gyms. I don't even own three pairs of shoes.'

'Ooh, tell me more.' The little minx is interested now, her elbows on the table as she leans towards me, her bottom lip clamped between her teeth.

'There isn't much to tell, but look at these.' I tap on one of Franko's workout videos and turn my phone to Claire, who watches on in speechless wonder. 'We bumped into each other outside my house. That's why I was late.' I don't mention I'd also left buying Gran's birthday present and an outfit worthy of Mum's approval for the party tonight until the last minute, so I was already running late by the time I ran into Franko. 'I couldn't stick around, but he said to add him on Instagram so we could catch up.'

'On Instagram? Not in person?' Claire scrunches up her nose. She looks so adorable, I'm at a loss – as I frequently am – as to how she's still single (because it isn't for the lack of effort on Claire's part, believe me).

'He lives in Kent.'

Claire slumps back in her seat. 'That sucks. I'm sorry.'

'Don't be.' I shove my phone in the pocket on the front of my tabard and grab more chips. They're starting to grow cold now, but they're still irresistible. 'There's still hope. He's coming back for his mum's fiftieth birthday, so we can meet up and fall madly in love then.'

'When's his mum's birthday?'

I shrug, wiping my greasy fingers down the length of my tabard. 'No idea, but I've sent Franko a message, asking when he's back in town.'

'What if it's weeks away?' I've got up to head into the kitchen and Claire has followed me. We try to keep on top of the dishes, but with only two of us here for the lunchtime rush, they've piled up on the worktop. I open the dishwasher and start to load it up.

'Then it'll give me time to work a few things out.'

Claire slots a plate into the rack and stands up, placing her hands on her hips. 'What things? What did you do?' Her tone is half suspicious, half exasperated, as though I've done something stupid.

Which I have. She knows me too well.

'I sort of… bigged myself up.' I make it sound casual as I coolly stack the dishwasher. 'Nothing major. I just told Franko that I'm an award-winning editor of a women's glossy magazine.'

'You did what? Why?'

'I don't know.' I grab a handful of cutlery and divide it between the sections in the rack; knives in the front sections, forks in the back, just as Jed likes it organised. 'I suppose because he seemed so together. So *grown-up*. He's a business owner and I'm…' I spread my hands out and look down at my tabard. 'Still working here, all these years later. And it isn't just Franko. It's all of my childhood friends. Sienna and Shelby and Peter are all having babies, and Peter's a *doctor*. Even Spencer got married and that boy couldn't commit to a football team, never mind spend his life with one woman. And Demi – who I can't even remember from back then – has been on some BBC TV programme.' And it isn't just their careers that have me wanting to stick my head in the potato rumbling machine – I've checked out their social media, which is filled with evidence of fun and active lives. Spencer is a TikTok influencer and coaches an under-sixteen's football team, and Peter and his wife are part of a community choir and do a lot of charity work in their spare time. Primary school teacher Courtney has a balloon bouquet side hustle and teaches belly dancing and Shelby's days are packed with picnics and pregnancy yoga and spending time with her friends with girls' nights out and pamper nights in and she has so many fancy meals out that I doubt she even owns an oven. And then there's Demi, who has a range of soft furnishings and several (real) awards for interior design and seems to be besties with a daytime TV presenter. My heart sank with every 'living my best life' boast I saw. 'What have I done with my life? I didn't travel the world like I said I would. I didn't become a journalist. And worst of all, I still live with my mum and dad.'

Claire snorts. 'What's wrong with that? You live there for practically nothing and your mum still does your washing and cooks your meals. It sounds like paradise to me.'

'It sounds like I'm a teenager in a twenty-five-year-old's body.'

'You should just tell him the truth.'

'And I will.' I hand Claire the mop and bucket. If she's going to dole out sensible advice instead of encouraging my nonsensical behaviour, she can have the crappy jobs.

How To Survive Family Parties:

1. *If you think you have enough alcohol, buy more*

2. *Don't get trapped in the kitchen with the pervy 'uncle'*

3. *Try to keep the buffet in your line of vision at all times until it's opened. The difference between grabbing a chicken drumstick and finding an empty platter is a nanosecond*

4. *If you think there are enough chicken drumsticks for the buffet, YOU ARE WRONG*

5. *Seriously, buy more alcohol*

Chapter Three

Mum's waiting for me when I step out of the shop, tapping the steering wheel to Boyzone (she only has one CD in the car, which is a Boyzone greatest hits collection, and she plays it over and over again. From the beat of her fingers on the steering wheel, I'd guess it's 'Picture of You'). She obviously doesn't trust me and is under the impression that I wouldn't have gone straight home to help set up the party without her supervision. Like Claire, she knows me too well.

'Oh, Mum's here. I can't come back to yours and help you to pick out your outfit after all. Good luck with your date tonight. Wear the teal tea dress with the wedges that tie around your ankles.'

Claire tilts her head to one side. 'That dress is mega short.'

'Exactly.' I pull the door shut and wave to Jed, who's back from his curling session and is getting ready for this evening's trade. 'You have the legs to pull it off and you look amazing in it, trust me.' Claire doesn't look convinced, but I don't have the time to persuade her as Mum's stopped tapping on the steering wheel and is now jabbing at her watch. 'See you on Thursday. Give Arlo a big kiss from me. And text me later, yeah? Or leave me a comment on Instagram. Make me look popular.'

'Picture of You' blasts out as I open the car door, but Mum turns the volume down as I climb inside. 'Thanks for the lift. What a nice surprise.' I smile sweetly at Mum even though inside I'm mourning the loss of the glass of wine I'd planned to have while we rifled through Claire's wardrobe for the perfect ensemble. It's her third date with this particular bloke, and she doesn't get many of those (Claire has *the worst* taste in men) so we're at a crucial point in her romantic life and we need to tread carefully. She doesn't want to appear too keen (this is usually her downfall. That and she picks complete turds to pursue), but nor does she want to be off-puttingly cool.

I may be more invested in Claire's love life than my own.

Speaking of which... I slide my phone out of my hoodie pocket and open Instagram.

'Yes!'

Mum's eyes are wide with panic at my sudden outburst, but I couldn't keep it in. Franko – sorry, *Paul Franks*, according to Instagram – has followed me back. *And he's sent me a DM.*

> Hey Cleo great to meet up this morning even if I did knock you into that bush lmao can't wait to catch up again Paul xxx

My stomach gives a happy little flip (which has nothing to do with the dip in the road we've just driven through). I'm going to ignore the lack of punctuation (nobody likes the grammar police) and focus on the positives. Paul (it's a bit weird thinking of him as anything other than Franko, but I'll get used to it) can't wait to catch up again. He's looking forward to our date as much as I am!

'Your dad is going to keep your gran away as long as possible, but we really do have to get a move on with the party prep. I've made the sandwiches but I'll need to warm up the sausage rolls and the quiches…'

Mum's blathering on about the party as I tap out a reply but I zone her out and float into a daydream where Paul (still weird) and I meet up for our first date. I'm wearing a floaty, floor-length dress with delicate straps at the shoulders (because daydream me is more sophisticated than reality me who doesn't own this outfit) and I'm bare-foot as I make my way down the steps to the beach, which is strangely deserted even though the weather suggests it's the height of summer. Paul's waiting for me on the sand, surrounded by a circle of flickering tea lights (will have to watch my floaty dress while near those) and in the centre of the circle is a small, bistro-style table and two chairs, with two silver cloches covering what I imagine will be a sumptuous meal.

'You look beautiful.' Paul murmurs the words, shaking his head in wonder as he watches me approach. I'm suddenly aware of the music playing softly from invisible violins as Paul takes my hand gently in his and grazes his lips against my fingers. 'I have waited so long for this moment. You're the most unique girl I've ever met, do you know that?' I didn't realise my rainbow dreads were back, but he has one in his fingers, twirling it between his finger and thumb as his lips move slowly towards mine. 'Cleo? Are you going to sit there all day?'

Damn it! The daydream is whipped away – Paul, the delicious meal, every last grain of sand – and I'm back in the car with Mum. We're outside Gran's house and Mum is reaching into the back seat.

'I've brought your new outfit. We won't have time to go home so you'll have to change here.' She dumps the carrier bag on my lap before climbing out of the car and heading for the boot. I try to conjure the daydream again (I'm not bothered about the meal, but Paul was about to snog my face off) but it isn't forthcoming, especially as Mum's yelling at me to grab the platter of sausage rolls and pork pies from the boot. I check my phone as I drag myself from the car but Paul hasn't replied yet.

–

There's music blasting from upstairs as we stagger into Gran's house with arms full of flimsy disposable platters crammed with party food. I can barely see over the stack Mum's shoved into my arms and I nearly stumble over a box in the hall.

'I thought Gran was out?' The Buzzcocks are jamming at top volume upstairs (and yes, I have fallen in love with someone I shouldn't have fallen in love with, Buzzcocks. Dane turned out to be a rather unsavoury character who I wish I'd never clapped eyes on. Thanks for the reminder).

'She is.' Mum sounds out of breath as she staggers along the hall towards the kitchen. 'She must have left the radio on.'

That must be it, because the Buzzcocks aren't really Gran's cup of tea. I'm only familiar with the song because Russell's obsessed with Seventies music and plays it in the shop all the time. I could probably name more songs and artists from the Seventies than I could from the current charts, and if that isn't tragic, I don't know what is.

'How many people are you expecting?' It's a relief to dump the platters on the kitchen worktop, but I know it's only a brief respite because there's more food waiting to be transferred from the boot.

'Just us and a few of Gran's friends.' Mum checks the time on the oven. 'We don't have much time so we'd better get cracking. I'll grab the rest of the food and get it set up in here if you'll blow up the balloons?' Mum waits for confirmation (a barely supressed sigh seems to be sufficient) before striding off back into the hall. 'Oh, and can you bob upstairs and turn that racket off first? It's giving me a headache. I think we should check the batteries in your gran's hearing aid when she gets back.'

Mum's left a packet of balloons on the side, and I shove them in the front pocket of my hoodie before peeling the layer of cling film off one of the platters and wriggling a vol-au-vent free. I'm chewing on my creamy mushroom bounty as I head up the stairs, wincing at the increasing volume of the Buzzcocks. The music isn't coming from Gran's bedroom as I expected it to be, but the back bedroom. Decades ago, it was Dad's childhood bedroom, but it's now the guest bedroom. The door is half open, the music painfully blaring out, and I can see movement coming from inside – a shadow shifting across the carpet, an arm reaching out – and someone's singing along with Pete Shelley.

What the hell?

I'm frozen to the spot, my mind telling me to march into Gran's guest bedroom to confront the intruder while my cowardly heart is telling me to scarper down the stairs to get Mum. I still haven't decided which option I'm going to plump for when a bloke appears in the doorway. He's tall, with dark brown hair curling around his face

25

and almost reaching his shoulders. He has a neat, closely cropped beard and brown eyes beneath dark brows. I suppose you'd describe him as handsome, if you'd met him in a club rather than in your gran's house, mid-burglary.

'Hi.' He has to shout over the music, and his brow has furrowed. His stance has morphed into attack mode, his knees slightly bent, fingers slightly curled in front of him, ready to pounce. 'Who are you?'

'This is my gran's house.' I try to stand tall, to show him I'm not afraid, even though I'm in danger of peeing (or worse) on the hallway carpet. I wish I was armed with more than half a vol-au-vent and a packet of balloons. 'Who are *you*?'

'Cleo?' His brow smooths as a grin spreads across his face, and he takes a step forward, his hand reaching out to strike me. Instinctively, I take a step back, colliding with the mahogany dresser that sits between the back bedroom and the bathroom. I graze my hip on the corner and although I want to cry out all the swear words, no profanities are forthcoming. I am mute with fear, even when in pain. *He knows my name.* How?

'I'm James.' His hand hangs in the air, and I realise he isn't going to hit me – he wants to shake my hand. What the actual hell?

'*Mum!*' I finally find my voice as I spot movement at the bottom of the stairs. Mum's back with more food. She'll know what to do. She'll karate-chop the dude in the face or kick him in the balls. She'll do *something* other than stand here like a turnip.

'What is it, love?' Mum's jogging up the stairs, and the burglar inches forward so he can peer around the doorway. I finally, miraculously, conjure some courage from somewhere deep down inside and take a step forward, holding up my hand, palm out.

'Back off, buddy.' Emboldened when he does as I command and stumbles backwards into the bedroom, I move towards him, keeping him cornered. The last thing I want is for him to bolt, knocking Mum down the stairs in his haste.

'What's going on?' Mum's almost at the top of the stairs now, which is good because my courage is already fizzling away. My hand is still held aloft, but it's trembling.

'Him.' I curl my fingers into my palm, so there's only my index finger pointing at the burglar. Mum's reached my side now, and she turns towards the back bedroom, her body jerking in shock when she sees the strange man standing in the room.

'Who are you? And what are you doing in my mother-in-law's house?'

I knew Mum wouldn't crumble. I knew she'd take control. Take action. She doesn't stand for any nonsense, particularly from scummy opportunistic burglars of the elderly.

'I'm James Merchant.' The burglar holds up his hands, palms out. 'I'm moving in with Cordy. I take it from your reaction that she didn't tell you about me?'

'No, she didn't.' With one hand held up towards the burglar (or James, whatever) Mum holds the other out towards me. 'Phone, please. We need to sort this out.'

I hand my phone over, my hand still trembling. Mum keeps an eye on James (if that's even his name) while she phones Gran. Slowly, and explaining his actions before he carries them out, James turns the music off before returning to his spot near the door.

'Sorry about that, James.' Mum hands me the phone back. 'We had no idea who you were.' Some of us still don't. 'The thing is, we've organised a surprise party for Cordy and she's already on her way back, so we need to get a move on.' Mum turns to me. 'Forget the balloons for now. Food first and then we'll see if we've got time for decorations. And you need to get changed. I don't want you dressed like that when your gran gets here.'

I look down at my leggings-and-hoodie combo. I've got a patch of mushy peas crusting on my sleeve and a hole on the inside seam of my leggings near my left knee. She may have a small point.

'What can I do?' James steps out of the bedroom and into the hallway. 'I was unpacking, but that can wait.'

Thinking about it rationally, James isn't dressed for burglary. Instead of loose, running-away-from-cops type clothes, he's wearing fitted jeans, brown brogues, a navy sweater and matching blazer.

'You want to help?' Mum places a hand on her chest and tilts her head to one side. 'How sweet of you. There are still a few bits and pieces in the car – would you mind bringing them into the kitchen while I set out the buffet?'

From thief to hero in one swift move. What a charming bastard this dude is – and Mum's falling for it, hook, line and sinker. Well, I won't be falling for it. I've been taken in by smooth-talkers before, and look where that got me. I'm going to keep an eye on this James fella. A *very* close eye.

My Top 5 Drinks:

- *Coffee (can't function without it. My blood group is macchiato)*

- *Alcohol (any kind will do, though you know the party's started when the tequila makes an appearance)*

- *Smoothies (but not the ones with 'hidden' veggies – bleurgh)*

- *Hot chocolate (with marshmallows and cream if I'm feeling fancy)*

- *Tea (but only if none of the above are available)*

Chapter Four

I only manage to blow up three balloons before Mum sends me upstairs to change. Under normal circumstances, I'd have changed in the guest bedroom, but since Burglar James has somehow commandeered that room, I squeeze into the box room that is now Gran's sewing and craft room. I don't usually wear dresses, but I have to admit that I've picked a particularly pretty one that I think Mum will love (and definitely deem suitable for the party). The pale oyster skater dress is sleeveless, with a laced bodice and double-layered skirt that billows when I twirl (which I do in the limited space of the box room, until I start to feel dizzy). And the best bit is, it has *pockets*.

'Oh, Cleo.' Mum's in the kitchen, putting the finishing touches to the buffet while Burglar James hangs bunting from one end of the room to the other. Rather than sounding stunned by the beautiful dress I've chosen, she sounds... disappointed. 'You didn't buy new shoes to go with the dress?'

I look down at my feet. I'm still wearing my glittery Converse, which I happen to think work well with the dress. Plus, I won't be complaining of blisters and numb toes all night.

'I think you look great.' James is standing on one of the kitchen chairs and I idly wonder how injured he'd be if I gave the legs a swift kick and he tumbled onto the tiles.

'Do you really?' I run my fingers through my hair, which has been released from its messy bun and is tumbling around my shoulders. 'Or are you brown-nosing in the hope I won't see right through you?'

'Cleo.' Mum's tone is dark, but I won't back down on this. She may be okay with this dude moving in with my elderly grandmother (who would *kill* me if she knew I'd described her as such) but I smell a rat. A big, stinking rat. I've listened to enough true crime podcasts to spot the signs of a con man so James may have charmed my mother, but I'm on to him.

'What exactly are you going to see?' James doesn't have the grace to face me as he questions me. He's turned back to the task of tacking the bunting above the sink.

'You're up to something.' I narrow my eyes as I watch him press a drawing pin into the wall. 'Are you planning to seduce my gran?'

The chair wobbles as James spins around, the string of bunting falling from his fingers and the pin bouncing into the sink. 'You *what*?'

'For goodness' sake, Cleo.' Mum scrunches the cling film in her hand into a ball. 'Your grandmother is eighty-five, and James is… How old are you?'

'Twenty-eight.' He plucks the drawing pin out of the sink and pulls the bunting back up towards the wall. 'And no, I'm not planning to seduce Cordy. The tenancy is up on my house and the landlord didn't want to renew because his daughter wants to move in instead, so Cordy's letting me stay here for a few weeks until I sort something out. And I'll be paying her board, I assure you.'

'Why do you keep calling her Cordy?'

James secures the bunting in place and hops down from the chair. 'Because that's her name?'

'Her name is *Cordelia*. Only her friends call her Cordy.'

James shifts the chair over a few inches and climbs back up. 'I guess I'm one of her friends then.'

I do not like this guy, and I don't buy his story for one minute. Why would my grandmother invite some random guy to move in with her? Where did they meet and when? How long has this guy been working on my gran, earning her trust and worming his way into her affections? And why the hell is my mother okay with this? I'm about to ask when the doorbell rings. Giving me a warning look, Mum dashes off to answer the door.

'I don't trust you.'

James shoves another drawing pin into the bunting. 'You've made that loud and clear.' He hops down off the chair and moves it along again. 'And I get it. I'd be a bit suspicious if some bloke moved in with my grandma without warning, but it isn't my fault Cordy never mentioned it to you. I assumed she'd told you about me. She's told me all about you.' He turns so he can smirk down at me, and I'm tempted to kick the chair over again. There are no witnesses...

'Cleo! Long time no see.' Jerry, one of Gran's oldest friends, strides into the room and pulls me into a too-tight hug that makes my ribs ache. I'm torn between begrudging Jerry's presence (he can be a bit much) and relief that he's here and can therefore turf James out on his arse. Although he's inching towards his nineties, Jerry's still a sturdy-looking man with broad shoulders and an intimidating height. 'You must be James. Cordy's told us all about you.' Jerry has released me and is looking up at Gran's new lodger, holding out his hand for him to shake.

For God's sake. Isn't *anybody* else questioning this guy's motives? I can't be the only one who was engrossed by *The*

Puppet Master: Hunting the Ultimate Conman on Netflix! This guy has Robert Hendy-Freegard written all over him.

'Jerry?' James hops down from the chair and takes his hand. Jerry's delighted that he's been identified (how is James doing this?) and he pumps James' hand up and down until James has to wriggle his hand free. He has to mask his discomfort with a chuckle when Jerry slaps him – audibly – on the shoulder.

'It's good to finally meet you.' He climbs back up onto the chair (out of harm's way. His shoulder is probably dislocated after Jerry's overeager greeting).

'What do you mean by "finally"?' My eyes narrow as I look up at James. 'How long have you known Gran?'

'About a year?' James shakes a drawing pin from the box onto the worktop. 'Maybe a bit more.'

'And how did you meet?' Gran retired years ago, but she isn't one for staying in the house. She keeps herself busy with volunteer work: she's a lollipop lady, works in the local charity shop, and she's the Brown Owl at the Brownie pack at the church hall. She also dog-walks for an animal shelter and helps to raise funds in any way she can. And on top of all this, she has a better social life than I do. James could have met her anywhere on her travels, but he doesn't get the chance to answer as Jerry's wife bursts into the kitchen, bringing a gagging cloud of too much perfume and booze with her.

'Hello. You must be James.' Gwen leans against the worktop so she can gaze up at James, her eyes all fluttery and her lips pushed out into a ridiculous pout. She's actually very pretty, but she masks it with these gormless expressions. 'Kitty said you were ruggedly handsome.' She bites her bottom lip as she plays coquettishly with her hair. As well as being the town's biggest gossip, Gwen's also Clifton-on-Sea's biggest flirt. 'And she was right.' She giggles while I mime sticking two fingers down my throat. James catches me and I whip my fingers away.

'Can you give us a hand getting everything ready?' I grab the packet of balloons and, smiling sweetly, push them into Gwen's hands. 'Thank you so much.'

Leaving them to it, I head into the living room and pour myself a glass of wine and drink half of it in one go. A few more of Gran's friends have arrived and are taking up the sofa and chairs so I stand next to the drinks table. I'm going to need all the booze I can get my hands on to survive an entire evening with Jerry and Gwen, especially if she's in flirt mode.

'Everything sorted in the kitchen?' Mum dashes into the room and heads straight to the window, shifting the blinds to check for any sign of Dad and Gran.

'Gwen offered to blow up the balloons.' I smile at Mum, placing a hand on my chest. 'Such a lovely woman. So helpful.'

Mum's eyes dart towards Gran's friends as she scuttles over, leaning in close to me and lowering her voice so it's barely audible. 'Those balloons will be filled with gin fumes if she's blown them up. Keep them away from any naked flames.'

I raise my wine glass in acknowledgement of the instruction, but pause before I take a sip. 'Did you describe James as *ruggedly handsome*?' I force the last two words out and try not to choke on them.

'Well, he is.' Mum shrugs and heads back to the window, pulling the blind aside so she can peer out on to the street. She suddenly jumps in the air, her arms flapping about as she makes a strangled squeaking noise. 'They're here! Reggie and Cordy are here!' She flaps a bit more as she dashes across the room and throws herself out of the door. When she returns, she ushers James, Jerry and Gwen into the room, shushing everyone and instructing me and James to hide. Gran's friends are excused from concealing themselves behind pot plants and squeezing behind furniture (which makes it pointless for the rest of us to do so, but Mum insists). I'm planning to slot myself between the sofa and bookcase but James has beaten me to it. There isn't time to find another hiding space – I can hear the front door clicking shut and Gran's muffled voice as she moves along the hallway. I'm going to have to squash myself onto the sofa with Gran's friends and try to blend.

'Quick.'

My hand is tugged suddenly, and for the second time today, I find myself taking a tumble. This time it isn't a bush that breaks my fall but James, who caused me to fall down in the first place. Steadying me, he inches back so there's room for both of us to crouch beside the sofa, a split second before the living room door opens.

'Surprise!'

It's Mum who practically screeches the word in her enthusiasm as she pops out from behind the curtains. James and I jump up from our position beside the sofa while the others simply twist in their seats to look up at Gran as we chorus the sentiment.

'Oh.' Gran clasps her hands together as she looks around the room at her loved ones, a beam stretched wide across her face. 'How lovely to see you all. I had no idea. You.' She points a finger at Dad, but she's still smiling. 'No wonder you insisted on all those cups of tea, you devil.'

She hugs her son before moving on to Mum and then Gwen, who's caught en route to the drinks table.

'You've met James then.' Gran has made her way around the room, hugging and kissing friends and family before she ends up at the bookcase, where I've inadvertently blocked James in. 'I hope you've made him feel welcome.' Gran places a hand on my cheek. 'I'm sure you have. You're a good girl.'

My cheek is hot beneath Gran's touch, because I haven't made James feel welcome. But then why should I? I'm looking out for her, because nobody else seems to be up to the task. Mum can't seem to see past his 'rugged handsomeness', Gwen's making eyes at him from across the room, and Dad doesn't seem to have clocked that there's an interloper at the party at all. Can nobody else see how inappropriate this is? What kind of twenty-eight-year-old man moves in with an octogenarian who he isn't related to? Especially when her actual relatives have never even heard of him until he's half unpacked his stuff in the guest bedroom?

I'm about to air these musings when I feel a buzzing from my pocket. I have a message. From Paul. *Finally*.

5 Things That Make Me Happy:

1. Imagining all the ways Dane can live unhappily ever after (the latest episode includes an extremely itchy crab infestation)

2. Watching Waiting on You with Gran

3. The first coffee of the day. And the second, third, fourth, fifth…

4. When Mrs Hornchurch tells me I make the best fish in Clifton-on-Sea (especially in front of Bossy Bridget)

5. Making lists in my bullet journal

Chapter Five

Gwen is jiggling the final drops out of a bottle of wine when I approach the drinks table for a top-up. It's been an hour since Gran arrived and Gwen has spent that time working her way through the wine Mum's been stock-piling over the past few weeks.

'Gone.' Gwen shrugs and drops the empty bottle onto the table, where it wobbles before toppling over. 'S'all gone.' She drains the contents of the glass, shaking it over her open mouth to dislodge every last drop.

'I'll go and get some more.' I grab the upended wine bottle but Gwen gives a dismissive wave of her hand and clumsily unscrews a bottle of vodka. She moves her hips from side to side, almost in rhythm with the music playing from the stereo, as she glugs vodka into her glass.

There's a box under the kitchen table that's already starting to fill with empty bottles, and I add the latest one to the collection. Gran's recycling bin is going to be overflowing at this rate.

I catch Gran's eye as she steps into the kitchen. 'She's started on the vodka.'

'Already?' I haven't even named anybody, but Gran knows who I'm talking about. 'But it isn't even six o'clock yet. And we haven't even got round to starting on the buffet.'

This is typical Gwen behaviour. She always ends up being half carried from parties and folded into the car, with Jerry begging her not to throw up until they get home. Every birthday party, every Christmas lunch, even family christenings. If there's alcohol, she'll consume it until it's removed or she falls down and can't get up again unaided. It's worrying, but Gwen is adamant she is simply a social drinker who likes to have a good time and insists to anyone who suggests otherwise that they're party poopers.

Gran grabs a paper plate from the pile on the worktop and starts to add a few nibbles. 'Here, go and take that to her. It might help soak up the alcohol.' She passes the plate to Mum, who takes a fortifying breath before she strides out of the room. It's just me and Gran and a cargo ship's worth of food left in the kitchen. If Gwen is allowed to start on the buffet, does that mean it's open to the rest of us?

'Have you had a nice birthday?' I inch a little bit closer to the sausage rolls. The lingering smell of them warming in the oven is making my stomach rumble, despite the chips I wolfed down earlier.

'It's been lovely.' Gran hands me a paper plate with a wink and I start to load it up with goodies. 'I'm very lucky to have such wonderful family and friends, and it's a good chance to introduce you all to James. He did a good job with the bunting.' She gazes up at the window, where the yellow and pink gingham triangles swoop perfectly and symmetrically. 'What do you think of my new lodger?'

I swerve the tuna sandwiches (bleurgh – fish should be battered and served with chips) and plump for an egg and cress. 'I think you're mad.' I add a mini pork pie and half a scotch egg. 'He could be anyone, Gran. A serial killer. A con man. You watched *The Tinder Swindler* with me.

You know what these men are like. He hasn't asked you to change your will yet, has he?'

'Oh, Cleo.' Gran tuts and rolls her eyes. 'James is a lovely young man, and I'm looking forward to having a bit of company about the place for a little while. I've been rattling around this house on my own since your grandad died. I haven't said anything, but it's been quite lonely and I've been struggling for a while.'

'How can you be lonely?' I pause my buffet harvest, even though I'm almost up to the big bowl of crisps. 'You never stop. There's always something to do – stuff with the Brownies, the charity shop, meeting up with your friends. And I'm here most days. When do you get the chance to get lonely?' I honestly don't understand it. Gran is the most positive go-getter I know. She doesn't have a spare second to feel isolated.

'Why do you think I do all those things?' Gran spreads her arms out before letting them fall to her sides. 'I try to pack my days, but it's the evenings. When you've gone home and there's no work to do. And the mornings, when everybody's busy getting ready for the day and I'm wandering around this empty house. This house isn't meant for one. It's supposed to be full of life, like it was when your dad was small.'

'I could move in with you. I'm here all the time anyway, and wouldn't you feel safer living with someone you know rather than a stranger who's probably going to steal your pension and siphon off your savings?'

Gran's eyebrows lower and she shakes her head. 'Oh, Cleo, *no*. That's the very worst thing that could happen.'

I try not to feel offended but fail, big time. I know I can be a bit messy, and I don't know what all the buttons and dials mean on the washing machine, and I'm constantly forgetting to replace the empty loo roll, but Gran and I get on so well. She's more of a friend than a grandmother. My mood had already plummeted when I read Paul's message earlier, but now I'm definitely out of the celebratory mood, even if I have a plate full of party food.

Three months. That's how far away Shona Franks' fiftieth birthday is. *Three months* until I get to see Paul again and live happily ever after. And what if he meets somebody else in the meantime? Somebody who doesn't still live with their mum and dad. Someone who doesn't have to pretend to have a career because they're actually doing something with their lives other than serving fish and chips in a small seaside town. Whoever Paul ends up with will be a *woman*. A proper grown-up, with life goals and prospects.

'Oh, Cleo. Don't look so gloomy.' Gran places a hand on my cheek and smiles. Gran has lovely cheeks: plump and doughy and rosy, and they go all crinkly when she smiles. 'You know you're my favourite person in the whole world. I love the very bones of you, girl. And that's why I can't think of anything as horrifying as a young woman like you moving in with an old wrinkly like me. You should be out there, spreading your wings and living life to the full, not moving out of your childhood bedroom into my guest room.'

'Reggie wants to do presents before food.' Mum's back in the kitchen, and she whisks my paper plate of buffet nibbles away and plonks it on the side. I watch it mournfully while Mum starts to usher Gran from the kitchen. 'He can't wait to give you his present from us. He's practically pink with glee, bless him.' She waits until Gran is out of the room before she hands me a small wrapped box. 'I wrapped the perfume for you.'

We head into the living room, where Gran's surrounded by Dad (who *is* pink with glee) and her friends, plus a host of gifts. I'd totally forgotten to wrap the perfume. I bet whoever Paul ends up with wouldn't turn up to a party with an unwrapped gift, because she'll be a proper grown-up. There's no way Paul will want to live happily ever after with someone who still lives like a teenager, relying on Mummy for everything.

But then I have three months until I see Paul again. Three months in which I can finally get my act together and be the grown-up I should have been all along. I'll get my own place and learn to drive so Mum doesn't have to ferry me around like an unpaid taxi driver, and I'll start an actual career and smarten myself up, replacing my tired old leggings and hoodies with garments with non-elasticated waists (which doesn't sound nearly as comfortable but at least I'll be taken more seriously clad in trouser suits and killer heels). I'm probably not going to become an award-winning editor in three months, but people change careers all the time. My mind is swimming with all the ways I can become a more refined version of myself as Gran starts to peel the paper from the large box in front of her, revealing a wooden box with a domed roof and a small opening at the front. Dad pounces on the box, telling us all about the hedgehog house with the in-built motion sensor camera that they can capture the prickly garden critters on. But I'm not really paying attention, because I'm thinking of the things I can change to become the grown-up I described to Paul, the grown-up he will fall madly in love with in three months' time. I need my bullet journal, so I can get organised and make a list. A grown-up to-do list that will bag me my dream man.

The Grown-Up To-Do List:

- *Start a career*

- *Move out of Mum & Dad's*

- *Learn to drive*

Chapter Six

It isn't an extensive list I've come up with, especially as it's now Thursday, five days after my light-bulb moment, but I'm finding it difficult to pinpoint exactly what makes you a proper grown-up. I've asked around – Mum said she felt like a grown-up when the midwife handed me over, all gooey and screaming my little head off, but I don't want to go as far as having a baby. That's quite a drastic move. Besides, I only have eighty-six days until Paul's back in Clifton-on-Sea, and I'm not sure being knocked up by someone else would be all that enticing for him.

Dad said he still feels like a kid (and Mum said this is a Man Thing while giving the biggest eye-roll I have ever seen) which doesn't help me in the slightest. Gran said she felt like a grown-up the day her mum died and she held her sobbing father before making him a cup of tea. She was *seven*, and I can't quite shake off the sombre feeling her contribution left me with.

'When did you start to feel like a proper grown-up?' Gran asked James the question while I died a little inside after the grieving father story. We were sitting in front of the telly, waiting for our favourite daytime soap to start. It was a recording, so we could have fast-forwarded to the start, but Gran likes to watch the ads, old-school style. James hadn't actually been invited to join us in the viewing, but he'd plonked himself on the armchair, sneering with derision when Gran told him our plan for the evening. Yes, James, we do watch 'that garbage', because we enjoy it, you massive bellend.

James had contemplated Gran's query as though it was the final question on *Who Wants to Be a Millionaire?*, his brow furrowed, his lips twisted up to one side as he tapped a finger on the arm of the chair. I expected to see a bead of sweat rolling down his temple. Did he want to phone a friend?

'I suppose it was when my divorce came through.'

I have to admit his answer gave me an unexpected jolt. Divorce? But he's only three years older than I am. I haven't been in a relationship that spanned more than five seasons, yet James has not only been married, he's had enough time to allow the relationship to grow so sour they've split up and divorced? How is that even possible at the age of twenty-eight? Obviously I discounted James' contribution (and not just because he's a massive bellend). Eighty-six days isn't nearly enough time to squeeze in a marriage and a bitter divorce.

So I asked my bosses the question, hoping for better insight. Jed said he felt like a proper grown-up when he came out to his parents at the age of thirty-two, because he felt like he'd finally accepted himself for who he was. It was a rather sweet answer, but unhelpful for my cause, and Russell's participation wasn't any more beneficial.

'Growing up is for losers. Live, love and dance the night away and you'll be a happy chap. No growing up involved.'

Jed had shaken his head and given a little sigh. 'Russell has Peter Pan symptoms.'

'It's Peter Pan *syndrome*, you turnip.' Jed has a habit of getting sayings slightly wrong. I'm not convinced it's

46

accidental, myself. I turned back to Russell. 'Didn't you feel like a grown-up when you married Jed?'

Russell had tipped his head back to look up at the ceiling for a moment before he shrugged. 'I felt hung-over. Very, very hung-over. That was one hell of a stag night.'

So I've only got three items on my list, which isn't a bad thing if you think about it. Three items to tick off is easier than a dozen, right?

'When did you feel like a grown-up?' Claire has finally arrived for work. She isn't late, but I've been desperate to talk to her about my list and I haven't seen her since we shared that shift on Saturday. We've texted, but mostly about her date at the weekend and when we think he'll phone her. Very soon we'll start to call him a bastard and try to work out why he never called. It's a weekly routine we have.

'When I found out I was pregnant with Arlo, I guess.' Claire heads into the little room at the back of the shop, where there's an old, splintered table and two wonky chairs, and I follow, bringing my bullet journal and its paltry list with me. 'You have to grow up pretty quickly when you see those two blue lines. Why?'

I sit down at the table, my heart leaping when the chair shifts sideways, even though I should be used to its wobble by now. 'I'm making a grown-up to-do list, so I can present the best possible me to Paul when he comes back.' I place my journal down on the table and turn it to face Claire. 'I haven't got very much so far.'

'You don't say.' Claire sits down opposite me, her hands slapping down onto the tabletop in a panic. She isn't accustomed to the wobble yet either. She reads the list (it doesn't take long) and nods. 'Start a career. Good start. So, what do you want to do?'

That's a good question. A very good question indeed. It's a pity I don't have an answer to it. 'I wanted to be a journalist when I was younger.'

'Do you still want to be a journalist?'

I pick up my pen and click the nib in and out while I think about it. I wanted to be a journalist so I could unearth juicy celeb gossip, but it's much easier to just buy a trashy mag and read about it, to be honest. 'Not really.' I scrunch up my nose. 'Not at all, actually.'

'What *do* you want to do?'

I click the pen in and out, again and again until Claire snatches it from me. 'I have no idea, but there has to be something better out there than serving fish and chips. Something more fulfilling. Something less greasy.'

'Then that should be the first item on your to-do list.' Claire hands the pen back. '*Decide* on a career, because you can't start one without knowing what you want to do first.'

'Smarty pants.' I squeeze in 'decide on a career' at the top of the list. 'You're wasted here.'

'This is just temporary. Once I have my degree, I'm out of here.'

Claire didn't get the chance to go to university with her peers; she found out she was pregnant a couple of months before her A levels, and though she sat her exams, she didn't take the next step in her life plan, which had been torn up around the time she clapped tearful eyes on those double blue lines. Her life plan may have veered off course, but Claire is still determined to reach her goals. She's taking a different, slower path – part-time job working in a chippy while her son is at school and long-distance studying while he's in bed – and I have every faith she'll get there.

'Right.' I sit back, my heart leaping as the chair wobbles. 'Done.'

'You know that's the easy bit, don't you? You've now actually got to *decide on a career*.'

Claire is such a Debbie Downer as Gran might say (or a Donna Downer, as Jed might say).

'How do I do that?'

Claire shrugs. 'No idea. I've known what I've wanted to do for years. I've always loved sports, so it makes sense to have a career based on something I enjoy doing. What do *you* enjoy doing, apart from doodling while people are trying to help you?'

I drop my pen and flash Claire a sheepish look. 'Sorry. It helps me think.' And the sunglasses-wearing pig is pretty cute. 'I don't know what I enjoy doing. Drinking coffee? Can you get paid for that?'

'You must have a hobby.'

I think about it. Hard. 'I like watching telly, and you *can* get paid for that.' Gran and I like watching *Gogglebox* almost as much as *Waiting on You*.

'But it's extremely rare.' Claire stands, clinging on to the table when the movement causes another chair wobble. Jed and Russell really need to replace this furniture. 'You don't have any hobbies at all?'

'Nope.' I'm not like Claire, who somehow has time to squeeze boxing into her busy schedule of parenting, working and studying. Or Gran, who likes to sew and crochet and do crosswords when she isn't volunteering for a squillion organisations. Or Jed, who became obsessed with curling during the last Winter Olympics and joined a team in Preston. Or Russell and his golf and Seventies music. Or Mum and Dad with their car boot sales and gardening. Does *everyone* have a hobby, apart from me? Would having a pastime other than watching reality TV and listening to true crime podcasts make me more mature? I think about my old childhood friends, who all seem to have stuff going on in their lives that doesn't revolve around work, like community choirs, netball coaching, belly dancing.

I add 'Find a hobby' to my list.

Five items to tick off now. This thing is starting to snowball.

Possible Hobbies:

- *Podcasting (will need equipment. And somewhere private to record. And a topic I know enough about to discuss. Coffee? Horrible ways in which your ex can suffer excruciating and/or embarrassing pain?)*

- *Metal Detecting (sounds really boring, but the beach is right there)*

- *Mixology (fancy word for cocktail-making. What's a fancy word for YES PLEASE?)*

- *Baking (even though the last thing I 'baked' were Rice Krispie cakes with Claire and Arlo, and it wasn't as much fun as Bake Off would have you believe)*

- *Surfing (except I'd have to move to warmer climes, because there is no way I'm submerging myself in the Irish Sea)*

Chapter Seven

I've been chatting to Franko over DM – sorry, *Paul* – over the past few days, and we've been reminiscing about our schooldays and the years we've missed out on. Paul has been single for six weeks (enough time to have got over the relationship? I'm not sure how serious it was – must find out) and I told another teeny fib and said Dane and I broke up a couple of months ago, because I'd felt like a bit of a loser when I typed out that I'd been single for a couple of years. So I'd deleted it and fudged the numbers a bit. Not only did Dane hurt me when he cheated on me, he really knocked my confidence and I haven't been able to even *think* about dating, until now. Paul Franks is my saviour. My insanely hot, gym-owning saviour.

We're both on different shift patterns at the moment, with Paul working mostly during the day while I'm at the chippy from late afternoon until closing. It's usually after midnight by the time the clear-up is finished, so communication has been patchy, but it means the thrill whenever I see a message from him is intensified.

'Expecting a call?' Gran places a tea tray on the table and straightens the plate of biscuits (home-made chocolate chip. Divine).

'Nah.' I slide my phone into the pocket on the front of my hoodie (Paul hasn't replied yet anyway) and reach for a biscuit. 'Just checking Instagram.'

'Jerry said he'd followed you.'

I try not to grimace as I nod. Having an old geezer as my most active 'friend' isn't going to do much to make me look cool and sophisticated. Especially with some of the content he posts.

Gran eases herself onto her end of the sofa. 'I've had to *accidentally* unfollow him again, to be honest. Some of that stuff he shares is far too blue.' She reaches for the basket she keeps next to the sofa, pulling out an ancient quilted bag she calls her 'project bag'. She's always got a crochet project on the go, something to 'keep her hands busy' while we watch telly. It's blankets at the moment, which she's making for the dog shelter where she volunteers.

'Are we ready?' I have the remote poised, but Gran shakes her head.

'James is joining us.'

What? But this is *our* time. I was working late last night, so we've had to wait until this morning to catch up on *Waiting on You*, which we always watch together. It's *our* thing, mine and Gran's, and James made it perfectly clear that daytime soaps are beneath him.

'I'm teaching him to crochet, and this is the only time we're both free.'

A belly laugh bubbles up and rumbles out. 'James is learning to crochet? *Why?*'

'Because he saw me crocheting the other day and asked what I was making. You know, taking an interest. A nice thing? Anyway, I told him about the blankets for the poor little doggies, and he said he wanted to help.'

Oh, he's a clever sausage, that one. *Of course* he's letting Gran teach him to crochet. Not only does he get brownie points for being a caring citizen, he also gets to spend time with Gran. Bonding with her. Showing her what a delight he is. That he thinks of others, even poor, defenceless animals. That he isn't afraid of fighting against gender stereotyping. He's worming his way into her affections via the medium of wool. Sneaky.

'Will you teach me?'

I have no interest in crocheting – never have done, never will do – but if it means I get to thwart James' devious plans to charm my grandmother, I'll do it.

'You want to learn to crochet?' Gran looks at me as though I've just announced my intention to run naked along the seafront. Which is valid, I suppose. Running along the seafront in my birthday suit is preferable to crocheting. 'Brilliant. The more the merrier, and it'll mean more blankets for the shelter.' She reaches into the basket and pulls out an old pencil case, rummaging around until she produces a silver stick with a thick blue rubbery-looking handle. 'Here's your hook. What colour yarn would you like to start with?'

I couldn't care less if I tried really, *really* hard. 'I don't mind. Whatever you have to hand.'

'I've got a nice yellow here, or this rosy pink?' She's plucking balls of wool out of the basket, holding them up for me to look at before placing them down in the space between us. 'This is a lovely emerald. Or how about this cornflower blue? I have a deeper blue here. Or orange. You like orange. It'll match your jumper.'

I'm already regretting my decision, and we haven't even started yet. It was impulsive, rash. I should rescind my interest before we're in too deep. Let James drain her savings – if he's willing to put this much effort in, he probably deserves it.

'We're making granny squares. I've started James off with a really simple, single-coloured square. He's gone for lime green. Fun!' She checks her watch. 'He should be back any minute now.'

Back? From where? It's only just gone nine o'clock. Where has he been? Oh, God. Don't tell me he gets up early to start the day off with a run. I couldn't cope with it. The crochet is bad enough, but being super-healthy on top? Have a day off from being Mr Perfect, James.

'If you don't like any of these colours, I've got stacks upstairs in the craft room.'

'This one's fine.' I grab a ball of wool – I don't even look which colour. 'What do I do now?'

'Let's have a cup of tea first while we wait for James.' Gran shuffles forwards and reaches for the teapot. There are three cups on the tray. Why didn't I clock that before?

I scoff my chocolate chip cookie, but it doesn't make me feel any better about the situation I've landed myself in.

–

'So, let me get this straight. He's engaged to her, but she's having an affair with the dude with the twiddly moustache and round glasses – who looks like a badly drawn cartoon character, by the way – while he's secretly in love with the chef?'

Our crochet lesson has ended (thankfully, because that was an excruciating experience, especially as I couldn't keep my eyes from James' nimble fingers and comparing him to Tom Daley's poolside knitting, which is hot and James most definitely is not), and we're rewarding ourselves with yesterday's episode of *Waiting on You*. James is displaying his morning's effort on the coffee table (a slightly wonky but passable lime green crocheted square) while I've hidden mine down the side of the sofa. I don't think anyone wants to see the orange sausage-like clump I created while attempting to create 'chains' and 'double crochet', not even Gran, who made encouraging noises while I wasted her wool.

'No, no, no. Melvin, the chef, is engaged to Tegan, but she's having an affair with Rex – the moustache man – while he's secretly in love with Amber.' Gran explains the main drama of the soap to James as she pours another round of tea. 'But Melvin isn't the poor, innocent party here, because he's the father of Joanna's unborn triplets.'

'Even though Elvin thinks that *he's* the daddy.' I add a couple of sugar cubes to my tea and a glug of milk from the little ceramic jug that matches the teapot.

'Well, he would, wouldn't he? Being her husband. You'd just assume that was the case.' James takes the milk jug from me and adds a dash to his tea. 'It isn't so much a love triangle, or even a square. More like love spaghetti, with everybody connected somehow. They must be riddled with all sorts.'

I give him a long, hard stare while he stirs his tea. 'You don't have to watch it, you know.'

James holds his hands up. 'I'm just saying, it's a very busy restaurant where this soap is set, but the only thing they seem to be serving is themselves up on a platter.'

'It's a daytime soap. It isn't supposed to be serious, just a bit of fun.'

'Have you got a dictionary to hand, Cordy?' James picks up his cup of tea and takes a sip. 'I think we need to look up the definition of the word fun.'

I pretend not to hear, but in my head I'm sticking two fingers up at the judgemental prick, very enthusiastically.

- *Days Until Paul's Back In Town: 84*

- *Moments of Panic That I'm Nowhere Near The Grown-Up I Wish I Was: 3,654,397*

Chapter Eight

It's been a whole week since I saw Paul. I'm still working on my grown-up to-do list, but I'm struggling, to be honest. I have no idea what career I'd like to start and I still don't have a hobby. Crochet definitely isn't for me, even if I am keeping up the pretence so I can thwart James' cunning plan to fleece Gran, and I've crossed all the possible hobbies out on the list I made in my bullet journal, including mixology because I watched a few YouTube videos and it looks really complicated with all that bottle-tossing and spinning and stuff, not to mention the cost of buying all that booze. It's much cheaper and much less faff to order a cocktail in a bar.

My phone pings and I dive on it, hoping to see a message from Paul. We've been chatting through WhatsApp for the past week and I've liked every one of his new Instagram posts and stories. I *may* have scrolled through his grid to see if I could glean any information about the ex-girlfriend as well but I'd deny it under torture.

The message isn't from Paul. It's from Courtney, a girl we went to school with. She followed me on Instagram a few days ago, and I've had a nosy through her grid too. She has a beautiful house with two cars on the driveway and the interior is opulent without being too flashy. She posts photos of her home at least once a day, and who can blame her? I'd want everyone to be jealous if I lived in a house like that too.

I flick through my bullet journal and underline 'Move out of Mum & Dad's', adding an 'ASAP' at the end for good measure before opening Courtney's message.

> Hey, babe! It's been SO LONG since I saw you! When was it? Shelby's 21st? That was a MAD night! We DEFFO need to all get together again and catch up :)

I ignore the part about Shelby's twenty-first birthday party *since I wasn't invited* and say that a catch-up would be great. Sienna, Franko and the others were my whole life back in my mid-teens and I can't believe how far I've drifted from them, despite being in the exact same place I was back then. Every last one of them moved on during the few short weeks I was away: Sienna further across Europe before settling in New Zealand, Franko down to Kent, Peter and Courtney to university, and Shelby and Spencer to wherever they wandered off to, all of them leaving me behind. We kept in touch for a while, but the contact fizzled out over the years, even with Sienna, my BFF. To my shame, I don't even know her married name and she isn't listed on Instagram under her maiden name. I'm scrolling through Courtney's friends list, to see if I can find her that way, when Mum pokes her head through my bedroom door.

'I'm putting a wash on before I pop out to Asda. Have you got anything that needs bobbing in?'

I sit up on my bed and look down at the floor. There's a hoodie in the corner, an odd sock in front of the wardrobe and a pair of leggings with my knickers still tangled up in one of the legs poking out from under the bed.

'Nah, I'm all right for now.' I settle back down with my phone, scrolling through the hundreds of contacts Courtney has.

'What about your bedding? When was the last time you changed it?'

I have no idea. Do people really keep track? Probably.

'I'll do it later.'

Mum hesitates at the door for a few more seconds before she retreats. I scroll through a few more contacts before I grab my journal and flick it open at the grown-up to-do list. I really should learn how to use the washing machine – and change my sheets unprompted.

I stare down at my list, tapping my pen against the page as I contemplate the points. I still haven't a clue about the kind of career I'd like to pursue, so I move on to 'Move out of Mum & Dad's ASAP', which should be slightly easier once I've downloaded a property app to help me. Once I have the app open, I filter the properties by area (Clifton-on-Sea, because I still have to work at the chippy for now and I can't drive, though I have booked my first lesson. I add the booking of said lesson to my list now, just so I have something I can cross off). I leave the rental price at the default, because I have no idea what the going rate is – Mum and Dad only take a tiny, token amount from me each month. I only need one bedroom and a flat will do for now.

I tap the search button.

Nothing.

I change the property type to 'any'. Still nothing. Two bedrooms? Nope.

This isn't as easy as I thought it was going to be. I do vaguely remember Dad saying they should rename Woodland Road to Airbnb Road as half the houses have been bought to rent out as holiday lets, pricing out the locals (whatever that means). Maybe James wasn't bullshitting about his reason for moving in with Gran if there aren't any available properties for single people in town.

Or maybe he really is the snake I suspect him to be. How do you *know* if someone is a con man before it's too late and they've run off with all your worldly goods? I'm about to google it when I notice the time on my phone. I'm due at work in three minutes.

'*Mum.*' I scrabble off the bed and hunt for my shoes. There's a lime-green Converse by the window and a glittery one wedged between the wardrobe and chest of drawers. Is it too kooky to mix and match? '*Mum?*' I'm on my hands and knees now, peeking underneath the bed. There's a lot of crap under there, but I can't see any footwear.

'Mum!' With the odd shoes in hand, I scurry down the stairs, flinging myself from room to room. I find a black slider and a fluffy slipper on the way, but nothing suitable to wear to work. 'Mum?' I'm out of breath as I shuffle into the kitchen, leaning against the worktop for support. She isn't in here, but I can see Dad in the garden, crouched over his border with trowel in hand. He looks up as I make my way carefully over the patio in my socks.

'Where's Mum?' I turn back towards the house, as though she'll appear at the back door.

'She's gone to Asda.' Dad's attention is back on his shrubby things so he doesn't see me look up at the cloudy sky as I groan with frustration. I do vaguely remember her saying something about the supermarket but I wasn't really paying attention.

'But I need a lift to work.' I turn to the house again, wishing with all my might that Mum will be there, car keys in one hand and a matching shoe in the other. 'I'm going to be late.'

Dad shakes his head as he stabs at the ground with the trowel. 'Your time management is shocking.'

'Yeah, I'm aware.' It's another thing to add to the list. *Get to work on time*. 'You haven't seen one of these shoes, have you?' I hold up my mismatched footwear. Dad peers at them for a moment.

'I think there's a green one in the hallway. Your mum nearly tripped over it in the kitchen this morning.'

'Great. Well, not great about the tripping. You know what I mean. Thanks.' I'm babbling as I scamper back over the patio and dive into the kitchen. There's a shoe rack in the hallway, beneath the coat hooks, and sure enough there's a single lime-green Converse sitting next to Mum's work heels. I don't know why I didn't look here in the first place (probably because I never use the shoe rack – I'm not that organised). Dumping the glittery shoe on the rack (there's a first time for everything), I grab the green one and sit on the bottom stair so I can shove them on my feet. I'm officially late for work. Again.

The Fish & Chip Shop Around The Corner is only a quick dash away – a couple of streets to the park, skirt around the perimeter until you reach the church, head down towards the seafront, then a sharp right and you're there – but my chest is on fire and I think I may throw up by the time I fling myself into the shop, almost knocking Elliot over as he leaves after his shift. I'm supposed to be taking over from him, which cements the fact that I'm late. Claire and Bridget, who I'll be sharing the early evening shift with, are already behind the counter, which doesn't bode well since I'm their supervisor and should be at the shop before them. Especially as both Jed and Russell are here, witnessing my bad employee behaviour.

'Cleo, here at last.' Russell's tone sounds jovial, but then it always does. He's that kind of person. 'Can we have a word? In the back room?'

I shoot Claire a look of panic as I pass. This is it. My time management – or lack of it – is finally going to bite me on the arse and I'm going to lose my job.

'In you come.' Jed holds the door open for me and I shuffle inside the back room. I really *am* going to throw up now. I know I was going to leave anyway, to start my new, exciting and fulfilling career, but I wanted it to be on my terms. I didn't want to be sacked by two people I consider my friends as well as my employers, and being fired from your last job doesn't look too good on your CV.

'Take a seat.' Russell indicates the wobbly chairs. I take one and Jed lowers himself carefully into the other while Russell perches on the little filing cabinet. He clasps his hands on his lap, a sombre look I've never seen from him before on his face. The big, cheesy grin has limped away, his lips pressed into a thin line while his eyebrows have lowered, leaving him with a furrowed brow. This must be his 'you're fired' look. I do not like this look one bit.

'We need to discuss something serious with you.'

My heart is pounding and I'm sweating in places I've never sweated from before. I don't want to be fired, but I have to somehow prepare myself for it anyway, which basically means trying my hardest not to cry.

I close my eyes and take a breath as I wait for the blow.

Things NOT To Do Today:

- *Cry in front of bosses*
- *Get fired*
- *Cry in front of bosses again*

Chapter Nine

'You want me to what?'

I look from Russell to Jed, to check he's on board with this and his husband hasn't gone completely cuckoo with this suggestion without consulting him first. Jed, it seems, is not only aware but is fully on board. He leans on his elbows towards me, his eyebrows inching up his forehead in anticipation of my answer.

'We want you to take over managing the shop for a week or two while we go and stay with Mum.' The corners of Russell's lips flick upwards briefly. 'We know it's a big ask, and at such short notice, but Mum's not well and we don't trust anyone to run this shop more than you.'

My eyes flick from Russell to Jed and back again before roaming the room for a hidden camera, because this has got to be some kind of wind-up. I've just turned up late for my shift, for the billionth time, and I'm about as responsible as a toddler, and yet they want to leave me in charge of their business? Are they mad?

'Haven't you asked Claire?' She's way more reliable than I am – she's always on time, she doesn't sneak off to message her teen-years crush under the guise of 'stock-checking the wooden forks' when Jed and Russell aren't around, plus she's a mum, and there's nothing more challenging than being responsible for another human being. If you can manage that, you're a superhero in my books, and managing a seaside chippy during low season would be a piece of piss in comparison.

'Obviously we asked Claire first, but she said no. We even asked Elliot but he's got his exams coming up.' Russell snorts, the cheesy grin back in its rightful place. 'I'm kidding. Of course you're our first choice. You've been with us the longest, and you're already the assistant manager. You coped when we went to Tenerife last year for Mitchell's stag weekend.'

'That was for a *weekend*. Not a whole week.'

Jed holds up a hand. 'Maybe two. We're not entirely sure yet.'

'Exactly!' What do palpitations feel like? Because I think I'm experiencing them. 'I can't be trusted to run the shop. This is your baby, you always say that. Well, this place and Bolan.' Bolan is their cat, who they adore to the point of weirdness. 'What if I mess up?'

'You won't mess up. You already run the shop when we're both out anyway, and we'll always be on the end of the phone if you need us. Which you won't. You've got this.' Jed reaches across the table and gives my hand a squeeze. 'It'll be a doodle.'

I don't point out that it's *doddle*, but I do explain why it won't be one. 'You did see me walking in late just then, didn't you? I do it a lot when you're not here. Practically every shift.'

What am I doing? Two minutes ago I was scared of being sacked, and now I'm practically handing myself my P45. I need to *shut the hell up* before I find myself without employment at a time when I'm trying to prove I can be a grown-up.

'We know.' Jed gives my hand another squeeze. 'But you always get the shop open on time, and the customers *adore* you. You're an asset, despite not being able to tell the time.'

'And we were hoping you'd stay in the flat? So you'll be closer to work.' Russell places his hands together as though in prayer. 'And so you can look after Bolan for us.'

'You can't be late if you're living upstairs.' Jed smiles, but it's a dubious kind of smile. The kind that's too wide. Slightly manic. 'Right?'

'And there'll be a nice bonus in your pay packet, obviously, for the cat-sitting.'

The extra money does sound good, and maybe I'll even be able to cross off the 'Move out of Mum & Dad's' item on my to-do list (it says nothing about the move being permanent, after all).

'Can I think about it? The flat and cat thing?' It's one thing stepping up at work but taking care of someone else's property and keeping a living creature happy and healthy?

'Of course.' Jed's still holding on to my hand, and he adds his other hand for an extra big squeeze.

'But if we could have an answer quite soon?' Russell pushes his hands together again. 'Because we were hoping to set off first thing on Monday morning.'

Russell has the good grace to look sheepish as he delivers this last bit of information.

—

The teatime rush has already started by the time Jed and Russell release me from the back room. Claire and Bridget are frantically throwing scoops of chips onto paper or plates as the queue starts to snake out of the shop and onto the street. I don't have time to worry about the temporary manager position as I join them, shoving my hairnet and hat on as I take my first order (this is not correct, hygienic behaviour, and yet another reason why Jed and Russell are off their rockers).

'To eat in or take away?' I fasten the press studs on my tabard while my eyes roam the area under the counter for a pencil. There isn't one to be found, so I chant the order in my head so I don't forget it. *Two lots of fish and chips, sausage, chips and gravy, and a chip muffin.*

'Cleo, can you do mine, please?' Mrs Hornchurch, who is my very favourite customer, should be moving along the line to stand in front of Claire, but she's held herself back (and earned a few tuts from the queue behind). 'You do my fish just right. Light and crisp.'

Two lots of fish and chips, sausage, chips and gravy, and a chip muffin.

'I will, but you'll have to hang on for a minute.' I chant the order again in my head so I don't forget it.

'No problem, my dear.' Mrs Hornchurch lets the person behind her pass to Claire. 'You make the best fish and chips in Clifton-on-Sea, you know.'

I smile my thanks before I dash off to pinch a couple of portions of battered fish between the metal tongs, dumping them down on the greaseproof paper. *Two lots of fish and chips, sausage, chips and gravy, and a chip muffin.* I chant the order over and over again until it's fulfilled, and then I move straight on to Mrs Hornchurch's fish, making it from scratch and ensuring the coating is light and it's cooked to the exact shade of golden brown she prefers. I haven't even asked for her order, because it's the same every Saturday: fish (cooked to perfection by yours truly), chips and mushy peas with plenty of salt for Mrs Hornchurch, and a steak and kidney pudding with chips and gravy (no salt, bad for his blood pressure) for her partner. They eat it down on the seafront – on the beach if the weather permits or sitting on the little bench in the shelter on the promenade if not.

'What can I get you?'

Mrs Hornchurch is shuffling out of the shop with her warm paper packages and I've moved on to the next customer. It's Riley, another favourite customer, but he doesn't look as happy as Mrs Hornchurch did when he realises it's me who'll be serving him today. But it isn't because he dislikes me – I don't think Riley has it in him to dislike anybody – it's because he's *in lurve* with Claire and he'd much prefer to be chatting to her, even if it's only to place an order for a meat and potato pie and chips.

'Claire, can you take over this order for me? I really need to…' I make a vague gesture towards the kitchen, trying not to smirk when I clock the daggers my friend is sending my way. Riley may have a massive crush on Claire, but the feeling isn't mutual. Riley is much too sweet for Claire, who gravitates towards men who'll treat her like shit. The kind of men who'll charm her, promise her the world and then never call once she's slept with them. She needs a man like Riley, who'll deliver on his promises. She *deserves* a man like Riley.

I wink at Riley before buggering off to the kitchen. The dishwasher is full so I set it going before checking my messages. *Yes!* There's one from Paul. It's his day off and he's only just dragged himself out of bed, the lucky sod. He's off to the gym before meeting his mates in the pub.

> **What are your plans for the day?**

I could tell him the truth, that I'm working until late, and that it'll be after midnight by the time I go home and crawl straight into bed. But that sounds a bit boring.

> **Working late and then going into town with friends xxx**

That sounds more exciting, but I hesitate before pressing send. Teenagers go to clubs to get mashed with their mates but I want to present myself as more sophisticated. I delete the message and start again.

> **Finishing work soon and then going to a friend's for dinner xxx**

A dinner party is super-sophisticated, or so I assume, having never actually attended one. Maybe I should add it to my grown-up to-do list, and that way I won't be lying to Paul right now, it'll simply be a delayed truth. Or, better still, I can *host my own dinner party*. Now *that* would be super-sophisticated.

–

Claire and I are on our own during the late evening shift, but it's much quieter now the teatime rush is over. It'll pick up in a while, once the pubs start kicking everyone out, but for now we can enjoy the lull. Fleetwood Jack wanders in as we're looking up flats on my phone, and he's purple with rage as he spews about his day in court.

'Community service and a fine. It's a bloody joke. Loads of rock stars lobbed tellies out of hotel windows back in the day, and did any of *them* ever get pulled up for it? Did they bollocks. It's all this bloody woke shite. You can't do owt these days without someone telling you not to.'

'To be fair, Jack, you weren't even a paying guest at The Royal.' Claire has adopted the tone she uses when she's letting Arlo know he's doing something he shouldn't. 'And you caused quite a bit of damage, didn't you?' She raises her eyebrows at him, and he drops his gaze to the countertop. 'There was the telly, and the window. And the fire extinguisher that you used to create a *Stars in Their Eyes* effect.'

Fleetwood Jack looks up with a beam at this bit. 'Tonight, Matthew, I'm going to be... Paul McCartney!' His beam widens as he looks around the chippy as though it's filled with adoring, applauding fans, but there's only me and Claire here. 'I met him, you know. Paul. Good fella. Said I was going to make it big.'

'I'm sure he did.' Claire's tone suggests she is not sure at all. 'Did he also tell you that you were going to ride a floor lamp around the hotel lobby like a hobby horse? Or attempt to tap-dance on the reception desk?'

Fleetwood Jack rubs his left bum cheek. 'My arse still feels bruised from where I fell on it.'

'Do you think you should cut down on the booze and drugs?' Claire's tone is softer now. She isn't condemning or mocking, she's genuinely concerned.

Jack looks up at the ceiling through squinted eyes. 'Nah. What's life without a bit of fun and adventure, eh?'

He hands Claire a handful of coins and scoops up his packages. 'Smell ya later.'

We watch him leave in silence, not sure how to process the encounter. Claire goes back to my phone, angling it so I can see the screen.

'This place is all right. One bedroom, open-plan living area and kitchen, shower room. It even has a shared garden.'

I take the phone from her and study the listing. We've had to widen the net because there really aren't any properties to rent in town, but this one isn't *too* far away, and after checking on Google Maps I see it's within spitting distance of a bus route that passes through Clifton-on-Sea. This could be it, my new grown-up home.

'How much?' I gape at the amount they're asking for per month. I want to rent a one-bedroom flat, not a mansion with a swimming pool and more bathrooms than you could shake a stick at. I'll barely have enough left over to feed myself on my wages. I'll also need a deposit and I have zero savings. I don't even have a savings account. I'll need to open one and start actually putting money aside instead of spending it as soon as it's in my hand. Yet another thing to add to the ever-growing to-do list.

'If you take Jed and Russell up on their offer, you'll get a bit more money and you'll be able to save up a deposit quicker.' Claire takes her phone back and closes the app. She has a point, and the managerial position is only short-term. I can't mess it up *that* badly in a week or two, surely?

Absent-mindedly, I open Instagram and start to scroll. My eyes widen as I pause on a photo Paul posted a few hours ago. It's a gym shot, taken in front of the mirrors at the weights. In it, a topless Paul is holding his phone in one hand and a hefty-looking dumbbell in the other, his bicep bulging. *And just look at that six-pack.*

'I'm going to do it.' I try not to drool on my screen as I tap the like button. 'I'm going to take Jed and Russell up on their offer.' And I'm going to save enough money for a deposit so I can move out of Mum and Dad's – and tick off every item on my to-do list – so I can bag myself this god in front of me.

The Grown-Up To-Do List:

- *Decide on a career*

- *Start a career*

- <u>*Move out of Mum & Dad's ASAP*</u>

- *Learn to drive*

- *Find a hobby*

- *Learn to use the washing machine*

- ~~*Book first driving lesson*~~

- *Get to work on time*

- *Host a dinner party*

- *Open a savings account*

- *Save enough cash for a deposit on flat*

Chapter Ten

Sundays are my day off, so I've had a lengthy lie-in, a bacon butty and a decent cup of coffee from the coffee shop on the seafront, and Gran and I (and James, because he's got his feet firmly under the table now) have caught up on *Waiting on You*. He's gone out now, leaving me and Gran to have some quality grandmother–granddaughter time together. At least, it'd be quality time if I didn't have a crochet hook in hand.

'That's it.' Gran's watching me as I clumsily twist the hook and grab hold of the yarn. 'Yarn over and pull through. You've got it.'

I don't have it. I have absolutely no idea what I'm doing, other than trying to follow Gran's extremely patient step-by-step instructions while keeping a lid on my frustrations so I don't drop-kick the ball of yarn out of the window. James has picked it up and can produce a decent-looking granny square in an evening while I'm still flailing and haven't created a single square, decent or otherwise.

'Yarn over.' Gran nods encouragingly as I fiddle about with the hook again. I don't even know what 'yarn over' means. 'And pull through. Lovely. One more time. Yarn over… and pull through.'

'Can we take a break?' I drop the hook and knotted bit of yarn on my lap and wriggle my aching fingers.

'Shall I pop the kettle on? Make a nice pot of tea?' Gran pats my knee, and I nod, managing the teeniest of smiles. What I really want is a big, fat coffee but Gran's expertise lies in tea-making. She has beautiful teapots with matching cups, saucers and milk jugs, all of them older than I am, but the only coffee she owns is an ancient jar of home brand instant that's starting to clump. She doesn't drink coffee so she doesn't realise how nasty and bitter it is and I don't have the heart to complain (out loud) about it.

We have the cup of tea in the garden. It isn't quite warm enough and I have to bury my hands deep into the pocket of my hoodie, but at least it's a break from the stupid 'yarning over'. And the plate of home-made chocolate chip cookies makes me feel a bit less grumpy.

'You've made these a lot recently.' I brush the crumbs from my hoodie with a hand encased in its sleeve for warmth. 'Not that I'm complaining, obviously.'

'Edith likes them.' Gran pours tea into the floral-patterned cups. I have no idea who Edith is – a new friend from one of her volunteering posts? She certainly wasn't at Gran's party, and I've never heard her mentioned before. Still, if it means I get to eat more delicious cookies, I'm glad she's found herself in Gran's life.

'How's it going with James?' It's good I've finally got Gran on her own, so I can dig for any dirt. She can be honest now it's just the two of us, because she can hardly bad-mouth the guy when he's sitting in the same room within close proximity to a pair of scissors (tiny crochet scissors, but still sharp). We should have some sort of code word, something innocent-sounding that really means *get this scumbag out of my house*.

'It's lovely having him here.' Gran adds a tiny dash of milk to my tea. The drink's the colour of a wet terracotta pot (bleurgh). 'It's settling just to know there's someone else in the house, and he's great company. He likes a bit of gentle crime, so we've been watching *Midsomer Murders* in the evenings when he isn't working.'

Damn. He's got me there. I really can't sit through another episode, even for Gran. I'm more of a true crime girl, the grittier the better, and being crushed to death by a wheel of cheese does nothing for me.

'And he's a wonderful cook. You should come over for tea. I'll ask him to make his spaghetti Bolognese.' Gran leans towards me, lowering her voice. 'It's even better than your dad's. Don't tell your dad that, of course. I'll deny it under torture.' She chuckles as she adds a dash of milk to her own tea. 'Are you free on Tuesday?'

I shake my head as I plop a couple of sugar cubes into my tea. Gran tuts because I use my fingers and not the pretentious little silver tongs on the tray. 'I'm working the later shifts all next week. I'm managing the shop while Jed and Russell are away again.'

'That's wonderful. It shows how much they trust you.' Gran reaches across the table to give my arm a squeeze. 'Well done, Cleo.'

I shrug. I still think Jed and Russell aren't quite right in the upstairs department if they're willing to leave their pride and joy in my hands, but who am I to complain? I'll be getting a bit more money to put towards a deposit for a flat, plus they've asked Bridget to step in and help out because I can't physically be at the shop during opening times seven days a week without collapsing of exhaustion. Bridget's an ex-geography teacher who found herself bored out of her brain after taking early retirement and has been working at The Fish & Chip Shop Around The Corner for the past six years. She's bossy and forthright and thinks she knows absolutely *everything* and, because of our new roles, I won't have to share a shift with her for at least a week. Forget the money, this is reward in itself.

'I'm flat-sitting for them as well.' I pour in a decent amount of milk to get rid of the terracotta shade and give my tea a stir. 'So maybe *you* should come over to mine for tea?'

Does it count as a dinner party if you bung something in the microwave for your gran?

–

I'm having another go at crocheting when James stumbles through the door. I've finally figured out what yarning over is (it's when you do the twisty thing with your hook and make another loopy thing) and I've sort of mastered the treble crochet. I've almost completed a whole round of my granny square and am feeling pretty proud of myself.

'Cordy in the kitchen?' James' chin is tilted up so he can see over the large cardboard box he's struggling to keep hold of.

'Yes, *Cordelia* is in the kitchen.' *Yarn over and… pull through.* 'What's in the box?'

James uses his knee to nudge it upwards and clings on to the sides before it slips. 'Just some bits and pieces I had in storage. Cordy said I could bring some stuff over. Not the big stuff, obviously, but some home comforts.'

Home comforts? The dude really has got his feet under the table.

'What kind of home comforts?' I've turned back to my crochet (*yarn over and… pull through*) and when I look back up again, James has already staggered from the room without hearing my question. I finish my stitch before laying my crochet carefully on the table and marching after him. James is unpacking the box on the kitchen table. Home comforts, it seems, include a games console and a bunch of games, a pile of books, some framed photos, a David Bowie mug and… oh, sweet lord. *A coffee machine.* A really decent-looking coffee machine. She's a thing of beauty, stark black against shiny chrome, with dials and buttons and a *milk frother.*

I wonder if James will let me have a play…?

'Why don't you pop that over in the corner?' Gran indicates the space she's made on the worktop, where her cookbooks used to live. 'There's a spare socket, and I've made some room in the cupboard for the pod thingies.'

I peer into the box and nearly wet myself with excitement. There are a ton of coffee pods, of various types and flavour. Espresso, cappuccino, latte, Colombian, Brazilian, Ethiopian, vanilla, almond, caramel. I'm in coffee heaven.

'Shall we set it going? Christen it in its new temporary home?' James has set the coffee machine down on the worktop and plugged it in and I'm still gawping down at the caffeinated delights in the box. 'What do you fancy? I'm going for a hazelnut espresso.' James plucks one of the variety packs out of the cardboard box and shakes out a pod. He does a little shimmy with his hips as he crosses the kitchen, like an excited little boy with a new toy. 'Decided yet?' He's back again, the delicious nutty coffee smell wafting from his David Bowie cup.

'Can I have a vanilla latte macchiato? No, a cortado. No, the latte macchiato. Definitely the latte macchiato.' I fiddle with my messy bun, making it even messier than usual. 'Or maybe the cortado?'

'Tell you what.' James reaches into the box and grabs two pods, placing one in each hand before putting them behind his back. 'Pick one. Left or right?'

'My left or right; your left or right?'

James rolls his eyes. 'My left or right.'

'Right.'

'Right?' James starts to move his hand, and my eyes widen in panic.

'No! I was saying right, I understand, not picking right.'

'So you want left?'

I twist a loose strand of hair around my finger. 'I don't know. Maybe.'

'Oh, Cleo.' Gran sighs as she marches over. 'It's only coffee. Have this one.' She grabs one of the pods from behind James' back and peers at it. 'A cortado?'

James looks at me for confirmation and I give a limp shrug. I really want the caramel latte macchiato now the option has been taken away from me.

'Why don't you have this one later?' He holds up the cortado pod before putting it back into its box.

'I can have them both?'

James heads over to the coffee machine and pops the pod inside. 'Have as many as you like. Help yourself. Mi coffee es su coffee.' He grabs a mug from the cupboard, his back to me so he can't see the awe on my face. Is it wrong that I suddenly want to marry this man? Yes, yes it is, because he may be generous with his coffee pods, but I still don't trust him. This coffee business could be nothing but a ruse to hoodwink me. He's sensed my weakness and he's exploiting it so I'll turn a blind eye while he rips off my gran. Well, I'm not going to fall for it (though I *may* play along and drink his coffees).

'Thank you.' I take the coffee from him, my face back to its usual non-star-struck look. The smell is dreamy but I manage to keep my guard up. I'm going to have to be very careful with this one. He's even sneakier than I'd anticipated.

Life's To-Do List:

- *Enjoy the little things in life*

- *Eat healthily and exercise daily*

- *Drink more water*

- *Love yourself*

- *Pretend any of these things are going to happen*

Chapter Eleven

There's a lot of stuff in Jed and Russell's living room, but it's all neatly in its place. There's floor-to-ceiling shelves in the alcoves either side of the fireplace, one crammed with DVDs (retro, but maybe Jed and Russell are like Dad, who refuses to stream and still uses a DVD player) and the other filled with books, CDs (more retro-ness. Haven't they heard of Spotify?) and Jed's curling trophies. There are photos everywhere – canvases on the walls, framed photos on the mantelpiece, windowsill and sideboard, and even the throw cushions on the sofa depict their owners, with Bolan (the cat) in the middle and his humans either side. The cat is currently curled up in a hammock-type bed hung from the radiator, and he has another bed, an actual four-poster in miniature with a teal satin duvet and matching pillow, underneath the window.

'He's actually pretty low-maintenance.' Jed has spotted me looking at the mini bed with dismay. I mean, that's pretty weird, isn't it? Having a four-poster bed *for your cat*? It wouldn't look out of place in a boutique. If it was bigger and intended for human use. 'He eats twice a day – his pouches are in the fridge – and he's fully house-trained. His litter tray is in the hall.'

We've just passed through the hall, and I didn't spot a litter tray. I head back out there, just to be sure. Nope, no litter tray.

'It's really easy to manage.' Russell stoops down and flips the lid up off the brown leather ottoman in the corner. 'You can take the tray out and empty it really easily. I'll show you where the bag of litter is.'

There's a hole cut out of the side of the ottoman, so the cat can pop inside and do its business in privacy, but I don't have time to marvel over the luxurious kitty litter tray because Jed and Russell have already left the hall. I scuttle after them, passing back through the living room and into the kitchen. It's a tiny room, but it still manages to look showroom-like, with its geometric tiles, white glossy cupboard doors and gleaming chrome fittings.

'The kitty litter's in here.' Russell opens one of the cupboards. There are only three cupboards in the kitchen, but this one is dedicated to the cat's needs, with bags of kitty litter, a stack of little bowls, a grooming kit consisting of brush, comb and *a toothbrush and toothpaste*, and a tin of treats, which Russell takes out now. 'He has a treat *once a day*.' Russell eyes Jed as he says this, an eyebrow cocking as his head tilts to one side.

'What? Sometimes I forget he's already had something.' Jed looks down at the floor as he says this. He doesn't forget at all.

This cat means the absolute world to them, I realise as I follow them back through to the hall so they can show me the bathroom and bedroom. It's a little nerve-wracking, to be honest. I've never had to look after anyone before, unless you count Grandad after his stroke, but at least then I only had to follow Mum and Gran's lead. Now I have sole responsibility for a living thing. I need to add 'keep the cat alive' to my grown-up to-do list.

'I think that's it.' Russell claps his hands together. 'The new rota's on the fridge as well as downstairs in the shop.

One of the temps is starting tomorrow, but Bridget will show them the ropes, and she's going to deal with the early-morning deliveries. She's up at the crack of dawn anyway, apparently. You'll have to deal with the other temp on Tuesday, but you'll be fine. You've got this.' He clamps his hand down on my shoulder. 'You have got this, right?'

I bob my head up and down, trying to convince myself as well as Russell. 'I've got this. You go off and look after Pauline. I'll be fine. The shop will be fine. Bolan will be fine. I promise.'

Russell hesitates for a moment before he takes a deep breath, gives a curt nod of his head and picks up the holdall at the foot of the bed. Hitching it onto his shoulder, he grabs one of the suitcases and extends its handle before dragging it across the bedroom carpet and out into the hall. Jed grabs the other suitcase and a rucksack from the bed and follows while I ponder exactly why they have so much luggage for a week with Russell's mum. I have a few changes of clothes, my washbag and hairdryer (in case I'm inclined to use it. I'm usually not), a couple of pairs of pyjamas and my bullet journal stuffed into a carrier bag.

'You have our mobile numbers and the landline at my mum's.'

I've followed the guys down to the car, which Jed is busy packing their luggage into while Russell flaps a bit more. 'There's a bunch of emergency numbers on the fridge. The vet's is on there in case Bolan takes ill.' He performs the sign of the cross, even though he isn't religious and hasn't stepped foot in a church since his sister's wedding twenty-odd years ago. 'And there's the names and numbers of the plumber and electrician we've used in the past. Fingers crossed you won't need them, but they're there, just in case.'

'Better safe than sorrowful.' Jed closes the boot and joins me and Russell on the pavement. The pair look at the fish and chip shop, Russell with his lips pressed into a thin line, Jed swallowing hard as they gaze at the signage.

'You're not leaving the place forever.' I roll my eyes as I nudge them towards the car. I won't hesitate to slap them if they start to blubber. 'You'll be gone for a week. Two, max.' I catch Russell's eye, to make sure this is still the deal and they're not trying to pull a fast one.

'You're right.' Russell kisses me on the cheek. 'Take care of our babies, won't you?'

'I will.' I give them another nudge before standing back. They climb into the car, giving a cheery wave before they set off, T. Rex's 'I Love to Boogie' blasting from the stereo. I wave until they disappear around the corner and then head back up to the flat. My new home for the next week or two.

Bolan is still nestled in his radiator hammock, none the wiser that his owners have left him. I wrestle my bullet journal from the carrier bag I dumped on the sofa earlier and flip to my grown-up to-do list. I add the point about keeping the cat alive and cross out 'Move out of Mum and Dad's ASAP' before settling down with the remote. It may be cheating, since I haven't technically *moved out*, but it gives me a little boost anyway.

–

What's your favourite film?

I send the message to Paul while I'm browsing Jed and Russell's vast selection of DVDs. They have at least a hundred lined up on the shelves in the alcove but none of them are catching my interest. I'm the same with Netflix and Amazon Prime; I spend longer browsing than I do watching whatever it is I finally decide on. There are loads of films I know of on the shelf but have never watched (*The Breakfast Club*, *Vertigo*, all the Indiana Jones films) and some I've never even heard of (*East of Eden*, *Midnight Cowboy*, *St. Elmo's Fire*). There are films I've seen – some I've even enjoyed – but my eyes flick past them. A few hours into flat-sitting and I'm already bored and restless. Claire's downstairs, but she's working and she'll be picking Arlo up from school and doing 'mum' things once she's finished her shift, like feeding the boy, homework, bath and bedtime, all while trying to squeeze in her studies. Gran will be off doing her volunteer work and Mum and Dad will be at work.

My world, I realise, is very small. But Paul is going to change that. He's going to open up my world again, expand it beyond Clifton-on-Sea and The Fish & Chip Shop Around The Corner.

My phone buzzes with a message from him. His favourite film is *The Dark Knight*, which I'm pretty sure is a Batman film. It isn't my kind of thing, but I scour the DVDs anyway in search of it. Watching Paul's favourite film will make me feel closer to him. Russell and Jed have a copy of *A Knight's Tale*, but no Batman films. I slide *A Knight's Tale* off the shelf anyway – it's a close enough match, I suppose, especially as they both star Heath Ledger.

I manage approximately five minutes before I pick up my phone and message Paul again, and I have no idea what's going on in the film by the time the exchanges dry up. I stop the DVD and pop it back on the shelf before having a wander around the flat in search of something to do to stave off the boredom. I almost wish I'd brought my crochet project with me, just so I'd have something to keep me occupied.

I need to get out of this flat for some fresh air. Craziness has clearly started to kick in.

I walk around the corner to the seafront, my hands stuffed into my pockets to ward off the chill in the air. The seafront is pretty much deserted, with only a couple of dog walkers down on the beach and the odd person wandering past the shops, most of which are shuttered. It's low season now, but in a few weeks all the shops will be open and the seafront will be packed with tourists. The town will be bustling and we'll have to take on seasonal workers in the chippy to keep up with demand. High season is my favourite time in the shop. We're rushed off our feet and I always fall into bed in an exhausted heap, but the atmosphere changes in those few months. The tourists arrive to enjoy their holidays and days out, jubilant at the small window of freedom and relaxation. People are *happy* and their good mood spreads throughout the whole town, bringing the place to life again.

Across the road, a figure dressed in a navy suit catches my eye. It's the hair I recognise, the brown curls swept back into a short ponytail. James is striding past the shuttered rock shop, a takeaway cup of coffee in one hand and a paper bag in the other as he strides along the pavement. My hand is halfway out of my pocket so I can raise it in greeting before I come to my senses and stop myself, shoving it deeper into the pocket and out of harm's way. I was about to wave at James, the would-be granny seducer. The craziness has most definitely set up camp.

Head down, I scurry back to the flat and give *A Knight's Tale* another go.

What I Thought I Could Be Today:

- *A world-class chef (a female Gordon Ramsay without the swears)*

What I Actually Was Today:

- *Delusional*

Chapter Twelve

Gran's house is empty when I get there, but then I am earlier than usual. After watching *A Knight's Tale* while scoffing a chicken pasty (the branded paper bag James had been carrying tempted me, so I popped in the shop on my way back), I pottered about the flat, changing Bolan's litter tray even though it didn't need it, stacking the dishwasher (if putting a couple of mugs in there counts as 'stacking') and unpacking my carrier bag in Russell and Jed's bedroom, periodically checking my phone for messages and frantically bashing out a reply every time I spotted one from Paul. Russell and Jed said I could help myself to anything from the fridge, freezer and cupboards, which were crammed with food. The fridge in particular was bursting, mostly with fruit and vegetables (probably to make up for the fish and chips) and I didn't even recognise a good chunk of it. I didn't let this deter me. If I'm going to host a dinner party as part of my 'be a grown-up' kick, I'll need to learn how to cook, so why not experiment while I have a fridge full of ingredients and a stack of cookbooks on the shelf in the alcove?

After selecting a recipe for a 'hearty vegetable stew' from one of the books, I grabbed a load of leafy green things from the fridge and peeled and chopped while listening to an uplifting playlist on Spotify. The whole lot was chucked in a casserole dish with boiling water and an Oxo cube before being placed in the oven. I checked – and double-checked – for more messages while I waited for the hearty stew to do its thing, and Bolan finally dragged himself from the radiator hammock and curled up on my lap, which was quite sweet until he started to claw at my thigh in a weird, rhythmic way. I had to shoo him away when I heard the threads of my leggings rip, which earned me a look of pure disgust as he slinked his way across the room and disappeared into the hall, where he did a big dirty protest in his spotless litter tray.

After over three hours in the oven, I pulled the stew out, lifted the lid and almost vomited over Russell and Jed's kitchen floor. Hours later, and with all the windows open, the flat still smells like a teenage boy's gym bag and, unable to take the stench for another second, I've taken myself to Gran's house.

There's no answer when I ring, so I use my key to let myself inside. The downstairs rooms are all empty, so I head upstairs. I don't actually check inside the guest bedroom, though I do press my ear against the door to listen for any signs of life. I'm tempted to have a snoop, to hunt for evidence of James' wrongdoings – a stack of pension books, a false passport, that sort of thing – but I show great restraint when I take myself back downstairs instead. I find myself in the kitchen, facing the fancy coffee machine James installed yesterday, mug in hand. He *did* say I could help myself to his pods, but was his offer genuine, or was he playing out his kind, generous spiel for Gran's benefit?

I open the cupboard beneath the coffee machine and select a pod. If James' offer *was* genuine, then there's no problem with me enjoying a cortado. And if he was simply showing off in front of Gran with his phony offer, then it'll serve him right for being a smarmy, deceitful git.

The coffee is delicious, with an intense, bitter burst of flavour combined with creamy milk. I'm in heaven right now as I sip the drink on my way to the living room. I have a quick snoop around (just in case James has carelessly left any incriminating evidence lying around) before settling down with my crochet. I may as well – there's nothing else to do while I wait for Gran to get back. I really do need to kick-start my social life again. It'd be something to post on Instagram to show Paul how much fun I am to be around if nothing else and I consider the places I can venture out to (perhaps not the Red Lion just yet) as I work on my crochet. I'm on the second round of my granny square and it's oddly satisfying to see it changing shape. How has it gone from a circle to square-shaped? Baffling.

I'm on my second coffee by the time Gran and James get back (the first coffee pod has been stuffed right down to the bottom of the bin so it doesn't look like I'm taking the piss). Gran is chuckling as she steps into the living room and though she's still smiling when she spots me, her eyebrows rise in surprise. I've caught her off guard. She wasn't expecting to see me sitting on her sofa when she arrived back with the lodger.

'Have you two been out somewhere together?' Eww, they haven't been out on a *date*, have they? Because I'll chuck the cortado and cappuccino up over the sofa if they have.

'No, I was on my way back from Gwen's and James stopped and offered me a lift the rest of the way.'

I'm not sure I believe Gran's version of events. It all seems a tad convenient and doesn't explain the surprise –

or was it guilt? – when she spotted me. 'You're learning fast.' Gran nods at the crochet square in my hand. 'You're doing marvellous. We'll have a blanket out of you in no time.'

I suppose the crochet – being carried out voluntarily – could explain the astonishment on Gran's face a moment ago.

'I was bored.' I raise one of my shoulders in a shrug before going at the yarn with my hook. I'm on the final corner of round two, which means I'm almost halfway there. Two more rounds and I'll have a whole granny square.

I am definitely adding 'kick-start my social life' to my to-do list, because it's tragic how gratified I feel right now over a bit of knotted wool.

'Have you eaten?' Gran drops her handbag onto the other end of the sofa. I watch James for signs of interest in the bag but he's too busy shrugging off his blazer and draping it on the back of his chair. *The* chair. Not his, even if he does seem to have claimed it as his own. How long until he's claimed the whole house?

'Cleo?' Gran unzips her anorak. 'Have you eaten? I could make you something if you're hungry?'

I tear my eyes away from James. 'I'm good. I had something before I came out.'

'Something' was the pasty I scoffed before attempting to make the revolting stew.

'How's it going? Living away from home for the first time?'

'It isn't the first time.' I don't mean to sound sulky, but that's how it comes out. 'I went away for a bit, during my gap year with Sienna.'

The gap year that turned into a decade, because I never made it to university.

'Only for a bit?' James sits down on the chair. I watch him closely for signs of snark, but he seems mildly curious, if anything. He can't even be bothered to make eye contact as he reaches into the box beside his chair.

'I had to come home.' I focus on my treble crochet. I'm still slow and clumsy with the hook and yarn, so it takes a lot of concentration. 'My grandad had a stroke. He needed looking after.'

'I'm sorry. That must have been tough.' I see James looking at Gran out of the corner of my eye. He's still reaching into the plastic box he keeps his crochet kit in, but he's stopped rummaging.

'It was quite a mild one. He recovered well with the help of his family and we had a few more precious years together.' Gran stoops to kiss me on the top of the head, her lips nudging my messy bun. 'I'll go and put the kettle on. I suppose you two will want one of those fancy coffees?'

'I'm fine for now, thanks.' I nod towards the mug on the table. 'I used one of your pods. I hope that's okay?' The coffee churns in my stomach as I fleetingly meet James' eye. I shouldn't have stolen a pod – *two pods* – and now I feel guilty. 'I'll buy some more to replace them… it.'

'It's fine.' James places his latest granny square on his lap. It has a green centre, a cream inner layer and he's about to start a green outer layer, the show-off git. 'Like I said, help yourself. Your gran's being so generous, a few coffee pods is the least I can do.'

How generous? What's she offering up to this stranger?

'You are paying rent, aren't you?'

James snorts. 'Of course. What do you take me for?'

I keep quiet. I'm not sure James would appreciate the answer to that question.

'I've bought you a little house-warming present.' Gran's back from the kitchen, beaming at me as she carefully hands me a spotty gift bag. 'I know you're only at the flat temporarily, but I was passing that upcycling shop near the station and I saw this in the window.' I peer into the bag and see a bunch of leaves. Reaching gingerly inside, I feel around and find a cool, smooth pot. There's a handle, which I use to pull the object carefully from the bag. 'Isn't it perfect for you?'

The 'object' is a Starbucks mug containing some kind of leafy plant. It's a lovely gesture, and it's the perfect house-warming gift for the coffee-obsessed, but my stomach churns again. Not only do I have to take care of Russell and Jed's cherished cat, I also have to somehow keep this plant alive too. I mentally add another item to my mounting grown-up to-do list.

–

It's strange being in a bed that isn't mine. I've slept in other beds, obviously – the bed in Gran's guest room many times (the bed James is probably sleeping in right now. Icky thought. Let's move on), the fold-up bed Sienna used to squeeze into her bedroom for our sleepovers, the scarily narrow bed at Jerry and Gwen's caravan, and, briefly, the beds in the hostels Sienna and I stayed in during our travels. I found those hostel beds the most difficult to sleep in, and not just because we had to share a room with strangers. I hated being away from home, from Mum and Dad, and Gran and Grandad, and my friends. Travelling the world wasn't at all what I had expected it to be. I thought being away from home would be freeing, but it was exhausting and grimy, and the nights were the worst, when there was nothing to keep my mind off how homesick I was, even with Sienna by my side. At night I could admit to myself that I wasn't happy, that I missed my old life and wanted to go home. So sleeping was hard and the only thing that helped was putting on the playlist Sienna and I had made before we left Clifton-on-Sea. It was made up of memories – the song we jumped around with abandon to during our primary school's leavers' disco; the song we listened to during Sienna's first break-up, when she was heartbroken and couldn't express the feelings swirling around her thirteen-year-old body; and the song that picked her up again and made her a fighter. Songs that we listened to on a loop during our first residential school trip, and songs we belted out the lyrics of as we staggered home after a night in the Red Lion. I grew up listening to these songs and it didn't matter that I was hundreds of miles away from home while that playlist was blasting through my earphones.

I have the playlist on Spotify, and I set it going now. Bolan, it seems, doesn't sleep in his fancy four-poster bed during the night. He curls up on the end of Russell and Jed's bed, but he's a quiet sleeper and at least it means he's forgiven me for shooing him away earlier. I close my eyes as Avril Lavigne tells me the story of the sk8er boi and the snobby, judgemental girl who threw away her chance to be with him. I can picture Sienna and I jumping around the hall of our primary school, the room filled with balloons and banners. Jessica Smithson was crying in the corner, being comforted by Mrs Langley and Miss Paris, and at the time I'd thought she was an attention-seeking baby. But I get it now. We were leaving one stage of our lives behind and moving on to the next but Jessica wasn't ready to let go. I wonder what happened to Jessica Smithson. We didn't go to the same secondary school and I never saw her after we left Year 6. She's probably acing life like all the others. High-flying career. Gorgeous house. Husband (or wife, let's not make assumptions). Kids.

I'm feeling gloomy again, but a message on my phone perks me up. It's from Paul, saying good night (with *three kisses*). For the past seven years, my life has been on hold, suspended between my teenage years and adulthood, but Paul 'Franko' Franks will be back in my life in eighty-two days and I'll be nudged back on track again.

The Grown-Up To-Do List:

- *Decide on a career*

- *Start a career*

- ~~*Move out of Mum & Dad's ASAP*~~

- *Learn to drive*

- *Find a hobby*

- *Learn to use the washing machine*

- ~~*Book first driving lesson*~~

- *Get to work on time*

- *Host a dinner party (<u>do not</u> serve 'hearty vegetable stew')*

- *Open a savings account*

- *Save enough cash for a deposit on flat*

- *Keep the cat alive*

- *Keep the plant alive (not as important as the cat, but will mean a lot to Gran)*

- *Kick-start social life*

Chapter Thirteen

I'm zipping around the flat, scurrying from room to room to feed the cat (who doesn't deserve nourishment after he woke me up by standing on my face at too-early o'clock this morning but I'm providing the little git with it anyway) and to shove yesterday's clothes in the washing machine (I haven't got time to actually read the instructions Jed left for me to set it going. Will do that later) while hunting down my left shoe. I can hear Mum honking the horn down on the street but I haven't brushed my hair yet and I'm going nowhere wearing one shoe. Russell and Jed's flat is immaculate (at least it was until I descended) so how can I have misplaced it?

I fly at the window and part the blinds when Mum honks again, sticking two fingers up to the pane of glass (symbolising 'two minutes' – I'm not flicking her the Vs). The shoe hunt continues as I drag a brush through my bedhead hair. There it is! Poking out from under the cushion printed with Russell's face. I shove the shoe on my foot and gather my hair into its usual messy bun before grabbing something quick to eat from the kitchen. I haven't had breakfast yet (despite being woken up ridiculously early by the demon ball of fur) and I'm *starving*. I don't have time for a proper breakfast, so a couple of fun-size Snickers will have to do. They're practically Crunchy Nut Cornflakes in bar form, but I'll add the breakfast thing to my grown-up to-do list later. I definitely don't have time now – Mum's three quick-fire honks have morphed into one very long, very agitated beep.

'At last.' Mum gives the clock on her dashboard a pointed look as I clamber into the car. 'I'm going to be late for work.'

'Sorry.' I shove the last bit of Snickers into my gob and buckle myself in. I have an appointment at the bank, to open some kind of high-interest savings account thingy. I was hoping to sort it out online, but it seems I have to go into the branch, and at least it's something to cross off the to-do list. I seem to be adding way more stuff than I'm achieving so I need to pull my finger out. Paul will be back in town in eighty-one days and I don't want to let him – or myself – down.

'How's it going staying in the flat on your own?' Mum pulls away, Boyzone's 'I Love the Way You Love Me' wafting from the CD player. 'Got any washing you need me to pick up later?'

'Mum.' I sigh, short and sharp. 'I'm a grown-up. I can do my own washing.'

Mum huffs. 'Since when?'

'Since now.' I shuffle down in my seat and shove my hands under my armpits. 'And staying at the flat has been great. Really great. I'm loving it.'

'So you haven't missed us then?'

'Why? Have you missed me?'

Mum sneaks a quick peek at me as we wait at a junction. 'Missed the extra washing and the shoes and clothes left lying around the place and causing a trip hazard? Of course I've missed you.'

I feel a flicker of a smile and try to tamper it down. 'I've missed you too. A little bit. But you know I'll be moving out for good one day soon?'

Mum nods, but I'm not quite sure she believes that's true.

The appointment at the bank goes well and my new savings account is activated. There isn't much in there yet, but it's a start. The woman who sorted it for me was lovely, and she seemed to enjoy her job. Plus, the knotted scarf she was wearing as part of her uniform was cute. A possible career direction? Something to think about, at least.

I'm not due at the chippy until mid-afternoon, so I have a little mooch around town (and I grab a coffee and pastry to make up for the rubbish breakfast) before heading for the bus stop. It's started to rain and I have neither a coat nor an umbrella. Why did I put a regular jumper on this morning instead of a hoodie, which would have at least provided a bit of extra cover?

A car approaches and I take a step back, away from the puddle that's forming at the gutter. But the car slows down and stops in front of me. The window lowers and someone leans across to peer at me.

'Cleo?' It's James, with someone else in the passenger seat. 'Are you heading back to Clifton?' I nod, my teeth chattering so violently I'm unable to speak. 'Get in. I'll drop you off.'

I don't like James. I don't trust him as far as I can throw him. But it's raining so hard my hair is plastered to my skull and I'm in danger of developing hypothermia in my sodden clothes.

'Thanks.' The simple word ends up having three syllables due to my chattering teeth.

The passenger door opens and a youth unfolds himself onto the pavement. He's tall and gangly and looks a lot like James but without the beard. He looks me up and down and heaves a huge sigh before he drags the back door of the car open and slumps inside.

'I'm a bit soggy. Sorry.' Still, I throw myself into the car before James can rescind his offer of a lift.

'No worries.' James closes the window, so I'm no longer getting spattered with rain, and sets off.

'No worries for *you*.' The youth in the back of the car shifts in his seat so that his knees press into my back. I know he's spectacularly tall for a kid, but I'm sure he does it on purpose. 'I've got to sit in that seat after.'

'Seth.' James' tone is low as he glances at the kid in his rear-view mirror.

'Dad.' The tone is reflected back by the kid, and I almost give myself whiplash as I twist my neck so fast to look at him. *Dad?* James is this kid's *dad*? But he's, what? Thirteen? Fourteen?

'Ignore him. He's grumpy because we've just had a trip to the dentist and now he has to go back to school.'

James is speaking, but I don't turn back around. There's another kid in the back, this one younger and female. She smiles shyly at me as our eyes meet.

'Hello.' I smile back. Or grimace, I'm not sure. The attempt is there but I'm shook. I turn to face James. 'Are these your kids?'

'Seth and Edith.' James eyes the rear-view mirror briefly again. 'This is Cleo.'

'Cordy's your granny.' The little girl smiles shyly again as I shift in my seat to face her.

'You know my gran?' I'm hit with a memory of sitting in the garden with Gran. There's a plate of chocolate chip cookies. *Edith likes them.* I'd assumed Edith was a friend of Gran's, not a sweet-looking little girl. She has James' curls, but they're a golden blonde, held back from her face by two sparkly blue butterfly clips.

'She helps us to cross the road.' Edith wiggles two fingers to make a walking gesture. 'And she gives us sweeties on Fridays. Just one.' She holds up a finger to demonstrate, her brow furrowed in earnestness. 'Rhubarb and custards are my favourite.'

I shift in my seat, so I can face James. 'Gran's your kid's lollipop lady? Is that how you met?'

I wasn't expecting *that.* Of all the scenarios I've run over in my head since Gran's birthday, this one had never even occurred to me.

–

'James has got kids.'

I've just flung myself into the chippy after racing up to the flat to bung my wet clothes in the washing machine, throw on a new set of clothes and blitz my hair with the hairdryer (I did need it after all). I've even set the washing machine going, thanks to Jed's instructions stuck on the front of the fridge, and it turns out it isn't that complicated after all. There are a load of settings and buttons, but you only need to know what a few of them actually do (daily cycle, forty degrees and start, in this case). I am now one step closer to being a proper grown-up, so I can proudly cross that one off my list later.

'Who?' Claire is wiping down one of the tables, having a good go at a dollop of congealing ketchup (gross). Danny, one of the temps Russell and Jed organised to help out during their absence, is here but there are no customers as it's in that quiet period between the late lunchtime stragglers and the early tea-timers. In a few weeks, this lull will feel like a luxury, but it's a bit boring during the low season, to be honest.

'James... thingy.' I'm sure he told me his surname, in that awkward moment when I thought he was a cat burglar, but my brain hasn't held on to the information. 'The bloke who's living with my gran. Not *living* living with her. The lodger.' I plonk myself down at the now clean table. 'And he's got kids. Two of them.'

'So what?' Claire straightens the little wire basket of condiments on the table and slips a menu behind it.

'*So what?* He's my age, pretty much, and he's got *two kids*. And one of them is like a man-child. He's taller than me. *Way* taller. The other one's younger. About Arlo's age, I'd guess. She said Gran's her lollipop lady, so she probably goes to the same school. Does Arlo know an Edith... something?'

I know very little about this man. He lives with my gran and yet he's still a stranger. I don't know what he does for a living, or even his surname. I'm going to have to do some subtle digging the next time I go over to catch up on *Waiting on You*, though I'll have to do a better job than I have done with Paul. I attempted to find out more about his past relationship but all I know is that her name is Daisy (cute) and there was 'no drama' when they broke up.

'The name doesn't ring a bell, but then Arlo thinks all girls smell like poo at the moment.' Claire picks up a small stack of plates and swipes the area they've been sitting on with the cloth before she heads into the kitchen.

'It's a bit weird though, isn't it?' I follow Claire into the kitchen and help to stack the dishwasher. 'Him having these secret kids?'

Claire shrugs. 'Not really. He's your gran's lodger. Paying the rent on time and tidying up after himself is all that's expected of him. His private life is his business. And if your gran is the little one's lollipop lady, they're not a secret to *her*.'

Why do people have to be so bloody reasonable? Why can't they simply agree with you to keep you happy?

'I just don't get the maths of it all. James is twenty-eight. This kid is, like, sixteen.' This is an exaggeration, but I want Claire to feel as shocked as I do about this revelation. 'James must have been about twelve when he fathered him.'

Claire nudges the dishwasher closed. 'Why do you care so much?'

I stare at my friend for a moment, my lower jaw slowly descending towards the tiled floor. 'This guy lives with my gran. I'd quite like to know what sort of person he is. To know that she's safe.'

'And you don't think she is because he has kids?' Claire speaks slowly, her face crumpling in confusion.

'No, because he was a *child himself* when he had kids.'

'And that's your business because…?'

'Because…' I fold my arms across my chest and tap my foot. 'Because…' Claire waits patiently for my answer, but I don't have one. Not one that doesn't include the fact I just don't like him, so there.

'Why are you so early anyway?' Claire eventually lets me off the hook by changing the subject.

'Am I?' I pull my phone from my pocket and check the time. I *am* early. We're not due to hand over for half an hour. This is a first. 'Be on time for work' is getting crossed off the list as well tonight. 'I guess I just love this place so much I can't keep away.'

'You love this place so much you can't keep away? I thought you were planning on leaving.' Claire gives me the crumpled-face look again. 'Speaking of which, I've got something for you.'

Ooh, a present. I follow Claire into the room at the back of the chippy, my steps light and skippy as I imagine what she's brought for me. A fairy cake she baked with Arlo? A gossipy mag she's finished with?

Or a dog-eared, boring-looking prospectus for long-distance learning.

'Thanks?' I take the prospectus, which is three years out of date, and flick through it as though it may be of interest.

'I know it's old, and we can get you a new one, but in the meantime I thought it might help you decide on your new career.'

I pull out a wonky chair and flop down on it, almost giving myself a heart attack when it lurches. I flick through the first few pages of the prospectus; there's motivational guff about achieving my ambitions, what the courses can offer and what I need to do to get started, and advice on choosing the right qualification. I feel my shoulders tense as I flick to the next page: how long your qualification will take. I don't have any ambitions, and I certainly wouldn't have any time to achieve them if I had. Or the money to pay for the course. Paul will be back in Clifton-on-Sea in less than three months and these courses take *years*. I don't have the time or funds to go back to basics. I need to start a new career, and pretty fast.

Dinner Party Checklist:

- *Set budget (as small as possible)*

- *Pick a date and time (my next evening off)*

- *Create a guest list (list is very small – see budget)*

- *Choose party games (none. Can't think of anything more cringey)*

- *Plan the menu (aka cook the most sophisticated thing you can manage. NOT VEGGIE STEW)*

- *Grocery shop (that was HELLISH. Not sure I will recover any time soon)*

- *Iron tablecloth, napkins etc (big fat NOPE)*

Chapter Fourteen

I can sort of see where Gran was coming from when she said she was lonely living on her own. I've only been in the flat for a week and I almost tap-dance with glee when I spot a real-life person (the canvases and cushion photos in the flat are of no comfort whatsoever). I've been working the later shifts at the chippy over the past week, so it's past midnight before I drag my weary carcass up the stairs and crawl into bed, but those few hours between waking and starting my shift are boring as hell. Mum, Dad and Claire are working, and Gran's either busy volunteering or visiting her friends (once again, I am appalled that my grandmother has a better social life than I do), so I'm left to potter around the flat with only Bolan for company. Despite curling up to sleep at the end of my bed every night, I'm pretty sure the cat despises me. He has this look – this really dirty look that I didn't think an animal was capable of giving – that he treats me to whenever he's awake (which isn't that often, to be fair) and he seems to store up his poops until *just after* I've changed the litter in his tray.

I've watched a lot of Russell and Jed's DVDs to try to ease the boredom this week, and I've been working my way through the extensive collection of Seventies music from the shelves while I doss about on Instagram, messaging Paul and searching for the elusive Sienna. Plus (and I hate to admit this) I resorted to finishing off my granny square. For some strange reason, I'd popped the little square, ball of yarn and the crochet hook in my bag when I was last at Gran's and brought it back to the flat with me, and now I have my first granny square. It looks okay – a bit wonky, perhaps, and some of the stitches are a bit loose, but I'm kind of… proud of it. *I made this*.

The week has passed slowly, but I've survived it and even gained some life skills along the way. I know how to use the washing machine (*and* the dryer – bonus) and I've built up my directory of things I can cook, adding baked potatoes, pasta bake (from a jar) and scrambled eggs to my (limited) repertoire. I'm so confident in my abilities in the kitchen, I'm hosting a dinner party. Tonight. For actual people.

The menu I'll be offering my guests consists of tuna pasta bake (currently in the oven) served with garlic flatbread (shop-bought) and a side salad (from a packet), followed by strawberry cheesecake (from a box, defrosted and waiting in the fridge). There's a long road ahead of me before I reach Nigella levels of cooking, but I'm baby-stepping my way there.

The doorbell rings as I'm sprinkling cheese on top of the pasta dish (from a packet, pre-grated. Don't judge me). Wiping my hands on the apron I found hooked on the back of the kitchen door (which has the image of a sausage spiked on a fork and the slogan: 'Wanna see my sausage?' Keeping it classy, guys), I hurry down the stairs and take a deep breath before I fling open the door, welcoming smile in place.

'Claire. Thank God it's you.' I pull her into the flat and squeeze the life out of her, the forced smile sliding away. For some strange reason, my stomach is a jumble of nerves about tonight. And it isn't as though I've invited royalty over, or even Paul. 'Hey, you.' I offer my hand to Arlo for a high five and he obligingly slaps my palm as hard as he can. 'Do you want to come upstairs and meet my friend's kitty?'

I'd begged Claire to come to my dinner party, which wasn't supposed to be a dinner party at all. The intention of the evening was to have Gran round for tea. No pressure. No stress. Just the two of us eating something hopefully edible. But Gran got the wrong end of the stick and assumed I was inviting her *and* James over for the evening, after some conversation we supposedly had last week in the garden. Anyway, she'd already extended my offer of hospitality to James before I could correct her mistake, and so I'd begged Claire to join us, to make the evening at least bearable.

'I'm not sure I can get a babysitter at such short notice. I only have you and Mum to help, and Mum has her Pilates class on Monday nights.'

'Bring Arlo with you. It isn't going to be anything fancy – this is me we're talking about.'

'A night off cooking?' Claire had tapped her finger against her chin in mock thought. 'I'm in.'

So it's going to be the five of us. Six, if you count Bolan, who's currently enjoying a chin tickle from Arlo. He has his eyes closed as he lifts his face up for easy chin access, and he's *purring*. He's never purred for me.

'Would you like a drink?' I've stocked up on wine for the grown-ups and juice for Arlo. I could only find fancy crystal wine glasses in Russell and Jed's cupboard, so I've bought a little plastic beaker with a picture of cartoon dogs in various emergency services uniforms on the front for the boy.

'Yes, please.' Arlo continues to tickle Bolan's chin. The cat continues to enjoy the fuss. 'Does the kitty have any toys?'

I almost splutter at the question. *Any toys?* The spoilt feline has tons of them, stored in a circular velvet storage box next to the fireplace. There's everything a kitty could dream of playing with: mice on string, little plush birds and fish, feather-duster-type things on long sticks, balls that jingle, sparkly pom-poms, *finger puppets*. I show Arlo the storage box of playthings before heading to the kitchen to check on the pasta bake (the cheese is starting to bubble – good sign) and pour drinks for Claire and Arlo.

'Can I help with anything?' Claire has followed me into the kitchen, and she accepts the glass of wine and takes a sip.

'No, I think everything's under control.' The table has been laid, the salad is prepped (tipped from packet to bowl and shoved in the fridge) and the garlic bread is waiting to be popped into the oven when the timer on my phone goes off. 'Thanks for coming. I really appreciate it. I owe you one.'

Claire holds the glass of wine up to her lips, eyeing me coyly as she takes a sip. 'Do you think I can cash in that favour on Sunday? I've got a date but Mum can't babysit…' She widens her eyes and flashes a little half-smile at me.

'Of course I'll babysit.' It's the least I can do. Without Claire, I'd be on my own with Gran and James without the distraction of *Waiting on You* or granny squares. 'Who's the date with?'

'Danny.' Claire smiles, properly this time.

'Danny? The temp?' We've been on the same shift a few times and he seems all right. Fun, blokey, likes to get drunk at the weekends. And on weekdays. In fact, I don't think he's worked a shift when he hasn't been at least a little bit hung-over. He can eat a meat and potato pie in three bites, and he's proud of it.

'He's fit. Don't you think he's fit?'

I shrug, not committing either way. He is good-looking (though not a patch on Paul, obviously) but the tattoo on his face is a bit off-putting. It isn't anything grotesque, like lizard scales covering his entire face or an alarming teardrop, and I'm not against tattoos – I have three myself and I wouldn't rule out getting more in the future. But on my face? That's a step too far for me.

The doorbell rings, saving me from having to elaborate on the shrug. I press the plastic beaker of juice into Claire's hand before hurrying to answer the door.

'You look lovely.' Gran pulls me into a hug before stepping into the little entrance hallway. I've made more of an effort than usual with my clothing and styling choices, wearing an ankle-length black dress with white spots that Claire kindly let me borrow for the occasion. Of course, I've teamed the dress with my glittery Converse, because I'm not wearing heels, dinner party or not. And instead of scraping my hair into a messy bun, I've washed and dried it and left it loose around my shoulders, which is the most attention I've paid to my hair in a very long time.

'You look lovely too.' Gran's wearing a pale blue dress with a matching cardigan and low-heeled court shoes, and she's curled her hair. 'Very Queen Mary Berry. This way, Your Majesty.' I indicate the stairs behind us before peering around her to acknowledge James with a brief wave.

'Thanks for having me over.' Gran has moved past me and started to climb the stairs, and James closes the gap between us, hesitating for a moment before he thrusts a bottle of wine at me. For a second there, I thought he was going to lean in and peck me on the cheek. I flash a smile of thanks before turning and legging it after Gran, just in case.

'This place is gorgeous.' Gran nods appreciatively as we step into the living room, her eyes taking in Russell and Jed's décor. The room is cosy and inviting, with its forest-green feature wall, jewel-coloured furnishings and the plush rug that your feet sink into. The myriad of photos – of Russell, Jed and their friends and family, plus Bolan – add another layer of warmth. 'You won't want to leave. Russell and Jed will have to forcibly evict you when they get back. I bet you were ecstatic when they said they were staying for the extra week after all. Not that you'd wish ill health on Russell's mum, obviously. How is she, by the way?'

'Getting there, according to Russell. They should be back at the weekend.' I move fully into the room and head towards Claire. 'Gran, you remember Claire and Arlo? Claire, this is James, my gran's lodger.' It still feels so weird saying that. 'James, this is my good friend and colleague, Claire, and her son, Arlo.'

'Hello, James.' Claire lifts her hand and wriggles her fingers. 'It's good to see you again, Cordelia. Arlo, come and say hello to Cordelia and James.'

The boy drops the little stuffed flamingo toy he's trying to entice Bolan with and joins his mum on the sofa, pressing his cheek to her chest. Claire kisses him on the top of his head.

'He's a bit shy.'

'My daughter can be the same.' James sits down on the armchair, a safe distance from Arlo, who eyes him through lowered lashes. 'But once she starts chatting, there's no stopping her. Her brother, on the other hand, doesn't speak because he's a surly pre-teen rather than being shy.'

'How old are your kids?' Claire sneaks a peek at me, and I can see the unaired question: *pre*-teen? Because didn't I claim the child was sixteen or something the other day as I attempted to process the new information?

'Edith's seven and Seth's eleven.'

I avoid her second peek and study the ceiling instead, focusing on the intricate coving. In my defence, the kid is extremely tall, and James wasn't even allowed to legally drink when Seth was born. He was practically still a kid himself.

'Arlo will be in the year below Edith then.' Claire and James start chatting about the school – Edith is in Mr Thompson's class while Arlo is in Miss Higginbottom's class – so I leave them to it and back away into the kitchen to pop James' wine in the fridge for later. After checking on the pasta, I pop the garlic bread in the oven and check my phone for any messages from Paul. I told him about the dinner party earlier, to show him how sophisticated I've become since we left school, but I haven't heard from him since.

'Jeez, Cleo.' Claire has joined me in the kitchen, and she hisses in my ear as I slip my phone in the pocket of my dress. 'You didn't mention how fit James is.'

'He is?' Frowning, I lean so I can peep out of the kitchen and into the living room. James is sitting cross-legged on the rug with Arlo, dangling a fish attached to a miniature fishing rod at Bolan, who's lying on his back and batting at the fish with his paws. Arlo's cheeks are pink with delight, his mouth gaping open as he laughs at the game. Both child and feline are thoroughly charmed.

Claire nudges me. 'Don't pretend you haven't noticed. He's *gorgeous*.'

'He is?' I have another peek. James is laughing as Bolan clutches the little fish with his claws, bringing up his back legs so he can kick the toy repeatedly. Arlo is clutching his stomach, his cheeks bright red now as he giggles his little socks off.

'He is.' Claire fans herself, which I think is a bit much. Okay, fair enough, the man is good-looking behind all that hair, but gorgeous? I wouldn't go that far.

'Do you want me to set you two up?' I assume James is single, otherwise why would he be lodging at Gran's?

Claire has a long look at James before she scrunches up her nose and shakes her head. 'Nah. He's too wholesome-looking for me.'

'You mean he looks a bit like Jesus with the long hair and beard?'

'No, I'm totally on board with the beard and long hair.' Claire shivers with delight. 'But look how he's dressed. He could be a teacher or a librarian.'

He *could* be a teacher or a librarian – I still have no idea what he does for a living. My sleuthing skills are shite.

'I think he dresses smartly.' James is currently wearing a pair of skinny jeans, a soft grey jumper and a charcoal blazer. It's the most casual attire I've seen him wearing, but it's still elegant and stylish.

'Exactly.' Claire gives a slow nod. 'I like my men a bit… rougher around the edges.'

'Rough like having tattoos on their faces?'

'Exactly.' Claire sucks in a huge breath before letting it out in a dreamy rush. 'That's exactly my type.'

I don't think I have a type. My last three boyfriends have been as far apart, looks and personality-wise, as they could be. Bradley was short but buff with jet-black hair (too jet-black to be natural, though he claimed otherwise) and a bit of a poser. Mo was super-tall and skinny with a wild Afro that gained him far more attention than he was comfortable with, and Dane was a gentle giant. He had the physique of a rugby player but he was kind and attentive (*too* attentive, it turned out, when he lavished attention on the Red Lion's barmaid). And then we have Paul, who's a mix of all three; he's almost as tall as Mo, and he has an amazing body like Bradley, and he has piercing blue eyes like Dane. Maybe I do have a type after all, but I've only picked out little bits of it along the way so far. But now I have the perfect package and in seventy-five days we'll get to start our perfect life together.

Thought of the Day:

There's no I in 'teamwork'

(there's also no I in 'coffee', so does that mean James' pods are up for grabs?)

Chapter Fifteen

'The thing is, I don't have a passion like you do.'

A grin spreads across Claire's face as she flicks her gaze towards Danny, who's hefting a bucket of sliced potatoes up to the fryer. I tut and push the distance-learning prospectus along the counter towards her.

'Not that kind of passion. I mean this.' I tap on the cover of the prospectus, which I flicked idly through before bed last night. I was buzzing after my first successful dinner party, but this sent me off to sleep with no trouble. 'You've always known what you wanted to do. I wasn't even sure I wanted to go to uni after my A levels – it was just expected of me, I suppose – and then Grandad got ill so I didn't end up going anyway. And I didn't miss it. I was fine with staying here in Clifton-on-Sea, and working here, but now I want more. I just don't know what that more is.'

'And none of these courses sparked even a bit of interest?' Claire picks up the prospectus and opens it at random, turning it to show me the page. 'Art history?'

I scrunch up my nose. 'I have no interest in the history of anything, to be honest.'

'Anything creative at all? Creative writing? You like doing your journal thing.'

I shake my head. 'That's just for fun. It's a load of nonsense, usually. Top celebrity crushes, favourite films, to-do lists, that kind of thing. It isn't anything deep and meaningful.'

'It's meaningful to you.'

'But not something anyone is ever going to pay me for.'

Claire returns to the prospectus. 'Languages? Religious studies?'

I flick the brochure closed. 'I need to start my career *now*, not years down the line when I have a qualification.'

'How about working with the elderly? They're crying out for care assistants.'

'Can't think of anything worse.'

'But you looked after your grandad.'

'Because he was my grandad, and Mum and Gran never made me wipe his arse.'

'How about… working with kids then?'

'Okay, I can think of something worse than working as a carer.'

'So that's a no then?'

'A very big one.'

Claire looks as though she would quite like to strangle me right now, and I can't blame her. This career stuff is frustrating when you have no drive whatsoever. Instead of wrapping her hands around my neck, she opens the prospectus again but whips it away and plasters on a smile when the door opens and a customer steps inside. But the smile slides away when she spots Riley shuffling towards the counter. He's already blushing, bless him, and he hasn't even made eye contact with her yet.

'I'll leave you to it. Stuff to do.' I raise a hand in farewell and back away, making a heart shape with my hands once I've passed Riley. I can tell Claire wants to shoot me daggers, but she won't want to draw attention to my symbol of affection. Instead, she focuses on taking

Riley's order while I make swooning gestures as I back out of the shop.

Bolan glares at me from his four-poster bed when I step into the living room of the flat, and I glare right back at him. *I'm* still peeved that he woke me up at four o'clock this morning by walking across my face, but I'm not sure what *his* problem is with me. I'm due at Gran's in half an hour, so I settle down on the sofa with a brew and my crochet. I have to remind myself that I'm twenty-five and not a pensioner, but I'm getting pretty good at granny squares now. I still have to read the instructions Gran noted down for me carefully, and while James can knock out a granny square during a couple of back-to-back episodes of *Waiting on You*, it takes me several hours to complete the rounds. But I *have* mastered the colour change, and my current granny square, which I'm trying desperately to finish before I head over to Gran's, is made up of *three colours* (magenta, electric blue and forest green, inspired by Russell and Jed's décor).

'Get off.' With a tut, I snatch the yarn away from Bolan, who has just leapt from the coffee table onto the sofa to attack the stringy forest-green foe. The yarn's movement only encourages the cat, who rolls onto his side and hooks the yarn with his claw and brings it to his mouth. '*No*. Bad kitty. Play with Mingo.' The flamingo plush toy is on the sofa, but Bolan isn't interested, not even when I waft it in front of his face. Only the yarn will do, apparently. 'No, not happening.'

I pick up the cat and pluck the yarn from his claws before placing him back in his four-poster bed. I need to get this square finished in the next twenty minutes or so, and I'll never manage that with a feline gnawing at the yarn.

'I did it.' I hold up the jewel-coloured granny square for Bolan to inspect, but having settled on the bed, he doesn't even bother to flick his eyes from their position glaring at the wall. I'm well and truly in the doghouse with the cat.

I have just enough time to weave in the ends, pack my crochet things into a plastic bag and water the plant Gran bought me (she was very pleased to see it was still flourishing at the dinner party last night) before I head out, calling a cheery farewell to Bolan before I pull the door closed behind me. I peek in the chippy as I pass, waving to Claire and Danny and making the heart gesture when I spot Riley still sitting inside with his chips and a can of Coke. Claire gives a gesture of her own in return, but it isn't a friendly one.

Gran puts the kettle on as soon as I arrive, and I eye James' fancy coffee machine. Would it be cheeky to swipe another pod? I've already raided his selection so many times I've lost count, but they're so deliciously tempting.

'Look at this.' Gran opens the fridge, but instead of taking the bottle of milk out of the door, she swings it shut again before opening it with a flourish. I study the fridge for a moment before looking at Gran for elaboration. She tuts and rolls her eyes before reaching for the milk. 'The light. It works again. James changed the bulb for me.'

'I said I'd do that for you.'

'Yes, you did.' Gran nudges the fridge door shut. 'Before Christmas.'

'I was busy and…' I forgot. Plus, I don't know *how* you change a fridge light bulb, or even where you'd buy a new one. 'You could have asked Mum or Dad.'

'Your mum already does too much. The poor woman never has five minutes to herself, what with work and running after me and your dad and… everyone.'

Me. She means running after me, even though I should be perfectly able to look after myself by now. And I am starting to. I can wash my own clothes now, and I'm finding my feet in the kitchen, and I've got my first driving lesson in a couple of days so I'll be able to run myself into town very soon. We'll ignore the fact that Mum has paid for my first ten lessons to set me on my way (she says it's an investment, that she'll save money in the long run if she no longer has to taxi me around. Gran has also offered to go halves on the rest of my lessons. It isn't an investment for her, she's simply ace).

'Anyway, in the end I didn't have to ask anybody. James took it upon himself to fix it.' Gran pours milk into the little jug set out on the tea tray. 'Just like he took it upon himself to fix that squeaky floorboard on the landing and bleed the radiator in the bathroom.'

Lucky Gran, having St. James to fly to the rescue and sort stuff out, no bother.

'He's mended that gap in the fence as well. You know the bit where next door's dog keeps squeezing through and messing on my lawn? He's a godsend, honestly.'

Sod it, I'm having one of his coffee pods. Mr Perfect can spare another one, surely.

I'm halfway across the kitchen when I hear the front door open. I freeze, my coffee pod-pinching plans flying out of the window as James strides into the kitchen.

'I can't stay long.' He shrugs off his blazer and drapes it over the back of one of the chairs at the table. 'I'm on my lunch break. Are you having a coffee, Cleo?' He passes me, opening the coffee pod cupboard and I feel a stab of guilt that I was about to pilfer one behind his back. I should have a cup of tea, as penance.

'Is there a latte going?' I am very bad, but I can't help it. Caffeine is the devil.

'Regular, caramel or vanilla?' And James really is a flipping saint. Why can't he be a knobhead so I can hate him with impunity?

'Caramel, please.' If there are any left. I've had at least four since the coffee machine's arrival, all of them when James hasn't been around.

'Excellent choice. I think I'll have the same.' My stomach tightens as James rifles in the cupboard, but he produces two caramel latte pods and sets them going at the machine. With the drinks sorted, we all sit around the kitchen table so we can get cracking on the final part of our blanket project for the dog shelter. James and I have produced lots of granny squares (James way more than me, but who's counting?) but neither of us has enough to create a large enough blanket (my squares would barely amount to a tea towel) so we're going to combine our efforts.

'These are very good.' Gran's inspecting my granny squares, nodding in approval as she runs her thumb over the stitches. 'They're going to make a beautiful blanket. I'm proud of you.'

She's going to be super-duper proud of me in a second, because I've held the best square back. The triple-coloured granny square is still in the plastic bag on my lap, but I pull it out now, placing it down on the table, and try not to look too smug. Unfortunately, James chooses this moment to dump his own granny squares on the table, totally overshadowing my poor triple-coloured effort with his fancy-ass, multi-coloured squares.

'What the hell is this?' I pick up one of the squares between finger and thumb and thrust it at James. This is no ordinary granny square, and not just because it's made of *four colours*. The centre is made up of a white circle, surrounded by red, petal-like stitches, which are framed by larger, rounded stitches in a navy-blue yarn. The final layer is a dark grey, which takes the circular design into a square.

'It's a sunburst granny square.' James picks up another *sunburst granny square*, this one in alternating rounds of red and yellow. 'The effect is really good, but they're much easier to make than you'd think.'

The effect *is* really good. So much so that they make my basic efforts look like dog shit. Thank you, James. Thank you very much.

–

It turns out that it's quite difficult to sulk when you're concentrating on sewing together crocheted squares, and the excitement of seeing the blanket coming together overtakes my misgivings of James' superior (smug?) crocheting skills, but James is determined to keep my mood down as he shoots off the worst dog-based dad jokes as we put together the blanket for the animal shelter.

'A three-legged dog walks into a bar and says "I'm looking for the man who shot my paw".'

Gran titters politely while I roll my eyes practically right up to the clouds.

'What kind of dog did Dracula have?' James pauses for a second, leaning forward as he prepares to deliver the punchline. 'A bloodhound.'

'Can you stop?' I hold up the crochet squares I'm joining together. 'I'm trying to concentrate.'

James can't – or won't – stop. 'Why do dogs make terrible dance partners? Because they've got two left feet.' James cracks up, belly-laughing at the terrible joke, and I have to fight the urge to kick his shin under the table. 'I wanted to see lots of dogs at the zoo, but they only had one small dog. It was a shih-tzu.'

That one, I hate to admit, was actually quite good, and this time I'm fighting the urge to crack a smile. But I win the battle and manage to keep a straight face until James gets up to set the coffee machine going. Even then, I hide my smirk with my hand and am fully recovered by the time he places my mug down in front of me. The second latte is incredibly soothing and I've pretty much forgiven James for his show-off crochet skills and the horrifically bad jokes by the time he slips his blazer on and heads back to work. I still have a bit of time before I'm due to start my shift at the chippy so I stay with Gran and finish building the blanket from our crocheted building blocks. It's a hodgepodge of colours and designs, but it works in a quirky kind of way. My fingers are aching by the time I leave, but I have a warm feeling of satisfaction in the pit of my stomach as I head back to the flat. Tomorrow, that blanket will be going to the dog shelter, and some little pup will really appreciate its warmth. They won't care that some of the squares are sunbursts and others are not-so-fancy basic ones. We've done a Good Thing here, and I'm proud of both of us.

I'm in an incredibly good mood as I climb the stairs up to Russell and Jed's flat, but it evaporates as soon as I step into the kitchen and spot the Starbucks mug Gran bought me. The poor plant is half in the planter and half on the floor, with soil spilling everywhere. The handle has broken clean off and when I pick the mug up, it comes apart in two pieces. Bolan is sitting in front of the fridge, cleaning his paws. He pauses and eyes me, and I almost expect him to shrug and say, 'Yeah, I knocked it off the side. So what?' This is revenge. For the yarn thing this morning. He *knows* I'm trying to be a grown-up, and that keeping this plant alive is important to me, so he's sabotaging my plans.

Okay, I may have had too much caffeine today. Cats don't do revenge or sabotage, even if this particular mog is looking me dead in the eye as he *ever so slowly* licks his paw, challenging me. Testing me. *What are you going to do now, Cleo?*

What I'm going to do is get a grip and stop imagining my kitty flatmate is a supervillain. I'm going to find something to put this poor plant in temporarily, and I'm going to throw the mug away before sweeping up the loose soil and porcelain fragments. And quickly, because I'm due at the chippy in three and a half minutes. Bolan may have put my 'keep the plant alive' task in jeopardy, but he will not make me late for work.

Things I Can't Say Out Loud:

- *To Mum: I would quite like to frisbee your Boyzone CD out of the car window*

- *To Dad: Can you PLEASE make Mum put another CD in her car?*

- *To Gran: Your garden is amazing and beautiful but I would rather fill my bra with broken glass and perform star jumps than get my hands dirty out there*

- *To Claire: I want to put you in a headlock and repeatedly drag my knuckles over your scalp every time you mention bad boys. THEY SUCK*

- *To Russell & Jed: Your cat is the devil in fur*

Chapter Sixteen

I'm trying to forgive Bolan for the plant thing, but he's making it pretty difficult when he's standing on my head at half past six in the morning. I didn't leave the shop until almost two o'clock last night (or this morning, technically) so I am *not happy* about the early wake-up call. I've pushed him off my face several times but he isn't giving up and his paw is currently sliding from my forehead towards my eye. I've seen what he can do with those claws so, with a heavy sigh, I throw back the covers and stamp my way into the kitchen. I've tried locking the damn cat out of the bedroom, but he mews constantly until I surrender and open the door so he can curl up on the bed. Russell and Jed have spoiled him and turned him into a brat.

I try not to gag as I spoon gourmet salmon and whole shrimp cat food into Bolan's dish. The smell is revolting during normal waking hours of the day, but it's even more horrendous as it plops into the dish first thing in the morning. Bolan has no qualms about the stench, happily wolfing it down as though he hasn't been fed for weeks, and I leave him to it, staggering back to bed. But I can't drop off back to sleep and I end up giving up and dragging myself to the shower.

I make myself some scrambled eggs and strong black coffee to ward off the zombified mood due to the lack of sleep. I'm getting pretty good at scrambled eggs – I was afraid I wouldn't cook the eggs properly and poison myself at first, but I've survived so far. The telly's on in the background, some breakfast-news-type programme, but it feels weird once my breakfast has been dispatched with and I have nothing to do with my hands. I'm used to crocheting granny squares, but the project is over and I left my stuff at Gran's yesterday. I have a scroll through Instagram, but it's still early and my feed is pretty dead. Paul posted a meme earlier, and I tap the like button even though it isn't that funny, before having another fruitless search for Sienna. I really wish I knew what her married name is, but I never made it to the wedding as it was so far away and I was afraid Grandad would have another stroke – or worse – while I was away, and it never occurred to me to ask her new surname. I guess we'd started to drift away from one another, even back then.

With nothing else to do (other than shoot daggers at Bolan, who's curled up in his four-poster bed for a snooze) I head out of the flat and wander down to the promenade. The only shops open are the cafes and coffee shops, so I treat myself to an espresso and the fresh air and the caffeine is enough to jolt me fully awake. I don't feel like going back to the flat, so I grab another coffee (just to make sure I'm fully alert) and make my way to Mum and Dad's. They're at work, so the house is empty and it feels odd being back even though I've only been away for just over a week. I pick up a few things – a couple more sets of clothes, my lime-green Converse, a packet of chocolate digestives that I vow to replace – before locking up again. I still don't feel like going back to the flat (my feelings towards Bolan still aren't favourable) so I take a detour to the upcycling shop Gran mentioned. If I can buy a replacement mug planter, I won't have to admit to Gran that her gift ended up smashed on the kitchen floor.

The shop's just opening up when I get there, and although there are no more Starbucks planters, I buy a different replacement for the poor plant currently residing in an empty Pot Noodle container. The new planter is made from a cute penguin mug, and I end up buying a lavender-filled teapot planter for Gran. I pop over on my way back to the flat, hoping she's back from her morning lollipop lady duties, and find her pottering about in the front garden with a pair of secateurs. She's stooping over some kind of flowering shrub, but she straightens as I open the gate.

'Look at this beautiful lawn. James dragged the mower out of the shed yesterday and had a tinker until he got it working again. He's a marvel, that boy. He really is.' She returns her attention to the shrub, nipping at it with the secateurs. 'My borders were letting the garden down, so I thought I'd have a tidy-up.'

I hope she doesn't ask me to help. Dad's the gardener in our family, and he definitely didn't pass on the gene. I hate gardening – it's a grubby, bug-filled, back-breaking chore that I'll avoid at all costs. I've already formed an excuse to get the hell out of here should Gran suggest I don a pair of floral-patterned gloves and muck in.

'I'm glad you're here.' Gran nips at the shrub again and takes a tiny step back to judge her handiwork. 'You can help me with my new project.'

'Actually, Gran, I can't stay. I only came to drop this off.' I hold up the paper bag hand-printed with the upcycling shop's logo. 'It's a little gift.'

'For me?' Gran's eyebrows rise as she looks up from the shrub.

'The cat broke the planter you bought me, so I went to the shop to buy a replacement. They didn't have the same planter, so I had to get another one. It's cute. See?' I pull the penguin mug-turned-planter out of the bag. 'I hope you don't mind about the original one. I wasn't even there when it happened. I found it on the kitchen floor.'

'Accidents happen.' Gran pats me on the arm. She's removed the gloves, and I realise we're making our way down the side passage towards the kitchen. I'm supposed to be making my excuses and legging it, not sticking around.

'Anyway, like I was saying.' I stop halfway along the passage. I won't go any further. Once I'm in that kitchen, I'll be in it for the long haul. The kettle will be on. Floral gardening gloves will be donned and I'll be prodding at the ground and praying there are no worms or spiders about. 'I can't stay. I just came to drop this off.' I reach into the bag and find the handle of the teapot. I manoeuvre it out of the bag, careful not to break off the lavender sprouting from its middle. 'I thought you might like it?'

'Oh, Cleo, it's lovely.' Gran had continued down the passage, but she heads back to my safe-ish spot halfway along. 'You sweet, sweet girl. Thank you so much. Let's go and pop it on the kitchen windowsill and I'll make us a nice cup of tea.'

'The thing is, I need to get back to the shop. There's a delivery due. Spuds. Lots and lots of them, and Elliot can't manage on his own. He's only a kid, really, and Bridget will be busy getting the shop ready for opening.'

But Gran isn't listening. She's marched along the passage and has disappeared through the gate and into the back garden, which is most definitely the Danger Zone.

Once you're in the back garden, you're practically in the kitchen and being roped into helping out.

'Gran?' I edge my way to the gate, poking my head around but not actually stepping foot into the garden. 'I need to head off now. Okay?' I wait a moment. Nothing. 'Gran?'

I could just go. Run off before I find myself elbow-deep in compost. But I can't. My mind wants to flee but my body is refusing to leg it. Instead, I'm shuffling into the garden. The steps leading up to the kitchen are *right there*. Danger! Danger!

'Kettle's on.' Gran's back at the door, beaming at me briefly before she disappears again.

'I can't stay. I have to be at the shop for a delivery.'

I'm in the kitchen. The most perilous place to be. I need to get out of here, and fast.

'Doesn't it look lovely?' Gran's gazing at the windowsill, where she's placed the teapot planter. It does look pretty, with the light beaming in through the large window. 'Are you having a cup of tea or one of James' coffees?'

It's tempting. Very tempting. But I know that one minute I'll be enjoying a vanilla latte, the next I'll be in the garden with damp patches on my knees and my skin itching at the possibility of a bug invasion.

'I think you'll enjoy this new crochet project more than the granny squares.' Gran turns to wink at me as she turns the tap on at the sink to wash her hands. 'And you'll have a head start on James this time.'

Crochet project? Not gardening?

I'm across the kitchen and flinging open the coffee pod cupboard at lightning speed. 'What are we making this time?'

Thought of the Day:

All work and no coffee makes Cleo a grumpy girl

Chapter Seventeen

It could be argued that gardening, with all its dirt and bugs and backache, is much more preferable than the new crochet project, and I would head up that debate with a passion. Because Gran has somehow got it into her head that after producing bog-standard, okay-at-best granny squares, I'm ready (and willing) to move on to making toys. She's volunteered herself to make stripy crocheted sausage dogs, which will be raffled off at the dog shelter's Easter fair, and seems to be under the impression that I'm capable of contributing to the cause. Admittedly, the picture on the pattern is adorable, but they're a bastard to make and I'm ready to hurl hook, yarn and pattern out of the window. I've only been at it for half an hour and I've had to learn new words, phrases and techniques (amigurumi, magic loop, double crochet into the same stitch). It's too damn complicated, and I haven't even started properly yet because the magic loop, *the very first step*, is defeating me. Gran's been very patient with me and showed me repeatedly how to do it, but I can't get the hang of it, and every time she demonstrates, I want to toss her out of the window too. I should have taken the opportunity to dash back to the shop and the imaginary potato delivery while I had the chance.

'I know it seems really, really complicated at the moment, but you will get it and it'll be a doddle.' Gran pats my knee, and a horrible thought flashes through my head: would it be even more satisfying to chuck her out of one of the *upstairs* windows?

'Can't we watch *Waiting on You* instead?' I'll be much calmer catching up on the soap, and I won't have worrying granicidal thoughts. Plus, the last episode ended on a cliffhanger, with Elvin walking in on his wife getting it on with the chef. The shock of being caught out was enough to break Joanna's waters, so now she's in labour with the triplets.

'We can't. Not with James being at work.' Gran picks up the black yarn and wiggles it in front of my face. 'Come on, give it another go. You nearly had it last time.'

I snatch the yarn and wrap it over my fingers, just like Gran's demonstrating with her own yarn. 'James doesn't even like *Waiting on You*.'

'Of course he does. He's getting into it. Didn't you notice his surprise when Tegan broke off her affair with Amber?'

'I believe his surprise was that she'd had time to have *another* affair, as well as holding down a full-time job.' I follow Gran's instructions with the hook. So far so good. 'He also said he couldn't believe anybody could keep that many relationships going without needing medical assistance.' And then he'd said the show was a steaming turd when Gran had popped into the kitchen to put the kettle on during the ads, but I don't repeat that now.

'He's definitely getting into it. He'll be upset if we watch it without him.' Gran peers at my fingers entwined with the yarn and nods. 'That's it. Now hook the second loop... And twist the hook... brilliant. Yarn over... Pull it through... Perfect! You did it!'

I did it! I've made a magic loop! I slide it off my fingers *ever so carefully* and stare down at it in wonder. It doesn't look like much, just a little circle of yarn, but it's the start of a whole new project. Plus, I've finally managed to do something before James. I'm one step ahead of him and I'm going to run with it.

'What's next?'

Gran reads out the next bit of instructions from the pattern. I do the stitches required – with a bit of help from Gran, obviously – and somehow, *magically*, the circle closes up and I'm left with… well, it's a blob. I've messed it up. I'm going to have to start all over again. So much for being a step ahead of Mr Perfect.

My shoulders have slumped in defeat. I don't think I have it in me to unravel the blob and start from scratch for the millionth time. But wait, Gran's reading out the instructions for the next round as though I can plough on regardless. It's a bit fiddly, but I do the stitches as per the instructions and slowly, round by round, the blob starts to take on a new non-blob shape. Dare I say it, it starts to look like a tiny dog's nose.

I spend the next few hours with Gran, both working on our own sausage dogs on the sofa with daytime telly on in the background. I learn how to increase stitches and decrease them again, and by the time I have to leave to go to work, I have a complete stripy head of a dachshund. I can't say it looks much like a dog's head at the moment – it has more of a look of a misshapen Christmas bauble – but it looks similar to Gran's and she assures me that it'll look the part once we add the eyes and ears later.

I'm feeling quite proud of myself as I walk back to the flat, and I'm in such a buoyant mood, I say a cheery hello to Bolan, despite the glare I'm greeted by. I have just enough time to repot the plant into its new penguin mug before I head downstairs to the shop to take over from Bridget. The shop is empty of customers, but it won't be long until the local horde of teenagers descends for an after-school snack. Some of the kids are cheeky and gobby, but they're mostly harmless. There's a group of girls who always sit in the corner, a plate of chips sitting on the table between them that they pick at while tapping away at their phones, occasionally giggling and passing the phone around to share whatever has amused them. Every now and then they'll look up from their phones, usually when one of the more boisterous teen boys is in the vicinity, and they'll pout and flick their hair and take the giggling up a notch. They make me smile, those girls, because they remind me of myself when I was their age, sitting with Sienna and gossiping about the boys we fancied. It was always Franko – *Paul* – I used to talk about, while Sienna's crush would change on a week-by-week basis. It's why I was so surprised when she settled down so quickly with Cam; they met in Vietnam four months into her six-month travels and spent the next two months together. By the time Sienna was due to fly home, she was engaged and planning to settle down in Cam's native New Zealand.

'I just knew, as soon as I saw him, that he was the one for me,' Sienna told me once. Of course, Cam was bronzed, toned to perfection, and dripping wet from the sea at the time, which helped (Sienna painted quite the picture, even over the phone). Did I know that Paul was the one for me as soon as I saw him? That would be a big, fat no. I've known Paul Franks since we were in reception class, back when he cried for his mummy every morning until the teacher pulled him onto her lap and read him a story. When he had a constant snotty nose that he wiped periodically on the sleeve of his jumper. And even when we moved up to high school, he still wasn't crush-worthy. He no longer had a snotty nose, and I hadn't heard him cry for his mum for years, but he was just Paul Franks, a short, puppy-fat-faced boy who shared some of my classes. But then something miraculous happened during the summer before our GCSEs. He shot up so that he towered over most of his classmates, the puppy fat went, and he grew his hair so he had to flick his head every thirty seconds to stop it from flopping into his eyes. And it wasn't just his looks that were transformed. He was more confident, louder, and he became 'one of the lads', swaggering down the corridors, giving smart-arse answers to the teachers and making the class erupt in giggles and jeers. All the girls had a thing for Franko after that summer, but it would take another three years until I finally kissed him. I smile to myself as I replay the moment in my head.

'Hello?' There's a hand waving in front of my face, and I blink the memory away. There's laughter from the corner of the chippy, and I see the group of girls giggling behind their hands as they watch what's happening over here. One of the teenage lads is leaning against the counter, his eyes flicking from me to the girls and back again, a grin spread across his face. I hadn't even realised we had customers, but Ross, the other temp Russell and Jed organised, must have served them while I was daydreaming of the past.

'Can. I. Get. Some. Ketchup?' The teen speaks slowly, his eyes flicking towards his audience again when they giggle.

'Yes. You. Can.' I speak just as slowly as I cross my arms and rest them on the counter. 'If. You. Say. Please.'

There's a pause, where the teen tries to come up with a witty response to entertain his entourage. I could have let him have his big moment in front of the girls and simply handed over the ketchup, but where's the fun in that?

'Whatever.' The teen pushes himself away from the counter and swaggers towards the door. 'Didn't want ketchup anyway. I was just messing with you.'

The girls giggle again as he saunters out of the shop. They're obviously easily impressed, but we've all been there, right? I know Franko didn't have to do much to make my pulse quicken when I was their age – a hair flick, eye contact, walking into the room. I thought the boy was a god, but it's nothing compared to what I think about him now. My relationship with Paul has been a major slow burn, but it'll be worth the wait when we finally get together in seventy-three days.

Today's To-Do List:

- *Supermarket shop (remember to take shopping list this time)*

- *First driving lesson (help!!!)*

- *Show Ross – again – how to wrap chips (scrunch-and-roll doesn't look pretty and the chips end up falling out)*

- *Water plant (???)*

- *Ask Gran how often I should water plant*

Chapter Eighteen

Breakfast this morning is a bowl of Russell and Jed's granola. The box is almost depleted, so I add it to the shopping list I've been keeping on a scrap of paper on the front of the fridge, like Mum does. I also need bread, milk, eggs (because I am a scrambling *queen*), biscuits to replace the ones I nabbed from Mum and Dad's cupboard, and some coffee pods to replenish James' stock. Although I actively dislike the man, I can't supress the gnawing guilt of my coffee raids any longer – I had three yesterday while crocheting with Gran, which adds up to about two gazillion guzzled coffees. But before I can head over to the supermarket, I have my first driving lesson to get through. I'm booked in for nine o'clock, which is less than half an hour away and why I'm tipping most of the granola in the bin and my hand is trembling as I slot the bowl in the dishwasher. I'm incredibly nervous, but I'm finally at the point where I'm willing to give learning to drive a go. This doesn't mean I think I'll actually be able to pull it off; in fact, I don't know whether I should laugh or cry at the prospect of me, in the driving seat of a car, attempting to control it. But I have to try. I have to be brave, because standing in the pissing-down rain and freezing my arse off at bus stops isn't fun, and there's nothing grown-up about being ferried around by your mum.

My instructor is called Connie, and I'm not sure what I was expecting, but it isn't the woman climbing out of the plum-coloured Toyota outside the chippy. She's quite short, but the blonde beehive hairdo and the heeled Mary Janes give her height a boost. She's wearing a pink tweed blazer and matching skirt with a frilly-fronted white blouse, and I feel extremely underdressed in my usual leggings and oversized hoodie combo.

'Cleo?' She's striding towards me, hand outstretched, showcasing impeccable French-tipped nails and a massive pink sapphire ring. Her grip is firm but brief as we shake. 'Hello. I'm Connie, and this is Pixie.' She indicates the car as she strides back towards it. My nerves are still in situ as I slide into the passenger seat, but Connie doesn't give me the chance to overthink things as she goes through the formalities before we set off. It isn't so bad, sitting here in the passenger seat as we drive through town, but I know that in a few minutes we'll be switching places and I'll be in control of the vehicle. All too soon, Connie's pulling up at the side of the road and unbuckling her seat belt, and my nerves shoot up a gear when I realise we're on Woodland Road, three doors down from Paul's childhood house. The house I know his mum still lives in. What if she comes out of the house and spots me? Mentions it in passing to Paul?

'Remember that girl you went to school with? The one who used to have the rainbow hair? I saw her having a driving lesson the other day.'

Because there's no mistaking I'm in the middle of the driving lesson – the big red L on the roof of the car is a dead giveaway – and I don't want Paul to know that I only started learning to drive to impress him.

'Are you ready, my love?' Connie's opened the door and has swung her Mary Janes out of the car, yet I'm frozen to my seat, still buckled in, still staring at Shona Franks' house.

It still has the same red door, with the same slightly crooked number 26 screwed above the brass knocker. I used to slow down as I approached this house, just in case Franko – *Paul* – was inside, perhaps on his way out and we would bump into each other, but now I want to run away as fast as I can.

'Come on, it won't be as scary as you think.' Connie twists so she's fully back in the car and pats me on the knee. 'We'll take it one step at a time, okay?'

I end up in the driver's seat, but I don't really have the chance to feel sick with nerves as there's so much going on: there are seats and mirrors to adjust, pedals to learn, instructions to try and get my head around. I even forget to worry about seeing Shona going about her business three doors down. And then the next thing I know, we're on the move. The car is in motion and I'm supposed to be the one in control of it. I'm in the middle of the road – but at least I'm still *on* the road, I guess.

I'm not good at this. I feel like a buffoon and definitely not in control of the car, but at least my instructor's here to keep everyone in the vicinity safe. Connie is calm despite the hash I'm making of everything, and she coolly advises and encourages as we move along Woodland Road. We must be travelling at a snail's pace, but it feels like I'm taking part in a Formula One race (or Mario Kart, Rainbow Road, 150cc, to be more accurate). I only take three positives away from the lesson when I emerge onto the pavement on jelly-like legs:

1. I only swore once (a teeny 'Oh, shit' as we set off for the first time. If Connie heard, she didn't acknowledge it).

2. When I saw a squirrel dashing across the road, I didn't point it out all excited and childlike (as I would under any other circumstance). I didn't run it over either (does this count as another positive?).

3. I survived intact, if shaken.

'See you in a few days, my love.' Connie waves before rolling the window up again and pulling away.

I can't wait.

–

'I'm proud of you.'

It's a few hours after the driving lesson and I'm still a bit jelly-like in the legs department. I've just told Claire all about it, and she's somehow translated the horror of an imbecile behind the wheel to something to be delighted by.

'You wouldn't be if you'd been there to witness it.' We're in the shop's kitchen, Claire slicing the potatoes into hearty chips while I'm preparing the batter for this evening's fish. 'I was all over the place. I can't steer around corners properly, I can't change gear, and I nearly gave us whiplash every time I applied the brake.'

'It was your first lesson. Give yourself a break. Gently, so we don't get whiplash.' Claire grins at me and I stick my tongue out at her. 'Seriously, you'll get there. It just takes practice. And think about the freedom you'll have once you've got your licence. You'll be able to go anywhere. No more being stuck in crappy Clifton-on-Sea.'

'I like crappy Clifton-on-Sea.'

I mean, it'd be even better if we had a Primark, and a post office that wasn't in danger of being shut down every five minutes, but we have the beach on our doorstep, the best fish and chip shop in the north-west (the country?) plus a Costa *and* a Starbucks *and* a couple of independent coffee shops. What more could a girl ask for? I was desperate to leave town like most of my peers when I was a teen, but I'll miss this place if Paul asks me to move to Kent with him, but I guess I'll be able to pop back any time once I can drive.

'My whole plan was almost scuppered today by that stupid driving lesson.'

Claire looks up from the chopping board. 'How?'

I tell her about the start of the lesson, of sitting a few doors down from Shona Franks' house in the learner car.

'Why didn't we think about his mum before?' Claire scoops up the potato wedges and drops them into the bucket on the side. 'What if she sees you working in the chippy? If you and Paul do get together, she's bound to mention it.'

I shake my head. 'I've worked here for years and I don't think I've ever seen Shona in here. She's over on Woodland Road, so she probably goes to The Plaice is Right. It's just around the corner from her house.'

'Still, you'll have to be careful.'

Which is another worry to add to the list, along with maiming someone with an out-of-control car.

The late afternoon quickly passes into evening and we're kept busy with the teatime rush. I pass on my chip-wrapping expertise to Ross, who finally manages to produce a neat package that doesn't spill its contents as soon as you pick it up. Claire puts a Seventies music channel on the TV bolted to the wall in the corner of the chippy to remind us of Russell, and we sing along to T. Rex's 'Get It On' as we scoop, salt and vinegar, and wrap the chips. Ross doesn't know the words, but he plays air guitar and drums his palms on the counter with admirable enthusiasm. Russell would be proud.

Riley arrives at the tail end of the teatime rush, and I'm not surprised to see him. He seems to know Claire's work rota better than I do. He hangs back, pretending to muse on the menu board even though he's going to order his usual, and would you look at that, it's Claire who ends up serving him. Clever boy.

There's a quiet period afterwards. Claire goes for a break in the little room at the back while Ross practises his new chip-wrapping skills on the handful of takeout customers and I wipe down the tables and set the dishwasher going. Custom picks up again later when the local slimming group session ends.

'Two pounds off this week.' Babs, as usual, is beaming, and she does jazz hands at me and wiggles her hips. Her joyfulness is why she's one of my favourite customers, because you can't be sad while Babs is around. 'One more and I'll have hit the three-stone mark. That's the same weight as my grandson, that is.' She chuckles as she rummages in her handbag for her purse. 'I'll have my usual, please.'

Babs' usual is half a portion of fish with the batter taken off ('You'll have to take it off for me. I've no willpower. If it's there, I'll scoff it') and a small serving of peas, and once a month ('Never, ever let me have them more frequently, I'm begging you') she has a tiny helping of chips.

'How did you get on this week?'

Babs' slimming group friend, Katrina, is next, and she holds up four fingers.

'Four pounds? Wow. That's amazing. Well done. Are you having your usual?'

Katrina's usual is a cone of chips, no salt, with a drizzle of gravy. 'Are you kidding me? I lost four pounds this week. I deserve a proper treat. Give me your biggest fish, a portion of chips and a battered sausage, please.'

Another slimming group member leans on the counter beside Katrina. 'I'll have the same.'

'Are you celebrating too?'

She shakes her head. 'Commiserating. Two pounds on, for the second time in a row. I'll be up to my starting weight if this carries on.' She holds up a hand. 'But don't worry, I'm back on the diet tomorrow and I'm starting "Couch to 5k" again and I'm going to get past week two this time.' She nods at the condiments on the countertop. 'Don't scrimp on the salt and vinegar, love.'

It's late by the time I lock up the shop. The Fish & Chip Shop Around The Corner may be small and it may still be low season, but it's sometimes hard to keep up with demand, even with three members of staff, so I'm knackered as I head upstairs to the flat. As exhausted as I am, I still send Paul a message, as I usually do before going to sleep. I'm in bed, Bolan curled up by my feet as I tap out the message. Claire sent me a link to a careers test earlier, and I take it while I wait for his reply. I take the test three times, skewing my answers and downright lying to try to get a result that doesn't involve social care (not happening) or something cooler than data entry or telesales, but there still isn't a response from Paul and I can't keep my eyes open a second longer and I fall asleep without hearing from him.

Possible Careers According To 'The Planet's Most Accurate★ Careers Test – Take The Online Quiz NOW★★':

- *Teacher*

- *Sales Representative*

- *Artist*

- *Social Worker*

- *Politician or Diplomat*

★am seriously doubting this right now

★★cool your jets, son. I'll take it when I'm good and ready and definitely after my coffee

Chapter Nineteen

I take the careers test again in the morning, to see if it'll throw up any careers I'm actually interested in, but it gives pretty much the same list, even when I keep fudging my answers to the multiple-choice questions. I'm not majorly impressed with the results. Teacher? No, thank you. Kids are okay in very, very small doses. Politician or diplomat? I don't know the first thing about politics, other than it makes Dad shout at the telly a lot, and he refuses to discuss it with Jerry since a near punch-up during the lead-up to the Brexit referendum, and I have no idea what a diplomat is or does and I'm in no rush to google it. I do quite like the idea of being an artist, but I don't think a few doodles in my bullet journal show a real passion for the arts. I had a chat with the careers advisor back when I was at school, who thought I'd be suited to becoming a nursery nurse as I enjoyed a bit of painting ('Creative traits are useful when it comes to working with children!'), but it turned out she'd told all the girls that they should become nursery nurses (and the boys mechanics) so I didn't give her opinion much weight.

Paul still hasn't replied to last night's message and I'm itching to tap out another, to prompt him to respond. Is that too needy? Probably, so I grab my crochet from the 'project bag' I bought myself at the supermarket yesterday as a distraction. It isn't a real project bag like Gran's, but the sunshine-yellow packed-lunch bag with the elephant squirting water on the front was too hard to resist, and it's the perfect size to store my yarn and hook.

I've started on the body of the stripy sausage dog now and have got to the stage where I'm lengthening the trunk by repeating the same stitch over and over again, which is oddly therapeutic. So therapeutic, in fact, that I forget to check my phone for messages from Paul, and I jump a mile when it starts to ring. There's an unknown number on the screen, and I consider ignoring it (it's probably one of those annoying have-you-been-in-an-accident-that-wasn't-your-fault type calls) but my thumb taps the answer button and I press the phone to my ear.

'Hello?' I carefully move my crochet from my lap to my project bag on the coffee table, hoping I don't dislodge any stitches.

'Cleo? It's James.'

I unwedge my little scissors from where they've fallen down between the sofa cushions and toss them into the bag while grunting with reluctant acknowledgement.

'It's Cordy. She's had an accident.'

I'm fully alert now, and Bolan starts as I leap up from the sofa, pressing the phone tighter against my ear.

'Don't panic. She's okay.'

Too late, mate. 'What's happened to her?' *What did you do?* I *knew* I couldn't trust James. How could I have left her with him, vulnerable and naïve to his scheming?

'She slipped on the stairs.'

Slipped? Or was pushed?

'I popped back to the house on my lunch break and found her at the bottom of the stairs. She was awake but a bit woozy. She thinks she banged her head, and she's hurt her wrist. I've phoned for an ambulance. Cordy said not to, that she was fine and just needed a cup of sweet tea for the shock, but I think she needs to be checked over.'

I'm already making my way down the stairs as James is talking, my feet thundering on the steps in their haste. 'I'm coming over.' I end the call and shove my phone in my pocket as I yank open the door. I leg it all the way to Gran's, cutting through the park to shave a few minutes off the journey, listening for the sound of sirens over the racket of my laboured breathing and the pounding in my ears. I'm worried about missing them, about Gran being taken away without me seeing her and reassuring her that she's going to be okay, but my concerns are unfounded as the ambulance isn't even there when I reach the house.

'Oh my God. Gran.'

She's in the hallway, her back leaning against the wall and her arm resting on a throw cushion on her lap.

'I'm fine. Honestly, it's all a fuss over nothing.' Gran smiles at me, but the smile looks wobbly and her skin is pale and slightly clammy. She looks so small, sitting there on the floor. James is kneeling next to her and although he hasn't taken a tumble down the stairs, he looks visibly shaken too. Concern – or a guilty conscience?

'They said not to move her.' He stands and heads for the door, which is still open behind me. He peers out. 'What's taking them so long?'

'They'll have real emergencies to get to, not daft old women who trip over their own feet.'

'You're not a daft old woman.' I crouch next to Gran and place my hand against her forehead, like Mum used to do when I wasn't feeling well.

'I don't even know how it happened. One minute I'm coming down the stairs, the next James is waking me up

152

in a flap. I think I nearly gave him a heart attack, the poor boy.'

'Waking up? So you passed out?'

Gran sweeps a loose strand of hair off her forehead with her good hand. 'Maybe, but only for a minute or two.' She peers past me. We're the only ones left in the hallway as James has wandered out to the pavement. 'I didn't tell James that. Didn't want to worry him even more.'

'Oh, Gran.' I take her good hand in mine and give it a gentle squeeze. 'You shouldn't be thinking about other people at a time like this. And when the paramedics get here, you have to tell them everything, okay? It's important.' I give her a hard stare, and she responds with a minute nod of her head. 'Who was here, Gran, when you fell?' I ask the question gently, trying not to glare out of the door towards James.

'Nobody. James was at work. I'm lucky he popped home when he did. I could have been lying here until teatime.'

So James didn't hurl my gran down the stairs then. He's donned his cape to be the superhero again rather than the villain, only this time I'm grateful for his actions.

'Can I get you anything? A cup of tea?'

'They said not to give her anything to eat or drink.' James is back, striding into the hallway but still looking behind him at the street.

'Not even a paracetamol, and my head is banging.' Gran reaches for her head and winces. 'That's all I need, really. A paracetamol, a cup of tea, and a sit-down for a bit. I'll be right as rain once I've got over the shock and embarrassment.'

'Then that's what the paramedics will advise.' I give Gran's hand another squeeze before turning to James. 'Do Mum and Dad know what's happened?'

'I phoned your mum after I'd phoned for the ambulance. She's picking your dad up from work and coming over.'

Gran tuts. 'There's no need.'

'They're worried about you. We all are.' James is pacing up and down the hallway, peering out of the still-open door whenever he reaches that end.

'I'm a little chilly, James. Could you be a dear and grab my blanket from the back of the sofa for me?' Gran waits until James is out of sight before she lowers her voice. 'I'm not really cold – I just had to give him a little job to do. The lad's going to wear a path through my carpet if he doesn't stop pacing.'

I feel a knot of guilt for suspecting he'd had something to do with Gran's fall. From now on, I'm going to have nothing but Good Thoughts about James, and I'm definitely going to stop plundering his coffee pods.

–

Mum and Dad arrived about twenty minutes before the ambulance (by which point, James had worked on his hallway path a bit more, until Gran instructed him to keep watch outside, just to save her carpet). The paramedic examines Gran before giving the verdict she's been dreading – she has to go to hospital. Mum goes with Gran in the ambulance while James offers to give Dad and me a lift.

'Don't you have to get back to work?' Dad watches as the ambulance turns off the street before heading for James' car.

'Don't worry about it. I rang them earlier to warn them I probably wouldn't be in for the rest of the day.'

'You're a good lad.' Dad claps James on the back and I feel that stab of guilt again. I've severely – and unfairly – misjudged the man. He's been nothing but charming – good company for Gran, helpful around the house, generous with his coffee pods – and I've painted him as a monstrous grifter who's only interested in getting his mitts on Gran's pension. If I had my bullet journal with me, I'd add today's lesson to it: 'Never Make Snap Judgements'. I'd dedicate an entire page to it, using my most decorative (and practised) fonts and illustrating it with doodled flowers and maybe a fox, because I'm pretty good at foxes.

It takes an age to find a parking spot at the hospital, and we end up tucked away in a corner, as far from A & E as we could possibly be without leaving the grounds.

'You all didn't need to come.' Gran shifts in the plastic chair when we find her in the waiting room, her lips pressed together with the discomfort the movement has brought. 'I feel like an idiot, wasting your time like this.'

'It isn't a waste of anybody's time.' I sit next to Gran, noting with alarm that bruising has started to appear on her arms and cheekbone. 'We want to be here, to make sure you're all right. We'd only worry even more if we were stuck at home.'

'Will you at least do something to stop him from pacing?' Gran nods at James, who's already tracing a path along the length of the packed waiting room. She smiles fondly as he turns smartly at the table of grotty-looking magazines and marches towards the desk.

'Come on.' I get up and thread my arm through James'. 'Let's go and find a vending machine. I need coffee, even if it's of the disgusting kind.' There's a vending machine in the corner of the waiting room, but I pretend not to have noticed it and lead James through the swinging doors and into a corridor. My Converse squeak on the glossy floor as we wander through a maze of corridors, finally chancing upon another vending machine.

'Thanks for everything you've done today.' I feed coins into the machine and select from one of three coffee options (black coffee, coffee with milk, coffee with milk and sugar).

'I didn't really do anything.' James digs in his trouser pocket and produces a fistful of change, which he holds out to me. I shake my head. The least I can do is buy the man a crappy cup of coffee after all the pods I've pinched from the cupboard.

'You found Gran. You phoned the ambulance.' I move the cup of vile-looking coffee out of the way and add more coins to the machine. 'You phoned me and Mum. You gave me and Dad a lift here. You kept calm. Ish.' I grin at him. 'You really need to stop the pacing.'

'I know, but I can't help it. You should have seen me when Carla was in labour with Seth and Edith. I nearly wore a hole in the floor of the delivery suite. At one point, Carla threatened to tie me to the chair if I didn't stop.'

I didn't know his ex-wife's name until now. There's a lot I still don't know about him because I haven't bothered to find out.

'You're only three years older than me.' I indicate that James should select his drink of choice. 'How is it possible you have two kids already? I mean, my best friend from school has two kids, but they're tiny. How old did you say Seth was?'

James pushes the 'coffee with milk' button. 'He's eleven.'

'But that would've made you…' I do the calculation in my head. 'Seventeen when you had him?'

'Yep.' James lifts the cup carefully and grimaces when he clocks the browny-grey liquid inside.

'*Seventeen?* That's so young.' I add more coins to the machine and select 'tea with milk' for Mum. 'I was still hanging out with my mates and getting pissed on cheap cider in the park when I was seventeen. I can't imagine being responsible for another human being at that age. I'm struggling taking responsibility for a cat at the moment.'

'I didn't have much choice. It happened, so we had to deal with it as best as we could. It wasn't ideal, but we've done our best and we had a lot of support from Carla's parents. They've been great.'

'What about your parents?' I've gone from zero interest in James' life to nosy bugger in a matter of seconds.

'Mum's done her best, I suppose, but we don't have the best relationship. I don't get on with my stepdad and Mum's stuck in the middle. It's all a bit awkward.' James goes to take a sip of the minging coffee but changes his mind. 'Dad's never really been a major part of my life. He doesn't have much interest in his kids – I think he's lost count of how many he's got, to be honest. So when Carla was pregnant with Seth, I knew I had to do better, whatever it took.' James shrugs and takes the plunge, taking the tiniest sip of his coffee. I can see he regrets it immediately. His eyes search the corridor, but there's nowhere to dispose of the foul drink – not even a handy potted plant – so he's forced to swallow it.

'For what it's worth, I'm amazed. I couldn't have been so grown-up at that age. I'm not even grown-up now.'

'Being grown-up is overrated.' James grabs the cup of tea and I select another one for Dad. 'It didn't feel amazing when all my friends were going off to college and university and starting the careers of their dreams and I was taking any crappy job I could get that only just managed to cover the bills. I was pretty miserable in the early years, but I was determined to provide for my son, whatever it took.'

'I'm lucky, I guess.' We start to head back along the corridor, more slowly this time with the cups of hot drinks. 'I've always loved my job, and I'm good at it. I like chatting with the customers and some of them even like chatting back. I'll miss it when I leave.'

'You're leaving?' James uses his elbow to open the door at the end of the corridor and stops it swinging shut with his body so I can pass through.

'It's part of this whole growing-up thing I've got going on. I'm learning to drive, looking after myself more instead of relying on Mum, and I'm going to start a fabulous new career.'

'Doing what?'

I shrug (carefully, so I don't spill the minging drinks). 'No idea yet. I'm still working on it. What do you do?'

'I'm an accountant.' He pulls a face. 'Not the exciting career of my dreams, believe me.'

'What did you want to be?'

James looks down at the floor, where his shoes are squeaking with each step. 'I wanted to be a performer. I was in a band and everything, but then Seth came along...'

'And you ended up being an accountant.'

'Eventually. I've done all sorts in between – bar work, waiting tables, I even went out on the trawlers for a bit, which was bloody hard graft. But then Carla's uncle took me under his wing and offered me an apprenticeship at his firm, and that's where I've been ever since.'

'And do you enjoy it? Being an accountant?'

James gives me a half-smile. 'I wouldn't say enjoy, but I don't hate it and it's a warm and dry nine-to-five kind of job so I can't complain.'

We've reached the A & E department, where Gran's still sitting on the plastic chair, looking bruised and miserable. Mum and Dad are sitting either side of her, and I sit next to Mum and hand her the cup of tea.

'Any news?'

'Nothing yet.' Mum blows on her tea. There are flaky white bits floating on the top. 'Hopefully it won't be too long before they call us through though.' She leans over to place the cup of vileness onto the table in front of us. 'Your gran's in a lot of pain. She's pretending not to be, so we don't worry, but I can tell.'

Gran tuts, but she's cradling her hand and her face is pinched. 'I'm fine. Embarrassed more than anything, and annoyed with myself for wasting everyone's time.'

'You're not wasting anybody's time, Mum.' Dad's tea, I notice, has been abandoned on the table too.

'You should be at work, and Kitty and James. Cleo too, probably. Instead, you're all sitting here, on these uncomfortable seats with that revolting-looking tea. Where have they dredged it from? A septic tank? If there's one positive of chucking yourself down the stairs, it's that you're nil-by-mouth until they've assessed you. I hope they didn't charge you for that muck.'

Mum catches my eye and raises an eyebrow. 'See? Crabby. That means she's really suffering.'

The Grown-Up To-Do List:

- Decide on a career

- Start a career

- ~~Move out of Mum & Dad's ASAP~~

- Learn to drive

- Find a hobby

- ~~Learn to use the washing machine~~

- ~~Book first driving lesson~~

- Get to work on time

- ~~Host a dinner party (do not serve 'hearty vegetable stew')~~

- ~~Open a savings account~~

- Save enough cash for a deposit on flat

- Keep the cat alive

- Keep the plant alive (not as important as the cat, but will mean a lot to Gran)

- Kick-start social life

- ~~Eat a proper breakfast that doesn't involve chocolate~~

Chapter Twenty

Gran's eventually assessed, and an X-ray reveals she has a broken wrist. It isn't a bad break, but Gran's admitted for an overnight stay due to the bump she took to the head on the way down the stairs. She isn't happy about it, but she doesn't put up a fight and she's soon settled on the ward with a stack of magazines, a cup of 'decent enough' tea and a bunch of flowers Dad bought from the hospital's little shop.

'You two can get off now.' Gran's finally had some painkillers, but she still winces as she shifts position on the bed, her eyes flicking between me and James. 'I think you're only allowed two visitors, so Reggie and Kitty will keep me company for a bit before I send them packing too.'

'I'll come and see you tomorrow.' I stoop down and kiss Gran's cheek. She's got a bit more colour to her now, but she looks frail for the first time. I always assumed Gran was invincible, but today has been a stark reminder that she's no spring chicken (not that I would ever dare say this out loud to her).

'I'll be home tomorrow.' Gran may look diminished tucked up in the narrow bed, but her voice rings clear.

'Then I'll come and see you at home. You'll need help around the house now you've got a busted wrist. I'll help you out with cooking and stuff.'

'Haven't I suffered enough?' Gran chuckles as she reaches out to take my hand with her good one. 'I'm kidding. That would be very helpful. You're a good girl.' She squeezes my hand before turning her attention to James. 'And you're a good lad. Thank you for everything today. I'm not sure I would have been able to drag myself up off the floor. You do realise this means you two will have to crochet all those sausage dogs yourselves now, don't you?' She lifts her plaster-casted arm gently off the pillow it's been resting on. 'I'll be out of action for about six weeks, according to the nurse.'

'What?' I look from Gran to James and back again, my mouth gaping. 'But I'm rubbish at it. I can barely make a granny square. How am I supposed to make a whole dog on my own?'

'Not just one whole dog. Several of them. As many as you can manage. I promised the shelter we'd deliver a whole litter.' Gran winks at me. 'You'll be fine. You've already got the hang of it. It just takes practice, and you can help each other out. And I'll be there to advise, even if I can't physically do much.'

'But…' I look at James for support, but he simply shrugs and starts to back away. Just when I was starting to warm to him.

'I'll see you tomorrow, Cordy. Let me know if you need anything. I can pick you up once you're discharged?'

'Could I get a lift with you now?' Mum grabs her handbag from under the chair and hooks it onto her shoulder before turning to Gran. 'I'll go and grab some bits and pieces for you – your own nightie, some clean clothes, toiletries, that sort of thing.'

'My reading glasses are on the coffee table.' Gran nods towards the stack of magazines on top of the bedside locker. 'And I'll need my night cream and a hairbrush.' She pats her bedraggled hair. 'I must look a state.'

'You look as beautiful as ever, Cordy.' Mum stoops to kiss her on the cheek. 'I won't be long.'

We head through the maze of corridors and trek across the car park to James' car. I'm miffed about the sausage dog thing, so I hang back, trailing after Mum and James as they chat, mostly about Gran. It isn't James' fault I've been roped into the project, but he could have backed me up just then. As far as I know, James hasn't even attempted the sausage dog pattern, so although he aced the granny squares, he could be totally crap at whimsical amigurumi pets. Magic loops may be the undoing of him.

I slip into the back seat of the car, spotting signs of James' family life back here, from the child's booster seat on one side, an abandoned blue teddy bear with a pirate's patch over one eye, and a pocket stuffed with empty crisp packets. I still can't believe he's a father, even with the evidence right in front of me.

Mum and James are still chatting as we set off, and I'm still slightly miffed at the sausage dog thing, so I tune them out and take my phone out of my pocket. I haven't spoken to Paul all day, I realise, so I send him a quick message about Gran, assuring him she's okay but leaving enough room for a bit of sympathy for her worried granddaughter. He replies almost straight away.

> That sucks glad she's on the mend though
>
> xx

Two kisses. I'm still grinning about them when James pulls up outside The Fish & Chip Shop Around The

Corner, until I remember poor Bolan hasn't been fed since early this morning and he's usually demanding his 'evening' meal by mid-afternoon. I rush straight up to the flat to feed the cat, whose hunger is so great he zigzags between my feet and nearly sends me flying across the kitchen. With Bolan wolfing down his organic chicken and lamb casserole, I head downstairs to relieve Bridget, who has stayed on to cover my absence. The teatime rush is imminent, so I hurry to wash my hands and shove my tabard, hairnet and hat on before getting stuck into the prep for the evening's trade. It's a Friday, so I'm kept busy until closing. I have Ross out the front with me, while Elliot is in the back, keeping us stocked up with sliced potatoes and loading and unloading the dishwasher. Babs is back, smiling even as she tells me about the super-stressful day she's had at work ('But *please* don't let me have chips. I shouldn't even be in here at all…'), along with Riley, who's miffed that Claire has switched her shift with Ross so she can finish off an assignment that's due in tomorrow, and Fleetwood Jack, who's meeting Ross for the first time.

'I'll give owt a go, me.' Jack lifts his shoulder in a casual shrug. 'I once snorted a line of baking powder that my mam hadn't cleared up off the kitchen worktop, just to see if it had the same effects as coke.' His shoulders slump. 'It didn't. Shame, really. It's much cheaper.'

Poor Ross doesn't know how to respond and simply gapes at Jack, unblinking, uncomprehending, until I swoop in, nudging Ross aside so I can serve Jack and have him on his way. I should have taught him about Jack before we mastered chip-wrapping.

I'm so busy in the shop, I don't have the time to worry – about Gran and the sausage dog project – until I flop into bed. I'm exhausted but my mind won't switch off with what ifs. What if James hadn't come home for lunch? What if James hadn't moved in with Gran and she'd been left slumped at the bottom of the stairs for hours? What if the bump to her head had been more severe? What if she hadn't walked away with a broken wrist and bruises? What if…?

My bullet journal is on the bedside table, and I grab it to take my mind off the questions buzzing around my brain. Flicking through my grown-up to-do list, I'm dismayed to find I've only managed to cross off five items of many, especially as I need to add 'find permanent flat' because Russell and Jed will be back tomorrow, and unless I'm planning on claiming squatter's rights, I'll be moving back home to Mum and Dad's. I've missed them, obviously, but it's definitely time to move out and get some independence.

Pushing a hand against my mouth, I stifle a yawn as I plonk the journal on the bedside table. Tomorrow, I'm going to stop messing around and start taking this growing-up thing seriously.

Things To Do Before Russell and Jed Get Back:

- *Empty dishwasher*

- *Make sure all the CDs are back in their cases*

- *Make sure all the CDs are back in alphabetical order*

- *Clean the bathroom and kitchen*

- *Change bedding*

- *Make sure the stain on Russell's photo cushion is hidden*

- *TIDY ALL ROOMS*

- *Pack (don't forget penguin plant)*

Chapter Twenty-One

Blondie's 'One Way or Another' is blasting from the stereo as I run the hoover across the living room floor, picking up stray cat toys, abandoned mugs and the little pair of scissors I misplaced along the way. I've already washed the bedding and it's currently tumbling in the dryer, there are new sheets on the bed and the duvet cover has been changed (which was a deceptively *exhausting* task, FYI) and I've given the bathroom and kitchen a thorough going-over until they sparkled. Russell and Jed aren't even due home for a couple of hours, so I'm feeling rather pleased with myself. Gran's hopefully going to be discharged this afternoon, so I'm hoping I'll have time to do the handover with Russell and Jed before dashing over to Gran's to welcome her home before my shift starts. I've already packed my stuff and the bags are waiting in the hallway. I'll miss the flat (though maybe not the early-morning wake-up calls from my furry flatmate) but I'm determined to find my own place and have already saved a couple of promising flats on the properties app to look into when I'm not so busy blitzing Russell and Jed's place for their arrival.

'What do you think?' I've switched the hoover off, but I still have to raise my voice so Bolan can hear me over the music. 'Clean enough for your owners?'

The cat glares at me from his radiator hammock. Okay, so we haven't exactly bonded during my two-week stay, but at least I've managed to keep him alive. I'm going to take great satisfaction striking that one off the list, because surely there's nothing more grown-up than taking care of another living thing? I should get bonus points for keeping my shit together during the six a.m. pawings to the face.

With the flat gleaming, I sit down on the sofa (carefully, so as not to disturb the plumped-up cushions) and open Instagram on my phone. Paul hasn't messaged me this morning, but I can tell by the gym selfie posted earlier that he's been as busy as I have. I like the post before scrolling through the rest of my timeline. My friends list has grown, and my old schoolfriends Shelby, who has posted twelve near-identical photos of her sleeping baby, and Spencer, who seems to post nothing but football gloats and rants, have followed me back. I wonder vaguely if James is on Instagram, but I still don't know his surname so I can't look him up.

I'm at a loose end once I'm up to date with Instagram, so I grab my project bag from the hallway and add a few more rounds to my sausage dog's body. If Gran's serious about the responsibility of the crochet project resting on the shoulders of me and James, I'm going to need all the practice I can get.

I've growled at the stupid crochet sausage dog three times and sworn at it once (I won't repeat it, it was that bad) when I hear footsteps on the stairs. Confusion, quickly followed by alarm, floods my body, until I hear the familiar whistle of Russell. He's over an hour earlier than expected, so I'm glad I was up early for the flat-cleaning mission. Flinging my crochet into my project bag, I leap to my feet to greet my boss and friend, but

Russell isn't interested in me. He heads straight for the cat, who springs from his radiator hammock like it's on fire. He circles Russell's feet in a figure of eight a couple of times before he flops onto his side, lifting his paws for a belly rub.

Where has this friendly cat been hiding for the past two weeks and why have I been stuck with his miserable twin?

'Who's a good boy? Who's a good boy?' Russell scoops the cat into his arms and they nuzzle each other. 'Did you miss me? Because I missed you. Yes, I did.'

'Would you two like some privacy...?' I tiptoe towards the living room door, only half kidding. Russell stops rubbing his nose into the cat's furry neck and puts him back down on the carpet.

'How's everything been? Any problems?'

I think about Bolan and his insistence that I get up at the crack of dawn every morning, plus his attempt to kill my poor plant. 'Nope, everything's been fine. Shop, flat, cat – no problems at all.'

'Good, good. Glad to hear it.' Russell claps his hands together and sucks in a breath. 'Especially as I have another massive favour to ask. Well, it's the same favour really, just an extension, if you like.' Bolan is circling his feet again, so Russell scoops him up. The cat rumbles with pleasure as Russell scratches under his chin. 'The thing is, we sort of need to stay in Manchester for a bit longer.'

'How much longer?'

Russell pauses his chin-scratching. 'A month? I know it's a lot to ask, and at such short notice, and we'll totally understand if you say no. There's no pressure. At all. It's just that we trust you, and we know how good you are with the customers and everything, and you've clearly taken great care of the flat and our precious Bolan. But, like I said, no pressure.'

The way Russell looks at me, all wide-eyed and thin-lipped, adds a teeny bit of pressure. If Bolan wasn't in his arms, he'd definitely have his palms pressed together. But then I don't think I want to say no anyway. I like having my own space here at the flat, and the extra money will sit nicely in my new savings account.

'I am going to take Bolan back with me. We've missed him too much already.' He sticks his face into the cat's neck again. 'So that'll be one less thing to worry about. If you say yes, obviously, which you're still under no pressure to say.'

'Okay.' I make my way back to the sofa, flopping down and making sure I cover the stain on the Russell photo cushion. 'I'll do it.'

'You will?' Russell joins me on the sofa, with Bolan curling up angelically on his lap. 'Seriously?'

'Seriously.' I reach across to stroke Bolan since he's in such a good mood. 'I'll need to get myself a new alarm clock if you're taking this gorgeous little furball with you though.' I laugh until I spot Russell's confused face. 'You know, because he likes to wake you up early in the mornings by pawing – gently – at your face?'

'You've been letting Bolan sleep in the bed with you?'

'No. Of course not.' I look down at the cat, who I *swear* is grinning slyly up at me.

'Good, because that's a big no-no.'

'Obviously.' *The sneaky furry bastard.*

'So how did he paw at your face to wake you up?'

That cat is definitely smirking at me now. He's loving watching me squirm. He's probably been waiting for this moment since his owners left two weeks ago.

'Didn't you know he can open doors?'

Russell looks down at the cat, who's started doing that rhythmic clawing thing on his lap. 'He can?'

'He's a very clever kitty.'

Too clever.

I can't believe I've been outwitted by a ball of fluff.

–

Russell pops into the shop before he has to dash off back to Manchester, to say hello and check I haven't trashed his business over the past two weeks (he denies this last bit, but he does disappear into the little room at the back for a nosy at the paperwork). Claire, who's been overseeing the running of the shop during the early afternoon shift, says she's happy to carry on with her increased hours for a few more weeks, and Russell assures me that he'll have a chat with Bridget to make sure she's still on board (she will be. It's been reported back to me that she's in her element bossing people around) and liaise with the temp agency to ensure we have sufficient cover.

'I hope it's Danny working with us again.' Claire sighs dreamily as we wave Russell off. Bolan is strapped into the passenger seat in a pet carrier, and it's oddly gratifying to see him behind bars. He's out of my care now, which means I can strike looking after him off my list.

'I'm sure Danny will jump at the chance to carry on working with us.' I nudge Claire. 'Or you, at least.' They have their date tomorrow, so I'll be swapping my pet care duties for the child variety. A Sunday afternoon is an odd time to have a first date, but with their shifts and Claire's parental responsibilities, it's the only chance they have.

Russell's car disappears from view and we head back into the shop. It's a drizzly day, so it's pretty quiet and the lunchtime rush is more of a shuffle. There are only a couple of customers waiting to be served at the counter while a disappointed family slouch at one of the tables, their buckets and spades tossed aside while they pick at their food.

'So what happened to your big career plans?' Claire is back behind the counter and I lean against it while she works on the first order.

'What do you mean?'

Claire nimbly wraps a portion of fish and chips and places it on the counter, chatting with the customer and completing the transaction before she elaborates.

'You were supposed to be starting a whole new and exciting career, but you've just signed up for another month of this.' She spreads her arms wide to indicate the chippy.

'I couldn't say no, could I?'

'You could have.'

I lean my forearms on the counter and rest my head sideways on them. 'You're right. I could have, but I didn't want to. I love working here, so this can be my way of saying goodbye.'

'By still working here...?'

'For one last month. And then after that...' I stand up straight and click my fingers. 'I'm gone. I'll have a month to decide what I want to do and go on interviews and stuff, and by the time Russell and Jed get back, my career will be ready to take off. Then I'll have a whole month to settle into my new job before Paul gets back.'

Claire gives me an odd look, as though she doesn't think I can pull this off. But I absolutely can. I have a plan now and I'm going to stick to it. I'm going to take it seriously – I have to, because time's running out. I'm going to use the next seventy days to become the best version of Cleo Parker as I can, and Claire will be looking at me with awe rather than the scepticism she's sending my way right now.

I grab myself a plate of chips and sit at the table next to the miserable-looking family. The drizzle has turned into a proper downpour now, with rivers of water flowing down the windowpanes. Any hope of building sandcastles has been dashed and one of the kids has started to wail. The incessant noise is putting me off my chips, but thankfully they pack up and trudge out into the rain, buckets and spades dangling by their sides. As they leave, they pass Riley, who looks like a drowned rat. His usually floppy hair is plastered to his skull and his rain-spattered glasses have fogged up from the warmth of the shop. Still, he manages to hone in on Claire, despite the limited vision, and the rain may have soaked through his clothes, but it hasn't dampened his spirit. He's his usually cheery self as he chats to Claire as she fulfils his order. He's a nice bloke, and I can't understand why Claire won't give him a chance. Why does she always go for the idiots who revel in treating her like crap?

Riley waves a chirpy goodbye before he heads back out into the downpour, his shoulders already hunched against the onslaught before he makes it over the threshold. The sky has taken on an ominous grey hue and the rain doesn't seem to be in any hurry to leave, so I decide to stick around in the shop even though my chips are long gone. I've been checking my phone every few minutes but there's been no word about Gran being discharged from the hospital yet. I do find a selfie Paul uploaded on Instagram of him and his (extremely beautiful) personal trainer colleague, but I quickly scroll past it without liking it.

Finally, the message I've been waiting for comes through, and I dash up to the flat to grab the pack of coffee pods I bought earlier in the week before legging it over to Gran's. The rain has slowed to a mild drizzle, so I'm more damp than sodden when I get there. Gran is still en route from the hospital, so I shove the coffee pods in the cupboard and have a bit of a tidy-up. I thought about presenting the coffee pods to James, to show how considerate I am, but then I'd have to explain the extent of my coffee-pilfering so I've decided to go with the no-fuss approach.

There isn't much to tidy, to be honest. James, it seems, is pretty neat. I put away the bowl and David Bowie mug from the draining board, but there isn't a visible crumb on the worktop or a stray teaspoon resting on the corner of the sink (there's usually a little collection before I think to deal with them) and even the tea towel is folded and draped over the handle on the oven door. And it's a similar story in the living room; there are no mugs lying around, no magazines tossed aside or odd shoes causing a trip hazard in the middle of the room. I'm actually thankful it's James who'll be here with Gran, because this place would be a pigsty within minutes if it was down to me.

It's an unsettling thought after projecting nothing but resentment over James' presence at Gran's house for the past few weeks, but I don't have time to dwell on it as his car has just pulled up outside and he's helping her out onto the pavement. I rush out to help, but Gran bats us both away.

'No fussing, please. I've had enough of that over the past twenty-four hours. I just want to sit in my chair, with a cup of *decent* tea and the remote control. Do you know how much sleep I got last night?' Gran's gait is slow as she makes her way along the garden path, but she shoots James daggers when he attempts to take her arm. 'About four and a half minutes. In total. There was so much noise on the ward – coughing, snoring, moaning about being too hot, too cold – that I was woken countless times. I want to sit quietly, with no clucking around me, so I'm afraid I'm going to have to ask you to vacate the house, for a couple of hours minimum.'

'We can't leave you, Gran. You've just got out of hospital.'

'You can.' Gran steps aside, so James can unlock the door. I'm surprised she let him take charge of that, to be honest. 'And you will. James, my dear friend, can you please make me one of your lovely cups of tea and then drag my dear granddaughter away for a little while?' Gran touches my arm with her good hand. 'I appreciate your concern, honestly I do, but I just need to decompress. Get my bearings. And I promise I will phone you if I need anything at all.'

'Anything? Even if you drop the remote and need it picking up?'

Gran is clearly holding in a sigh, but she nods. 'I'll promise that if you promise to take James to the pub to say thank you for everything he's done?'

I hesitate. I don't want to leave Gran, but I do want to kick-start my social life and the pub is a great place to start. As long as it isn't the Red Lion.

I suggest heading over to the Fisherman, even though it's way across town, because I'm still not ready to bump into Dane or the skanky barmaid. James seems nonplussed by my choice of venue, until we arrive at the pub and he discovers there isn't a pool table and everyone else in the pub is a pensioner. I get the first round in and we sit by the window so we can look out across the harbour. The grey clouds have finally drifted away and the water is shimmering.

'I get the impression Cordy isn't going to be an easy patient.'

I shake my head. 'Not easy at all. She's usually the one looking after other people and she's fiercely independent, unless it comes to mowing the lawn or DIY. But here's a tip for you: never, ever refer to her as a patient in front of her. She will not like that at all.'

The corner of James' lips quirks upwards. 'Thanks for the warning.' He takes a sip of his pint. 'So. These sausage dogs. Are you ready for the challenge?'

'Nope. But I don't think we have much choice.'

James snorts, and his face lights up with mirth. I feel a little glow inside, but that could be the wine working its magic.

'We'll be fine.'

I arch an eyebrow at James, and I feel that glow again when he laughs.

'We will. And if not, we'll buy some handmade toys from Etsy and pass them off as our own.'

I raise my glass to that idea. 'I like your style. Can that be Plan A?'

James gives a sad shake of his head. 'Emergency Plan B only, I'm afraid. I don't think Cordy would let us get away with it.'

'I think she'd let *you* get away with anything. She's taken a real shine to you. I don't think you could do any wrong in the eyes of Gran. You've fast become her favourite grandchild and you're not even related.' I smirk at James, but I'm not even kidding.

'Let's see how she feels after six weeks of me playing nurse.'

'Good luck, James. You're going to need it.' I raise my glass again and this time James clinks his pint against it.

Favourite Childhood Activities:

- *Sleepovers at Sienna's (listening to mixtapes, talking about boys, eating mint chocolate chip ice cream)*

- *Building sandcastles with Grandad (and eating candyfloss on the way home)*

- *Baking with Gran (licking mixture from the bowl at the end was the best bit)*

- *Going to the playground with Dad (he pushed me higher than anyone on the swings)*

- *Snuggling up on the sofa on rainy days with Mum (with hot chocolates, with gooey marshmallows bobbing on top)*

Chapter Twenty-Two

With Bolan being away, I managed to have a well-deserved lie-in this morning but it means I'm running late. I said I'd be at Claire's for eleven, to give her time to get ready for her date, and it's already quarter to and I'm still in my pyjamas and shovelling muesli into my mouth. It's almost half past eleven by the time I collapse against Claire's front door, wheezing from the sprint across town with only just enough energy to press the buzzer for her flat. I don't even have the energy reserves to weep at the thought of climbing the stairs up to the second floor.

'Sorry. I'm. Late.' I'm doubled over, my hands resting on my thighs as I gulp down oxygen when Claire opens the door to her flat. When Paul and I meet up again, we should definitely start working out together. I'm so unfit, and there's no better motivation to work out than getting to see Paul with his top off.

'It's okay. You're just in time to help me decide what to wear.' Claire leads the way to her bedroom, where there are three tops hooked on to the front of her wardrobe door. 'I'm definitely wearing these.' She picks up a pair of ripped skinny jeans and rests them against her body. 'But I can't decide which top. We're going bowling, so is this too dressy?' She unhooks a white low-cut top with voluminous sleeves and holds it above the jeans. It's a beautiful top that's fitted at the bust but flares out with pleats underneath to give a floaty effect.

'The sleeves may become a problem if you're bowling.' I pinch one of the sleeves between finger and thumb and stretch it out. That's a lot of fabric for a sleeve.

'I really like this vest.' Claire hooks the white top back on to the wardrobe door and grabs a cropped floral vest top. 'But it's a bit… blah, for a first date, don't you think? Yeah, definitely blah.' She tosses the vest onto her bed and plucks the third and final top from the wardrobe door. 'What do you think?' She holds the dusty rose-coloured sweater against her body. It's off the shoulder to one side with oversized three-quarter-length sleeves.

'I think it's perfect.'

Claire gives a decisive nod. 'Me too.'

I leave Claire to get changed and head into the living room, where Arlo is building a racetrack out of bits of orange and green plastic while keeping one eye on the telly. He doesn't seem to notice I'm in the room as I sit down on the sofa, moving the abandoned bowl of browning apple slices from the seat to the coffee table, but he doesn't start when I speak.

'What're you watching?'

Arlo's eyes flick to the TV screen. '*ThunderCats Roar.*' He picks up a bit of orange track and slots it into the structure he's working on.

'Is that for your cars?'

Arlo nods and carries on slotting bits of track together.

'We're going to be spending the day together. What shall we do?'

Arlo shrugs, his attention firmly on the track in front of him.

'It's a bit rainy today. Do you have any wellies? We could go for a stomp in the puddles.'

I wait for a reply, or some sort of response to show that the kid has heard me.

Nothing.

Today is going to be Fun.

'Cleo?'

I jump up from the sofa, grateful for Claire's distracting call, and head back to her bedroom. She's wearing the jeans and the sweater and, although it's a casual ensemble, she looks stunning. This girl could wear a bin bag and still look like a goddess.

'How shall I do my hair?' She gathers a section of hair and twists it on top of her head. 'Messy half-up topknot?' She drops the hair before gathering it to the side. 'Chunky fishtail?' She releases the hair again and combs her fingers through it. 'Or shall I just leave it down?'

'Topknot.' I take my phone out of my hoodie pocket under the guise of checking the time, when really I'm checking for messages from Paul. 'What time is Danny picking you up?'

'I'm meeting him there at twelve, but it doesn't matter if I'm a bit late. It'll keep him on his toes.'

I nod, though I'm not really paying attention. I've sent Paul two messages already today – one to say good morning and the other to let him know I may not reply to his messages straight away because I'm babysitting this afternoon (I will absolutely reply straight away, but the being-in-charge-of-a-kid sounds grown-up). He hasn't replied to either message yet and he hasn't liked the photo I took of our drinks in the pub yesterday, to show off the fact I was partaking in a bit of daytime drinking with my friends (it was just one friend, who isn't actually a friend, and we were only there because Gran made us, but Paul doesn't have to know that).

–

I last approximately ten minutes with Arlo before we pack a little bag of snacks and toys and head over to Gran's. He lost interest in his car track and the TV as soon as Claire headed out and I've failed to find anything to occupy him since. But Gran will know what to do. I used to love spending time at Gran's when I was a kid, and there was always something fun to do, whether it was baking fairy cakes, or having a teddy bears' picnic in the garden, or gluing and sticking at the kitchen table.

'When's Mummy coming back?'

Arlo's clomping next to me in his wellies, his clammy little hand in mine as we walk across town. I try not to take offence that he's bored of my company already.

'In a little while. She's meeting a friend, but she'll be back before teatime. Look, there's a big puddle. Go and jump in it.' I wriggle my finger towards the giant puddle taking up half the width of the pavement, but Arlo simply looks up at me with his big brown eyes, still clomping along beside me. 'Not a fan of puddles, eh?' What a waste of a pair of wellies. If I was wearing something more watertight than my Converse, I'd be bouncing up and down in there like a shot, but perhaps that says more about me than it does about Arlo. 'What do you like doing?'

'Eating ice cream.'

'Me too!' Now we're on the same page, kid. 'What's your favourite flavour?'

Arlo takes a moment to consider his response, but this time the silence isn't awkward. Deciding on a favourite ice cream flavour takes careful deliberation.

'Pink, with sticky sauce and a wafer.'

'Ooh, good choice.' We pass the giant puddle and I resist the urge to jump in. 'My favourite is mint chocolate chip.'

Arlo scrunches up his little nose as he looks up at me. 'Yuck. Mint ice cream tastes like brushing my teeth. I *hate* brushing my teeth.'

'How about raspberry ripple then?'

Arlo nods. 'I like raspberry ripple.'

'That's my second favourite, I think. Or maybe Neapolitan.'

'What's nepapoltan?'

I try not to giggle at the mispronunciation. 'Neapolitan is three different flavours in stripes – vanilla, chocolate and strawberry. I like it because you get to eat three flavours at the same time.'

'That sounds *awesome*. Nepapoltan is my new favourite.'

I feel a little glow. Something I said sounds *awesome*. We're bonding here. 'Maybe we could go for an ice cream after lunch?'

'Is that when Mummy's coming back?'

The glow dims, but I get a different kind of joy when my phone pings with a new message from Paul. It's short but sweet ('Have fun!') but it comes with *three kisses* at the end. Although it pains me to do so – even more so than avoiding another giant puddle – I slide my phone back into my pocket without replying. I have the very important, very *mature* task of looking after a little boy today, so Paul will have to wait. At least until we get to Gran's.

I expect to find Gran convalescing, perhaps in her armchair with her favourite blanket over her knees and a cup of tea within easy reach. What I do not expect – and what I actually find – is Gran in the kitchen, somehow making sandwiches one-handed while she jiggles her bum along to T. Rex.

'What are you doing?' My hands plant themselves on my hips as I observe the scene before me. Gran turns, still jiggling away to 'Jeepster'. It's one of Russell's favourites.

'Hello, love. I didn't hear you come in.'

'Well, you wouldn't, would you?' I head over to the little portable stereo and turn the volume down. 'I didn't know you were into glam rock.' And not at top volume on a Sunday afternoon.

'I'm not really.' Gran turns back to her sandwich-making, layering sliced tomato on top of lettuce. 'It's one of James' CDs. It was left in the stereo and I thought why not? It's easier than trying to get another one out of its case with this thing.' She lifts her cast and rolls her eyes up to the ceiling.

'And yet you're managing to make sandwiches. Hey, Gran. Why are you making sandwiches when you should be resting? And why so many?'

'Seth and Edith are on their way.' Gran lays the last piece of tomato down and repeats the process with sliced cucumber. 'Carla will be dropping them off any minute now.'

'And where's James? You know, their *dad*.' I'm going to kill him. Or hurt him really badly. He said he'd look after Gran. I *trusted* him. But he's not only shirked the responsibility on day two, he's got her running around after *his kids*.

'I sent him out to the shop for milk.' Gran crosses the kitchen and opens the fridge, where there are two unopened bottles of milk. 'I needed to get him out of my hair for five minutes. Don't get me wrong, I love having the boy around, but he doesn't half fuss. My feet have barely touched the ground since I got home from the hospital. He wants me glued to the darn chair all day while he fetches and carries for me.' She returns to the task of sandwich-making while I stare at her, open-mouthed. 'Hello there, Arlo. You're being very quiet. I didn't even know you were there.'

Arlo's peering out at Gran from behind my legs, his fingers clutching at my coat. 'I want my mummy.'

'How about a sandwich for now? Do you like tomatoes?'

Arlo shakes his head, still hiding behind my legs.

'What about cucumber?'

'What about you going to sit down while *I* make the sandwiches?' I give Gran my most severe look, to show I'm not kidding around and, miraculously, she shuffles off to the living room. It's with a heavy eye-roll, and she's muttering to herself about not being a child, but it still feels like a victory.

'Okay, mister, what would you like on your sandwich?' I help Arlo to take his coat and backpack off and hook them over the back of one of the chairs. 'It looks like we have ham and salad here.'

Arlo scrunches his nose up. 'Don't like salad.'

'No, me neither.' I make a face of my own. 'But why don't we have a little bit of it, just to make us big and strong? I'll put some on the side, so we can have a nibble.' I finish off the sandwiches Gran was in the middle of constructing and make a couple of plain ham sandwiches for myself and Arlo. 'Hey, this can be the Hulk.' I hold up a couple of slices of cucumber and place them in front of my eyes. 'Do you know who the Hulk is?'

Arlo looks at me as though I've sprouted another head. 'Er, yeah.'

I plonk a cucumber slice next to the ham sandwiches and pick up two slices of tomato. 'And these can be Spider-Man.' I place them next to the cucumber and pinch two tiny fingerfuls of shredded lettuce. 'But who can this be?' I wiggle the lettuce in front of Arlo's face, which makes him giggle.

'The Green Lantern!'

I have no idea who that is, but I go with it. 'There you go, Mr Green Lantern. You sit next to Spider-Man and the Hulk.'

'And we'll gobble you up!' Arlo hops from foot to foot, his hands held out in front of him with his fingers bent so they look like Bolan's claws as he battles with his flamingo toy. 'Raar!'

'Raar!' I make the claw-hands and roar at the salad just as James steps into the kitchen with the milk.

'Having fun?' James ruffles Arlo's hair as he passes. 'Hello again, mate. Cool backpack. Bunny from *Toy Story 4*. Great film.' James is grinning as he swings the fridge door open, but it's wiped clean off his face when he spots the bottles of milk already in there. 'That little minx. I can't believe I fell for it again.'

'Again?'

'Cordy sent me out for batteries for the remote yesterday.' He slots the milk in the fridge before jabbing a finger at one of the kitchen drawers. 'Turns out there's a million batteries in there. Every size you could ever want.'

'She says you're fussing.'

'I'm just trying to make sure she's resting.'

I hold my hands up. 'I'm on your side. I caught her making these.' I indicate the sandwiches on the worktop. 'I've had to send her into the living room to sit down.'

'I caught her dragging the hoover out this morning. I had to wrestle the thing off her. She may be functioning with one hand, but she's still got some strength to her.'

I start to move the plates of sandwiches from the worktop to the table. 'She's a tough cookie, but she doesn't realise when she needs to slow down.'

'I've got a broken wrist, not broken ears, you know.' Gran's in the doorway, her eyebrows arched. 'I've just come to see if you need a hand with those sandwiches. I do still have one hand in working order.'

'It's all done.' I pull out a chair and indicate that Gran should sit. She ignores me and heads for the kettle. 'And I can do that. Please, Gran, sit still for five minutes. For me.'

The doorbell goes while I'm filling the kettle, and Gran's off before any of us can stop her. There's definitely nothing wrong with her legs. I think we're going to have to strap her to the bloody chair at this rate.

Top Five Flavours of Ice Cream:

1. *Mint Chocolate Chip*

2. *Raspberry Ripple*

3. *Neapolitan*

4. *Cookie Dough*

5. *ANY OTHER ICE CREAM*

Chapter Twenty-Three

Edith propels herself into the kitchen, honing in on James like a missile and almost knocking him off his feet as she throws herself into his body. He stumbles, but manages to stay upright.

'Hey, you.' Hooking his hands under her arms, he hoists Edith up and rests her on his hip. 'I think you've left scorch marks on the floor.' He kisses her forehead before easing her back down onto the ground. 'Do you know Arlo? He goes to your school.'

Edith observes Arlo before nodding her head. 'He's friends with Lola's little brother.' She clambers onto the chair next to Arlo, who's already eaten the superhero salad from his plate and is now nibbling at his sandwich. 'How old are you? I'm seven, the same as Lola. Lola's little brother is six. My brother is bigger. And *mean*.' She looks towards the kitchen doorway, her eyes narrowing to little slits and her mouth puckering as Seth slopes into the room.

'What have you done now?' James' chest has expanded, as though he's holding in a massive sigh.

'What? Nothing. *God*.' Puffing out a breath, Seth turns and thunders from the room, bumping into the woman passing through the doorway without apology. The woman shakes her head and holds her hands out to the side before letting them fall against her thighs.

'He hit me.' Edith rolls up the sleeve of her T-shirt and examines the flesh for some sort of mark. 'Really, really hard. It made me cry, but just a little bit.'

The woman reaches into her handbag and produces a phone. 'He found her playing on his phone. Needless to say he isn't getting this back today, so I'm afraid he's in a bit of a mood.'

The sight of the confiscated phone reminds me that I haven't replied to Paul's message yet. My fingers find the phone in my hoodie pocket but I leave it where it is for now.

'I'm sorry to drop and run like this.' The woman – Carla, the ex-wife, I'm assuming – smirks at James, displaying she's not in the least bit regretful. 'But I'm meeting a friend for coffee and I'm already running late.'

'No worries.' James steps forward and pecks her on the cheek. 'I'll drop them off at about seven?'

'Perfect.' She kisses the top of Edith's head and raises her hand in a general farewell to the room before she dashes off.

The kettle clicks off, so I make a pot of tea for Gran and pour juice for the kids. Gran has finally sat back down at the table while James has gone in search of Seth for 'a little chat'. I send a quick message to Paul ('I just got a 6 year old boy to eat SALAD. How amazing am I?') before joining Gran and the little ones at the table. James and Seth eventually make it back into the kitchen, leaning against the worktop to eat their sandwiches as there's no more room at the table.

'Can we have ice cream now?' Arlo dumps a crescent-moon-shaped bit of sandwich on his plate and swipes the sleeve of his T-shirt across his mouth.

'Can *I* have ice cream?' Edith looks at her dad, her eyes wide and a tiny but hope-filled smile on her lips.

'I was going to take Arlo over to the ice cream parlour in the park. He wants to try nepapoltan, don't you, mate?' I ruffle Arlo's hair while leaning in towards James and whispering, 'That's Neapolitan to you and me.'

'Can we go?' Edith's eyes are even wider now. 'I want to try nepapoltan ice cream. Please?'

'I can take Edith with us. And Seth.' I'm not quite sure why I'm offering to take charge of two more kids – perhaps the superhero-salad-eating thing has gone to my head. I'm suddenly Mary Poppins with no fear of small humans. Or giant, gangly ones, in the case of Seth.

'Why don't we all go together?' James takes his plate to the sink and turns the hot tap on. 'It's been years since I've had nepapoltan ice cream. Do you fancy an ice cream, Cordy?'

'I think I'll stay here.' Gran catches my eye briefly before looking away. 'And rest.'

'You'd better.' Grabbing Arlo's plate, I tip the leftovers into the compost caddy and James takes it off me to wash. 'If you touch the hoover – or any other household appliance – there'll be trouble.' I grab a tea towel and dry the plates, because I know if I leave them, Gran will take it upon herself to do it while we're out.

–

The ice cream parlour is situated conveniently close to the play area of the park, though the swings and climbing frame are empty right now due to the persistent rain. Stepping into the shop is like stepping into another world; while it's grey and drizzly outside, inside there's an explosion of sugary-sweet colour, with gleaming pink and white tiles on the floor, pastel-coloured seat cushions, and blocks of soft shades on the walls. There's an octagonal counter in the centre of the room, with three sides containing trays of every conceivable flavour of ice cream, two more containing a rainbow of toppings and another filled with jars of cones and wafers of various shape and size. The remaining two sides are lined with tall stools, which Edith and Arlo attempt to clamber up onto as soon as we step inside.

'What would you like?' I'm helping Arlo onto the stool, but I turn to Seth, whose expression is as dark as the clouds outside.

'Whatever.' He shrugs before sloping off to one of the booths by the window, dropping into the end seat so nobody can sit next to him.

I look at James and shrug. 'Five nepapoltans then?'

It seems like a simple choice, but at Alessandra's there is so much more to a Neapolitan ice cream. I have mine in a sundae glass, with whipped cream, chocolate sauce, rainbow sprinkles and a chocolate-filled rolled wafer. And it is a thing of beauty. So much so, I take a photo of it and post it to Instagram before digging in.

'What do you think? Is nepapoltan your favourite?'

Arlo has chosen to have his ice cream served in a chocolate-dipped cone, with raspberry sauce and mini marshmallows on top. He's only a few licks in and his face is already looking sticky.

'Nepapoltan is the *best*.' Arlo grins at me before taking an extra-long lick that leaves him with a blob of raspberry sauce on the tip of his nose.

'It's Ne-*a*-pol-*i*-tan.' Edith slides down from her stool and heads over to the mini chalkboard menu propped up on the counter above the trays of ice creams. She points out the words and spells it out for us again.

'So it is.' I hit myself lightly on the forehead. 'You're a very clever girl.'

'Mummy says I'm a genius.' Edith shrugs and clambers back up onto her stool. 'But I'm just good at reading.'

'Daddy says you're a genius as well.' James straightens on his stool, throwing his shoulders back. 'I'm always telling you how clever you are.'

'*You* tell me I'm a ratbag.' Edith's chosen to have her Ne-*a*-pol-*i*-tan ice cream served in a wafer bowl, and she's mixed the scoops into a marbled, gloopy soup which she's now spooning up and dropping back into the bowl.

'That's because you *are* a ratbag. But you're a clever ratbag. And a messy one too.' James wrestles a serviette from the metallic dispenser on the counter and leans over to wipe up a splash of ice cream soup. He grabs another and wipes the sticky sauce from Arlo's nose. 'And speaking of mess, what do you think your gran's up to while we're out? Deep cleaning the kitchen? Clearing the gutters?'

'She's probably using the opportunity to have the attic clear-out she's been meaning to do for the past decade.' I'm joking when I say this, but it fills me with worry, because I wouldn't put it past Gran to tackle a huge task like that single-handedly (literally).

'She's definitely a determined woman.' James plucks the fan wafer from his ice cream and bites off the pointed tip before dipping it back into his ice cream.

'I think the word you're looking for is stubborn.'

'Capable?'

'Stubbornly so.' I catch James' eye and smirk. 'Seriously though, the woman's like a machine. Not in an emotion-less way – far from it – but she just gets things done, you know? She doesn't let anything get in her way. Broken bones, well-meaning grandchildren…'

'Or lodgers.'

I nod as I dig my spoon into my chocolate scoop of ice cream. 'Or lodgers. Or even my mum, who's also a force of nature. When you put the two of them together, there's no stopping them. Like when my grandad had his stroke. I came home to help out and they'd already put their heads together and devised a rota so there would always be someone there to help Grandad, day or night, and the housework and the shopping and the cooking all got taken care of. I wasn't much good at the cooking or the personal care, but I helped out with other stuff – washing up, hoovering, that kind of thing – and I'd sit with Grandad, reading the newspaper to him when he was too tired to do it himself or watching his favourite films with him while Gran rested.'

'It sounds like you all came together to help your grandad.'

I give a one-shouldered shrug. 'It's what families do.'

'Why didn't you go off again on your travels, once your grandad was okay? Or go to university?'

I give another one-shouldered shrug and dig into my bowl again, filling the spoon with vanilla ice cream this time. 'I don't know.' I do know, but I don't want to say it out loud, in case all the other bits come out and James sees what a monster I am. 'Everything had changed, I guess. People had moved on and I'd lost the passion for celebrity journalism.' I grin at James, my face belying the guilt that's squirming around inside and making the ice cream curdle in my stomach.

'Daddy?' Edith has slipped down from her stool and she's standing in front of James, her head tilted to one side and her hands pressed together, palm to palm. 'Can I show Arlo how to play on the pinball machine?'

'Go on then.' James reaches into his jeans pocket and pulls out a handful of change, sifting through for a couple of pound coins, which he passes to Edith. 'Seth? Do you want a game?' He holds up another quid and nods towards the pinball machine. Seth looks up briefly from his ice cream to sneer in reply. 'Go on. It might be fun?' He waves the pound in front of Seth's face and though he rolls his eyes, he snatches the coin and shuffles over to the arcade machine. '"Pinball Wizard" by The Who.'

'What?'

James scoops ice cream on the remaining half of his wafer. 'That's what you were humming just then.'

I hadn't even realised I was doing it until James pointed it out. 'Actually, it was the Elton John version.'

'Are you into Seventies music?'

I shrug. 'Russell – my boss – is, so I have to listen to it whether I like it or not. You're a fan too, I'm guessing. I caught Gran dancing along to T. Rex in the kitchen earlier.'

'Ah, yes. I was listening to it last night while cooking. Must have forgotten to take it back upstairs.'

'Well, Gran seemed to be enjoying it. It was quite cute, actually.' Gran's usually into Diana Ross or the Bee Gees rather than glam rock, so I smile at the memory of her shaking her bum while she made the sandwiches.

'Edith and Arlo seem to be enjoying the pinball.'

I twist in my seat so I can see the machine. Arlo and Edith are standing on either side of it, each taking control of one of the flippers, their faces lined with concentration as they hammer at the button constantly, no matter where the ball happens to be. Arlo hasn't asked when his mum's coming back for a while, so he must be having fun. First the superhero salad and now this. I am acing this babysitting thing.

'Even Seth looks like he's getting into it.' I watch as Seth's head jerks left and right as he follows the path of the pinball, his face more animated than I've ever seen it. Is that… a smile almost forming?

'He's a good kid underneath all those surly pre-teen hormones.' James pushes his ice cream away. 'I don't think the divorce helped. Edith was so young, she just took it in her stride, but Seth didn't react too well to the split. It's taking him a bit more time to adjust.'

'He'll get there.' I nearly reach out to squeeze James' hand but shovel another spoonful of ice cream into my mouth instead.

James nods, eyes still on his son, who's up on his toes now to get a better look at the flying pinball. 'I hope so.'

My Favourite Childhood Family Games:

- *Buckaroo! (even with Mum saying 'this is how I feel getting the big shop home' EVERY TIME we piled the poor donkey up)*

- *Guess Who? (Embarrassing fact: I had a secret crush on Hans, even with the massive moustache)*

- *Mouse Trap (The anticipation of trapping the mouse was, admittedly, more fun than the actual clunky reality)*

- *Operation (I have a very steady hand. Is it too late to become an actual surgeon? THAT would be an impressive career)*

- *KerPlunk (Even though Dad would yell 'I'm losing my marbles!' EVERY TIME he caused them to tumble)*

Chapter Twenty-Four

It's stopped raining by the time we leave the ice cream parlour. Arlo and Edith skip ahead of us during the walk back through the park to Gran's, while Seth hangs back, keeping at least five feet between us at all times.

'I still can't believe you've got two kids. I've kept a houseplant alive for a couple of weeks and I'm giving myself major kudos, so you must be covered in bruises with all the patting on the back you give yourself.'

James snorts. 'Hardly. An afternoon eating ice cream and playing pinball is lovely, but you haven't seen the everyday stuff. The arguments over homework. Trying to get them to brush their teeth. The nagging to bring washing down from bedrooms.'

An image of my bedroom back at Mum and Dad's pops into my head and I feel a wave of shame crash down over me when I see the piles of dirty laundry strewn about the place. I've kept on top of my washing while staying at Russell and Jed's and I vow not to slip into bad habits once they're back.

'Seriously though, you're like a proper grown-up.'

James moves out of the way as a cyclist passes, putting his arm out to shield me even though there's plenty of room. 'And you're what? A pretend grown-up?'

'Not even that. I'm a teenager languishing in a twenty-five-year-old body.'

James laughs. 'You what?'

I stop and stretch my arms wide. I see Seth panic out of the corner of my eye, his own feet shuffling to a halt so he doesn't catch up with us.

'Look at me.'

James gives a slow nod of his head, his eyebrows pulling down low and causing his forehead to crinkle. 'I'm looking.'

I pull at my hoodie. 'I still dress like I did a decade ago. I'm still doing the job I did when I was at college, and I technically still live at home with my mum and dad.' I set off again, ignoring the baffled look on James' face. 'And then look at you with your shit together.'

'Hardly. I'm renting a room at your gran's, remember.'

'Because you're divorced.'

'You think getting a divorce is grown-up?'

I shrug. 'It is the way you've done it. I saw the way you were with your ex earlier. There was no screaming and shouting like when my best friend from school's parents split up. I sometimes think she moved to New Zealand just to get away from the arguing.'

'I suppose it's because Carla and I never fell out. There was no animosity or drama. We just realised we wanted more from life. We were really young when we got married – too young – and we'd settled for a life we thought we were supposed to have. I still love Carla – she's the mother of my children, the person I've shared everything with since I was seventeen – but it isn't the all-consuming love you should feel for your significant other. And Carla feels the same. We both deserve more than what we had.'

'So you're not at all jealous about this friend she's meeting up with today?'

'What do you mean?'

'This friend she said she was meeting.' I glance behind me, to make sure Seth is out of earshot. 'It's obviously a bloke.'

'Is it?'

I roll my eyes. 'Of *course* it's a bloke. How long had you been with Carla? Forever, right? You know her friends, so if she was meeting up with one of them, she'd have said their name. *I'm meeting Susan.*'

'She doesn't have a friend called Susan.'

I shove James and roll my eyes again. 'You know what I mean. The fact she didn't name the "friend"' – I make the air quotes – 'means it was a bloke. She was trying to be subtle about it, but it's obvious.'

'Right.' James nods, but I'm not sure whether he believes my theory or not.

'Would it bother you? If she was meeting a bloke?'

'Not at all. I want her to be happy.'

'See? *This* is what I'm talking about. You're a proper grown-up. *I* want my ex to live miserably for the rest of his life.'

'Why did you split up?'

I tuck my hands in the sleeves of my hoodie and shove them under my armpits even though it isn't cold. 'He cheated on me with one of the barmaids at the Red Lion.'

'Is that why you made us go to that old man's pub?'

'The Fisherman isn't an old man's pub.'

James quirks an eyebrow. 'We were the youngest there by at least four decades.'

'It was the afternoon. Only the pensioners weren't at work.' I scrunch up my nose. 'And yes, I was avoiding my ex and his skanky barmaid.'

'The prick deserves to live miserably for the rest of his life for cheating on you.'

I catch James' eye and smile. 'He does, doesn't he?'

'See, I'm not such a grown-up after all. And why would I want to be? I'd much rather be like those guys.' He points ahead, where Arlo and Edith are having a sword fight with a couple of lengthy twigs they've picked up along the way. Edith taps Arlo on the chest and he falls dramatically to the ground, groaning loudly before he starfishes his arms and legs out and allows his head to loll to one side. He lies very still, his eyes squeezed shut and his tongue sticking out.

'Come on then.' Grabbing James' arm, I march off towards the trees, ignoring the small twigs snapping underfoot.

'What are we doing?' James watches me as I stop to search the ground. I spot a large enough twig and stoop to pick it up before handing it to James. 'Are you serious?'

'Deadly.' I grab another twig – it's not as long as James', but it's chunkier and will make a fine sword. 'En garde!' Wielding the twig in front of me, I move my left leg back and bend at the knees.

'You're serious.' James' arms are still by his side, his twig dangling from his fingers. He is defenceless. I lunge, poking him with the twig on the left arm before scuttling backwards. I could have gone in for the kill straight away, but where's the fun in that? 'You're actually doing this?' James shakes his head, but he laughs and leaps out of the way when I lunge at him again.

'Victory will be mine.' I lunge again, aiming my twig at James' right arm but he twists and avoids contact.

'You think?' James springs forward, brandishing his twiggy sword. Yelping, I leap out of the way before counterstriking. James is light on his feet, bouncing out of harm's way with ease. When I go to strike again, he blocks my move with his sword and bounces once, twice, three times, back and forth before he attempts a strike.

'God, you're so embarrassing.' Back over on the foot-path, Seth is watching on in horror as he quickens his pace.

'What was that?' James turns towards his son, and I take advantage of the distraction and attack. My twig pokes James in the side, in the fleshy bit below his ribs.

'*Yes!*' I raise my sword in the air and skip from foot to foot. 'Victory is mine!'

'What? No way. That didn't count.' James turns away from Seth, who's striding towards the park's iron gates at a pace.

'It counted. I win.' I lower my sword and do a little running-man victory dance. It makes James laugh, even though he should be starfished on the soggy ground with his tongue lolling.

'Okay, okay, you're quite the swordswoman.' James tosses his twig on the ground and we catch up with Arlo and Edith, who have abandoned their own sword fight to chase a bunch of poor pigeons. Seth has already left the park, and we find him sitting on the wall outside Gran's house.

'Fancy a go on the Xbox with your dad?' James nudges Seth, who shrugs but slides off the wall and saunters towards the door. 'It's set up in my room. Choose a game and I'll be up in a minute.' He unlocks the front door, but he pauses before he swings it open. 'Brace yourself.' He tilts his head to listen for the sounds of Gran not resting as instructed. But there are none and, miraculously, we find her sitting on the sofa when we troop into the living room. It's only the yellow dusting cloth poking out from under the cushion that gives her away.

–

'Do I *have* to go home?'

A glow of smugness blooms from my chest at Arlo's words as I'm helping him into his coat. We've spent the rest of the afternoon at Gran's, dusting off the board games that have been dumped in a corner of the craft room for years, and painting at the kitchen table. Later, while Arlo and Edith burned off some ice-cream-induced energy in the back garden and Seth remained glued to the games console upstairs, James and I cracked on with our crochet sausage dogs under Gran's supervision. I'm pleased to report that James has struggled with magic loops as much as I have – if not more – and I'm firmly ahead on sausage dog production.

It's been a fun afternoon, but it's time to get Arlo home.

'I'm afraid so. Mummy's waiting for you.' Claire called when she arrived home to an empty flat, wondering where we were. 'But we can hang out again, can't we?'

'Will Edith be here?'

The smugness dims a little. So it isn't *me* who Arlo is reluctant to leave but his new pal, even though it was *me* who invented superhero salad and bought him a massive ice cream.

'We'll have to arrange a play date, won't we?' I zip the coat up carefully and hook the Bunny backpack onto Arlo's shoulders. 'Ready? Shall we go and find Mummy?' I'm dying to know how her date went with Danny – I haven't been on a date myself for so long, so I have to live vicariously through my friend. 'Don't forget your paintings. They should be dry by now.'

'You can keep this one.' Arlo passes me one of his paintings. He's painted three pictures, all of them depicting his new favourite ice cream, and I'm touched by the gesture.

'Thank you. That's very kind.' I crouch down so I can hug the boy. 'I'll take it home with me and put it on my fridge.'

We have bonded. I can't wait to tell Claire about our day – after she's spilled all the juicy goss from her date, obviously.

Claire has already changed out of her jeans and sweater by the time we get to her flat. She's wearing a pair of flannel pyjamas, her face scrubbed of make-up and her hair is wrapped in a towel. She smiles from ear to ear when she sees her son, but I can tell she's missing the sparkle of an amazing first date.

'Well? How did it go?'

With Arlo transfixed by kids' TV, Claire and I have sneaked off to the kitchen for a post-date dissection.

'It went really well. We had a laugh, and it felt easy and comfortable, you know? Danny already knows about Arlo, so I didn't have to worry about if or when I should tell him, so I could just relax and have fun.' Claire places her 'nepapoltan' painting onto the front of the fridge and secures it with a Blackpool Zoo magnet. 'And we had a *lot* of fun.' She crosses the kitchen and closes the door. 'We went back to his, and you know… But afterwards, he changed. Went all cool and dickhead-like. He said we should be just mates. I didn't even have my knickers back on at this point.'

'Oh my God. What a knob.'

'What the hell is wrong with me, Cleo? Why do I do this to myself?'

'There's nothing wrong with you, other than your shitty taste in men.' I pull Claire into a hug and give her a big squeeze until she giggles and tells me I'm going to crack her ribs.

'I think I'm going to give up on dating. It isn't worth it.'

'Or – and this is a crazy idea – you could try dating men who don't have tattoos on their faces?'

Claire shrugs. 'Maybe. I just don't want to settle for someone boring. Why can't I find someone edgy and exciting who'll fall head over heels in love with me? Is that too much to ask?'

'Definitely not, and your perfect guy is out there somewhere, wondering when he's going to find a gorgeous, vivacious woman who'll fall head over heels in love with him. But he probably doesn't have a tattoo on his face.'

'You're really not into facial tattoos, are you?'

'Nope. Because I'm normal.'

Claire snorts. 'You? Normal? Since when?' She nudges me playfully, and I'm happy to see a smile lighting up her face again. Claire may have been bruised by Danny, but she'll dust herself off and move on. Just like I am, with Paul. Dane may have emotionally bruised me, but I'm not beaten and I deserve to be happy.

It's as I'm dropping off to sleep that night when Paul finally replies to my earlier 'I just got a 6 year old boy to eat SALAD. How amazing am I?' message. It's only a thumbs-up emoji, but he's probably been busy working. I reply with an emoji of my own – a simple smiley face – and drift off to sleep while mentally planning our future together. A future where I'm successful in both love and career.

Today's _must do_ to-do list:

- _Apply for a job. _Any_ job_
- _Find out how to remove stains from soft furnishings_
- _Survive second driving lesson_

Chapter Twenty-Five

I'm staring at Russell's face, debating with myself whether this is the right thing to do. Either it'll make everything perfect again, or I'll make things ten times worse. But what choice do I have? I can't leave the situation as it is, and I trust the advice Gran has given me.

Right.

Here goes.

Scooping up a spoonful of the washing powder, water and white vinegar mixture, I *very slowly* place it on Russell's cheek, wiggling the spoon until most of it has dolloped onto the cushion.

'Please work, please work, please work,' I'm chanting to myself as I rub the mixture into the coffee stain, my bottom lip pinched between my teeth. I've already tried washing it three times – twice with stain-remover stuff – so if this doesn't work, I'll have to come clean and tell Russell and Jed that I've ruined one of their photo cushions.

Most of the stain seems to have lifted with Gran's magic concoction, so I bung the cushion cover into the washing machine before it changes its mind and the stain returns. There was a moment of mild panic this morning, when Jed almost made an unplanned return to Clifton-on-Sea after the temp agency contacted him to let him know Danny (the face-tattooed bastard) would no longer be covering the required shifts, and my mind went straight to the cushion cover. The *stained* cushion cover that I managed to hide from Russell a few days ago but would not go unnoticed once Jed was living back in the flat. The crisis was averted when the temp agency got back in touch to confirm they'd arranged alternative cover and Jed's return was cancelled, but I decided I couldn't put it off any longer. Either the stain had to go or I'd have to come clean, because I couldn't take another scare like that again.

Maryam will be starting as our new temp today, and I wanted to pop down to the shop to show her the ropes before lunchtime, even though it's my day off, but I've got my second driving lesson with Connie so I'll have to leave her in the capable hands of Claire. Maryam will be fine, as long as Claire doesn't try to sleep with her too.

I'm fizzing with nervous energy as I wait for my driving instructor to arrive. I can't remember anything from the last lesson as it's all a blur of fear and major panic, which makes the situation a million times worse. I try crocheting to calm myself down, but my fingers feel fat and useless, and even stalking through Paul's Instagram isn't helping. Bizarrely, I find myself scrubbing the shower cubicle. Even more bizarrely, it seems to take the edge off my nerves, and I find myself singing along to one of Russell's Seventies compilations (he has many, along the lines of *Best of 70s Hits*, *The Greatest Hits of the 70s* and *The Ultimate 70s Chart Toppers*, but they all seem to have the same songs, just shuffled in a different order). I'm feeling much more Zen-like by the time the shower cubicle is gleaming, but the nerves come rushing back as soon as I spot Connie's plum-coloured Toyota pulling up outside. I wonder if I'm actually going to throw up as I trudge down the stairs, or if the swishy, acidic sensation is going to remain with me for the duration of the lesson.

'Good morning!' Connie's tone is as bright and jarring as her outfit, which consists of a knee-length mustard skirt and matching jacket with a magenta blouse and teal-coloured tights. She looks as though she's going for a business meeting at Willy Wonka's chocolate factory.

'Yeah, um, good morning.' My tone is flat as I shuffle towards the car. There's a grid to the left of me that I can throw up into if this queasiness amplifies, but what will I do if I have to hurl while I'm in the car?

'Are we ready for our next lesson?' Connie's smiling at me, all toothy and gummy, but I can barely lift the corners of my mouth. Why am I doing this again? Ah, yes. Paul. Being a grown-up. Self-sufficient. Not having to rely on Mum to ferry me around. 'We'll go over what we did last week – moving off, what happens when we approach a junction – and then we'll get going.' She climbs into the passenger seat, ducking her head low so her beehive hairdo doesn't get damaged, and I creep towards the driver's side, my gaze finding the grid one last time before I drop into the seat.

My legs feel like jelly as my feet find the pedals, and my hand is visibly trembling as I put the car in gear, but the nerves seep away as we move along the narrow road and turn on to Woodland Road, past Shona's house and the church and Arlo and Edith's school. The overwhelming fear of maiming people trumps nerves, it seems.

I somehow survive another lesson, which included passing two buses (when did they get so BIG?) and some bastard beeping at me, but he can go fuck himself because I *drove a car*. Badly, but whatever. Connie seems happy with my progress (though I think she's incapable of feeling anything but joy) and I'm oddly looking forward to my next lesson.

I pop into the shop afterwards so I can meet Maryam. She seems lovely and chatty, and she can already wrap chips better than Ross. I manage to pull Claire into the back room, so I can check in on her after the whole Danny thing, but she seems fine. Says she's 'totally over it' and has chalked it down to a bad experience she'll eventually roll her eyes over.

'I can't believe he left us in the lurch like that though.' I flop down on one of the chairs, experiencing the usual momentary pant-shitting fright as it wobbles. 'Maryam seems nice though.'

'She's great.' Claire pokes her head out of the door, to check on the shop. 'Fab with the customers, even Gwen, who told her the story of her finding that porno in the *Dumbo* video case without Maryam batting an eyelid, and she's more than capable with the fryer. Needs a bit of work on her potato slicing though – her chips are far too thin. But then she did work at The Plaice is Right last summer, and their chips are crap. We'll soon teach her the right way. Uh-oh.' Claire pulls a face. 'Fleetwood Jack's just turned up. I'd better get back out there before he scares Maryam off and we end up having to find a new temp tomorrow.'

I slip out while Jack's recounting the story of how he toured with Led Zeppelin and head up to the flat to sort my washing out before it starts to smell damp in the machine. Most of it is put in the dryer, but I drape the delicates, plus the now stain-free (hurrah!) cushion cover, over the radiators. I feel a little bit sad as I cover the spot that Bolan's kitty hammock used to take up. He was a pain in the arse at times (usually at six in the morning when he was pawing at my face) but I miss him. Perhaps I'll get a cat of my own once I have my own place. A cat that enjoys a lie-in and doesn't take its anger out on my pot plants.

With the washing taken care of, I stick one of Russell's Seventies compilations on and settle down on the sofa with my crochet bag. I'll be going over to Gran's later and I want to have at least two finished legs, and not just to rub my superior sausage-dog-making skills in James' face. I want to show Gran that she can take it easy over the next few weeks, that she doesn't have to worry about her commitments. A temporary lollipop lady has been installed outside the school, her shifts at the charity shop are being covered, and James and I have the sausage dog project in hand. All Gran has to concentrate on now is healing.

–

'So Melvin *isn't* the dad of the triplets?'

I take a deep breath, holding it for a few seconds before I release it slowly. 'No, because he had the snip last summer.' Seriously, we've been watching *Waiting on You* together for a few weeks now and James still can't keep up? Either that or he's deliberately winding me up. 'And her husband, Elvin, isn't the dad either, because he was working away when the babies were conceived.'

'So Elvin is really bad at maths then?'

'No, Joanna fudged the dates, so he thinks he's the dad, but *she* thought it was Melvin.'

'And Melvin didn't think to tell Joanna he'd had the snip so couldn't be the father nine months ago? Why did he have to wait until she was being wheeled into theatre to blurt it out? *In front of her husband*, who now knows she cheated. So now Joanna's a single mum to three babies with no idea who the father is, because let's face it, it could be anybody from that restaurant, employee or customer. It really is mind–numbing trash.'

I lay my crochet down on my lap and raise my eyebrows, making sure James has finished his mini rant before I speak. 'Just when I was starting to like you, you go and diss one of the best shows on TV.'

'*Starting* to like me? You mean you didn't like me straight away? How did you manage to hide it so well?' If James is offended by my previous mistrust of him, he's better at hiding his true feelings than I am as his face is alight with mischief. His features fall, however, when he looks down at his crochet. 'Can you show me how to make a magic loop again?'

James has completed the head of his sausage dog and has moved on to the body, but he's had five goes at a magic loop and hasn't managed it yet. Not that I'm counting his failures, or feeling in any way smug that I can make a magic loop without the aid of Gran or YouTube tutorials now.

'Like this.' I demonstrate the procedure slowly, waiting until James has carried out each stage before I move on to the next. 'There you go. You've done it.'

'Thanks.' James consults the pattern to see what the next step is. 'I'd have been trying to do that all night without your help.'

I shrug, but I feel a little glow. I think it's another helping of smugness at first, but it feels different. Nicer. Sort of warm and fluffy and not tinged with bitterness.

We sit in companionable silence as we work, one eye on our crochet, one on the TV, until my phone beeps with an alert from the job–search app I signed up to earlier in a bout of proactiveness. It's become quite clear I have no direction when it comes to a career path, but time is marching on so I'm going to have to wing it and apply for any office-based job.

'Do you think I could be a payroll officer?' My finger's hovering over the apply button. The salary looks pretty good, and it's a nine-to-five so no post-midnight locking up, and it's on the outskirts of Preston, so not too far away.

'Do you *want* to be a payroll officer?' James doesn't take his eyes off his crocheting as he asks, his fingers moving with alarming swiftness. He'll have finished the body before the end of this episode of *Waiting on You* if he carries on like this, and then I'll only be two legs ahead.

'It isn't a career option I've ever thought about, to be honest, but I have a maths A level and I've been taking care of the admin side of the chippy while Russell and Jed have been away, so the idea isn't too out there.'

'What's happening with the chippy?' Gran shuffles forward to reach for one of the chocolate chip cookies on the table, shooting me daggers when I shift in my seat to help her out. 'You haven't been fired, have you?'

'No, nothing like that.' I slouch back down against the sofa, my finger still hovering above the button on my screen. Still undecided. 'I'm just looking for somewhere I can start a career. *Finally.*'

'But you love your job.' Gran frowns at me. 'Why would you give that up?'

'Because it's hardly high-flying, is it?'

'So what? There's more to life than high-flying careers, you know. I was a dinner lady when your dad was small, and I loved it. It was only a few hours a day, and the money was pitiful, but I have such fond memories of that time, of the other ladies and the kiddies.' Gran sighs and shakes her head. 'I gave it up, once Reggie went to big school and didn't need me around so much. We needed the money, you see. So I took a full-time position as receptionist at the doctor's surgery that used to be over by the church. Dr Redman was a miserable bugger, God rest his soul, and I hated every minute of that job. I couldn't wait to retire, and not because I wanted to sit in my slippers watching television all day.' Gran harrumphs and lifts a slipper-clad foot. 'Anyway, my point is, why would you give up something that you enjoy? Not everyone can boast that they're so happy with their job.'

I *do* love working at The Fish & Chip Shop Around The Corner, but I can't help thinking about my old school friends and how much they've achieved since that summer they all went their separate ways while I remained stuck in a weird time loop. And I think of my to-do list that I still need to fulfil before Paul's return. As much as I love working at the chippy, working with Russell and Jed, and Claire, and as much as I adore our customers and look forward to each day, it's time to move on.

I tap the apply button and push away the sadness it brings.

- *Days Until Paul Returns: 60*

- *Items Still On My Grown-Up To-Do List: 9*

- *Jobs Applied For: 18*

- *Interviews so far: 0*

- *Anxiety Level: Through The Roof*

Chapter Twenty-Six

Connie's wearing a burnt-orange pencil skirt and a turquoise top with a scooped, ruffled neckline under a red blazer for today's driving lesson. The colour choices are strange but, oddly, they work. Either that or I'm becoming accustomed to her clashing outfits. Not that I can judge anybody's fashion choices; I'm wearing my uniform leggings and hoodie combo, and there's a milk splodge from my breakfast down the front. I really need to go shopping for some new outfits because I have several interviews lined up, with the first happening in *two days*. The fear is so overwhelming, I want to weep every time I think about putting myself through them, so I've been trying not to dwell on it too much, which is why I still don't have anything suitable to wear.

'No need to look so glum.' Connie tips her face up to the sky and closes her eyes. 'The sun is shining today. I didn't think the weather was ever going to pick up.' She takes in a huge breath and spreads her arms out wide as she releases it. 'Shall we get going?'

It's my fourth driving lesson, and while I pull away from the shop pretty confidently, there's no way I'm going to be anywhere close to taking – let alone passing – my driving test before Paul's return to Clifton-on-Sea. It was a ridiculously overambitious plan, so I'm not surprised that I'll be unable to cross this item off my list in the next couple of months, but I'm still proud of myself for taking the leap.

'We'll be turning right at the junction ahead.'

I carry out the routine and turn on to Woodland Road. There's a bus ahead, but I don't feel the same panic I felt the first time I saw one looming in front of me. It pulls up at a bus stop and I'm cautious rather than fearful as I pass.

'Nicely done.' I feel a glow of pride at Connie's praise. 'We'll take the next right, after the silver car.'

We end up on the seafront, with the open windows bringing in the salty breeze. The road is pretty quiet, but in a couple of weeks this road will be rammed as the schools close for the Easter holidays and the town fills up with tourists. Russell and Jed are so happy with the way I've been running the business, they've left me in charge of filling the high-season vacancies at the shop, and I've already managed to secure a couple of students to cover the extra weekend shifts. Ross and Maryam have made it clear they'd like to stay on until the end of the summer season, if not beyond, but I still have a few more spaces to fill, including my own, because if these interviews over the next few days go well I'll be leaving very soon.

I swallow the lump that's formed in my throat and focus on the road ahead. There's a set of traffic lights coming up, currently on red with a couple of pedestrians crossing.

Connie groans besides me, and I feel a flutter of panic that I've done something wrong. 'That's my ex-husband, crossing up ahead. And the tart he left me for. If you speed up and take them out, I'll give you your next set of lessons for free.' There's a brief pause before Connie barks out a laugh and slaps her thigh. 'I'm kidding. Of course I'm kidding. Don't do that.'

She laughs again, but there's no mirth there, and when we stop at the lights, her eyes are firmly on her blazer, picking at imaginary lint as the couple pass by the window.

'Pull up on the left once you've found a safe place, please.' Connie stares straight ahead until I've pulled over. Once I've applied the handbrake, she gives a tight smile before her eyes find the rear-view mirror. She peers into it, her eyes narrowed as she tracks her ex-husband's movements. He disappears from view and she takes a deep breath, gives a nod and releases it. 'Move off again when you're ready.'

I can't help feeling sorry for Connie, because I've been where she is, stuck between her old life and an unexpected new one she has to forge alone. I remember how lonely I was when I returned to Clifton-on-Sea and everybody had left me behind to start their new lives. And then there's the Dane thing. The Red Lion is up ahead, to the right, and I vow that one day soon I'm going to walk in there with my head held high. I'm finally ready to move on and I'm looking forward to becoming the new, grown-up Cleo and showing her off to the world.

–

'You don't have to keep buying these, you know.' James is stooping to reach into the coffee pods cupboard, and he straightens, holding out the fresh box I put in there when I arrived at Gran's earlier. It's a pack of vanilla lattes, because I've been stealing those most often lately. It's become a habit to pop a box of coffee pods in my shopping basket when I do my weekly shop.

'It doesn't seem fair, me drinking all your coffees. This way, I don't feel so guilty when I nab them.' Because I still probably drink more than I replace. I can't help it – they're far too tempting, sitting there in the cupboard, all delicious and caffeine-packed.

'Think of them as payment for all the help you've given me with Bratwurst. He'd still be several balls of yarn if you hadn't helped me with the magic loops.'

Bratwurst is the name James has given to his completed crocheted sausage dog. He's currently sitting in a clear plastic bag with Chorizo (the sausage dog I completed first – only just – after staying up all night so I could claim the victory, if only inside my own head). In a couple of weeks they – along with any other sausage dogs we manage to finish – will be off to the Easter fair at the shelter.

'I still can't do them.' James opens the box of pods and takes a couple out. 'It's too fiddly and complicated.'

'You *can* do them.' I hand James his David Bowie mug, which he places on the coffee machine. 'It just takes you thirty tries and all of your patience.'

'*You* use up all of my patience.' James is narrowing his eyes at me, but there's a smile threatening to break out so he turns and concentrates on the coffee-making.

'She uses up most people's patience.' Gran wanders into the kitchen, winking at me. 'And speaking of patience, how's that cup of tea coming along? I'm gasping and *Waiting on You* will be back on any second now. I can make the tea. I'll be quicker, even one-handed.'

'You can boil a kettle quicker than us? Really?' I catch James' eye and smirk.

'You've probably put too much water in.' Gran straightens the little milk jug I've set out on her tray. 'The more water there is to heat, the longer it takes, and you're only making a pot for one. There's no need to fill the kettle.'

'What was that thing about trying people's patience?' I guide Gran back towards the door. 'Go and sit down. Your tea will be with you within minutes. Pause *Waiting on You* if it comes back on.'

'Am I allowed to do that in my condition?' Gran gives me a pointed look before she leaves the kitchen, muttering to herself about how she manages quite well to make a pot of tea when James is at work all day.

'That woman.' I shake my head as I move over to the cupboard, reaching for a mug for myself. 'I love her to death, obviously, but…' I shake my head again, but there's a smile forming on my lips.

'You're not going to take the guest room when I move out then?'

I hand the mug to James, who switches it with his David Bowie one at the machine and pops in a new pod. 'You're moving out?'

'Of course. This was only a temporary thing, remember? Until I found something more permanent. I love your gran to death as well, but I need my own space, and I'd quite like to have my kids staying over for weekends again. I know I see them all the time, and I take Edith to school most days, but it isn't the same.'

'Oh.' I'd forgotten this was just a stopgap for James, and I've grown accustomed to him being around despite my aversion to his presence a few weeks ago. I'll miss competing with him over sausage dog creations (even if it's only the one-sided competition taking place in my head) and I suppose I'll have to purchase my own fancy coffee machine.

'It doesn't look like I'll be moving out any time soon though.' James sighs. 'You'd be more likely to see your gran mooning from the top of the Ferris wheel on the pier than finding an affordable vacant house round here.'

'Tell me about it.' The kettle clicks off, so I pour water into the pot that I've already spooned loose tea leaves into. 'The nearest I've come to finding a flat was a pigeon-filled place near the vet's.'

'The one above the betting shop?' James pulls a face. 'Yeah, I viewed that one too. They said it was a two-bedroom flat, but I don't think a bit of plasterboard down the middle of a room counts. One side had the window and you had to pass through the first so-called bedroom to get to the other.'

'And there was pigeon shit *everywhere*.' I want to puke just thinking about the smell.

'It needs some TLC, that's what the agent told me. TLC? It needs a wrecking ball.'

'It looks like you'll be sticking around here for a while then, and I'll be going back home.'

'Would that be so bad?'

I think about it for a moment. 'I guess not, but it feels like taking a step backwards.' I think about telling him about Paul and the fibs I told him, but the words won't come out and Gran's calling us from the living room. *Waiting on You* is back on and the continuity announcer says there's a 'shocking twist' coming up.

'Is the shocking twist that they're putting something decent on instead?' James picks up the mugs and heads for the door. I pick up the tray and stick my tongue out at him.

'Are you two doing anything tomorrow? At half past five?' Gran is holding the remote but she hasn't pressed play yet.

'I'm free.' James grabs his new sausage dog, which is nothing but a snout at the moment. 'Do you have an appointment to check your wrist?'

'No, nothing like that.' Gran turns to me. 'Any plans?' I shake my head. I'm starting to interview for the seasonal staff but I'll be done by mid-afternoon. 'Great. Because I've told the shelter you'll walk a couple of the dogs. I'd do it, but...' She lifts her plaster-casted wrist. 'Thanks so much, guys. You'll love it.' She presses play on the remote. If she sees my look of outrage, she doesn't let on.

Pros of Dogs:

- *They're cute*
- *Instagram content with guaranteed likes*
- *Walking = daily exercise*

Cons of Dogs:

- *Picking up poop*
- *Some of them smell*
- *No excuse not to exercise daily*

Chapter Twenty-Seven

Rain has been pouring all afternoon, trying its best to wash away the entire town, but the grey clouds have moved on by early evening, making way for a bright blue sky. There's a nip in the air from the breeze, but I'd been dreading taking the dogs for a walk in the downpour so I'm not too bothered about a bit of cold as I head to the animal shelter.

James is waiting for me outside, his hands shoved in his coat pockets and a sage-green hat covering his curls. He pulls a hand out of his pocket when he sees me, raising it in greeting.

'Ready for this?' He nods towards the shelter, which is an L-shaped single-storey building with peeling white paint.

I shake my head. 'Absolutely not. I don't know how Gran manages to talk me into this stuff. I need to learn the word *no* and how to sound like I mean it.'

'Who could say no to Cordy?' James reaches for the door, tugging it open but hanging back so I can pass through. 'It'll be fine.'

'Are you sure about that?' I step into the reception area of the shelter, which is made up of a small office area, separated from the public by a high counter with dog paw prints painted on the front in a rainbow of colours, and a couple of worn high-backed chairs in front of the window.

'Absolutely not.' James shrugs and strides towards the desk, where he tells the woman in the royal-blue polo shirt that we're here on behalf of Gran.

'We're just getting the dogs ready. Won't be a minute.' She steps out from behind the desk and disappears through a set of doors to the right, returning a couple of minutes later while James and I are browsing the carousel of leaflets next to the desk. 'Here we are. Meet your new friends: Sabre, Star, Fizz and Baby.'

I look at the dogs. I look at James. I look at the polo-shirted woman and her polo-shirted companion. I look back at the dogs again.

'*All* of them?' I look at James. Is he seeing four dogs? Hearing four names? Because Gran said a *couple* of dogs, not several, and not one that's the size of a small horse.

'I hope that's okay?' The polo-shirted woman – Carole, according to her name badge above the embroidered paw print on her top – looks startled. 'We're low on volunteers at the moment but Cordelia said you'd be fine doubling up.'

Cordelia was wrong. Very wrong. I was dubious about this whole dog-walking thing when I assumed it'd be one pup each and I didn't imagine we'd be saddling up a horse, so I'm beyond doubtful as I take in the four (four!) hounds before me.

'It's fine. We'll be fine.'

My head whips around, my mouth gaping as I look at James. Is he nuts? A cat gave me the runaround while we were contained in a flat so how am I supposed to cope with two dogs out in the open? 'We will?'

James nods. 'We will. Absolutely. Shall I take this beauty?' He steps forward and reaches for the lead of the stallion. Carole hands it over, a watery smile of relief on her face.

'This is Baby.'

I snort. *Baby?* Baby what? Elephant?

'She's a Rottweiler, around three years old, and although she looks...'

Menacing? Intimidating? As though she'd happily take a chunk out of your arse?

'...Forbidding, she's actually a big softie. Aren't you, Baby?' Carole crouches down and fusses the beast, Baby's ears flapping about as Carole rubs and scritches behind them. 'She really is a lovely girl, and so patient and loving. She's got great recall but we would like you to keep all the dogs on their leads today.' She passes the lead for one of the other dogs, a tiny blob of sandy fluff, to James. 'This is Fizz, our six-year-old Pomeranian and the source of that thing you smell.' Carole flashes an apologetic look at James. I'm a few paces behind and haven't caught a hint of anything other than the general whiff of dog that hit me as I walked through the door, but I'm almost knocked backwards with the stench as it reaches me now. It's a combination of burning rubber and rotting food waste and I place a hoodie-sleeve-clad hand to my nose and mouth to try to block it. The dog has farted and it is the most rancid thing I have ever had the misfortune to smell.

'She does that a lot.' Carl, Carole's polo-shirted companion, smirks. 'But you won't really notice it once you're outside.' He holds one of his leads out to me, which is attached to the smallest of the dogs. It's not much bigger than a guinea pig, thankfully. Maybe this will be okay. 'This is Star, who's a pug, obviously. We think she's around a year old. And she's blind.'

I hesitate, whipping away my outstretched hand. I get a blind dog? What if it walks into a lamp post? Or mistakes a leg for a tree and wazzes up it? Maybe this will not be okay after all.

'Don't worry. She'll trot along happily with the others on the lead.' Carl pushes the lead at me and I take it gently between finger and thumb, not quite committing. 'And last but not least we have Sabre.' Carl places the back of his hand to the side of his mouth, as though shielding his next words from the dog. 'We're not sure what he is – a mix of everything, probably.' He grins, letting his hand drop. 'But he's a very loveable chap. He can be a bit…' He looks at Carole for help.

'Spirited. He's one of our older dogs at *twelve years old*.' She widens her eyes at the dog and places her hands on her cheeks. 'But he still thinks he's a puppy.'

He doesn't look like a puppy. He's quite chunky and long-legged and while his fur is various shades of brown, he has white bits around his snout and eyes. But he isn't as humongous as the inaptly named Baby so I take the lead while Carole further instructs us about our dog-walking duties. Armed with poop bags and the four (four!) dogs, James and I head out of the animal shelter and make our way to the park. The breeze picks up the stench from the Pomeranian and delivers it to our nostrils, disproving Carl's reassurance that we wouldn't really notice it once we were outside, and although the park is only a ten-minute walk from the shelter, we're assaulted six times by the stench before we hit the gates.

Still, the walk is drama-free, with Baby leading the pack, striding purposefully while Fizz and Star scuttle after her on their little legs. Spirited Sabre likes to dart off to the side to sniff damp walls or to try to snaffle the floor snacks the seagulls have yet to find but I manage to keep him mostly on course until he spots a squirrel as we're wandering through the wooded area of the park and he nearly takes my arm out of its socket as he attempts to take off in pursuit.

'Are you okay?'

I nod in response to James' concern because I've somehow managed to keep my arm attached to my body. 'Pity about my shoes though.' I lift what was once a lime-green Converse but is now a sludgy brown due to the mud.

'We picked a bad day for it with all that rain earlier.'

'Would there be a good day for this?' I flash James a *see what I mean* look as Sabre veers off to the side, nose to the ground, taking me with him. He sniffs his way around a tree, winding the lead around the trunk. James holds Star's lead for me while I untangle Sabre.

'I don't know. It's quite fun, isn't it?' James hands the lead back once I've extricated us from the tree. 'Edith would love this. She'd love a dog but Carla was bitten by her aunt's poodle when she was little and she's terrified of them now, and I'm not in a position to be taking on a pet right now.'

'What about Seth? Is he a dog person?' I pull Sabre back as he tries to dash to the left, right into the path of Baby's lead.

'He'd love to have a dog but not the responsibility of having one.'

'Sensible kid.' I pull Sabre out of Baby's path again before we end up with spaghetti leads. 'What does he like, apart from video games?' I feel like I know a lot about Edith from the short time I spent with her while I was babysitting Arlo but Seth was more of a closed book.

'He loves basketball. He's really good at it.'

'He is *very* tall.'

James nods. 'That helps, but he's fast on his feet as well and an amazing shot. He's a great team player as well.'

'You sound very proud.'

Baby stops suddenly and squats to wee, which sort of ruins the moment of fatherly pride. We pause but avert our gaze to give her a sense of privacy.

'I'm very proud. I go to all his games. Wouldn't miss one.'

'Does he play for his school team?'

James shakes his head, stepping back as Baby flicks up leaves and mud with her back feet. 'He's in a local league. He's a Clifton Clipper, but he's hoping to get into the national junior league.'

'Maybe he'll make Team GB one day.' We set off again, feet splodging in the mud. My Converse are caked in it, with a sprinkling of brown leaves for added decoration. 'I'll be able to watch him on the telly during the Olympics.'

'Or on MTV.' James sidesteps a gnarly tree root stretching out of the mud. 'As well as becoming a world-class basketball player, he also wants to dominate the world musically.'

I bump my arm against James'. 'It must run in the family. Weren't you in a band?'

'I was, but Seth is much more ambitious than I ever was. My son has big plans for the future. Massive. His band's already got its first gig coming up.'

'Really? Wow.' The breeze causes the leaves to ripple on the ground and I try to shake the fresh ones off my shoes.

'It's only at the Easter fair, unpaid, but everyone has to start somewhere and Seth's really excited about it. I can tell by his grunts when I ask him about it. They're much more animated than usual.' James stops as Fizz's lead has gone taut. She's a few paces behind, refusing to move. Maybe she's stuck in the mud? She only has tiny feet and it's very squelchy. 'I'm excited for him. He's going to have the absolute time of his life on stage.'

'Do you miss it? Being in your band?'

James tugs gently on the Pomeranian's lead and makes encouraging noises until she takes a couple of steps towards him. 'I do. I loved performing.'

'You should get back into it.'

James scrunches up his nose and shakes his head. 'I'm a bit too old for all that now. Too many responsibilities.'

'Ugh. Responsibilities.' I shudder, over-dramatically, which makes James laugh.

'What happened to the grown-up thing?'

Fizz takes a few more steps and we start to move again. 'It's ongoing. In fact, I have an interview tomorrow.' My stomach flips and I feel a bit queasy. 'It's my first interview since Jed and Russell sat me down in the little room at the back of the chippy and asked when I could start. I don't think this one is going to be quite so easy.'

'You'll be fine.' James stops as Fizz starts to paw at his ankle, leaving little muddy marks on his jeans. 'Hey, what's up?' He stoops to stroke the ball of fluff on the head. Fizz paws at him again and she refuses to move when James straightens and attempts to continue our walk. She whines as she lifts herself up onto her hind legs so she can place both paws on his legs. She gives a little bounce and claws at his legs, as though she's trying to climb up him like a beanstalk. 'Are you tired, little lady?'

'You're not going to pick it up, are you?' My jaw is slack as I watch James lift the furball up and tuck her under his arm. 'It's a stinking time bomb.' I can smell the lingering pong of her last fart and it can't be long before she lets another one go.

'She's knackered. She's only got tiny legs.'

'She's only got a tiny arse but it's foul.'

'We'll be fine. Won't we, girl?' James smiles as the pooch stretches to lick his chin with her tiny pink tongue. We set off again, me a few paces to the right so I'm not directly in the path of Fizz's wall of funk. The wind picks up again and I pray it doesn't bring with it a fresh wave of stink. It doesn't, but it does cause a leaf to rattle past, which Sabre mistakes for a squirrel. The daft mutt takes off in pursuit, yanking me with him so forcefully I'm knocked off my feet and land cheek down in the mud.

'Are you all right?' James crouches down, peering closely at my mud-speckled face. It's at that moment, when she's mere inches from my nose, that Fizz lets rip, as though she's been holding on to cause maximum damage.

'I hate my life right now.' Still somehow managing to cling on to both dogs' leads, I scramble up to my feet. I've got mud on my face, my Converse are ruined, and my clothes are damp and grubby.

'Shall we get these four back to the shelter and go to the old man's pub?'

'Yes, please.'

I attempt to hold my head high as we set off but it's quite a difficult task when you look as though you've been wading through a swamp.

Interview Dos:

- *Be Prepared (google company beforehand, have questions ready, plan route)*

- *Make a Good First Impression (no leggings, hoodies or messy buns)*

- *Appear Interested & Engaged (ask questions, smile confidently, make eye contact)*

- *Listen (don't switch off and decide which coffee you're going to treat yourself to on the way home)*

- *Focus On Your Strengths (frying fish???)*

Chapter Twenty-Eight

I've been practising walking in my new shoes all morning, wobbling across the living room carpet with my arms outstretched as though I'm tentatively making my way across a tightrope without the security of a harness or safety net. And it isn't as though I've gone for full-on needle-thin heels; the shoes I'm sporting have a reasonable two-and-a-half-inch heel, yet I'm stumbling about the place as though I've been on an all-day bender. I need to concentrate, put one foot confidently in front of the other and walk like a normal person, because my interview is in an hour.

My stomach churns at the thought and if I'd been able to face breakfast this morning, I'm sure it'd be coming back up again right about now. I've never actually had a proper job interview before – I'd simply popped into The Fish & Chip Shop Around The Corner after seeing the notice for Saturday staff in the window, declared my interest and started my employment a few days later. I've been googling interview techniques ever since it was arranged so I can be as prepared as possible, and I'm wearing a brand-new non-leggings-and-hoodie outfit that is smart but comfortable (wobbly shoes aside). I've gone with classic black trousers with a soft grey sweater over a white blouse and I've pulled my hair back into a simple but sleek ponytail. It was as I was tying it back in front of the bathroom mirror that I thought a haircut was probably due, because faded pink tips hardly scream professionalism. I should have them chopped off and go for a sophisticated jaw-length bob, but it's too late for today's interview so the trousers and sweater will have to do.

I pause halfway across the rug, wobbling slightly but managing to keep upright. Why didn't it occur to me yesterday, as I stood in front of the mirror in the changing room pre-purchase, that it looks like I'm wearing my old school uniform? All I need is a horrible red-and-gold striped tie and a bulging backpack to complete the look. Why do I always seem to go backwards while everyone else is moving forwards? My friends all moved away while I ended up back in Clifton-on-Sea, and even now, when I'm taking a massive, scary leap, I've ended up looking like my sixteen-year-old self again. I bought more clothes yesterday, but do I have time to change? My train leaves in twenty minutes and, if I miss it, there isn't another one for forty-five minutes, meaning I'd end up missing the interview. A full outfit change is probably pushing it, so I peel off the sweater and throw on a single-breasted blazer. It has sharp shoulders and pointy lapels and is definitely the most sophisticated item of clothing I've ever owned. I can feel myself standing taller as I observe myself in the full-length mirror in Russell and Jed's bedroom, and it has nothing to do with the heels.

Satisfied I no longer look like a schoolkid, I shuffle back into the living room and make sure I have everything I need for my interview: handbag with purse (double-check I have enough for train fare and the fanciest coffee treat I can find afterwards), a copy of my not-very-extensive CV, and my phone so I can message Claire as soon as it's over. I have one more practice lap of the living room before I set off for the station, my stomach a riot of nerves while my head screams at me to kick off the shoes and run back home.

I make it on to the train and log on to Instagram on my phone, scrolling through Paul's feed in the hope it will distract me from my churning stomach as we set off. Paul's face is a comfort as I slowly move from a gym selfie he took earlier this morning to a selfie he took post-shower. I'll be looking at this gorgeous face in the flesh soon. I wait for the butterflies to take flight, but my stomach is too busy performing somersaults right now to feel any hint of joy. I'll come back to it later, once the interview is out of the way and I'm capable of feeling things other than nauseating dread.

I have another quick look at the website for the company I'm interviewing for, trying to memorise the facts should they be needed later. I doubt the interviewer will ask me when the company was founded, but I'll have the answer to hand just in case. I'm pretty much prepared to appear on *Mastermind* with the specialist subject of T C Fire Protection, 1994 to present day, as we start to approach my stop. My stomach rolls and I clutch hold of my seat as I take deep breaths to calm my nerves. I consider staying on the train until we reach Preston – I could grab a coffee and wander around the shops for a bit – but I force myself out of my seat and shuffle towards the doors, taking deep, even breaths as I go.

The station leads out on to a busy road, which I've seen many times on Google Maps as I plotted my route to the industrial park and made sure I could get there without any hiccups. It's only an estimated three-minute walk away, which my feet are thankful for as although I've managed to stop wobbling by now, the stiffness of my new shoes is starting to pinch my toes.

T C Fire Protection is the third building on the industrial park. It's a long, grey L-shaped building with tiny windows and a flat roof. It's hardly an inspiring exterior, but I'm sure the inside will be much more pleasant. And it turns out it is, if you're inspired by cold, characterless spaces.

'Can I help you?'

There's a woman sitting behind the desk in the corner of the room, squashed up against the wall even though there's plenty of space in the reception area. I take a couple of steps closer so I don't feel I have to raise my voice to be heard.

'I have an interview.' My voice comes out scratchy, so I clear my throat and throw my shoulders back and continue with a more confident tone that belies my jellied legs. 'It's with Susan Chambers, for the payroll administrator position. My name's Cleo Parker.'

'Take a seat.' The receptionist indicates the row of beige chairs pushed against the wall to the right. They blend in with the beige carpet, making the bare space look even emptier than it is. Other than the desk and the three beige chairs, the only other pieces of equipment are the photocopier in the corner to my left and the trio of fire extinguishers attached to the wall, which give the only pop of colour in the room as there are no paintings on the stark white walls or plants to cheer the place up. This does not look like a fun place to work, and I'm starting to feel as though I'm sitting in a large custard cream in some weird, biscuit-filled dream. I can't imagine breaking out in song here, my colleagues joining in with whatever Seventies hit happens to be playing, and it doesn't seem like the kind of place where every day is different. It seems like an extremely monotonous place where you find yourself checking the clock every two minutes to see if it's time to go home yet.

I check the time on my phone. It's on silent, but there's a message from James, wishing me luck for the interview. Glancing around the barren, joyless room, I'm not sure whether that's a good thing or not.

'Cleopatra Parker?'

I look up from my phone to see a new woman standing in the reception area. She's wearing a pale sand-coloured pencil skirt with a matching long-sleeved blouse and nude court shoes. Is colour banned in this place?

'It's Cleo.' I shove my phone in my bag and stand up, wobbling ever so slightly on my heels.

'I'm sorry?' The walking sandcastle blinks at me.

'It's, um, just Cleo. Not Cleopatra.'

She tilts her head to one side. 'You don't like Cleopatra?'

'My name isn't Cleopatra. Cleo isn't short for Cleopatra. It's just Cleo.'

'Just Cleo?' Her eyes have gone all squinty and she shakes her head, as though she can't compute this information. 'Well, *Cleo*. I'm *Susan* Chambers. Would you like to come this way?'

She indicates the door behind her. I would not like to go that way but I do, with careful steps on my new heels. The door leads to a corridor (beige, but with a jaunty white horizontal stripe to liven the place up), which I follow Susan down, past three cream doors and stopping at a fourth. Susan opens the door, holding it for me to pass before she follows me, striding to the desk and sitting behind it. The desk, I'm gladdened to see, contains two photo frames, even though I can't see the pictures they hold. I'm also relieved to see a plant on the windowsill, sitting in a yellow pot with the word 'MUM' picked out in pink, blue and orange paint on its side. Finally, a bit of life!

Susan nods at the chair on the near side of the desk and I sit, trying not to fidget with the CV on my lap. I place it on the desk in front of me, out of harm's way.

'So. *Cleo.*' Susan flicks her lips outwards, briefly flashing her teeth. 'You've applied for the position of payroll administrator.' I nod, while Susan links her fingers and places her hands in front of her on the desk, on top of a buff folder. 'Why do you think you would fit this position?'

I take a deep breath and grasp at the answer I've practised in front of Jed and Russell's mirror. 'I think I would be a good fit for this position because I'm good at organisation and paying attention to detail. I have excellent communication skills and the ability to work well within a team or on my own. In my current position, I'm responsible for the administration of the company, ensuring employees are paid correctly and promptly.'

Susan's eyes drop to the file on the desk. She flicks it open and scans the document inside. 'You currently work in a *fish and chip shop*?'

'Yes.' I don't like the way Susan said that, as though she was checking I had just admitted to pulling spiders' legs off for fun, in a *he loves me, he loves me not* kind of way. 'As assistant manager, but I'm currently acting as manager. So that means I'm responsible for employees' wages, making sure their time sheets are correct and up to date and processing the data.'

Susan smiles at me, her head to tilting to one side. 'And making sure the salt and vinegar shakers are topped up?' She tinkles out a laugh and I push a smile on my face.

'Of course. Attention to detail, like I said.'

'Quite.' Susan links her fingers again and rests them on top of my CV. 'And what are you looking for in a job here at T C Fire Protection?'

Kudos, mainly, from having an office job. So I can face Paul without still working at the chippy where I earned a bit of extra cash when I was at college.

I don't tell Susan this, obviously.

'I'm looking for a new challenge, where I can push myself and expand on my current skills.'

Susan nods, her face as neutral as the colour scheme of the office. 'Can you describe to me a time when you worked as a team?'

'I work as part of a team every day. We all work together to deliver the best customer experience we can, from the moment the food is prepared until it is served, fresh and delicious, to the customer. If any part of that chain isn't up to scratch, the customer will leave disappointed and may not return.'

Susan unlinks her fingers and lays her hands flat down on the desk. Her features haven't shifted one bit. She's still flying the flag of neutrality. 'What three words would your friends and family use to describe you?'

Dread swirls in my stomach. I have not prepared for this question and I can't tell her the truth: juvenile, unsophisticated, addicted to coffee (especially coffee that doesn't belong to me). I need to lie through my teeth, and fast, because Susan's eyebrows are starting to inch up her forehead, the mask of impartiality slipping.

'I think my friends and family would describe me as loyal, trustworthy and excellent with numbers.'

I nod, satisfied with my answers, and it isn't totally untruthful. I am loyal and trustworthy and my maths has never come into question while handling money at the chippy or helping out with the admin.

'Loyal, trustworthy and good with numbers?' Susan's lips lift, but it isn't exactly in a smiling motion. It's more of a smirk. 'Not quite *three words*, but let's move on, shall we?'

–

I manage to get back to the chippy before Claire finishes her shift and has to dash off to pick Arlo up from school. I fill her in on the interview, which went as well as could be expected when I don't have any experience of working in an office environment and I'd already decided I'd rather tap-dance barefoot over a floor of upturned drawing pins than work in that bleak building – and that was before Susan had collected me from reception for the actual interview. Mum texted me when I was on the train back and I told her similar, though I left out the tap-dancing bit.

'So your fingers aren't crossed that you'll get the job then?'

'Not very tightly.' I shrug the pointy-shouldered blazer off and drape it over the back of a chair. 'I don't think I'm destined to have a job I love.' I flop onto the chair, resting my elbow on the table so I can drop my head onto my hand for support. I've been for one measly interview that lasted no more than fifteen minutes, and yet I'm exhausted.

'Unless you stay here.' Claire joins me at the table, her fingers rummaging for the grips keeping her hat in place. 'You like it here. You *love* it here.' She drops the grips onto the table, followed by her hat and hairnet.

'But it isn't a career choice, is it? You'll be gone as soon as you've got your qualification, Elliot will be leaving for uni in a few months, and Bridget's only here because she was bored of retirement.'

'It's true.' Bridget's wiping down the counter, even though Claire has already done it. 'Plus, I'd quite like a conservatory and I'd be long dead before I could save enough on my pension.'

'Nobody stays here forever. Ross and Maryam will move on to other jobs and the only ones still here will be me, Russell and Jed.'

'I still don't see why that's a problem.' Claire unfastens her tabard and pulls it over her head. 'You love it here, so why leave? Do you actually *want* to leave, or is it just because you told a little white lie to Paul? Because you've hardly thrown yourself into job searching. There's less than two months to go before Paul comes back and you've been on *one* interview.'

'I've applied for loads of jobs.' I fold my arms across my chest and frown down at the table. Is it my fault that people aren't willing to even interview me based on my crappy CV? 'And yes, I do love it here, and yes, my main motivation to move on is Paul, but so what?'

'If he's as great as you say he is, and he likes you as much as you like him, he won't care what job you do. And if he does, then he's a knobhead who doesn't deserve you. If you enjoy your job, isn't that the most important thing?'

'You sound like my gran.'

241

'Your gran is very wise.' Claire gathers up her things and shoves them into a tote bag, which she hooks onto her shoulder. 'I can't hang around – I got chatting to one of the dads in the school playground this morning and I'm hoping to accidentally bump into him again. He is *mega gorge*. Wish me luck!' She crosses her fingers and raises them in the air as she dashes across the shop and flings herself out of the door. She blows me a kiss through the window and then she's gone. I can't imagine Susan Chambers blowing me a kiss – she barely cracked a smile during my interview – but I'm sure I'll find colleagues just as warm and friendly elsewhere.

I head up to the flat to change into something more comfortable, something that I won't mind so much if it gets splashed with batter or oil. I quite liked how sophisticated the pointy-shouldered blazer made me feel, but I sigh with contentment as I push my feet into my glittery Converse. This is more like it. This is more *me*.

Bridget's still cleaning when I go back down to the shop, going at the floor with the mop as though she's trying to wear the tiles clean away. I have to wrestle the mop from her hands and send her home while we still have a floor to stand on. Maryam's arrived for her shift but pre-teatime is always quiet. We have a handful of schoolkids popping in on their way home from school, with a chip-fight breaking out between two of the more boisterous lads (I kick them out while Maryam sweeps up the potato missiles) but then it's completely dead. The shop's still deserted by the time I've prepped the fish for the teatime rush, so I make myself a coffee and sit by the window with a magazine one of the teen girls left behind. It's one of the really trashy celebrity mags, where they praise an actress in one issue and tear her apart in the next. The kind of magazine I adore, especially when it comes with a special pull-out feature for *Waiting on You*. I'm poring over the biography of Joanna (which consists mainly of affairs) when it occurs to me that I should replace my reading matter of choice with something a bit more mature. Something less superficial, where famous women minding their own business on a beach aren't snapped in their bikinis just in case there's the tiniest patch of cellulite that can be blown up and highlighted for the joy of its readership. Something my mum would read, with features on boosting women instead of bringing them down, and tips on creating the perfect home. The latter would come in handy when I finally get my own place. Accommodation in or around Clifton-on-Sea is proving to be problematic – I have an alert set up on the property app on my phone, and so far I've only been notified of a three-bedroom cottage becoming available over by the harbour, which looked lovely and cosy but way too big for a single occupant and eye-wateringly expensive – but I'm still hopeful I'll find something, even if I have to widen the perimeters of my search.

Even as I'm contemplating upgrading my reading material, I'm still gobbling up the sordid details of *Waiting on You*'s latest love spaghetti scandal, and it's only the arrival of a customer that forces me to close the magazine.

'We don't usually see you on a Wednesday, Mrs Horn-church.' I head behind the counter, pushing a loose grip back into my hair to keep my hat secure.

'I'm not usually stuck in the council offices all day.' Mrs Hornchurch presses a hand to her stomach and grimaces. 'I missed lunch and I'm hungry enough to feast on a rabid dog carcass.'

'I'm afraid we're all out of rabid dogs today. Will fish and chips do instead?'

'Lovely. Two portions, please. It'll be a nice surprise for Tom.' Mrs Hornchurch's face lights up as she mentions her partner, and I hope I'll be that in love one day, where a mere name causes my lips to pull up into an involuntary smile and my cheeks to pinken.

'What were you doing at the council offices?' I've prepared Mrs Hornchurch's portions of fish just as she likes them and lowered them into the fryer. They'll take a few minutes and there aren't any more customers, so we have time for a little chat.

'I had an appointment with Gordon Meadows.' Mrs Hornchurch says the name as though I'll know who he is, but unless he's rumoured to star in the new Marvel film or is a contestant on a reality TV show, I won't have a clue. 'The councillor? Supposedly responsible for this ward?' I shake my head. I wouldn't know the dude if he walked through the door right now. 'Anyway, I've been emailing him for months about trying to clean up the town, the seafront in particular. It's a right mess, and it's only going to get worse once Easter's here. Gordon Meadows *says* he understands and cares deeply about the town, but where's the action? I finally got an appointment and he kept me waiting for *hours*. Urgent meetings, apparently, but what's more urgent than a filthy, litter-filled seafront? Because people won't want to come here for their day trips and their holidays if it continues, and it'll be the local economy that suffers.' Mrs Hornchurch slaps a hand on the counter. 'I think Mr Meadows thought I'd get bored and go home if he left me waiting long enough, but he's about to learn a very valuable lesson about this old bird. I'm like a dog with a bone when I get a bee in my bonnet. I won't give up until he follows through on the promises he made that got him elected in the first place. I went to Greenham Common, you know, so I'm well versed in patience and perseverance. I won't be fobbed off or left to fester on uncomfortable plastic chairs all day long. I'll fight this, and do you know what?' Mrs Hornchurch leans towards me across the counter, her eyes narrowing and her jaw setting. 'I'll win.'

I believe her. Her eyes may be mostly obscured by crinkly, fleshy bits of skin but the fire in them is shining through. I've never had any interest in politics – local or otherwise – and so I have no idea who this Gordon Meadows bloke is, but maybe I should find out if he's so important to the running of this town. I *should* be politically knowledgeable. I *should* know who's responsible for the town. For the *country* (I obviously know who the prime minister is, but I haven't the foggiest who the others are when they pop up on the news, never mind what they stand for). I'll look them up, and when politicians are on the telly, I'll actually pay attention to what they're saying. In fact, I'll seek them out and tune into those Sunday morning politics programmes instead of catching up on *Hollyoaks*. I'll add 'become politically motivated' to my grown-up to-do list and impress other people with my knowledge and new-found passion. I'll even find out where Greenham Common is and its significance to Mrs Hornchurch and her fortitude. I can feel myself growing as a person already.

I'm fired up by the idea of being one of those proper grown-up people who uses words like 'shadow home secretary' (and knows what one is) or one of those proper grown-up people who can stride into a polling station and put their cross in the box with confidence, because they know who they're voting for and why. I'll actually rock up to the polling station and vote, because I haven't bothered so far. I'll be one of those proper grown-up people like Mrs Hornchurch and my dad. I'm so fired up, I don't drag myself straight into bed when I lock up the shop like I usually would. I don't even message Paul, because I have important knowledge to absorb. Instead, I google local politics (best to start small and build up my understanding at a reasonable pace) and discover who my MP is. There's a wealth of information online, and I'm cross-eyed by the time I place my phone on the bedside table and crawl into bed.

I won't be adding 'become politically motivated' to my grown-up to-do list after all, because it turns out politics is really, really boring.

What Not To Do During An Interview:

- *Turn up late*

- *Dress inappropriately*

- *Forget to turn your phone off*

- *Get the name of the interviewer wrong*

- *Get so flustered, you pretty much forget your <u>own</u> name*

Chapter Twenty-Nine

My next interview is much closer than T C Fire Protection and I can catch a bus that'll drop me off practically on its doorstep. I'm wearing my new shoes and the pointy-shouldered blazer again, but this time I've chosen a pencil skirt, a silky cream blouse and black tights. I look like my old maths teacher, but I'm sure this is a Good Thing because I've applied for the role of credit controller, which is number-orientated, right?

The bus was due six minutes ago, but it's okay because my interview isn't for another half an hour and the journey is fifteen minutes, max. As long as the bus arrives in the next five minutes – ten, even – everything will be fine.

Seven and a half minutes later, I'm still waiting at the bus stop. But it's okay, because I still have a couple of 'buffer' minutes, and I'm sure the bus is going to appear around the bend any second now... Any second... I'm sure of it... See? There it is! No, wait, that's a coach. Where is the bloody bus?

My stomach feels leaden, and my armpits are prickling as I stare ahead, willing the bus to appear at the top of the road. The number one rule of attending interviews is DO NOT BE LATE, but I'm in real danger of shattering that rule – and it isn't even my fault. I was at the bus stop in plenty of time – I made sure of it – but the bus actually turning up is out of my control. As, it seems, is my breathing, which is coming in rapid, panicked little puffs as I check the time again.

The bus eventually trundles into view, making its way to the stop at a painstaking crawl. I have the money for the fare ready in my clammy hand, but I'm in such a flustered state I almost forget to take the ticket that's spewed from the machine. The bus is rammed, with every seat taken apart from half an aisle seat towards the back. The woman sitting in the window seat has a gazillion shopping bags spilling into the neighbouring seat and although she attempts to shift them over, I'm still only left with a few inches to park myself onto, with my legs swinging out into the aisle. Still, I sink down, grateful to take the weight off my feet in my new shoes after standing at the bus stop for so long.

The bus stops to cram more people on at *every single stop*, eating into my precious time and causing a hot, claustrophobic atmosphere as people squeeze into every millimetre of floor space, jostling past my legs and tutting when I can't move them out of the way. I'm a frazzled mess by the time we approach my stop, three minutes late for my interview. I need to pass my driving test – and fast – so I don't have to put myself through this on a daily basis.

Pressing the bell, I lever myself out of my seat but there's an odd pulling sensation on the back of my tights. When I look down, I see a string of chewing gum trailing from my tights to the blob stuck to the side of the seat. My stop is quickly approaching (the bus has been crawling for the entire journey, but *now* the driver decides to channel Lewis Hamilton) but I'm tethered to the seat by the gross, chewed-by-someone-else gum. I have no choice but to touch it, my face scrunched up with disgust as my finger and thumb clamp on to the sticky thread. I pull, but it simply stretches. I pull again, and again, but the gum seems to have magical, ever-increasing properties.

'Wait!' The bus has reached my stop, but the doors are now swishing shut again. 'I need this stop!' Grabbing a clump of my tights with one hand, I yank at the gum with the other, finally managing to dislodge the yucky mass. Unfortunately, the force on my delicate tights is too much and I'm left with a small hole at the top of my calf.

Still, I don't have time to worry about that right now as the bus has started to pull away.

'Hey! Wait!' Shaking the string of gum from my fingers, I edge my way through the tightly packed throng of standing passengers and make my way towards the front of the bus. I'm panting by the time I reach the driver. 'That was my stop. I need to get off.'

'Sorry, love.' The driver shrugs. 'I can't stop again until I get to the next stop. Health and safety.'

'But you drove off from the stop before I could get off.' We've just passed the building I needed to be in three minutes ago and I can't see another bus stop ahead.

'There was nobody at the doors. I can't hang around all day, love. People have places they need to be.'

People like me. 'I rang the bell. I was trying to get to the front but I had chewing gum stuck to my leg and there are too many people to get through. *Please* can you let me get off? I've got an interview and I'm already late.'

We've stopped at a set of traffic lights. There still isn't a bus stop in sight, even though we stopped at one approximately every twenty seconds until now. The driver sighs as he looks me up and down through the clear plastic barrier.

'I'll do it just this once.' The doors hiss open and I make a bid for freedom. The doors close again and the bus sets off as I start to scurry my way back along the pavement as fast as I can while my movement is restricted by my pencil skirt and new shoes. I'm clammy and out of breath by the time I make it to the office block, and I'm sure my make-up has melted and pooled on my chin but I don't have time to nip into the loos to check. I'm already several minutes late and I'm ushered straight into a small, windowless room next to the reception area.

'Cleo Parker.' The receptionist announces my arrival to the man sitting behind a small desk, and when I turn to smile my thanks, I find she's giving me an odd look, focused on the lower half of my body. I follow her gaze and find the source of her scrutiny. The small hole I created when I yanked at the chewing gum has grown into a larger hole, with a huge ladder snaking down my calf and bleeding over my ankle before it disappears into my shoe.

'Good... morning?' The man behind the desk lifts his wrist, angling his arm so he can check the time on his watch. 'Yes, it is still morning. Just about.' The corners of his lips flick upwards but the rest of his face remains stony as he indicates the chair opposite his desk.

'Sorry about being late.' I fling myself into the chair, hoping he hasn't clocked the state of my tights. I don't want to add a sloppy appearance as well as arriving late to my charge sheet. 'The bus didn't turn up for ages.'

'Hmm.' He isn't really paying attention to my excuse as he's too busy running his eyes over the copy of my CV on the desk in front of him. 'Tell me about yourself, Cleo.'

God, I hate this question. I mean, it's such a vague request, isn't it? Can't he be more specific? What *exactly* does he want to know about me? I'm pretty sure he doesn't want to know about my unhealthy love of coffee, or how obsessed I am with daytime soaps. His interests surely lie in my employment history, which is noted right in front of him (and it won't take him long to read through it, seeing as I've only ever worked at The Fish & Chip Shop Around The Corner).

Fortunately – or unfortunately, actually, given the circumstances – I'm prevented from answering the question by a loud and obnoxious ringtone. Which is coming from my handbag. In all the drama of getting to the interview, I've forgotten to switch my phone off.

This interview has plummeted from bad to worse. Really, is there any point continuing the misery?

–

The phone call, it turns out, was from Claire. I phone her back when I'm on the bus home (which turned up right on time, naturally). She's in such a buoyant mood after securing a date with the school-gate dad for tomorrow night that I don't tell her about the interview she inadvertently interrupted. She sounds so joyful and carefree (the exact opposite of how I'm feeling) and I don't want to bring her down.

'He's taking me out for dinner tomorrow night. And not somewhere local. He says he wants to take me somewhere more upmarket.' Claire sighs, long and softly, and I can picture her twirling a strand of hair around her finger as she daydreams about the date to come. 'Nobody has ever taken me anywhere upmarket. I don't think I'm that kind of girl. Oh, God.' The buoyancy has dropped from her voice. 'What am I going to wear?'

I chat through Claire's wardrobe choices until my stop approaches (I don't want to miss another) but instead of going straight back to the flat I make a detour to one of the coffee shops on the seafront. I deserve a calorific caffeine hit after the morning I've had, and a mug of instant isn't going to cut it.

'Hey, you.' James is on his way out of the shop as I push the door open, a takeaway cup and a paper bag in hand. 'You're looking smart.' His eyes drop to my decimated tights. 'Ish.'

I twist to the side, to try to shield the tatty-looking tights. 'I had a fight with a blob of chewing gum and lost.'

'Ah.' James shoots me a look of sympathy. 'Grim.'

'It hasn't been the best day, to be honest.' I move out of the way of the door to let someone else in behind me. 'Which is why I'm here. I need cheering up. I'm thinking a caramel cortado might be up for the job.'

'What's happened?'

I cringe. I'm not sure I want to relive the horror of the interview from hell quite so soon. Because it only got worse after the phone-ringing incident when I accidentally called the interviewer Richard (his name was Nigel, so not even close) and got myself into such a tizzy, I couldn't even remember what year I left school or the name of the company I was interviewing for – or what they did. I don't think I'll be on the receiving end of a job offer for this one.

'Bad interview.'

'Bad' doesn't even come close to describing the car-crash interview, but I can't bear to acknowledge the details out loud.

'Oh.' James' shoulders drop, but then he brightens, his arms spreading wide. 'But hey, you can learn from this, right? Take it as a positive.'

'Believe me, there's nothing positive to be taken from this interview.'

'I bet there's something.'

I shake my head. Today's interview was completely void of positivity, unless you count the fact that it's over and I'll never have to come face to face with Nigel what-shisface ever again.

'To be honest, I just want to forget it ever happened.'

'Then I'll shut up about it.' James mimes zipping up his lips, the paper bag in his hand crinkling. My stomach rumbles as I imagine what's in there. Perhaps I'll need more than a coffee to cheer me up. 'Anyway, I'd better get back to work. I've got a ton of emails to reply to and I can't put them off any longer.' James' shoulders have slumped so much, they're practically down to his knees, and I think it'll take more than the coffee and whatever's in the bag to wipe the glum look off his face.

I feel a little bit sad for James as he leaves the shop, but also for myself. Because what if that's me in a few weeks, sloping off to do a job I dislike while being begrudgingly grateful it's paying the bills? I've been fortunate to do a job I love over the past eight years, but from the interviews I've attended so far, I think my luck's about to run out.

'Oh. Cleo.' James has stopped a few paces away, and he turns to face me again. 'I'll see you this evening?'

He will?

James must clock my bemused face. 'Dog-walking the fearsome foursome?'

Oh, God. The dog-walking wasn't a one-off. Gran has somehow manipulated us into making it a regular thing, *every other day*, at least until her wrist has healed. My luck has definitely run out.

Thought of the Day:

Whoever said a dog is man's best friend is either a humongous liar or completely off their rocker

Chapter Thirty

It turns out that Gran isn't the only one who can manipulate people, and I'm seriously considering adding the skill to my CV when Claire actually turns up to help us with our dog-walking duties. Her phone call interrupting my interview came back to bite her on the arse because she couldn't say no when I dropped that little fact into our conversation, could she? And when I pointed out we could discuss her upcoming date with the school-gate dad, the deal was sealed. Obviously, I didn't prewarn Claire about stink-bomb Fizz (otherwise there's no way she'd have agreed to join us, even with the disruptive phone call) so she gets a nice surprise as we turn out of the shelter's ground and on to the pavement and she's assaulted by the rancid smell.

We head down to the beach this time, because it's a nice day and I have zero desire to return to the mudbath park. James takes charge of Sabre (because I absolutely refuse to engage with the 'spirited' little shit) while Claire takes on Baby and I'm stuck with the farting fluff ball and Star (who's no trouble at all, despite not being able to see where she's going). Arlo is skipping along beside us, in his element that he gets to walk *four dogs*, and I wish I could share his enthusiasm. The beach is pretty much deserted despite the pleasant weather but we still keep the dogs on their leads as per the instructions from

Carole. We wander along the sand, James chatting to Arlo about school and cartoons while Claire and I have the very important discussion about what she should wear for her date. It lessens the guilt over emotionally blackmailing her into joining us when we settle on the perfect outfit.

'Old man's pub?'

We've dropped the dogs off at the shelter, promising to return soon, when James makes the suggestion. I'm not covered in mud this time, but the idea of a beer is extremely appealing right now.

'I can't.' Claire nods down at Arlo. 'Bath and bedtime for this one. But you guys have fun.' She pulls me into a hug. 'Thank you for your advice. And sorry again for the phone thing.' She releases me and takes a step back. 'This was fun. Let me know when you're going out with the dogs again.'

'You want to do this?' I thrust a thumb at the animal shelter we're leaving behind. 'Again?'

Claire shrugs. 'I'm a single mum. I don't have much of a social life apart from going on terrible dates with terrible men. It makes a change to do something that doesn't end with me feeling like C.R.A.P.' She spells the word for Arlo's benefit. 'So, yeah, I'd love to do this again.' She lifts a hand in farewell and I'm left wondering about her choice of words. Social life? Is that what this is? A social event? I suppose we do chat while we walk, and then there's the pub afterwards. Perhaps I can tick an item off my list, which makes breathing in Fizz's foul smells almost worth it.

–

True to her word, Claire joins us for our next dog-walking stint. And she isn't the only one who wants to volunteer.

After hearing about our walks and seeing the photos of the dogs on Claire's phone, Maryam asked if she could tag along to the next one. And when Ross found out we were going on a team-building exercise, he insisted on joining in too (nobody sold it to him as team building, or anything to do with the chippy, but I suspect he has a little crush on Maryam and saw an opportunity to spend an hour with her away from the grease and hairnets).

Claire is working during our fourth walk, but with Maryam and Ross on board, we have a dog each, which feels much more manageable. James sticks with Baby, Maryam falls head over heels for Star and, with a choice of stink-bomb Fizz and 'spirited' Sabre, I opt for the super-smelly one as I haven't forgotten about the mudbath I was treated to in the park. I warn Ross about Sabre's sudden pursuit of anything that moves but the mischievous mutt trots along by Ross' side perfectly, which I take as a personal insult.

Walking as a foursome feels like much more of a social event, as does the drink in the pub afterwards. Maryam and Ross insist on going to the Red Lion (Maryam because her grandad drinks in the Fisherman and Ross because he'd walk off the cliffs into the sea if Maryam said it was a good idea) and when James joins in the coaxing, I feel outnumbered. So, for the first time since my break-up with Dane, I step into my old local, and do you know what? It's fine. Nobody points at me or even looks at me, knowing I'm the girl whose boyfriend was stolen by the barmaid. I can't see Dane or any of my old mates and after a few minutes I forget to look as I'm having such a good time with my new friends. After a few drinks, we head home via the chippy, where Bridget scowls as she serves us our chips.

'Nobody told me there were team-building exercises going on.'

'Would you have come if we had?' I take the bag of chips, unfolding the paper even though I'd intended to eat them up in the flat. I'm starving after all that exercise and fresh air.

'Walking dogs? Not a chance. Can't stand the flea-bitten things.' She pulls a face before turning to scoop more chips into paper. 'But it would have been polite to ask.'

'Bridget.' I pluck a chip from my bag and blow on it. 'Would you like to come dog-walking with us next time?'

Bridget starts to aggressively wrap up the next portion of chips. 'And who would run this place?'

I roll my eyes and shove the chip in my mouth, catching Claire's eye behind the counter, who shakes her head in despair at our colleague.

'You guys are all up for it though?' I look at James, Claire, Maryam and Ross in turn and I'm strangely pleased when they all say yes. Maybe this dog-walking thing isn't so bad after all, and my social life has definitely been kick-started. That bad boy is getting ticked off my list.

My Top 3 Dates:

- *The opening night of a new club in Preston. It was supposed to be filled with celebs, but we only saw a former Big Brother contestant (which I was giddy about but my then-boyfriend, Bradley, was extremely disappointed)*

- *A picnic on the beach for my second date with Mo. It was super-romantic, even if I did end up eating literal SANDwiches*

- *My first date with Dane. I'd just been ghosted by Mo and thought I was too hideous to date, so being asked out by someone as gorgeous as Dane was a real ego boost*

Chapter Thirty-One

My third interview didn't go nearly as badly as the one before it (I don't think that's even possible, unless I accidentally burned the building to the ground and performed the Macarena on the ashes) and it seemed like a more enjoyable place to work than the beige box I'd found myself in last week. The role was for a receptionist at a car dealership just outside Clifton-on-Sea, where the staff all seemed friendly and happy in their jobs. The sales manager who interviewed me was welcoming and approachable (it helped that I arrived on time, without a hint of chewing gum stuck upon my person) and I headed home feeling much more optimistic. So it's pretty galling to find the rejection email sitting in my inbox just two days later as I'm waiting for Connie to arrive for my driving lesson. It throws me off so much, I stall the car three times during the lesson and mount the pavement while attempting to parallel park. And I can't even creep away to the flat to lick my wounds as my shift is about to start. Still, at least I'll be working with Claire today, which is always a laugh.

Or almost always.

'Hey, what's up?'

Claire's slumped against the counter, her head resting sideways on her arms as she stares out of the window, and she sighs before she stands up straight. Mud's 'Tiger Feet' is playing on the radio (we still haven't got out of the habit of listening to Seventies music even though Russell's been away for over a month) but while Claire would normally be jiggling away to the irresistible beat, she can't seem to muster even a foot tap.

'My love life is a disaster.' Claire sighs again, which turns into a low growl. 'Why are men such utter bastards?'

'Not *all* men, surely?' I think about James, who's been nothing but lovely to my gran, and who has a weirdly pleasant relationship with his ex-wife. And Paul, obviously, who's so gorgeous it hurts.

'Every. Last. One. Of. Them.' The shop is empty, so Claire follows me into the little room at the back, where I dump my bag and throw on my tabard. 'They're bastards. The lot of them. I've had it with them and their selfish, unfaithful ways.'

'Lewis has cheated on you already?' Blimey, that's a record, even for Claire. She only got chatting to him in the school playground last week, and they've only been on one date. A date Claire hasn't stopped gushing about since the weekend.

'He hasn't cheated *on* me.' Claire pauses. For dramatic effect, I suspect. 'He's cheated *with* me. *On his wife.*'

I'm about to plonk my hairnet on my head, but I freeze, the hairnet suspended in the air by my fingertips. 'His what?'

Claire nods as she slowly folds her arms across her chest. 'His wife. No wonder he didn't want to take me somewhere local – he had to keep me away so he didn't get caught out. And there I was, bragging about how *sophisticated* and *quaint* that little restaurant was when really it was just out of the way so I could be his grubby little secret. I may not have high standards when it comes to men, but I draw the line at being the other woman.'

'How did you find out?' I stretch the hairnet over my head and make sure there are no loose strands sticking out.

'I saw them together, at the school, picking up their little boy. Lewis tried ducking behind a tree, but I saw him. I assumed the woman was the boy's mum, which isn't damning in itself – they could have been separated or whatever – but the trying to hide thing was a major red flag. So I texted Lewis and he spilled it all. They're married, happily as far as the wife is concerned, with no plans to split up.' Claire drags out a chair and slumps onto it, swearing under her breath when it wobbles. 'And now I feel really guilty. Because what if she finds out? I'd be devastated if I was in her shoes, and the thought that *I'd* caused all that pain makes me feel sick.' Claire places a hand over her stomach and grimaces. For a moment, I'm worried she really is going to throw up, but nothing presents itself all over the table.

'None of this is your fault.' I plonk my hat over the hairnet and secure it with a couple of grips. 'You didn't know he was married. *He's* the only one in the wrong here, and if his wife does find out, it'll be *him* that's caused the pain, not you.'

'But I'm part of it.'

'Accidentally.' I check my hat is sitting right in the mirror above the filing cabinet. 'And now you know, you're going to steer clear of him, right?'

Claire's jaw drops. 'Obviously. I don't date married men. Knowingly, anyway.'

'At least you didn't sleep with him.'

Claire brightens at this, and there's a hint of a smile on her face as she scrapes back her chair and stands up. 'You're right. Thank God for periods, eh? Sorry, Ross. That was probably too much info.'

I hadn't noticed Ross' arrival for his shift, but he's standing in the doorway, trying his best to mask the stricken look on his face. 'Sorry. Didn't mean to interrupt.' He holds his hands up as he starts to back away. 'I'm just going to, um, go away now.' He dashes away before Claire can divulge any more bodily functions, and I find him in the kitchen, busily prepping the potatoes for the teatime trade. Embarrassment, it seems, is a great motivator when it comes to chipping spuds.

The teens arrive for their late-afternoon snacks but the real work starts in the evening, when the queue starts to snake out of the shop and on to the street. The orders are generally larger during the teatime rush as there are more families in need of feeding rather than individual orders. Ross remains in the kitchen to keep us stocked up on chips while Claire and I serve as fast as we can to a medley of Seventies hits. I'm feeling pretty frazzled by the time the queue starts to dwindle, but the sight of Riley hanging back to make sure it's Claire who serves him invigorates me.

'I don't see why you won't give Riley a chance.' I lean in close to Claire and lower my voice as we both fill up trays with chips, our backs to the customers.

Claire glances behind us. She hadn't even spotted him. 'He's cute and everything, but he's too sweet. You know me, I like bad boys. Librarians just don't do it for me.'

I scoop a few more chips into my tray. 'He isn't a librarian. He works in a bookshop.'

Claire shrugs and heads back to the counter. 'Same thing. Salt and vinegar, Gwen?'

I watch Riley out of the corner of my eye as I serve the next customer. He's calculating the right moment to join the queue as he gazes up at the menu, and he times it to perfection so that it's Claire who serves him. If that isn't a skill to be admired, I don't know what is.

'Where has dating bad boys got you so far?' I hiss the question as we fill up at the chip station together again. Riley's at the counter, gazing lovingly at Claire as she fulfils the order he agonised over for so long (and yet is the same thing he orders every time). 'Why don't you give Riley a chance? He'll treat you better than Lewis and Danny and all the other idiots you've wasted your time on lately. He adores you. Don't you want to be adored for a change?'

'I guess it'd be quite nice, but...'

'But what? But he's too *nice*? Do you realise how ridiculous that sounds? After the way men have treated you?'

Claire sighs and rolls her eyes. 'Fine. I'll go out with him. But just for a drink, and I'm not having sex with him.'

'That is absolutely your choice. I'm not your pimp.' I am, however, a modern-day Cupid, and I will gloat for eternity if this works out.

–

I'm thinking about having a name badge made up, that I will wear for all occasions: *Cleo Parker, Cupid Extraordinaire*. Because Claire's date with Riley was 'all right, actually. Surprisingly fun', which is extremely high praise when you consider how many times Claire attempted to wriggle out of it. We had everything, from a 'doublebooking' (though Claire couldn't elaborate on what her other commitment was), 'working late' (even though I'm responsible for the shift timetable, and Claire wasn't working at all that night) and a simple 'I don't want to go'. But luckily I managed to talk her into it a second time, and she met up with Riley in the Red Lion and had an amazing time.

Okay, 'amazing' may be over-egging it, but Claire said she'd had fun and that Riley wasn't boring or book-obsessed (he mentioned Harry Potter once, but only because there was a bloke who looked exactly like Dumbledore propping up the bar, and it made Claire laugh so it was fine). Claire was true to her word and didn't sleep with him, but she did agree to a second date which, in my opinion, is even better. I'm thinking long-term here. Soulmates. The One. All that gubbins that ends with marriage and babies and living happily ever after. Naturally, as the *Cupid Extraordinaire* who brought the pair together, I will be Claire's maid of honour and godmother to their offspring.

'There's just one problem. Well, two actually.' It's Saturday morning and Claire and I are in Russell and Jed's little kitchen, leaning against the worktop with the coffees and pastries she brought with her for the date dissection while Arlo watches cartoons approximately three inches away from the TV in the living room. 'He wants to take me to some Victorian exhibition.' She scrunches up her nose. 'Which is probably going to be incredibly boring.'

'Or it could be really interesting.' I bite into my almond croissant, closing my eyes to savour the deliciousness. I would have channelled my inner Cupid ages ago if I'd known this was the reward.

'Maybe.' Claire shrugs. 'I'm willing to give it a go anyway.' I raise my hand for a high five because my mouth is too full of buttery pastry to speak, and Claire responds accordingly. 'But the thing is, Arlo was supposed to be with his dad this weekend but he's bailed – again. He says he's got the flu, but he's hung-over more likely. Anyway, I'd ask my mum to babysit, but she's on her way down to Brighton to see my sister. Plus, this is all your doing, so I was wondering…'

'Of course I'll babysit.'

'Really?'

I take a sip of my coffee. It's a caramel macchiato. Beautiful. 'Really. We had fun last time.' I've still got the ice cream painting stuck to the fridge behind me, and if I get Arlo to eat something healthy again, I can have a second badge made up: *Cleo Parker, Babysitter Extraordinaire*.

'Thank you.' Claire gives me a squeeze. 'You're the best.'

'I am that.' I raise my takeaway coffee cup and Claire taps her own against it. 'When do you need me?'

Claire flashes me a sheepish grin. 'Now? I said I'd meet Riley at eleven.'

'You'd better get going then.'

'Are you sure?' Claire's tone is hesitant, but she's already backing up towards the door. 'It's really short notice. I can cancel. It's no problem at all.'

'Go.' I point a finger towards the door. 'Have fun.'

Claire snorts. 'At an exhibition?' But she heads into the living room so she can say goodbye to her son before she leaves with a definite skip to her step. I have a Very Good Feeling about this date. A Very Good Feeling indeed. I wonder if they'll name one of their kids after me?

- *Weeks until Paul is back: 6*

- *How prepared I feel on a scale of 1-10: -67*

Chapter Thirty-Two

I finish off my coffee and croissant before bundling Arlo into his raincoat and heading out to Gran's. I may be Babysitter Extraordinaire but I'm not totally confident in my ability to take solo charge of a child, so I'll need Gran on hand as a backup in case it all goes horribly wrong. We stop off at the newsagents on the way so Arlo can choose a magazine (which is a massive ploy to keep him occupied, to be honest) and I browse the shelves while he decides between the magazine with the plastic mobile phone stuck to the front and the magazine with the plastic stethoscope. Instead of checking out the gossipy mags, I redirect myself to the more 'grown-up' publications, selecting a magazine which pledges help with updating my summer wardrobe as well as giving me pointers on saving cash (not buying a shedload of new seasonal clothes should be point number one, surely) and providing me with recipes for '5 Fat-Free Treats!' (which is an oxymoron, but whatever).

Arlo thrusts his magazine of choice at me (the stethoscope is triumphant) and we pay at the counter before heading back out into the rain. I wonder if that summer wardrobe includes wellington boots…

Gran's thrilled to see us and insists on putting the kettle on as soon as we step inside. I try to do it myself, but Gran's adamant, and short of wrestling the kettle from her hand, I have little choice but to let her get on with it.

'Honestly, you're as bad as James. He thinks I'm an invalid too. It was sweet at first but he's turning into a bit of a fusspot.'

'He cares about you.'

Gran smiles. 'I know he does, bless him, but I'm more than capable of making a cup of tea. Look!' She points at the table with her good hand, where there's a plate of home-made chocolate chip cookies. 'I've even managed a bit of baking.'

'Where is James?' I grab a cookie and hand it to Arlo before taking one for myself. It's cookie perfection; crunchy around the edge but gooey in the middle.

'He's gone to pick the kids up.' Gran stoops, resting her hands on her thighs so she's at Arlo-level. 'Edith will be here soon, so you'll have someone to play with.'

Ah, so that's why Gran's been baking cookies, which happen to be Edith's favourite. Why doesn't she ever bake my favourite treats? My inner monologue sounds extremely petulant, so I give myself a talking-to. Edith is a child and I'm trying to be grown-up. Besides, Gran's chocolate chip cookies *are* amazing.

'We can play with my stevvascope.' Arlo holds up his magazine, which is a bit damp but still readable.

'Lovely. I'm sure Edith would like that very much. Now, young man, would you like a hot chocolate to warm you up after all that rain?' I try – again – to offer my drink-making services, but Gran's having none of it. 'This machine does most of the work anyway.' She pops a hot chocolate pod into the coffee machine and pushes the button to set it going. 'I might have to buy one of these contraptions when James moves out. Did you know it can make Horlicks?'

The front door opens and Edith comes thundering into the kitchen, her cheeks rosy and her blonde curls matted down from the downpour. Her face lights up when she spots Arlo and she drags him – and the magazine – into the living room.

'It's nasty out there.' James wriggles out of his coat and drapes it over the back of one of the chairs. 'I only went from the car to the house and I'm soaked.'

'I'll make you a coffee to warm you up.' Gran opens the cupboard and reaches for the David Bowie mug. When James offers to make it himself, I tell him not to bother arguing.

'The battleaxe is determined to do it all herself. Look, she even baked cookies.' I offer the plate to James and then Seth, who's hovering by the door, his soggy coat still on while his face is fixed on the screen of his phone. Somehow, he clocks the plate of biscuits and takes one without his gaze ever shifting. He does, however, mumble his thanks as the biscuit reaches his mouth.

'Less of the battleaxe.' Gran shoots me a reproachful look, but I can see the sparkle in her eye. 'And less of the thinking I'm made of glass. I'm not going to shatter, you know. If a nosedive down the stairs didn't finish me off, making a cup of tea certainly isn't going to do the job. I'm a tough old bird.'

'I think you mispronounced *stubborn* old bird.' I arch an eyebrow at Gran, but I take her point and I'll try to ease up on the worry, especially if it means she'll make more of these chocolate chip cookies because they really are *amazing*. As soon as I'm back at the flat, I'm going to whip my bullet journal out and add 'learn to bake' to my grown-up to-do list, because nothing will make Paul fall madly in love with me more than something that tastes this good. He'd be on one knee and asking me to spend the rest of my life with him after one bite.

–

The kids are bored of the 'stevvascope' and the magazine and even the TV, so James and I decide to take them out for a bit to give Gran a rest. Edith wants to go to the park to sword fight with twigs again, but it's still pretty miserable out there and we've only just dried off, while Arlo requests a visit to Alessandra's for ice cream and pinball.

'I think you've had enough sugar for one day.' The only thing Arlo and Edith haven't grown bored of are Gran's cookies, which they would have polished off if it had been up to them. I want Arlo to enjoy his day with me, but I don't think Claire will be impressed if I return her child hyped up on sugar. 'How about the arcade instead? They have pinball machines there and loads of other fun stuff.' I look at James to gauge his reaction to the idea, and he gives a 'why not?' shrug.

Captain John's Treasure Chest, like most of Clifton-on-Sea, has been shut up for the past few months, but the arcade threw up its shutters a couple of weekends ago. Captain John, the life-size resin pirate, is sitting on his treasure chest by the entrance, the flashing LED-lit jewels spilling out of the chest and enticing people inside, where treasures of the tatty gift-shop variety lie. Edith and Arlo stand on either side of the pirate while James and I take their photos on our phones. I'll send it to Claire later – I don't want to disturb her date, on the off-chance she's having a good time at the exhibition.

The arcade somehow seems dark inside, despite the billions of flashing lights from the machines and pulsing disco lights above, but there's a happy atmosphere as families and groups of teenagers gather in clusters, pushing coins into the slots, the little ones whooping with joy as two-pence pieces clatter into the dishes below. Fistfuls of coins are collected and deposited into cardboard cups while strips of tokens snake from the machines, ready to be exchanged at the prize store later. Music is blaring out over the sound system, but you can barely hear it over the roar of collective voices, the clanging of coins spilling from machines and the clunk, clunk, clunk from the air hockey table.

'What would you like to do first?' I crouch down to Arlo and Edith's height and raise my voice to be heard over the happy din. Seth has already wandered over to the arcade games and is sitting in one of the high-backed chairs and clutching the steering wheel in front of him as he waits for the game to start. 'There's pinball. Or some little rides. Or you can play some games.'

The kids choose a racing game like Seth, but they're too short to reach the pedals so James and I have to help out. Arlo sits on my lap so I can control the pedals while he steers, with James doing the same for Edith.

'Ready?' James is grinning as his finger hovers over the start button, and I give a curt nod of my head, my gaze moving to fix on the screen in front of me. Arlo and I are going to win this, as long as there's no parallel parking involved.

On the screen, the red light changes to amber and then to green and we're off. I can see James' car ahead of us, moving straight into second place while Arlo and I lag behind in fifth. But not to worry. This is just the start, and who cares if Arlo has just steered us into the barrier and we're spinning out of control? We're in last place now, but there's plenty of time to catch up.

'Hey, that's cheating.' James' eyes are rapidly moving from his screen to my hands, which are gripping the steering wheel as I manoeuvre our vehicle around a tricky bend. Sixth place and nudging into fifth – yes!

'What?' I lift my hands off the steering wheel and shrug, my eyes wide as I attempt to feign innocence. If Arlo steers to the right, we could move into fourth…

'Hey!' James' mouth is a cavern of outrage as I flick the steering wheel to the right. I can see James' car again, just two places ahead of us. I steer to the left… now the right and quickly to the left again. Third place! James is just ahead. I'm gaining on him, and he's veering dangerously to the right. If I steer left, I can nip past him and into second place. Except…

My eyes flick to my side, and as I suspected, James is now taking full control of his machine and is steering to the left, blocking me from overtaking. I go right before swinging back to the left, hoping I'll be able to snatch the second-place position, but James manages to outfox me and sails ahead. I'm not giving up though. We have one more lap to go, which means I have one more lap to claim the victory.

'Hold on tight.' Arlo's ear is mere inches away, but I yell the instruction, both due to the noise of the arcade and the tension that has taken over me. Only the car on the screen is moving and we're stationary in our seat but Arlo follows my direction and clings on to my knees as I twist the steering wheel fully to the right as we zoom around the tricky bend. I ease up on the accelerator pedal until we make the bend and then I slam it back down again in a bid to catch up with James. He's just ahead, about to overtake for first position. He can't win. He simply can't.

Except he does, giving a victorious roar as he zips over the finish line. He's waving Edith's arms in the air and thumping his feet by the time Arlo and I limp over the line in third place.

'That was fun.' Arlo's grip has loosened on my knees, and he looks up at me, beaming painfully wide.

'I want a rematch.' I'm not beaming. There isn't even a hint of a smile on my face.

'Fine by me.' James shrugs. 'I've got no problem kicking your butt twice in a row.'

'No, not this again.' Lifting Arlo off my lap, I plonk him on the ground and twist my legs so I can wrench myself out of the stupid seat.

'What did you have in mind?' James rubs his hands together as Edith clambers off his lap.

My eyes roam the space before us, my mind rejecting each machine until I spy the one thing I'm guaranteed to win at. I spent my teenage years feeding my pocket money into the dance machine at Captain John's, and there's no way I won't be triumphant this time around.

'Limber up.' I lead the way towards the back of the arcade, past the fruit machines and the air hockey tables. 'And get ready to have that smug grin wiped off your face.'

My Summer Bucket List:

- *Be happy in my dream job*

- *Drive along the seafront with the windows open and summery songs playing on the radio*

- *Build sandcastles on the beach (haven't done this since I was little with Grandad)*

- *Have a barbecue in my own back garden*

- *Be head over heels in love*

Chapter Thirty-Three

'You're surprisingly agile.' I lean against the dance machine's rail for support as I try to get my breath back. 'And you have some rhythm.'

'You have no idea.' James leans against the rail at his neighbouring machine. 'My rhythm is legendary round these parts.'

I roll my eyes as I push myself away from the rail and hobble towards the whack-a-mole game, where Arlo and Edith are clocking up an impressive trail of tickets. I haven't managed to wipe the smug grin from James' face at all. In fact, I've made matters worse because he's just annihilated me on the dance machine. And not just once; after losing I demanded best of three, then best of five, and now I want to curl up and die, of exhaustion and humiliation. That was *my* game. Nobody could beat me on the dance machine back in the day, but my crown has been well and truly knocked from my head.

'Is there anything you're not good at? I bet you even have a decent shower-singing voice.'

'I was in a band, remember? Fronted it. My voice is fantastic both in and out of the shower.' James narrows his eyes as he looks up towards the ceiling. 'I'm pretty fantastic all round, really. I've even mastered magic loops.' He raises his eyebrows at me, the grin pulling at his lips again. 'I'm on my fourth sausage dog now.'

'*Fourth?*' I stop and stare at him, my arms folding across my chest. I'm still on my second, with two paws and a tail to go until I'm finished.

'Yup. I finished Chipolata last night and started Cumberland this morning.'

'Of course you did.' I throw my hands up in the air and stomp my way to the whack-a-mole machine. Arlo and Edith are wielding a mallet each, with Arlo making an adorable, breathy *huh* sound every time he swings it. I record a short video to show Claire later.

'I have really bad handwriting.' James leans in close to whisper his confession in my ear. 'Really, really bad. It's not writing at all, really, just a squiggle that vaguely resembles letters if you study it long enough.'

'That's it? That's your flaw? Your *handwriting?*' I lock my phone and slide it into my pocket. There's a message from Paul, but I'll read it later. 'Jeez, that must be so debilitating. How on earth do you cope?' I'm trying to sound disparaging, but the smile creeping on to my face is letting me down.

'It's a cross to bear, that's for sure.' James' shoulders rise as he takes in a deep breath before he lets it out in a long sigh. I elbow him lightly in the ribs and he laughs, holding up his hands. 'Okay, the handwriting thing was a bit lame. My *real* flaw is my inability to let women know that I like them. I'm terrible at flirting and I can't just come out and tell someone that I like her, because that would be utterly mortifying, especially if she doesn't feel the same way.'

'That's because you're out of practice. You were married for, what? A decade? And now suddenly you're single and you haven't flirted with a woman since you were seventeen. At least, I hope you didn't flirt with other women when you were married.'

James holds his hands up again. 'Not guilty, ma'am.'

'There you go then. You just need to dust off the old flirting skills and give it a go. You're a good-looking bloke, if you're into long hair and beards. Get out there and have some fun. Your twenties have almost passed you by – you've got some catching up to do.' The whack-a-mole game finishes and spits out the last of Arlo and Edith's tickets so I gather them up and pop them in my pocket for later. Seth's wandering towards us, probably out of money by now. 'Hey, Seth, how are you on the dance machine?'

Seth lifts one shoulder up lazily. 'All right, I guess.'

'Do you think you can beat your dad?'

Seth snorts. 'That old geezer? Easy?'

'Really?' James ruffles his son's hair. 'Bring it on then, twinkletoes.'

The pair head to the dance machine, feeding coins into the slot and ribbing each other with good-natured trash talk as the lights start to flash and the music starts. James gives it a good go, he's nimble and enthusiastic, but it's the junior version who's triumphant. I high-five Seth while James complains about the fact that Seth is younger and fitter and it was an unfair contest.

'Bad loser. That's your flaw.' I nudge James lightly with my elbow. 'What shall we do now?'

We play air hockey, even Seth, who doesn't slope off back to the racing games as soon as he has a fistful of pound coins, and we feed a ton of two-pence pieces into the coin-pusher machines until the kids start to complain that they're hungry. After exchanging the prize tickets for two bouncy balls and a handful of sweets, we head back home, where Gran's prepared a lasagne. It's just starting to bubble in the oven and Gran instructs us to sit at the table in the dining room, which has already been laid.

'I'm going to miss your cooking when I move into my new place, Cordy.'

'You're moving out?' I've been replying to Paul's message from earlier on my phone, but my head snaps up at this news and I frown at James. 'When?'

'As soon as I can get everything arranged. I've loved living here, obviously.' James smiles fondly at Gran. 'But it'll be nice to have my own space again, with the kids staying over at the weekends.'

'Where are you moving to?' Dread fills my stomach. What if he's moving out of town? Who will help me with the sausage dog crochet then? Because Gran isn't up to it yet, no matter what she claims, and the Easter fair is just around the corner.

'It's over by the harbour. It's only a small cottage, but it's cosy and it's had a loft conversion to make it into a three-bed.' James' gaze flicks to his kids, and a smile spreads across his face. 'Pretty perfect for us, really.'

'You'll still be able to help out with the sausage dogs though, won't you?'

James' brow furrows. 'Of course. Why wouldn't I?'

I'm relieved James is staying in Clifton-on-Sea, and that he's still on board for the crochet project, but a little bit of dread remains in the pit of my stomach and remains there for the remainder of the day, even after I've dropped Arlo off at Claire's and gone back to the flat. I've got used to James being around at Gran's, so I guess I'll miss him not being there all the time.

The dread has eased by the following morning, but I'm still left with an odd underlying feeling of mild panic that sneaks in whenever I let myself settle. I've tidied and scrubbed the flat to within an inch of its life to keep me occupied, updated my bullet journal and even created a new page with a bucket list for the summer, complete with colourful illustrations, and I've crocheted another leg for Saveloy the sausage dog. I'm about to start yet another leg when Claire texts, suggesting we meet up for a coffee and a date dissection, since I wasn't in the mood last night. I never turn down a coffee opportunity, plus I really, really want to know how the date went with Riley now the shock of James' imminent move is wearing off.

The rain from yesterday has shifted, making way for a clear, bright sky, so we decide to meet at the park so Arlo can run about on the playground while we chat. The park is already filling up with early picnickers, and there's a couple of footballs being kicked around on the fields while little rowboats bob about on the lake. The kiosk where you can hire boats has been shut up for months, but like the rest of the town, the park is slowly coming to life again.

'Sorry I had to rush off last night.' Claire is already at the park and has secured a bench outside the rainbow fence of the playground. I carried out a rapid drop and run with Arlo last night, claiming unexpected staffing issues at the shop when the truth is I was feeling weird and twitchy about the James thing and I knew Claire would question my odd mood.

'No problem. Sorry the date took so long. That was… unexpected.' Claire's trying to keep a straight face, but there's a grin itching to flourish across it. She takes the coffee and paper bag I hold out to her and twists in her seat as I flop down beside her. 'Oh, Cleo. You'll never guess what the exhibition he took me to was all about.' She leans in close and lowers her voice so it's barely audible. 'It was a Victorian *sexhibition*.' She straightens to observe my reaction, which is suitably shocked. 'I know, right? Who knew Riley had it in him? It was *pure filth*. Early porno pics, fallen women, *dildos*.' Claire checks all around her, to make sure none of the other parents – or worse, their kids – are in hearing distance. 'Riley clearly isn't the boring librarian I thought he was.'

'You slept with him, didn't you?'

'Obviously.' Claire places the coffee beside her on the bench and delves into the paper bag. 'We were surrounded by sex all afternoon. I've never been so turned on in my life. I'm surprised we made it back to my flat before I ripped his clothes off, to be honest.' She sinks her teeth into the raspberry and almond bake, trying to catch the bits of nuts that scatter with her hand.

'So you're seeing him again?'

Claire holds up a finger while she swallows. 'God, yes. It just goes to show that you shouldn't judge a book by its cover.'

I can't help feeling a little bit smug that I spotted Riley's potential months ago. I've definitely earned that Cupid badge, and the timing is perfect with Paul returning to town in six weeks. Claire and I can be properly loved up with our new boyfriends together.

We finish our coffees and cake and then I leave Claire to the playground duties and head to Gran's. The Easter fair at the dog shelter is taking place next weekend and I'm determined to present three stripy sausage dogs for the raffle. There is no way I can match James' four in the time available, but I've come to terms with it – mostly – and three will have to do.

James is in the kitchen when I get there, whipping up a brunch of French toast bacon sandwiches, waffles with whipped cream and berries, and a cafetiere of freshly brewed coffee. I can see why Carla stayed in the loveless marriage for so long if this was what weekends looked like in the Merchant house.

'Cordy's outside, deadheading.' James nods towards the open back door as he carries the plate of sandwiches to the table. 'I didn't even try to stop her this time.' He flashes me an apologetic look, but I shrug.

'There's no point. You'd be wasting your breath on the stubborn old bird.'

'Are my ears burning?' Gran steps into the kitchen, heading straight to the sink to wash her cast-free hand. 'This looks lovely, James. I really am going to miss your cooking when you've moved out.'

I must be hungry, despite a scrambled egg on toast breakfast followed by the raspberry and almond bake in the park, because my stomach twinges. I press a hand against the discomfort to try to ease it.

'Have you eaten?' James adds a pot of tea to the table, next to the matching milk jug. 'There's plenty.'

I think about the double breakfast I've already scoffed this morning for a nanosecond before pushing the thought away and plonking myself down at the table and helping myself to a bacon sandwich. James has added maple syrup and the sweetness against the saltiness of the bacon is heavenly.

'You're wasted as an accountant.' I place the sandwich down on my plate and lick the delicious grease from my fingers before helping myself to a coffee.

'Being an accountant pays the bills.' James grabs the teapot, and while Gran tuts and rolls her eyes at him, she lets him pour her a cup. 'I don't think I could make quite as much trying to flog bacon butties.'

'There's more to life than money.' I take another huge bite of my sandwich and resist the urge to groan in appreciation. This must be what Claire felt like as she dashed back to her flat after the exhibition yesterday.

'That's true, but there's more to my life than work. I have other less boring things going on. Things that might surprise you.'

'I doubt that.' Nothing could surprise me after the Riley revelation earlier. 'Unless you do a bit of Magic Mike-ing at the weekends?'

I shouldn't have said that, because now I'm imagining James peeling off his blazer very, *very* slowly while looking deep into my eyes, which is a disturbing enough thought in itself but made doubly unsettling with my gran sitting across the table from me.

'I liked that film.' Gran adds a drop of milk to her tea and gives a dreamy sigh as she stirs.

'I know. You made me go with you to see it at the cinema three times.'

'That's because Gwen wouldn't go and see it again. Twice was more than enough, she said.' Gran shakes her head. 'Such a prude.'

'Anyway.' I think it's time for a change of subject. Something as far from stripping men as possible. 'I've brought my crochet with me. I've nearly finished Saveloy and then I want to try and squeeze another one in if I can.'

Gran smiles at me across the table, her eyes almost disappearing in the crinkled folds. 'You've really caught the crochet bug, haven't you?'

Have I? I thought I was just being over-competitive with James, but I guess I have found it quite therapeutic to sit down for an hour or so with my hook and yarn, and I think I'll miss it once all the sausage dogs are complete and raffled off next week.

'What's our next project going to be then, Cordy?' James takes a bite of his sandwich, completely missing the look of surprise on my face (it turns out he is capable of surprising me after all).

'You're still going to crochet with us? Even when you've moved out?'

James wipes his mouth on a napkin. 'You didn't think you'd get rid of me that easily, did you? Who else is going to scoff at your silly daytime soaps?'

I'm feeling quite enthused by the time we've finished eating – so much so that I offer to wash the dishes. James dries and then we settle down with our current crochet project. Over brunch, we decided that once the sausage dogs are complete, we're going to make tiny hats for newborns, which Gran will send off to local neonatal wards. It seems I've inadvertently found that new hobby to cross off my list.

The Grown-Up To-Do List:

- Decide on a career (does 'any' count?)

- Start a career

- ~~Move out of Mum & Dad's ASAP~~

- Learn to drive

- ~~Find a hobby~~

- ~~Learn to use the washing machine~~

- ~~Book first driving lesson~~

- ~~Get to work on time~~

- ~~Host a dinner party (do not serve 'hearty vegetable stew')~~

- ~~Open a savings account~~

- Save enough cash for a deposit on flat

- ~~Keep the cat alive~~

- Keep the plant alive (not as important as the cat, but will mean a lot to Gran)

- ~~Kick-start social life~~

- ~~Eat a proper breakfast that doesn't involve chocolate~~

- *Find permanent flat*

- ~~*Shop for smart attire for job interviews*~~

- *Get a more sophisticated haircut*

- *Learn to bake*

Chapter Thirty-Four

'What do you think?'

I give my head a little side-to-side wobble as I stand in front of Mum in her living room. She's already seen and liked the photo I posted on Instagram of my new haircut as I sat in front of the mirror at the hairdresser's, cape still around my shoulders and the hacked-off, pink-tipped hair still clumped on the floor, but this is the first time she's seen it in the flesh. I already showed the new choppy, chin-length bob with long side fringe to Claire as I took a detour to the chippy on my way to Mum and Dad's.

'Oh, Cleo.' Mum beams at me as she reaches out and takes a strand of hair between her finger and thumb. 'It looks lovely. Very *chic*.'

I'm going to miss those pink tips, and it feels very strange not being able to scoop my hair up into a messy bun, but I like it. It *is* chic, and the choppy layers give it an interesting texture. I give my head another little wobble, just to see my new hair bounce around a bit.

'Your gran won't recognise you later at the fair.' Mum looks down at my hands and then back up at my face. 'Did you already drop the flapjacks off at the shelter?'

I pull a face as I slump down on the sofa. 'Not exactly.'

It's the Easter fair at the dog shelter this afternoon, and I attempted to bake a batch of the fat-free banana flapjacks from the magazine I bought the other day, but after nearly destroying Russell and Jed's kitchen and searing my fingerprints off when I forgot to don oven gloves before moving the tray to one side, I ended up with soggy, cardboard-tasting squares that nobody – not even the dogs – would want to eat. Learning to bake is never getting crossed off my list. I've made my peace with this fact, and my still-tender fingertips are grateful.

'So my contribution is just the sausage dogs.'

Mum sits down on the sofa and pats my knee. 'That's still brilliant. I'm very proud of you, and I know your gran is.'

Even though the disgusting flapjacks went straight into the compost bin, I was able to present three stripy crocheted sausage dogs to Gwen, who's volunteered to run the raffle stall, before my hairdresser appointment. They may be slightly flawed (Chorizo has one ear bigger than the other, Salami has an odd bulge around his middle, and Saveloy's tail is sitting at an odd angle) but, to me, they are perfect.

'Shall I pop the kettle on?' Mum pats my knee again before she eases herself out of her seat.

I check my Instagram post while she's in the kitchen, and my chest expands with joy when I see that Paul has liked the photo. I tap through to his grid, where I find a new photo of his own. It's another gym selfie (he posts a lot of those, but why wouldn't he?) but this time he's with the blonde colleague I've seen him with before. The pretty blonde one. Who even looks pretty with a serious post-workout sweat going on. She's tagged in the photo: Olivia Sharpe. I tap on her name, but her profile is set to private. I think about adding her as a friend, but that would be a bit weird, wouldn't it?

'It's only instant, I'm afraid.' Mum hands me a mug and settles back down on the sofa. 'I know how much you like James' fancy coffee machine. Even your gran has grown fond of it. I'm not sure which she'll miss most when he moves into his new place – James or her nightly Horlicks.'

'What have you missed most while I've been staying at Jed and Russell's? Me or the mess?'

Mum quirks an eyebrow. 'I haven't missed tripping over your shoes.' Her face softens. 'But I have missed you. Your dad has too. It's been too quiet around here, but I guess that's something we'll have to get used to if you're planning on flying the nest for good. Have you found anywhere affordable yet?'

I shake my head. Properties – affordable or otherwise – are slim pickings in Clifton-on-Sea and Jed and Russell are due back soon.

'You're always welcome here until you find somewhere.'

'Thanks, Mum.' I try to sound grateful, because I am, but I can't help feeling glum at the prospect of ending up back in my childhood bedroom. 'And I promise I won't be the same messy Cleo that I used to be, and I'll pay you proper rent, not a few quid like I usually do. I know how expensive stuff is now. Plus, I'm willing and able to use the washing machine. It's not just the hair that's new and improved.'

Mum nudges me lightly with her arm. 'I think I've mollycoddled you a bit, because you're my only child, my baby, but you're not a child any more. I think I've had a hard time accepting that, but you've really shown me how much you've grown up these last few weeks.'

'Thank you, Mum.' This time I don't have to try to sound grateful, because I cherish Mum's words. My plan is obviously working.

–

'You okay?' Claire links her arm through mine and rests her head on my shoulder.

'It's just harder to say goodbye to the little fellas than I thought it would be.' Claire straightens so she can give me an odd look. 'What? I crafted those little dogs with my own hands. You'd feel a bit sad if you were giving Arlo away in a raffle for a pound a strip.'

'Are you comparing my *child* with a *soft toy*?'

I am, but I pretend I was just kidding. Mums can get pretty feisty when it comes to their kids.

'How are you anyway?' I guide Claire away from the raffle stall as I can't bear to see my sausage dog pups with their please-don't-abandon-me eyes. 'Any word from Riley?'

Claire shakes her head. It's been a week since her date at the exhibition of Victorian smut but Claire hasn't heard from Riley since. He hasn't called or texted her, and he hasn't set foot in the chippy. Profits for the week have plummeted.

'I think I've been played. Who'd have thought sweet little Riley was just a regular bastard man?'

'There has to be a credible reason why he hasn't been in touch.' I unhook my arm from Claire's so I can drape it across her shoulders. 'Maybe he's been involved in an horrific car accident that's left him in a coma? He could be fighting for his life right now, barely clinging on with only the thought of seeing you again stopping him from slipping away.'

'I hope so.'

Claire and I make our way to the bouncy castle, where Arlo is propelling himself as high as he can into the air before thrusting his legs forwards so he can land on his bum. It looks like a lot of fun, but it'd probably be frowned upon if I kicked off my shoes and had a go myself. Still, there's nothing stopping me from rotting my teeth away with candyfloss, or making myself sick by gorging on chocolate eggs – why should kids get to have all the fun?

'There's James.' Claire points towards the bunny piñata, which Edith is viciously attacking with a stick while Seth stands to one side, his face fixed on his phone. 'I bet he wouldn't lure a woman into bed by taking her to a sexhibition and then never call.'

'I can't imagine James going to a sex exhibition.' I mean, look at him. It's the weekend, we're at an Easter fair, and he's still wearing a blazer, albeit with a T-shirt and jeans. He's even swapped his brogues for a pair of Converse, but he's still giving off the accountant vibe. I'm not saying James is uptight – far from it – but I simply can't imagine him shedding the composed, professional image and doing something wild and unexpected.

'Maybe I should ask him out. He's still single, right?'

I pull back my chin. 'You can't date James.'

'Why not?'

'He's hardly your type, is he?' James is a steady, practical kind of guy, and there's nothing wrong with that, obviously, but he doesn't exactly fit Claire's bad-boy ideal. They're completely mismatched and the idea of the two of them together makes me feel uneasy. 'His idea of a good night is sitting in with my gran watching *Midsomer Murders*.'

'I quite like *Midsomer Murders*.' Claire scours the pile of shoes on the mat, selecting a pair of PAW Patrol trainers. 'And we have other things in common.'

'Like what?' I glance over at James, who's trying to coax Seth into having a go with the piñata stick. The seed of uneasiness is growing, a feeling of mild panic fluttering in my chest as it spreads. Claire has been hurt enough recently, and although I don't think James would intentionally let her down, there are no guarantees.

'We're both parents.' Claire waggles the trainers at me. 'So he'll get how important Arlo is to me and understand if I have to duck out of dates at the last minute or if I show up with melted chocolate button fingerprints on me. Plus, he *is* gorgeous.'

'If you say so.' I wave as Arlo bobs his way to the end of the bouncy castle and slides onto the mat.

'I say very much so. Wouldn't *you* say so?'

I shrug and try not to look back at him, but fail miserably. He's throwing his arms up in the air in victory as Seth picks up the piñata stick. 'I'm not really into the beard and long hair thing.'

'Yeah, and those piercing blue eyes are minging as well, aren't they?' Claire rolls her eyes at me before crouching down to help Arlo put his shoes on.

James does have very nice eyes, actually. And I guess the beard wouldn't bother me too much – it's neatly trimmed and doesn't appear to have bits of cereal clogged in there – and the hair is quite nice. Quite sexy, in a Heath Ledger in *10 Things I Hate About You* kind of way, if you really think about it.

'Are you really going to ask him out?' I try to keep my voice even, to mask the alarm I'm feeling. *Please say no.*

'Nah.' Claire stands up, reaching her hand out to help Arlo to his feet. 'He's way too nice for me. Besides, things still might work out with Riley if he really has been mangled in that car accident.' She holds two entwined fingers up. 'And if not, I think I'm going to have a break from dating for a bit. I've got my course to finish, so I should be concentrating on that, really.'

'You're giving up on men?' I snort but manage to mask it as a small coughing fit. The day Claire Harris gives up on men is the day I develop Mary Berry-style baking skills and produce something edible for the bake sale.

'Just for a little while. I'm not going to join a convent or anything, but I'm not going to actively seek out the opposite sex. I'm going to concentrate on my course and my friends and this little dude, obviously.' She reaches down and scoops Arlo up, planting him on her hip. 'It'll be the summer holidays soon, so I was thinking about going on a little holiday before I start my dream career. Benidorm, maybe. Or Tenerife.'

'On your own?' I don't mean the question to sound so strangled, as though Claire has just told me she's planning on stripping off and having a go on the bouncy castle, but the mere thought of jetting off without a responsible adult is giving me palpitations. I tried that once before and I'm in no hurry to do it again.

'Well, I was planning on taking this one with me.' Claire kisses the top of Arlo's head. 'You'd like that, wouldn't you? A nice holiday at the beach.'

'We have a beach on our doorstep.' If the sound system wasn't blaring out 'You're the One That I Want' from *Grease*, we'd be able to hear the rhythmic crashing of the waves in the distance. 'You don't need to get on a plane and travel hundreds and hundreds of miles to sit on the beach.'

'You do if you want to sit on the beach without freezing half to death. Hi, James.'

I hadn't realised we'd gravitated towards the piñata, but the poor, bashed-up bunny is before us. Claire lowers Arlo to the ground and hands him a quid so he can have a go at battering the rabbit.

'Where would you rather spend your summer: freezing your Wotsits off as you overlook the grey Irish Sea or getting a tan as you look out over the sparkling blue Mediterranean?'

'Is this a trick question?' James looks from Claire to me and back again. 'The Mediterranean, obviously.'

Claire flashes me a smug look. I'm about to stick my tongue out at her but the sight of a squillion foil-wrapped chocolate eggs showering out of the piñata bunny's leg wound distracts me. I hope Arlo's in the mood for sharing with his favourite babysitter.

I manage to coax a couple of chocolate eggs out of Arlo before he races off to get his face painted. Claire's waiting with him in the queue with Edith and Seth, who's volunteered to watch his little sister out of the goodness of his heart, and not because his eyes went all love-heart-shaped when he spotted Claire. I won't break it to the boy that she's sworn off the opposite sex, or that he's at least a decade too young.

'Have you bought a raffle ticket?' James nods towards Gwen's stall, where our little sausage dogs are lined up, ready to be rehomed.

'To win something I made myself?' I lick a splodge of raspberry sauce that's dripping from the ice cream James has just bought me from the ice cream van.

'You might win one of my beauties?' James shrugs and reaches into his jeans pocket, producing a couple of raffle ticket strips. 'I've had a go. Edith has her heart set on winning one. I've told her I'll make her one if we don't win – after we've made the baby hats. I need a break from stripy sausage dogs right now.'

'I've got a pattern for a daisy garland that I thought I'd have a go at.' It was in the magazine I bought last week. Hopefully I'll have better luck with the crochet than I did with the baking. 'It'll be something pretty to hang above my bed if I ever manage to find a flat.'

'Still no luck?'

'Nope.' I've been checking the app for rental properties daily – sometimes by the hour when it's a slow day at the chippy – but there's been nothing in my price range that doesn't look as though a sneeze would bring the walls down. 'I guess I'll be moving back in with Mum and Dad for a bit.'

'Would that be so terrible?'

I lick my ice cream while I think about it. 'I guess not, but it feels like a step backwards.'

'A step backwards from what?'

'From growing up.'

There's a couple of plastic chairs free near the burger van, so we sit down while we wait for Claire and the kids.

'You can still be grown-up and live with a parent. It's about your attitude, not geography.'

I have another lick of my ice cream. 'Yeah, I guess so. Just because I'll be living with Mum and Dad doesn't mean I'll have to revert to my old ways. I can cook now – sort of – and use the washing machine, and I've stopped leaving my shoes lying around.' In fact, I've been tidying up after myself rather well. Mugs and plates are transferred to the kitchen after use rather than lying around the living room for days, and I've perfected the art of using the laundry basket for dirty clothes instead of the bedroom floor. I even have a cleaning schedule in my bullet journal. The changes have been so subtle, I haven't given myself enough credit. I may not have my own flat or an exciting career to boast about, but the new and improved Cleo Parker is definitely emerging.

'Thanks, James.'

'For what?'

I shrug and have another lick of my ice cream. 'For making me feel a bit better about my situation. You're a good listener. You should take on a second job as an agony aunt.'

'I already have a second job. It's only a recent thing, but I'm really excited about it.'

I frown. He's never mentioned this before. 'You do? Doing what?'

But James doesn't get the chance to answer as I'm distracted by my phone pinging with a new message. I snatch it up, assuming it's Paul commenting on my new hairstyle, but it's a message from Russell. He's back in town and wants to meet up for 'an urgent chat about the shop'. The ice cream curdles in my stomach. What have I done wrong? Did I forget to lock up last night? Leave the fryers on overnight?

'Do you think you could lend me your second job?' I look around for a bin to drop what's left of my ice cream into, because there's no way I can face eating it now. 'Because I think I'm about to lose mine.'

Things I Would Rather Do Than Have an Urgent Chat With Russell:

- *Drink nothing but revolting hospital vending machine tea for a ~~month~~ week*

- *Share a bed with stink-bomb Fizz*

- *Admit (out loud) just how superior James' crochet skills are to mine*

- *Listen to Mum's Boyzone CD on a loop for twenty-four hours*

- *Deep dive into politics*

Chapter Thirty-Five

I know that I'm going to be leaving The Fish & Chip Shop Around The Corner anyway, but it was supposed to be on *my* terms, when I had another job lined up. I have two more interviews scheduled for next week, but unless they buck the trend and a) go well and b) I'm offered the job, I'm up to my neck in the smelly brown stuff. I'd thought admitting to Paul that I still work at the chippy would be bad enough, but having to admit that I'm unemployed would be even worse. If moving back home is taking a step backwards, losing my job is taking a giant leap the wrong way, and it's going to have a domino effect. How can I afford my driving lessons without a job? Or afford my own place, even if one popped up right in front of me?

'I think you're jumping to conclusions. The message doesn't say anything about losing your job. It doesn't even say you've done anything wrong.'

It's been ten minutes since Russell's message came through and James is doing his best to calm me down, but it isn't working and I'm currently wearing the soles of my Converse out as I pace up and down in front of the plastic chairs.

'It could just mean that his mum is better and they're able to take the reins of the shop again.' He looks to Claire for backup, and she nods enthusiastically. She's left Arlo in the queue with Edith and Seth so she can help placate me, and she even typed out a reply to the message for me because my hands were trembling and my brain had turned to mush.

'But then he would have said that. He would have announced that they were *ba-ack*.' I do jazz hands to convey the zeal of this alternate message. I look at Claire, who winces, because she knows what I'm saying is true.

'Let me see the message again.' She holds out her hand and I press my phone into it. I know the message word for word by now:

> Hi Cleo. I'm back in town for the afternoon. Need to have an urgent chat about the shop. Can we meet ASAP?

'Maybe I've done the accounts wrong. Paid everyone double and now Russell and Jed are going to go bankrupt.'

'You didn't pay me double, that's for sure.' Claire hands the phone back. 'And you haven't burned the place down or flooded it – you'd have noticed when you popped by after your haircut. James is right – you're panicking over nothing. Meet up with Russell, see what's so urgent, and then deal with it. I'll even panic with you if the meeting warrants it, but I doubt it will.'

I nod, but the lump of fear is still growing in my throat, and I almost choke on it when a new message comes through from Russell.

'He wants to meet up at the flat. He's there now.' I press a hand to my chest. I can't breathe. I'm about to lose the job I adore and I don't even know what I've done to deserve it. Maybe Russell and Jed have got wind of the interviews I've been on and are pushing me before I have the chance to jump. I bet it was Bridget, who's always been a bit miffed that I was put in charge and not her.

'Do you want me to come with you?' James rubs my back with a soothing circular motion, and the desire to crumple into his arms and take him up on the offer is strong. But I resist.

'You need to stay and watch Seth's band perform. He'd be gutted if you missed it. *You'd* be gutted if you missed it.'

'I'll come.' Claire stands up but I shake my head.

'No. Thanks, but I'm a grown-up. I can do this.' Outwardly, I'm throwing back my shoulders and tilting my chin in defiance while inside I'm battling the urge to throw myself onto my knees while begging Claire to come with me and hold my hand. 'Besides, Arlo's looking forward to having his face painted as Spider-Man. I couldn't deny him that.' I give a wobbly smile as I back away. 'Wish me luck.'

I turn and practically run away from the fair before I hide myself away in the corner of the bouncy castle. I've got myself into even more of a state by the time I make it to the chippy, but I'm relieved to see it's still standing. In fact, it's looking pretty busy for a Sunday afternoon, with Bridget, Elliot and Ross all flitting around behind the counter as they serve the long line of customers. We've definitely moved into high season, but the question is, will I be part of it after this meeting?

I trudge up the staircase to the flat, prolonging the agony of not knowing with each step. Russell's in the living room, lounging against the Jed cushion as he listens to one of his glam rock albums. He smiles when he sees me, and not in a I'm-sorry-I'm-about-to-sack-you kind of way, which I take as a Good Sign. And I almost weep with relief when he envelops me in a huge hug, because he wouldn't do that if he was mad at me, would he?

'Cleo! It's so good to see you.' Russell squeezes me even harder for a brief moment before releasing me and holding me at arm's length. 'You're looking good. I like the new hair. *Très sophistiqué.*'

I reach up to touch my shorter style. 'I kind of miss the pink, to be honest. And it'll be a while before I can throw it up into a messy bun. It'll take me ages to style now it's shorter, which is backward, don't you think?' I'm babbling because I'm nervous and can't seem to stop. 'I'll have to blow-dry it and straighten it, and the fringe will be a nightmare. So high-maintenance!'

'Tell me about it.' Russell sniggers as he runs a hand over his balding head. 'Anyway, shall I pop the kettle on and then we can have our little chat?'

My innards drop to the floor, but I manage to push a smile onto my face. It droops as soon as Russell steps into the kitchen and I start to pace the living room. I'm still anxious about the 'little chat' despite the pleasantries.

'Sit down. You're making me nervous, pacing like that.' Russell returns with a couple of steaming mugs, which he places down on the coasters on the coffee table. I do as I'm told, folding myself carefully into the armchair while Russell turns the stereo down. He claps his hands together before he sets off pacing himself. The grimace on his face as he moves from one end of the living room and back again tells me I was right not to trust the pleasantries.

'Can *you* sit down?' My stomach is in knots, and the marching is making it worse.

'Sorry. Yes. Of course.' Russell attempts a smile, but it just makes the grimace more pronounced. But he does sit, perching on the edge of the sofa and angling his body towards mine. 'Cleo, I have a confession, and it's quite a big one.' He takes a huge lungful of air before releasing it at an agonisingly slow rate. 'My mum was never poorly. She's never been fitter, in fact. She's been doing that "Couch to 5k" thing. Runs every day now, and she does one of those park runs every weekend, and she's doing the Great North Run. Reckons she'll be going in for the full London Marathon next year.' Russell shakes his head in wonder. 'She's seventy-six, you know, but there's no stopping her. She's an inspiration.'

'Russell.' I clasp my hands together and lean forward in my seat. 'Why did you tell me your mum was ill? And what have you been doing all these weeks? Have you even been in Manchester?'

'Yes.' Russell's head bobs up and down. 'We have definitely been in Manchester. We didn't fib about that. But the thing is.' Russell takes another huge lungful of air, closing his eyes before he releases it. 'The thing is, we bought a bar.'

'A bar?'

'In the village. I spotted it was up for auction when I'd gone to visit Mum one time, and it played on my mind. You know, what if… A bit like when Jed and I bought the chippy.' Russell smiles wistfully, the grimace a thing of the past. 'Anyway, I took Jed to see it and we fell in love with the place and the idea of running it. And before we knew it, we were bidding on it – and we won!'

'But why didn't you say anything? Why did you say your mum needed looking after?'

The smile drops from Russell's face as he drops his gaze to his lap. 'We shouldn't have told those porkies, I know. But we were a bit apprehensive after the euphoria of having the winning bid at the auction had died down. It was an impulse purchase – and a massive one – and we didn't know whether we'd be able to do it. Running a chippy and a bar are two wildly different things. So we wanted a trial run before we told everyone, just in case it didn't work out. But Cleo, it has worked out.' Russell peeps up at me, and I can see he's itching to break out in a grin. 'We absolutely love it. It's a challenge and every day is different, but it's like we've woken up after a deep sleep. I haven't felt this alive in years!' He isn't able to contain it any longer – the grin breaks out, beaming across his face. 'We still love this place, obviously, but we want to give the bar our all. I'll be fifty next year, and Jed's already past that milestone, so we want to get stuck in while we still can.'

'Are you selling the chippy then?' The knots had started to loosen in my stomach, but they constrict again. The good news is I haven't done anything to warrant getting fired, but I could be out of a job anyway.

'No, no, no.' Russell reaches out between the gap between us and takes my hand in his. 'The Fish & Chip Shop Around The Corner will always be our baby. I'd sell my own dear mother before I sold this place. No, we'll be moving to Manchester, but we'll be putting a permanent manager in the shop. And we'd like that manager to be you.' Russell gives my hand a squeeze. 'You've done such a marvellous job while we've been away, and we trust you to look after our baby as though it's your own.'

Wow. I'm not losing my job. The opposite, in fact. My first instinct is to throw my arms around Russell while having a little weep of joy. But then I think of Paul and my grown-up to-do list. I'm supposed to be moving on from the chippy and beginning my new career. Onwards and upwards, not stationary on the ground. I know I'm lucky to have a job I love, a job I was moments ago devastated about because I thought I was going to lose it, but if I stay at the chippy now, I'll probably never leave.

'Can I think about it?'

Russell gives my hand a squeeze, but the beam on his face dims. 'Of course. I'm going to be in Clifton-on-Sea for a couple of weeks while I pack up the flat and tie up all the loose ends, so if I could have an answer by then? And don't worry – I'm not kicking you out of the flat, and all the big furniture's staying here. I'm going to stay with a friend while I'm here. I can't imagine living in this flat without Jed. It wouldn't feel right. And you're welcome to rent the flat, whatever you decide about the manager's position. It'd be a weight off our minds having a tenant we know and trust.'

This is one decision I don't have to ponder after the trouble I've had trying to find a suitable property. 'I would love to stay here.' I jump up off the chair and flop down next to Russell, throwing my arms around him. 'I should have known you weren't coming back when you took Bolan. How is he getting on?'

'He loves the new place. We're renting an apartment overlooking the canal, so Bolan spends his days people-watching on the balcony. He's got a bit of a spat going on with one of the dogs who has his daily walk along the towpath – they have a growl and hiss back and forth, all very ferocious but harmless – and the lady next door chucks treats over for him. She doesn't even have a cat of her own, she buys the treats especially for Bolan, so he's in his element, really.'

I kind of miss the little furry dude, although my plant is doing much better without him knocking it around.

I water it every day (and I've even started to talk to it. Should I be worried about that?) and it's started to produce tiny buds.

'Anyway, I'd better get going.' Russell downs half his coffee in one. 'I've packed up a few bits to take over to Don's. I'll be back tomorrow to start packing up the rest. I'll try not to get under your feet.'

I take the mug from Russell and he grabs a hefty-looking holdall from beside the sofa. 'What will you do, if I don't take the manager's position?'

Russell heaves the holdall onto his shoulder and stoops to pick up a smaller one. 'I guess we'll have to get someone temporary in from the agency until we find someone as wonderful as you.' He leans in carefully so the holdall doesn't swing at me while he kisses my cheek. 'I'll see you tomorrow. We'll get a tenancy agreement drawn up for the flat. Make it all official. Don't forget to invite us to your housewarming party, will you?' He winks at me, and then he's gone. I wander into the kitchen, emptying both mugs into the sink before stacking them in the dishwasher. I take a look around the room, at the kitchen that is now mine for the foreseeable future. A giddy feeling bubbles up from my stomach and I do a little jig on the spot. *This is my kitchen.* I run my hand along the worktop. *My worktop.* I tell the plant the good news before rushing down the stairs and on to the street. I need to share the news with Claire and James.

But I pause when I see the chippy. Bridget, Elliot and Ross are still flitting about as they fulfil orders inside, and the queue is now stretching halfway down the street. What am I going to do about this place? Do I go with my head and move on, or do I go with my heart and stay forever?

Reasons to Leave The Fish & Chip Shop Around The Corner:

1. *I won't have to admit to Paul that I fudged the truth about my job (office-based career change is more believable than me somehow ending up back at the chippy)*

2. *I'll finally have moved on from my seventeen-year-old self (new flat, new job, new Cleo)*

3. *I can cross the career bits off my Grown-Up To-Do List*

4. *I won't be quite so tempted to snack on chips so often*

5. *Better coffee in the staff room?*

Reasons to Stay at The Fish & Chip Shop Around The Corner:

1. *The customers are so wonderful (except Riley, who is a big, phoney pig)*

2. *The staff are more like friends than colleagues (except Bridget, who's a bossy old bag)*

3. *Every day is different and fun (who doesn't like dancing around to Seventies hits while mopping the floor?)*

4. *The commute is minimal (c. 25 steps from living room to shop door, and not a blob of chewing gum in sight)*

5. *I love it. Every last bit of it (even the wobbly chairs in the back room)*

Chapter Thirty-Six

I never thought I'd be back at school, but here I am, striding towards the gates in my pointy-shouldered blazer. It isn't my old school, but a primary in Cleveleys that has taken me two buses to reach. But I'm on time for my interview and I don't have chewing gum stuck to my trousers (I double-check before I step through the gates. Nope, nothing). The role is for an administrative assistant and I'm sure I can hit all the necessary criteria. I'm used to dealing with people, I've been keeping the admin up to date at the chippy for weeks now, and I know my way around Word and Excel. Plus, dealing with dinner money will be a piece of cake after being responsible for cashing up on a Friday night once the Red Lion's customers have piled into the chippy after a live performance in the pub, so I'm feeling pretty confident as I stride up to the school's reception and press the buzzer. I'm permitted access to the building and told to wait in the little reception area. The chairs are big and squishy and covered in a bright blue fabric, and the walls are covered in vibrant artwork from the kids, which gives the space a lovely jolly feel. I particularly like the painting of a rainbow-striped fish that uses every single shade of paint available. Yes, I can definitely see myself working here, surrounded by colour and joy every day.

It's been three days since Russell's confession, but I still haven't made up my mind about what to do about the job opportunity, and my friends haven't been much help. Maryam and Bridget think I should be brave and take the leap away from the comfort of the chippy and embark on a new adventure (though I suspect the real reason for Bridget's enthusiasm for my new venture is so she can swoop in and snatch the manager's position herself) while James and Claire can't understand why I'd give up a job I love so much to start a new one I may end up hating. So the decision still lies with me, which I am not happy about. I'd quite like somebody to take charge and tell me what to do, but that isn't what being a grown-up is all about. It's my decision, and I have to be the one to make it. Even if I really, really don't want to.

I'm not sure how the interview goes. I try my best to be charming and engaging, but the woman interviewing me is quite cold and isn't giving anything away. I make the return journey home with less confidence than I arrived with, but I haven't given up hope, even if it is the last interview I have scheduled. I've applied for loads of jobs, widening my options to include everything from trainee estate agent to data analyst to telephone counsellor – anything that's office-based, basically, so I don't have to confess my porkies to Paul – but the well has run dry. At this rate, I'll have no choice but to remain at the chippy indefinitely. How I'll explain it to Paul, I have no idea, but I'll have to come up with something. I'm already going to have to fudge the truth about the driving, because I'm nowhere near passing my test – I haven't even attempted my theory yet – so my options are to either tell Paul that I'm banned due to drink-driving (not ideal when you're trying to give the impression you're super-mature) or that my car is in the garage. For a really, really long time.

'How did it go?' Claire pounces as soon as I step into the chippy. My shift doesn't start for another three hours, but I've headed straight to The Fish & Chip Shop Around The Corner because my stomach has been growling since I caught a whiff of the school canteen on my way out of the gates after my interview. Who knew the smell of institutional cooking could be so appealing?

'Not sure.' I hold my hand up and tilt it from side to side. 'I'll just have to wait and see. And while I wait, I'll have a cone of chips, please.'

I've missed the lunchtime rush so I stand at the counter and chat to Claire while I scoff my chips. The radio's playing its usual Seventies hits, and I wonder idly if I'd change the station if I became the permanent manager. Because it would be up to me, wouldn't it? I could play anything I wanted on the radio – regional, commercial, talk, classical (if my personality changed dramatically).

'Are you even listening to me?'

I start, a chip freezing between the cone and my mouth, and I gape at Claire for a moment before I rally. 'Yeah. Of course I'm listening to you.' I shove the chip in my mouth, chewing slowly in case Claire asks me to parrot her last bit of conversation back to her, because it'll give me a precious few seconds to think of something to say.

'No, you weren't, because if you had been paying attention, you'd have told me what a *very bad* idea it is.'

I slow my chewing even more. What could she be talking about?

'There's no way you'd let me hunt Riley down at the bookshop he works at and demand answers. You'd tell me it'd be almost tantamount to stalking, and that I have far more dignity and class.'

I drop my cone of chips down on the counter and wipe my greasy fingers on a serviette. 'You can't go and find Riley. He said he'd call and he hasn't. You've tried calling him and he hasn't picked up. You've sent him texts that have gone unanswered. Going to the bookshop will come off as…' I wrack my brain for something less offensive than 'desperate' but still truthful.

'Pathetic? I know that. I'm not actually going to track him down – it was just a ploy to prove you'd zoned out.'

'Sorry.' I pluck a chip from the cone on the counter and bite the end off.

'What were you thinking about so intensely anyway?'

I shove the rest of the chip in my mouth. I'm delaying my answer because I don't want to tell Claire I was musing about the radio station I'd opt for if I was manager of the chippy, because she'd pounce on it, demanding to know why I was leaving if I wasn't 100 per cent certain about my decision. And I really don't have an answer for that one.

–

The rejection for the school admin assistant role comes through later while I'm on my break, as I'm sitting in the little room at the back of the chippy with a cup of strong black coffee, musing whether it would be in my remit as manager to install a coffee machine, squeezed between the kettle and the toaster. I'm checking my phone for any messages from Paul – as I do frequently throughout the day – but there aren't any. There is a comment from my old school friend, Shelby, about my new hairstyle, saying how cute it is and how much it suits me, which is nice. After thanking her and adding a smiley face, I idly open my email app and there it is, barely seven hours since my interview. The 'thank you for your interest but we wouldn't want to employ you if you were the only applicant and we were desperate to fill the position immediately' email. (It doesn't say that, obviously, but that's how it feels, especially when I see that the email was sent three hours ago. They clearly couldn't wait to turn me down.)

I jab at my phone to lock it and shove it into the front pocket of my tabard, as though hiding it away will erase the memory of the email and take away its sting. I should be used to these rebuffs by now, but I find myself feeling more deflated with each one that lands in my inbox. I haven't been particularly passionate about any of the potential roles, but having them snatched away is brutal and is starting to chip away at my self-esteem. I wonder if Russell and Jed would have offered me the promotion if they'd known how lacking every other employer within a ten-mile radius found me.

'Cleo?' Maryam's hovering in the doorway, her hand raised and fingers curled in as though she was about to knock on the open door but changed her mind at the last second. 'There's someone here asking for you.'

I forget all about my latest failed interview as I scrape back my chair and hurry out into the shop. Maybe it's Paul, arriving early to surprise me. It would explain why he hasn't called or messaged me all day if he's been driving here all the way from Kent. But of course it isn't Paul here to surprise me; he doesn't know I work in the chippy, and if he stumbled across me here, it'd be *him* on the receiving end of the surprise. The fact dawns on me a split second before I see the ponytailed teenage girl standing awkwardly by the counter, but I'm still disappointed not to see him standing there in her place.

'Abbie. Hello.' My heart rate has slowed to a more normal level after it spiked during the short trip from the back room to the shop, but I still sound flustered as I greet the girl. 'Do you want to come through to the back? We'll sort you out a tabard and everything and start with the basics.'

I'd invited Elliot's friend to come in during a quieter period between the teatime and supper rush so I could show her the ropes before her first shift starts at the weekend, but it totally slipped my mind as I've been focused on the interview this morning and the subsequent 'go to hell' email. (Okay, I'm starting to sound bitter now. Must stop and focus on Abbie, who's looking a bit pale and nervy.)

'Is this your first job?' I grab a tabard from one of the spare lockers and hand it to her. Our interview was nothing more than a quick chat, which mostly consisted of arranging suitable shifts, so I don't know much about Abbie, other than the fact she's a college friend of Elliot.

'Is it that obvious?' Abbie scrunches up her nose. 'I'm really, really nervous.'

'Don't be. It's a really fun job.' Unless you're sharing a shift with Bridget, but I don't mention this as I don't want to put her off before she's even begun. 'You get to have a laugh with everyone and get to know the customers. And it isn't obvious it's your first job. It's just it was *my* first job while I was at college. But don't worry – you won't end up still working here in ten years' time. You'll be off doing… what is it you want to do?'

Abbie slips the tabard over her head and fastens the press studs at the sides. 'I want to do something arty – illustrator, animator, something like that. I haven't decided yet.'

'That sounds really cool. And you won't have to wear one of these doing a job like that.' I hand over a hairnet and help Abbie to push her hair underneath it. 'Sorry, it isn't very attractive, but you get used to it and the hat covers most of it.'

Once Abbie's kitted out, we head into the kitchen where I show her how to use the rumbling machine that peels the potatoes before rinsing them. We sing along to the radio as we slice the potatoes into thick chips, and I take it as a Good Sign that Abbie knows the words to 'Mr Blue Sky'. It doesn't matter that she's never heard of The Who ('No, not Doctor Who. They're a band') or Mud ('Tiger Feet? Never heard of it') because she'll soon learn if the Seventies vibe remains.

'We all chip in – if you'll pardon the pun – with making the chips, so don't worry, you won't be stuck in the kitchen all day.' I lift the bucket of chipped potatoes and carry it into the shop. 'We'll get you serving customers as well, because that's the best bit of working here. Hello, Gwen. We don't usually see you on a Wednesday.' The chippy is empty, apart from Gwen, who's being served by Maryam.

'I know, love, but my Tim's over with his family for a week. Arrived this afternoon and they're already driving me up the wall. I love them to death, but I needed a break so I offered to treat us to an early fish and chip tea.'

'Salt and vinegar?' Maryam holds the salt shaker up.

'Yes, please, love. And I'll have a large brandy if you've got one handy back there.'

We all laugh, even though I don't think Gwen is kidding about the brandy.

'How are things at the charity shop?' Gran misses her volunteer work, especially the camaraderie of working in the shop on Saturday afternoons. She's slowly getting back to her normal routines after the fall – she's resumed her role of Brown Owl and she'll be returning to her lollipop lady duties after the Easter holidays – but the dog-walking and charity shop are still on hold.

'We had a rather… interesting donation the other day.' Gwen shuffles forward and leans her elbows on the counter. 'Now, I'm not going to name names, but a certain… mature lady, shall we say… brought in a bag of old clothes. Said she was having a clear-out and getting rid of the winter stuff she doesn't wear any more. Which is fair enough. Except, nestled in amongst her jumpers and cardigans was a pair of nipple tassels. I couldn't believe it! I mean, what would a ninety-odd-year-old woman want with *those*?' Gwen raises her eyebrows as she straightens up and grabs the bag from the counter. 'Anyway, I'd better get this lot back to Tim and the kids before it gets cold.' She raises a hand in farewell and then she's gone.

'Is it always like this?' Abbie's eyes are fixed on the window, watching as Gwen crosses the road.

'It can be.' I don't want to put Abbie off working here, but I also want her to be prepared, because that morsel of gossip is pretty tame by Gwen's standards. Her tales from the charity shop are legendary. They're yet another thing I'll miss if I jump ship.

'I think I'm going to like working here.' A grin spreads across Abbie's face as she watches Gwen disappear from view, and I can't help smiling myself.

'It is a great place to work, even if I could do with less of the old lady nipple tassels.' My phone starts to ring in the pocket of my tabard as the door opens and Babs steps into the shop. I must have forgotten to turn it off earlier.

'Here you go, Abbie. Your first customer. Want to have a go?'

Babs is the perfect customer to ease Abbie into the job; she wouldn't stop smiling even if the new girl completely ballsed the order up. Abbie bites her bottom lip, but she nods and heads for the counter without any hint of nerves. Leaving Maryam to supervise, I head to the back room to answer my phone. I wouldn't usually answer while working, but there have to be some perks to being manager, however temporary.

'Hello?' I don't recognise the number displayed, so I'm expecting it to be one of those annoying scam calls. Not that I have much money for them to scam from me.

'Can I speak to Cleo Parker?'

I pull out a chair in the back room and plonk myself down, holding back a sigh as I prepare myself for the spiel I've heard a million times before. 'Speaking.'

'Hi, it's Nigel Wolfenden, the HR officer from Brightman Rose Limited.'

I sit up a bit straighter, startling myself when the chair lurches to the right. HR officer. Some company that sounds vaguely familiar. This must be about a job I've applied for.

'You had an interview with us a little while ago.'

I slump down again. Of course. Nigel. Brightman Rose Limited. The chewing gum on my tights fiasco, followed by a terrible interview that resulted in an inevitable wouldn't-employ-you-in-a-million-years rejection email (it didn't say that, obviously, but I'm still feeling rather bitter about the whole process).

'And I'm delighted to offer you the role of junior credit controller.'

There's a pause while I try to get my head around the job offer. Nigel is presumably trying to persuade his voice to *sound* as delighted as he's claiming, because it currently sounds as flat as a pancake that's been run over by a monster truck. Repeatedly.

'But you already turned me down. You thanked me for my interest in the position but said you'd gone with a candidate with more experience.' And presumably a candidate who arrived for the interview on time and without a ladder running the length of their tights.

'Yes. That's right.' Nigel clears his throat. 'But that, er, didn't quite work out. So if you're still interested in the position…'

'Yes! I am.' I leap to my feet, almost knocking my chair over with my zeal. 'Very interested. Couldn't be more interested if I tried.'

I can't believe it. I've actually secured myself a new job. An office-based job with career prospects, just like I set out to do. And I'm sure once the shock has worn off, I'll feel absolutely *delighted* about it and the overwhelming urge to burst into tears will subside.

- *Days until I see Paul: 1*

- *Excitement level: Heart palpitations*

- *Grown-Up To-Do List score: 11/19 – could do better*

Chapter Thirty-Seven

Things move pretty quickly after the job offer. I hand my notice in to Russell at the same time as I sign the tenancy agreement for the flat, making it a bittersweet moment, and we agree that my last shift will be the early evening shift on the Friday before my Monday start date at Brighthouse Rose Limited (or whatever it's called). My final shift rocks around far too quickly and the shock hasn't had enough time to wear off, so I'm still feeling an overpowering sense of sadness at leaving The Fish & Chip Shop Around The Corner. But that's to be expected: I've worked there since I was seventeen, and it's the only job I've ever had, so of course I'm feeling bereft. But it'll pass and the excitement of starting my new job will take over, I'm sure.

'You can still wear them, you know.' Claire has caught me forlornly stroking my baggiest hoodie, and she places a hand on my shoulder, giving it a gentle squeeze. 'Imagine how great it'll feel to chuck your work clothes aside and sink into these babies.' We've been shopping for some office-attire staples that I can mix and match this morning, which are now sitting beside the cosy hoodies and worn T-shirts in my wardrobe. 'Shall we try out your new coffee machine?'

This purchase is much more cheering, and I manage a genuine smile as we head into the kitchen, where the coffee machine is yet to be unboxed. I've bought a shed-load of pods, which are filling Bolan's former cupboard, and I leave Claire to make her selection while I set the machine up.

'It'll be okay, you know. Starting your new job.'

We've moved through to the living room, where the sofa is now devoid of photo cushions. I kind of miss Russell, Jed and Bolan staring up at me, but Gran has promised to whip me up some new cushions on her sewing machine as soon as her wrist is up to it.

'I know.' I smile as sincerely as I can muster, so Claire will stop worrying about me. I am a grown-up, with a new grown-up credit controller career about to take off. There really is nothing to worry about. 'Everyone's nervous about starting a new job.'

'And that's all it is? Nerves?'

I admit, I had a bit of a wobble about leaving The Fish & Chip Shop Around The Corner, in between saying yes to Nigel whatshisface and handing in my notice, but it's the right thing to do. Everyone has moved on to bigger and better things since leaving school, so why should I be left behind? Paul's a business owner, Peter's a doctor and Demi – little Demi Marsh, who followed us around like an annoying shadow – is a well-respected interior designer who's been on the flipping telly. I didn't have a clue who Paul was talking about when we bumped into each other a few months ago, but it was the new haircut that finally solved the mystery. After Shelby commented on the photo, it received a like from the enigmatic Demi, who then friend-requested me. It all came flooding back as soon as I saw the photo from her profile; her hair may have been chopped into a spiky pixie style, and her skin had cleared and the braces were gone, but she was undoubtedly Courtney's cousin. A couple of years younger than us, she'd idolised us and we'd been unable to shift her, no matter how hard we tried. And now that irritating hanger-on is far more successful than I could ever imagine being.

'It's just nerves, I promise.' I grab my coffee, so I don't have to meet Claire's eye and she doesn't clock how dishonest I'm being. Because it isn't nerves that's causing the knot in my stomach. It isn't nerves that's making me queasy and tearful. It's almost grief-like, the knowledge that today will be my last shift at the chippy, but I have to do this. I can't be the only one left behind all over again.

–

'All ready for your new job?' We don't usually see Mrs Hornchurch in the chippy on a Friday evening, but she's shuffled her weekly plans around so I can serve her one last time, which I think is rather sweet.

'I think so.' I concentrate on jostling the salt shaker over Mrs Hornchurch's fish and chips so she can't see the grimace that appears whenever I think about Brighton Rose Limited (or whatever it's called. I really must commit the company's name to memory before Monday morning).

'Bit nervous?' Mrs Hornchurch reaches across the counter to give my shoulder a squeeze. 'That's to be expected, but you'll be fine once you get into the swing of things. We'll miss you though.' She gives my shoulder another gentle squeeze and I concentrate *really hard* on wrapping up the food so I don't burst into snotty tears. Because I'll miss Mrs Hornchurch too. I'll miss all the customers – even the most obnoxious teenagers who launch chips about the place – and I can't even think about the staff without wanting to bawl my eyes out. Even Bridget brings a lump to my throat. 'I hope you've trained them all up so they can make my fish just the way I like it.'

'Light and crisp, Mrs Hornchurch?' Maryam's bagging up her own customer's order, but she looks over at mine. 'Don't worry, we've all been practising.'

'Glad to hear it.' Mrs Hornchurch hands over the money for the fish and chips. 'Although I'll always have a soft spot for Cleo's. She makes the best fish in Clifton-on-Sea.' I want to thank her, but I think I'll burst into tears if I open my mouth so I simply give a wobbly smile as I hand over her change. 'Good luck in your new job.' She raises her hand in farewell and I do the same while pressing my lips together to hold in the wail that's hovering. Luckily, my next customer is Fleetwood Jack, so there's no danger of sentimentality there.

'What can I get you, Jack?'

'I'll have a chip muffin. No butter on the muffin.'

Oh, God. I don't think I can take any more. This shift is killing me. I'm even going to miss *Jack*. Turning away from him, I press a hand to my stomach and try to keep the guttural roar of grief at bay with a few deep breaths.

'Are you okay?' Maryam places a hand on my back, and I nod as I take another deep breath.

'Fine. Absolutely. But I think we need more chips. Can you…?' I waft a hand in Jack's direction before I flee to the kitchen.

I'm being ridiculous. People change jobs all the time, and it isn't as though I'll never see these people again. I'll still need my own fix of fish and chips, and I'm bound to bump into them in town. And at least I'll be able to hold my head up high when I meet up with Paul tomorrow, and there'll be a ring of truth to those little white lies I told the last time I saw him: the career, the driving, the being a proper grown-up.

'Hey, you.' Russell pokes his head around the kitchen door while I'm delicately slicing a mountain of potatoes into thick chips, fully aware I'll never work in this kitchen again. 'I've got a surprise visitor for you.'

My stomach drops to the floor. Paul. Catching me out at the very last minute. Just when I thought I'd managed to pull this whole thing off!

'*Jed.*' Relief and happiness and a dollop of melancholy flood my body as my soon-to-be-former boss appears in the doorway. 'What are you doing here?'

'I couldn't let my favourite employee swan off to their glittering new career without saying a proper goodbye, could I?'

I place the knife down on the chopping board and swipe my starchy hands down my tabard before rushing over to hug him, pulling Russell in too while trying my hardest not to cry.

'Speaking of a proper goodbye, we thought we'd take you out for a little send-off.' Russell places a gentle thumb on my cheek, where a pesky tear must have escaped. 'There's a T. Rex tribute band playing at the Red Lion tonight, so go and get glammed up and we'll pick you up in an hour.'

'But I'm not due to finish for another twenty minutes, and I'm in the middle of all this.' I indicate the potatoes, and while it isn't a task I'd normally fight for, I really don't want to leave a second before I have to. Because that'll be it then, won't it? I'll no longer work at The Fish & Chip

Shop Around The Corner. 'I'll finish my shift and then run upstairs to get ready.'

Russell shrugs. 'If that's what you want.'

I nod, though I'm not sure what I want any more. My determination to fulfil my grown-up to-do list seems to be wavering by the second.

–

I slice my last chip, dunk the basket into the fryer for the final time, and serve my last supper. I try to hang around for a bit longer – there's a bit of a queue forming and three tables need clearing – but Russell practically drags me out of the shop while Jed, Maryam and Ross applaud my departure, along with a couple of our regular customers. Russell nudges me in front of the window, so I'm standing underneath the arched lettering of The Fish & Chip Shop Around The Corner, and with Russell and Jed either side of me, Maryam takes a photo.

'Before you go and get ready for your *bon voyage* night out, we have a little gift for you.' Jed rummages in his pocket and pulls out a small gift-wrapped box. 'It isn't much, just a token to say thank you for being so brilliant, especially over the past few weeks.'

'The past few weeks where you lied through your teeth about what you were doing?' I give Jed and Russell a mock-stern look in turn, while my insides shrivel up a little more. Because this is really happening. I'm no longer an employee at The Fish & Chip Shop Around The Corner. Russell and Jed are no longer my bosses. On Monday, I'll have a new boss and new colleagues. I'll have a desk I'll have to sit behind *all day*, in restrictive clothing that I'll be longing to fling off as soon as I put it on. I won't get to chat to customers about weird charity shop donations, or their plans for the weekend, and there won't be any dancing around to Seventies hits or dodging chip missiles from rowdy teenage boys.

Okay, I won't miss the last one so much, but my heart feels heavy, the pressure building so much I'm convinced it's going to split in two. Gruesome.

'Yes, *those* past few weeks.' Jed hands over the little box and kisses me on the cheek. 'Thank you.'

The gift looks as though it's been wrapped while blind-folded, and there's so much tape I'm about to resort to using my teeth to tear through it when the paper finally gives, revealing a black hinged box. Nestled on the velvety pillow inside is a silver necklace with a little fish charm. His body shimmers with greens and blues while his face, fins and tail sparkle with tiny crystals. He is beautiful and sweet and perfect, and the thing that sends me over the edge.

'I'll wear it, always,' is what I attempt to say, but there's a lump the size of a boulder in my throat and my lips are trembling as I try not to cry in the street. I fail miserably, sobbing even harder as Russell and Jed gather me up in a massive hug. It's so tight, I can hardly breathe, but I don't care.

'No more tears, okay?' Russell wipes my tears away as best as he can with his thumbs and ignores the fact his own cheeks are wet. 'You're starting a new adventure, remember?'

I nod and wipe the rest of the tears away with the sleeve of my hoodie. I sneak a peek through the window, but quickly look away as more tears make my eyes burn. Maryam's returned to the shop and is laughing at some-thing one of the customers is saying as they gesticulate wildly while Ross is bopping away to whatever is playing on the radio as he shakes the basket of chips in the fryer.

'Now, young lady.' Russell starts to steer me towards the door that leads to the flat. 'You need to go and get ready for your big night out. The T. Rex tribute act is starting in…' He checks his watch and gasps. 'Twenty minutes. Go, go, go!' He pushes me the rest of the way and sighs as I take too long to wrestle my keys from my hoodie pocket underneath my tabard.

'If it's *my* big night out, why are we going to see a T. Rex tribute act? I'm more of a Barry Manilow girl myself.'

This isn't true, but it has the desired effect as Russell's eyes widen to painful proportions and his jaw drops to the pavement.

'Go and wash your mouth out. And wash your face while you're at it, it's all red and blotchy.' He pushes the door open as soon as I've turned the key, and I head inside, humming 'Copacabana' and relishing the vexed look I see on Russell's face just before the door closes behind me.

There isn't much in the way of party gear in my wardrobe, other than the dress I bought for the reunion with Paul tomorrow, so I change into the pale oyster skater dress I wore to Gran's birthday party. There isn't much I can do with my stupidly short hair, which is definitely far too high-maintenance for my liking – so I simply add a diamanté clip, which goes nicely with my new fish necklace.

'What took you so long?' Russell is still waiting outside the flat, and his finger jabs at the face of his watch. 'We're going to miss the start.'

'It isn't as though you gave me much notice.' And it took ages to mask the fact I've been blubbing. 'And we'll be even later if we stand here moaning about it.' I thread my arm through Russell's, which proves to be a mistake as I have to scuttle to keep up with his stride, which only quickens when we hear the low, filthy opening riff to 'Get It On' pulsing along the promenade. We have to push our way through the clusters of people spilling out onto the pavement outside the pub, and I recoil in shock and revulsion as one charming customer shoves his face up to mine so we're almost nose to nose and bellows the lyrics at me, his breath warm and pungent with tangs of beer and cigarettes. Russell pulls me to one side and leads me through the throng, parting the way with an authoritative outstretched hand.

'What are you having?' The pub is heaving, packed with hot, sweaty bodies, so Russell has to lean in close and yell in my ear.

'A pint, please.' I know I'm trying to be more sophisticated, but tonight I want to relax and enjoy myself and be *me*. The real me, not the version I'm trying to mould myself into, and I've got the rest of my life to be the new improved Cleo.

I'm jostled out of the way as Russell edges his way to the bar, and I'm forced to go with the flow until I end up near the low stage set up at the back of the pub where the band is playing. The lead singer is a pop of colour in the darkened pub, with his high-waisted gold satin trousers and a hot pink shirt with oversized lapels and the buttons open almost to his midriff. He's a bundle of energy, never seeming to stay still for a second as he marches across the small space on the stage, or stamps his foot to the beat, his fingers constantly moving on his guitar. He's fiery and passionate, oozing confidence and power. I try to shuffle around, to look for Russell as he'll hate missing a second of this, but it's too cramped to move and I'm finding it pretty difficult to tear my eyes away from the stage. The lead singer has a strange hold on me, as though he's reached out with invisible hands and grasped my face, holding it still so I can't look anywhere but at him. At his fingers on the guitar strings; at his shiny, flared trousers; at his hair, wild and bouncy, as though it has a life of its own. This is a man who is extremely comfortable in his own skin, even when that skin is clad in gold and pink satin, which should be off-putting but his confidence oozes and there's something mesmerising about that. Plus, his voice is sexy as hell.

'Cleo!'

I hear my name being called, and I make a half-hearted attempt to turn around again but my eyes don't want to move away from the stage.

'Cleo!'

There's movement behind me, and then Claire's squeezing in beside me, shooting daggers at the bloke next to her, who isn't pleased that he's been prodded out of the way.

'Hey, you.' I give her a quick hug before my eyes wander back towards the stage. 'What are you doing here?' I have to shout at the top of my voice to be heard over the music. It's so intense, I can feel the beat throbbing up from the floor.

'Russell said you'd be here.' Claire raises herself onto her tiptoes and searches the crowd. 'Where is he? And Jed?'

'Getting drinks.' I lean in towards Claire, but my eyes never leave the strangely magnetic lead singer.

'Here they are.' Claire thrusts her hand in the air and waggles it about. 'Russell! Jed! Over here!'

They manage to squeeze their way towards us, but instead of standing next to us, Russell grabs my free hand after passing me my drink and starts to pull me further into the crowd. 'We can do better than this. We can hardly see from back here.'

Like before, Russell somehow manages to make a path in the tightly packed audience until we're a couple of rows from the stage. The lead singer is looking down at his guitar as he plays, and my eyes are drawn to his fingers moving deftly over the strings until he looks up, throwing back his curls as the song comes to an end. The crowd erupts in applause, but I'm frozen, in shock, in amazement, as my eyes bore into the figure on the stage. Because the beard may be gone, and there may be glittery smudges on his cheeks and more eyeliner than Claudia Winkleman gets through in a month drawn underneath his eyes, but it's James standing up there in the gold and pink satin.

Thought of the Day:

Expect the Unexpected

(but surely there are some things that are too unexpected to expect?)

Chapter Thirty-Eight

I don't understand what I'm seeing. Can't comprehend how James, with his blazers and brogues and his snooze-fest job, can be the frontman of a T. Rex tribute act, performing with such confidence and vigour and radiating… what? Not sex appeal. It can't be sex appeal. This is *James* we're talking about. Steady-job James. Dad-of-two James. Quiet and unassuming James who watches *Midsomer Murders* with my gran and crochets stripy sausage dogs for charity raffles. How can *that* James be the one up onstage, pouting and strutting as he sings 'Solid Gold Easy Action', lapping up the reaction of the audience as they bounce up and down with the beat and clap along.

This can't be real. It's a joke, or a dream, or I've completely lost the plot and started to hallucinate.

'Oh my God.' Claire presses herself even tighter against me so she can shout in my ear. 'Is that…?' She looks at the stage, her eyes in danger of popping out of her skull when she turns back to me. 'It is! It's James!' She points at the stage, jumping up and down in excitement at the discovery. 'Did you know he did this?'

I shake my head, unable to conjure any words. I'd had no idea. I knew James was a fan of Seventies music, and I knew he used to be in a band before Seth was born, but I'd never heard him play or sing or hint at being part of a T. Rex tribute act. Oh! He did recently mention having a second job, but I just assumed it would be doing some-body's books on the side or something equally mundane. I had no idea it would be something like *this*.

'This is *amazing*!' Claire raises her arms in the air and claps along with the beat. 'Isn't this amazing?'

I'm not sure 'amazing' is how I would describe this situation. Incredibly unsettling would be more accurate, because I still can't take my eyes off James as he performs. I'm mesmerised, even though I know this isn't some random dude in orange and pink satin swaggering about up there. This is my friend. My predictable, blazer-wearing friend who is currently making my tummy go all funny every time he pouts or throws back his curls. This isn't the stuffy accountant I know. This James is energetic and powerful, someone who can somehow appear charis-matic despite the ridiculous outfit, and I've never seen him looking so happy. His face breaks out in a grin during a small instrumental gap, and how he looks right now is how I feel when I'm being silly at work, dancing around the chippy to 'Tiger Feet', or when Mrs Hornchurch tells me I make the best fish and chips in town, or when Russell and Jed put their trust in me to keep the chippy going during their absence. It hits me all over again what I've given up, only this time there's the niggling doubt that the trade-off doesn't seem worth it.

Claire nudges me, and I'm forced to drag my eyes off the stage. 'Ugh, look who's over there.' I follow her gaze and see Riley with his arm around the waist of a blonde woman with a Wotsit coating of fake tan and a way-too-short skirt. 'He isn't in a coma then. Shame.' Claire tips half of her glass of wine down her throat. 'I really am having a break from men. They're all pigs, so what's the point?'

It's approximately thirty-five seconds later when Claire grabs my hand in a death grip and hisses in my ear about the *absolute GOD* over by the bar. Some things never change, and I'm glad about that.

-

The band go out on a high, performing '20th Century Boy' as though it's the last time they will ever play together. The drummer's whole body is involved in the percussion, the guitarist is bouncing around the stage like a cattle-prodded Tigger, and James is utterly intoxicating. The audience erupt as the song comes to an end, and Russell is so caught up in the moment, he gathers me up in a massive hug, hoisting me up off my feet and spinning us in a circle in the tight space. Plonking me back down on the ground, he places his hands on Claire's cheeks and throws his head back, bellowing, 'That. Was. *Amazing*,' towards the ceiling.

'I think Russell enjoyed that.' Claire rubs her cheeks as Russell marches through the crowd towards the bar, but she's grinning. 'I think somebody else enjoyed it too. Or, rather, she enjoyed watching James.' I glance around the crowd, trying to working out who she's talking about.

'*You*, you great turnip. You were like this the whole time.' She places her hands underneath her chin and adopts a dopey-looking expression before heaving out a long sigh.

'I was not.' I roll my eyes, sneaking a peek at the stage. The drummer is still up there, chatting to a couple of blokes, but James has disappeared.

'You like him.' Claire shrugs. 'And why wouldn't you?'

'Because I'm meeting up with Paul tomorrow? You know, the bloke I've had a crush on *forever*.'

'The bloke you've stopped mentioning every five minutes recently? That one?'

I open my mouth to deny the accusation, but realise she's right. I don't talk about Paul as much as I used to, but that's only because it must be incredibly boring to hear about your friend's crush on a loop. And I no longer incessantly check my phone for messages because I don't need to; Paul and I will be meeting in the flesh in less than twenty-four hours.

'You've had a crush on Paul forever, but maybe it's time you moved on?' Claire grabs me by the shoulders and spins me around. The crowd has dissipated and I can see the bar now, where James is standing with Russell, nodding along to whatever he's saying. 'And speaking of moving on…' She twists me to the right, where the 'god' from earlier is making his way over towards us. 'Come and meet my next one-night stand.'

'That sounds really, really fun, but I'm lying and I'm going to slip away so you can flirt in peace.' Dodging Claire's grasp, I make a beeline for the loos, where I can shut myself in a cubicle for a few minutes to process what's happened tonight: I'm officially no longer an employee at The Fish & Chip Shop Around The Corner, and I seem to have developed a bit of a 'thing' for James after seeing him in a shiny pink and gold get-up (what is *that* about?) even though I'm meeting up with Paul tomorrow. It's been quite an evening, all things considered, but I can't remain holed up in the ladies much longer as there's a queue forming, judging from the sound of the disgruntled voices outside the cubicle and I don't want to give the impression I'm having a poo in here.

The pub is still busy when I emerge, but it's no longer heaving and Russell spots me and waves me over to the bar. James is still with him, and I edge towards them, my stomach doing funny little somersaults. I'm almost nervous, even though it's only James, as though the flamboyant outfit and lack of facial hair have transformed him into an entirely new person.

'I didn't know you did...' I turn towards the stage, where only the drummer and a couple of groupies remain. 'This.'

'I didn't. Not until recently. I mean, I've known those guys for ages. I went to school with Tom and Will, and we were in a band together until I left to change nappies and earn an actual living, but we've always kept in touch. Their lead singer left a few weeks ago — creative differences, something about him being an utter bellend — and they asked me to step in. I wasn't sure at first, but then I thought of you and said yes.'

'Me?' I frown, trying not to feel alarmed that I've somehow turned James from a blazer-and-brogues-wearing accountant into a shiny-trouser-wearing showman without even realising it. What will I cause him to do next? Trade his sensible family car in for a penny-farthing? Swap his new cottage for a canal boat (which sounds lovely, actually, but there are no canals in Clifton-on-Sea, and I'm not sure Seth would be seen dead on one).

'Yes, you.' James grins at me, and the movement makes the glittery splodges sparkle on his cheeks. 'You're so brave, doing all these new things, so I thought, why can't I do that too? Just go for it and do something that makes me happy? And I'm so glad I did, because that was... incredible.'

'I'm glad, though I still don't get why it's down to me. I haven't done anything like this.' The closest I've got to a glam rock performance is singing along to Russell's CDs in the shower, before he packed them up to transfer them to Manchester.

'You've done loads of new things recently. Driving lessons. Moving into your own place for the first time. Getting a new job. So, thank you, because there's no way I would have done that without your influence.' James closes the gap between us again and stoops down to kiss my cheek. It's only a peck that lasts a nanosecond, but this time it's me who takes a step back. Because something strange just happened as his lips brushed against my cheek, something that's making my heart race painfully fast and causing my insides to turn to mush. Something that's making me want to grab James' face in my hands and snog the life out of him. Which I'm obviously not going to do, especially on the eve of my reunion with Paul.

'I'd better get going.' I start to back away, but James grabs hold of my arm.

'Wait.'

I catch his eye, and I'm pretty sure that James felt whatever it was I just did too. But I can't stay and find out for certain. Wriggling free, I turn and scurry from the pub.

Tomorrow, Paul will be here and we can start the life I've been planning for over a decade.

Today's Very Important To-Do List:

- *Go to the hairdresser's*

- *Long soak in the bath*

- *Paint nails*

- *Make Paul fall head over heels in love with me (finally!!!)*

Chapter Thirty-Nine

I manage to get a walk-in appointment at the hairdresser's mid-afternoon so I can look my best for my date with Paul tonight. On a whim, I decide to get the pink tips put back in, and while my hair is still too short to gather up in a messy bun, I feel more like me when I leave the hairdresser's. I may have tweaked my job but I've realised I want Paul to see the real me tonight. I'm not sophisticated and probably never will be, but so what? I can't pretend to be someone else forever, so Paul is going to have to accept the rough-around-the-edges Cleo.

I celebrate my new mindset with coffee and cake, sitting in the window of the coffee shop so I can watch the families and couples on the promenade. High season is in full swing, so the beach will be packed every weekend for the next few months, bleeding into weekdays once the school summer holidays start. But I won't be in the thick of it this year, frantically serving customers in the chippy all day until it feels like I could collapse, exhausted but happy. The thought makes me sad, but I can't dwell on the past. I have a bright future ahead of me with Paul, so I have to focus on that.

I think about popping in on Gran after my afternoon treat, but I'm afraid of bumping into James and having to face up to those weird feelings from last night, so I head straight to the flat and have a long soak in the bath instead. Russell has cleared the shelf in the living room of his CDs and I miss the soundtrack of the flat, so I set up a Seventies playlist on Spotify. I have to lean out of the bath and skip one of the songs when I hear the intro to 'Get It On', because it conjures a snapshot of last night, of James with his head thrown back, fist held up in the air, the atmosphere electric and my stomach wonderfully squirmy. I think of Paul instead, squeezing my eyes shut and relishing the images of him from his Instagram. I play out the memory of that last night we had together: getting drunk in the Red Lion, spilling out on to the beach, Paul walking me home. His fingers playing with my hair. 'Your dreads are so cool. They make you one of a kind. Unique.' The kiss. Tonight is going to be amazing. It'll be like the past seven years haven't happened, as though we've slipped from that doorstep kiss to this moment, where everything can play out as it should have back then.

I haul myself out of the bath once the water starts to turn cold. I have loads to do before our date tonight, including painting my nails, updating my bullet journal and other things that will keep me busy. Too busy to think about James.

I paint my nails a rainbow of colours, as a nod to the rainbow dreadlocks. I've bought a new teal wrap dress for the occasion, which is cute and comfortable and swishes delightfully as I twirl around the bedroom until I feel dizzy. I was going to wear the shoes I've been wearing for my interviews (and that I can now walk in without stumbling) but I select my new pair of white high-top Converse instead, in a bid to further present the real me. The real me doesn't wear heels, even tiny, barely there ones, and while she may not have a boast-worthy career yet, she's working on it and she's beginning to see that her life is pretty fabulous.

With a bit of mascara, eyeliner and a nude lip gloss, plus my little fish necklace, I'm ready. Taking a couple of deep breaths, I lock up the flat and head for the pub to restart the life I put on hold almost a decade ago.

–

The Red Lion is busy, but it isn't heaving, and I feel a bit exposed as I step inside, my eyes darting first around the bar and then the seating areas in search of Paul.

'Cleo? Oh my God, it *is* you.'

A pair of arms are thrown around me before I've had the chance to identify their owner, but I pat her lightly on the back while trying to figure out who it can be.

'You haven't changed a bit.' I'm released from the hug and held at arm's length. 'Well, apart from the dreads. And the nose ring. Didn't you used to have an eyebrow piercing as well? Or am I thinking of Shelby? Never mind. We're outside in the beer garden. I only popped in for a top-up.' She holds up a couple of empty glasses and gives them a wobble. 'What are you having?'

She heads for the bar, and I follow, my mouth opening and closing as I try to figure out what to say. Her hair is slightly longer than the pixie cut from Instagram, with a more shaggy look, but it's definitely her. The question is, what is she doing back in Clifton-on-Sea?

'It's so good to see everyone again after so long, isn't it?' She's on her tiptoes as she tries to catch the attention of the bar staff, still as short as she was when she used to follow us around town. 'Courtney's already here with her husband. Have you met Neil? I don't think you came to the wedding, did you? It was lovely. Intimate but so much fun. Shelby's brought her whole little family – hubby and baby. He's so adorable – the baby, not the hubby.' She giggles, covering her mouth with her hand. 'Spencer's here. No wife. Says it's the first night off from the missus he's had in ages. Typical Spence, right? Peter can't make it, unfortunately. He sends his apologies but his wife is due in, like, three days and he doesn't want to travel too far, just in case. They're down in Buckinghamshire now. Gorgeous house. Five bedrooms with a self-contained granny flat. We were there for Nancy's baby shower a few weeks ago. I had *serious* house envy!'

Courtney, Shelby and Spencer are here? Even Demi, forever our little shadow.

'Shall I just get a bottle? Shelby isn't drinking, and Spencer, Liv and Paul are on pints, but it makes sense to get a bottle, doesn't it? Now you're here.'

'I guess.' I attempt to lift my lips upwards into a smile, but I'm so confused. What are they doing here, today of all days?

With the bottle of wine and a fresh set of glasses, we step out into the beer garden at the back of the pub, into the glare of the spring sunshine. And there they are, the faces I recognise from the past. Courtney hasn't changed much, apart from having much shorter hair that really suits her, and while Shelby's a bit rounder in the face and a bit puffy under the eyes (which probably has much more to do with the baby nestled in the sling attached to her front than the passing of time) she still looks like the school friend I remember. Spencer is much bulkier than he was at eighteen, with biceps the size of barrels and a neck that seems to have disappeared. His grip is alarmingly tight as we hug, and I feel a bit bruised as I sit down at the table. Opposite, Paul raises his pint in greeting, much less enthusiastic at my arrival than Spencer was. His other arm is slung around the back of the chair next to him where a small blonde woman sits. I recognise her from his Instagram posts. Olivia. The gym buddy. Except I don't think she is simply a gym buddy. I think I've been a bit foolish over these past few weeks, seeing things I wanted to see and ignoring the things I didn't.

This isn't a date.

This is a reunion of old school friends.

–

'Sienna's on her way!' Demi holds her phone up, where a text message has just come through. 'She's just got off the train so should be here in a few minutes.'

I've been feeling rather unsettled since I arrived and discovered that Paul hadn't been planning a date for two all this time but a group meetup, but I feel my spirits rise at the news of Sienna's imminent arrival. I haven't seen her since we hugged goodbye at the airport after Grandad's stroke. She'd offered to come back with me, but I declined; Sienna had grasped the whole travelling-the-world thing much more readily than I had, and she was loving the adventure. I couldn't drag her away, even if it was a wrench to leave her.

'She's come over from New Zealand?' A balloon of affection for my old BFF inflates in my chest, but one odd look from Demi puts a pin to it.

'Er, no. Scotland. She hasn't lived in New Zealand for two years.' She snorts in a didn't-you-know kind of way, which I didn't. 'She's in Edinburgh. Not that far from me.'

'How did she end up there?' The balloon has well and truly deflated now. Sienna has been back in the UK for a couple of years and she didn't even bother to get back in contact? I wouldn't have been hard to track down, being in the exact same place I've always been.

'It's where Cam's from?' Demi frowns at me, and I'm hit full-force by how little I know about Sienna's life after I'd got on that plane back home. Because I'd always assumed Cam was from New Zealand; it's where they lived, where they married, where they had babies. 'They moved back when Cam's mum was diagnosed. We only met up by chance – I was working on a refit of a shop next door to their local pub.' She grabs the bottle of wine from the table – the second since I arrived – and tops up the three glasses. 'Oh, I brought photos!' After shaking the last drops out of the bottle, she reaches into her handbag and pulls out a wallet of photos, taking them out and spreading them across the table. 'Look, here's Spencer and Courtney when they were Spentney. All loved up. How cute! Sorry, Neil. Gah, look at my hair in this one. I look like Morticia Addams.'

I grab one of the photos that was taken on the beach, with the Ferris wheel visible on the pier in the distance. It's a group shot, with Paul rubbing Spencer's hair with his knuckles on the left and Peter and Courtney laughing their heads off at something on the right. I'm standing in the middle with Sienna, my arm slung around her shoulders and my eyes squeezed shut as I kiss her on the cheek while she's sticking her tongue out at the camera and crossing her eyes.

'Look what a weedy tosser Paul was.' Spencer holds up one of the photos of Paul, who's posing on the steps leading down to the beach in a pair of paisley shorts. I look at the photo, waiting for the butterflies to take flight in my tummy, but I can't get excited about the

344

seventeen-year-old boy in the photo. I look across at Paul, who's giggling at another photo with Olivia, but I still feel nothing. Which is bizarre. I prepare myself for the punch in the gut as he nudges her playfully before leaning in to kiss her, but I don't feel much at all. Certainly no sting of jealousy.

'*I* was a weedy tosser? Look at the state of you.' Paul frisbees a photo towards Spencer, who roars with laughter when he spots his younger self splashing in the sea in his boxer shorts with Sienna and Shelby. It was taken that last night, before we all went our separate ways, the image grainy in the fading light of that summer night. It had felt so magical at the time, as though we were all on the cusp of amazing lives, but the camera hadn't managed to capture the enchantment the same way my memories have.

'Things were different back then, weren't they?' Shelby rocks the baby in the sling as she reaches for another photo, smiling wistfully at it. 'We were young and free. We could do anything. *Be* anything. Not like now. I'm dreading going back to the office once my maternity leave's finished. I mean, look at her.' Shelby holds up a photo of her younger self puckering up besides the Captain John statue outside the arcade. 'She'd be heartbroken if she knew she'd have to sit in an office all day, staring at a screen while hoping Bad Breath Brenda doesn't pop over for a chat.'

'Don't tell her about the commute.' Courtney rolls her eyes. 'An hour each way – on a good day. Soul-destroying.'

'At least you don't have to deal with yummy mummies and TikTok posers all day.'

I frown across at Paul. 'I thought you loved your job.'

He shrugs and reaches for his pint. 'I do, mostly, but no job is perfect, is it?'

Working at The Fish & Chip Shop Around The Corner felt pretty perfect. Even sweeping up missile chips thrown by teenage boys doesn't seem so bad when compared to wasting two hours plus of your life every day simply getting to work and back home again. The crush of the bus ride to my interview at Brightman Rose pops into my head, the panic of being late washing over me all over again followed by the revulsion of discovering I was tethered to the seat by someone else's chewing gum.

Oh, dear lord. What have I done?

'Did you become a journalist like you always wanted to be?'

I frown at Paul again, confused for a moment because I told him I had the day we bumped into each other outside my parents' house. But he can't remember, because it was three months ago and he hasn't carefully dissected every single exchange we've had since that day. Because he isn't interested in me like that. I doubt he even remembers that kiss on my doorstep, and there's no way he's obsessed over it all these years. I don't cause butterflies to take flight in his tummy whenever he thinks of me.

But then there are no butterflies fluttering around my tummy now either. The spell, it seems, has finally been broken.

'I'm starting a new job on Monday, actually.' I try to muster a smidgen of enthusiasm, but there is none forthcoming. I'll be joining Courtney on the commute and staring at a computer screen all day like Shelby, hoping Bad Breath Brenda doesn't descend.

'Congratulations!' Demi raises her glass, clinking it against mine when I half-heartedly follow suit. 'What will you be doing?'

I don't get the chance to answer because Sienna arrives, causing Demi to jump out of her seat with a squeal. Shelby's baby howls at being woken, while Demi bounces across the courtyard and flings her arms around Sienna.

Sienna's changed dramatically over the past few years. The waist-length brown hair has been chopped into an asymmetrical, pillar-box-red bob, and the jeans and T-shirts have made way for black tapered trousers, a leather jacket and a skull-printed scarf. I don't think I would have recognised her if I'd passed her in the street. The only sign of the old Sienna is the rose tattoo on her middle finger that we had done before we set off for our adventure around the world.

'Hey, guys.' Sienna drags her small suitcase over to the table, stopping to coo at the baby, who's still disgruntled but in a less fierce way. Her eyebrows shoot up when she spots me and she rushes over, flinging her arms around me in a forceful but brief hug. 'Cleo! It's been so long! You haven't changed a bit.' She drops into the empty seat between Spencer and Courtney's husband and pounces on the photos, pulling a face as she holds up a photo of her, Paul and me. Paul's in the middle, his arms slung around our shoulders as we all grin at the camera while squinting against the sun. 'Ugh. Look at the state of us. Proper minging.' She drops the photo and picks up another. 'Eww, I still have my braces in this one.' She runs her tongue over her teeth as she tosses the photo back down onto the pile on the table. 'I need a drink after seeing those.'

'I'll go.' Demi jumps out of her seat again. 'What are you having? The usual?'

Sienna's 'usual' drink when we were teenagers was a lurid alcopop (any would do) but I doubt that's her beverage of choice these days. Whatever it is, Demi seems to know and she heads back into the pub without needing any more clarity.

'Hey, Liv. All ready for your holiday?' Sienna's flicking through a handful of photos she's gathered from the table, but she looks across at Paul's girlfriend.

'Yep. Can't wait.' Olivia smiles, the action brightening up her whole face and making her look even prettier.

'You staying at Debbie and Marco's place again?'

I have no idea who Debbie or Marco are, but it sparks a conversation between Sienna, Paul and Olivia that I tune out of. While I have a shared history with Paul and Sienna, it's clear they have a shared present. They've all kept in contact over the years – attending weddings and birthday parties and baby showers – while I dropped off the radar until a chance encounter in the street outside my parents' house. The rose tattoos on our middle fingers were supposed to symbolise our BFF status, but Sienna and I are no longer even Fs, forever or otherwise.

'Oh, God. Do you remember when we got these?' I hadn't realised I'd been rubbing my rose tattoo, but Sienna leans across the table, slapping her hand down next to mine. 'I remember Paul trying to chat me up the day we got them. Told me how cute it was. How *unique* I was with my little rose tattoo, until I told him it wasn't unique at all, that you had the exact same one. That was the *whole point*.' She leans back in her seat and shoots Paul a disparaging look. 'He was always trying to get in my pants back then.'

Courtney snorts. 'Mine too. Even when I was with Spencer.'

'You what?' Spencer's jaw drops in outrage, but he laughs and shakes his head. 'You little shit. I had no idea.'

Neither did I.

I'd thought *I* was unique, with my rainbow dreads. But it turns out I was just the last in line when it came to snogging his female friends. I've clung on to the idea of being a star-crossed lover all these years, pining for The One Who Got Away, but it's all been a delusion in my own head. I mean nothing to Paul – to Franko – and I never have.

'You never told us about your new job, Cleo.' Demi's returned with a shot glass of amber liquid, which she hands to Sienna before sitting down.

I open my mouth to tell her that I'm about to become a junior credit controller, but I don't want to do that, because I don't want it to be true.

'I used to work in the chippy. You remember the one on Winden Street?' I scrape back my chair as I stand up. 'And hopefully I can still work there.' My fingers find the fish charm around my neck. 'Sorry, I have to go. It was great seeing you all again. It really was.'

Because now I can let go of the past and live the life *I* want to. I just hope it isn't too late.

The New Grown-Up To-Do List:

- *Be yourself*

Chapter Forty

I should feel like a total fool as I leg it from the pub, but I don't have time for self-flagellation. I'll give myself a major talking-to later but, at this moment in time, I need to concentrate on putting things right. I'm glad I chose to wear the Converse over the heels as I push my way through the pub doors and sprint along the pavement towards Winden Street. Jed dashed back to Manchester this morning, but Russell is still in town so he can tie up any remaining loose ends before the agency manager arrives on Monday morning.

'Is Russell here?' I collapse against the counter after bursting into the chippy, my breath ragged and chest burning after the race over here from the pub.

'He's in the back.' Bridget places a neatly packaged portion of chips on the counter, refusing to make eye contact with me. She's livid that she hasn't been given the manager's position and has somehow piled the blame on me.

'I'll just…' I lift a hand and wave it limply towards the back of the shop.

With supreme effort, I push myself away from the counter and limp to the back room, knocking on the door before stepping in. Russell's sitting at the table in front of a pile of papers, his eyebrows pulled down low as he concentrates. They lift up in surprise when he looks up and sees me on the threshold. My fingers find the little fish charm around my neck, and I hold it gently between my finger and thumb. Claire and James have been telling me for weeks that I'd be crazy to give up a job I love, but it's only now that I realise I've made a terrible decision for all the wrong reasons. I've sacrificed a job I love to try to meet an ideal I set myself in the hope of impressing a bunch of people I don't even know any more. I adored my job at The Fish & Chip Shop Around The Corner, so why couldn't that be enough? Not for Paul or Sienna or the others, but for *me*?

'I've changed my mind. About the manager position. I don't want to leave The Fish & Chip Shop Around The Corner. I love working here. I don't know why I ever thought it was a good idea to find a new job. I'm a fool. A massive fool.' I'm jabbering, throwing words at Russell at an alarming rate, getting them out there before I change my mind again. 'If the offer is still there, I'd like to stay and be the manager.'

Russell rises slowly from his chair and edges around the table towards me. 'Of course the offer is still there.' He reaches out to place a hand on my arm, but changes his mind and, with a grin spreading across his face, he pulls me into a hug that has me gasping for breath. 'I'm so pleased you're staying. The chippy will be in the very best hands.'

'It isn't too late? With the agency and everything?' I can barely get the words out with my chest being crushed, and Russell seems to realise and relaxes his arms so that only one is now loosely draped across my shoulders.

'We'll sort it. It'll be fine, don't worry.'

'Don't you have to discuss this with Jed?'

'Are you kidding me?' Russell takes my hand in his, squeezing gently. 'If he found out that I'd hesitated for even a *nanosecond* in accepting, he'd have my nuts for breakfast. Not a very pleasant breakfast, admittedly, but you get the gist.'

'Do I have to give the necklace back?' I pinch the little fish between my finger and thumb again. 'Because I won't give it up without a fight.'

'It's yours, forever.' Russell takes my other hand in his and we have a little dance around the back room until I drag myself away from the chippy, because there's one more thing I need to do tonight before I lose my nerve.

–

James is back to wearing his usual weekend attire of slim-fit jeans, a slate-grey T-shirt and a pair of brown brogues. He isn't wearing a blazer, but I know there'll be one knocking about, ready to slip on should he need to leave the house. I'm not disappointed though, because although the gold-and-pink-clad James was exciting and dynamic, the regular James isn't so bad either. He's fun and kind and bizarrely giving me butterflies as he stands at the front door of my gran's house.

'Hi.' I look down at the doorstep, willing my cheeks to cool down as I feel them start to blaze like a pair of glow sticks. 'Can I come in?'

'Yes.' The word is elongated, and when I sneak a peek at James, his face is scrunched up in bemusement. 'Of course you can.' He moves aside and I step into the house, turning to shuffle sideways along the hallway.

'Is this a bad time?' The hallway is filled with boxes so there's only just enough room to move down to the kitchen.

'The kids have gone to Cyprus with Carla and her parents and Cordy's at Gwen's, so I thought it'd be the perfect opportunity to get some packing done. I should be getting the keys to my new place on Monday. Big day, eh? You're starting your new job and I'm finally getting out of your gran's hair.'

'I've actually asked for my old job back.' My fingers find the little fish charm, and I move it gently up and down the chain. 'So I won't be starting my new job after all.' I push the thought of Nigel Wolfenden and the phone call we're going to have to have away. 'And it's all down to you.'

'Me?' James pulls back his chin, and his cheeks shimmer with a few flecks of stubborn glitter from last night. 'How did I do that?' He grabs a couple of mugs from the cupboard, none of which are his usual David Bowie one, which I assume is now wrapped in newspaper and sitting in one of the boxes in the hallway.

'By being up on that stage last night, doing something you clearly love and not even caring that you were wearing a pair of shiny gold trousers and a pink shirt.'

James takes a small step back and opens his arms wide. 'You didn't like my new look?'

I try not to think about James up on the stage in that outfit, because it's making my cheeks flush again and my palms are prickling with sweat. If I think about James in that outfit, I'll replay his sultry, highly charged 'Dreamy Lady' performance and my insides will jumble themselves up all over again.

'My point is, you looked like you were having the time of your life up there. You looked so happy, and I want that for myself, but I know that if I really did leave The Fish & Chip Shop Around The Corner and start working at that

Butter Rose place, I'd be miserable. So yes, you inspired me to do what makes *me* happy.'

'I'm glad. You *should* be happy. You deserve it.' He reaches into the cupboard and holds out a coffee pod in each hand for me to choose from. I step forward and tap the vanilla latte pod. Being closer to James causes a weird sensation in my stomach, as though there's an octopus in there that's decided to have a good stretch of all its tentacles, in a not entirely unpleasant way.

'*You* make me happy.'

My cheeks feel as though they're actually on fire right now, and I expect the smoke alarm to shriek into life at any moment. I can no longer allow my gaze to rest on James and am currently appraising the worktop to his left, where the kettle sits. I don't know if James feels the same way about me – I could just be the annoying granddaughter of his landlady, but I hope not because these last few weeks have been wonderful. I had thought it was the idea of meeting up with Paul that brought me back to life, but it wasn't. It was James. Spending time with him, getting to know him, falling in love.

'I do?'

I still can't quite look at James, and I can't gauge his reaction from those two tiny words, but I decide to plough on anyway, to get everything out in the open before I chicken out. I never told Paul how I felt and look how that turned out. I pined for the man for almost a decade, and for nothing, because he didn't feel the same way. Isn't it better to take a risk, to find out one way or another?

'Yes, you do. Even though you're always so much better at everything than I am. Crochet, arcade games. Even the *dance machine*.'

'You won the sword fight in the park.'

'See, you're even better at keeping score than I am.'

'I can't help being so perfect. It's a curse.'

'But you're not so perfect, are you?' I brave a glance at James to raise my eyebrows at him. 'What about your terrible handwriting?'

'Ouch.' James clutches his stomach. 'Hit me where it hurts, why don't you? I should never have revealed my flaw.'

'Is that really your only flaw?'

James places the coffee pods on the worktop and shakes his head. 'Can you keep a secret?'

'Yes.' As long as keeping a secret involves sharing it with Claire, because best friends don't count, do they?

'I'm a terrible kisser.'

Disappointment thuds heavily in my stomach. 'Really?'

'Let's find out.'

In one seamless motion, James has closed the gap between us, pulled me towards him and is kissing me. And I instantly discover his flaw, right there in my gran's kitchen: James Merchant is a great big fibber, because there is nothing terrible about this. Nothing. At. All.

Five Awesome Things That Have Happened Over The Past Six Months:

- I passed my driving test and bought my first car (a second-hand, sunshine-yellow Fiat 500 called Connie)

- The Fish & Chip Shop Around The Corner came runner-up in the Best Chippy of the North-West Awards (I celebrated by treating myself and the staff to a shiny new coffee machine and a new table and chair set for the back room)

- Claire asked me to be her maid of honour when she marries Ainsley (the god she met during James' performance in the Red Lion)

- We celebrated Edith's birthday with a barbecue in the little yard behind my flat, followed by sandcastle-making on the beach (Edith LOVED it and even Seth had a brilliant time – and we have photos of him smiling to prove it!)

- Adopting Chip from the shelter, who has transformed from the most timid cat in the world to a cheeky (yet still respectful of my plants) and playful little bundle of fluff (I hope he settles as quickly into James' place when we move in next week!)

A Letter from Jennifer

Thank you so much for choosing to read *The Grown-Up To-Do List*. I wrote the first draft of the book way back in 2020, during the first lockdown, squeezed in between home schooling and shuffling around the supermarket car park. It was a wonderful escape from reality at that time. There was no Covid in Cleo's world, no restrictions or lateral flow tests or face masks, and Cleo wouldn't have a clue what an R rate was. Clifton-on-Sea was a safe haven from what was happening around us and it was such a joy to slip away there for an hour or two each day and I hope *The Grown-Up To-Do List* brought you as much joy or escapism as it did for me.

If you enjoyed Cleo's story I would be so grateful if you would leave a review. I always love to hear what readers thought, and it helps new readers discover my books too. To keep up to date with my new releases, you can subscribe to my newsletter or follow me on social media.

Thanks,

Jennifer

Newsletter:
https://mailchi.mp/310b4ee4365f/
jenniferjoycenewsletter
Blog: www.jenniferjoycewrites.co.uk
Twitter, Instagram & TikTok: @writer_jenn
Facebook: www.facebook.com/jenniferjoycewrites

Acknowledgements

Thank you to Jennie Ayres and everyone at Hera for welcoming me to the team and feeling as passionate as I do about Cleo's story. Special thanks to Jennie and to Ross Dickinson for helping to shape the book and for making it as shiny as possible.

Thank you to my friends and family, for always encouraging me. As always, extra special thanks to the Joyces – Rianne, Isobel and Luna. You guys are the best.

And thank you to you, the reader, for choosing *The Grown-Up To-Do List*. I hope you enjoy Cleo's story.